"*Into the Go-Slow* tells the story of a place, a family, and a time through the worlds of a woman as she moves from grief to healing. Bridgett M. Davis writes with passion, precision, and a wide-open heart."

—Linda Villarosa, director, City College
Journalism Program and author of *Passing for Black*

"*Into the Go-Slow* spans continents and years, and traces the lives of sisters linked by loss and discovery. Bridgett M. Davis vividly renders the troubled, idealistic 1970s and the what's-left-to-dream-about 1980s, offering a powerful narrative driven by the all-too-human bafflement about how to resolve what could have been with what is."

—Farai Chideya, host of *One with Farai*
on Public Radio International

"*Into the Go-Slow* is an exquisitely executed journey enriched by the depth and complexity of the characters, the detailed specificity of the varied communities of Nigeria, and, above all, the poignant rendering of the yearning heart of the one who was left behind. Just beautiful."

—Wilhelmina Jenkins, moderator for Literary Fiction
by People of Color, Goodreads

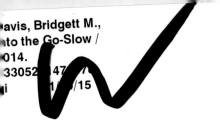
Into the Go-Slow

Bridgett M. Davis

THE FEMINIST PRESS
AT THE CITY UNIVERSITY OF NEW YORK
FEMINISTPRESS.ORG

Published in 2014 by the Feminist Press
at the City University of New York
The Graduate Center
365 Fifth Avenue, Suite 5406
New York, NY 10016

feministpress.org

 This project is supported in part by an award from the National Endow-
 ment for the Arts.

This book was made possible thanks to a grant from New York State
Council on the Arts with the support of Governor Andrew Cuomo and
NYSCA the New York State Legislature.

First printing September 2014

Cover design by Herb Thornby
Text design by Suki Boynton

Library of Congress Cataloging-in-Publication Data
Davis, Bridgett M., author.
 Into the go-slow / by Bridgett M. Davis.
  pages cm
 ISBN 978-1-55861-864-0 (pbk.) — ISBN 978-1-55861-865-7 (ebook)
 I. African Americans—Michigan—Detroit—Fiction. 2. African Americans—
Nigeria—Fiction. 3. Families—Michigan—Detroit—Fiction. I. Title.
 PS3604.A9556I58 2014
 813.6—dc23
                                                        2014023465

To the memory of my sister,

Deborah Jeanne Davis,

Whose shimmering brilliance still lights my way.

"In the world through which I travel,
I am endlessly creating myself."

Frantz Fanon, *Black Skin, White Masks*

HOME

ONE

SHE FOUND IT, BUT ANGIE HAD HOPED FOR MORE. FROM THE doorway, she saw that the turnout was low. An aging black man with a white ponytail was speaking to the tiny crowd. He stood beneath a giant sign that read "National Coalition for Black Reparations in America." His voice was hoarse. She entered the room reluctantly, already disappointed.

"This is what we must fight for, my brothers and sisters," croaked the speaker. "They ripped us from the shores of Africa and used our free labor to build their land of milk and honey! Reparations are our justice!"

The six or seven people forming an arc around the man nodded in agreement. A woman with dreadlocks hanging down her back sat behind a table of books about revolutions. Someone had hung up against a chalkboard the Ethiopian flag with its green, yellow, and red colors. Empty chairs formed a large circle, as though a lecture had already taken place hours before.

In one corner, a wide-shouldered man leaned against the ledge, arms folded. He seemed to be half-listening. Angie hesitated, feeling shy, but after a few moments she approached him.

"Excuse me," she said. "Is this the African Liberation Day celebration?"

"It is, yes." He had a British accent, and the faintest tribal markings scratched across his angled cheeks. She was certain he was Nigerian, which made her hopeful.

"Were more people here earlier?"

He gave a faint smile. "This, I'm afraid, is our critical mass."

He looked vaguely familiar. She wondered whether he'd known her sister Ella. It seemed to Angie that the handful of Africans who had found their way to Detroit had all known Ella.

She glanced back at the few attendees. "I thought it would be bigger somehow." She'd circled the date on her calendar, May 25, been excited when she'd read about the celebration in Wayne State University's campus newspaper. And for her to attend the same event that Ella had first attended when *she* was twenty-one had to mean something. Angie was wearing the tie-dyed caftan that her sister had brought back from Africa that year.

"They used to be very big affairs when I first came to this country from Nigeria," he said.

Angie beamed. She'd been right!

"Ah, but that was back when the idea of liberated African countries was still exciting," he noted.

The white-haired man droned on, punctuating his creaky words with a fist in the air, "We never got our forty acres and a mule, my people!"

Angie looked more closely at the Nigerian. "When exactly did you come here?"

"Nine years ago, in 1978," he said. "Back then, one hundred or more people showed up to these celebrations. We even had an after-party once, at a girl's house. Lasted until dawn. Fabulous party."

Angie nodded vigorously. "That was my house! I'm sure it was. My sister threw a lot of parties back then, Ella Mackenzie? That's whose party you went to, right?"

She vividly remembered that party because she was twelve

at the time, and had found a joint under the sofa cushion, wrapped in pink paper. She'd never had the nerve to smoke it. The wrinkled joint still lay inside her little wicker basket, one of several gifts Ella had brought her from Africa.

The Nigerian stood upright and stepped back slightly. "You're Ella's little sister?"

"Yes." Angie felt a pull of disappointment when he didn't say, *Of course! You look just like her.* No one ever said that.

He pointed to himself. "I'm Solo. Do you remember me?"

"Yes! I remember her talking about you." It was all rushing back to Angie now. "Solo, yes. She thought you had the coolest name ever." Ella had called him one of the finest-looking Africans she'd ever seen—chestnut-colored skin, high cheekbones, distinctly tall. Now Angie could see what Ella had meant.

He shook his head at time's passage. "You were just a little girl back then. How old are you now? Eighteen? Nineteen?"

"I'm twenty-one. I just graduated from here a week ago. From Wayne State, I mean."

"Ah-ha! I completed my PhD at this fine institution." Solo pointed his finger back and forth between them. "We are both alumni."

"One more thing we have in common," said Angie. This is what she'd been secretly hoping for—to be around someone who knew Ella, who would talk about her, not avoid saying her name. She wondered if Solo had ever dated her sister.

The aging nationalist had stopped lecturing, and the dread-locked woman was packing up her books. Angie and Solo watched as a young man wearing a mud-cloth dashiki took down the Ethiopian flag, furled it, and tucked it under his arm. The remaining handful of people filed out the door.

"Come, let me walk with you," said Solo, placing his hand in the small of her back as he guided her toward the exit.

Cars cruised along Second Avenue as they walked side by

side. Angie was nervous, wanting to seem sophisticated and worldly to this Nigerian man who'd known Ella. They passed by her favorite campus building, the historic Linsell House, with its white columns and air of distinction. She stared at its soaring Palladian window and tried to think of something interesting to say.

"So you met my sister right after you came here?" she finally asked.

"Yes," answered Solo. "She'd been to Lagos, so she and I had much to talk about, since that is where I grew up."

"I remember everything she told me about that trip," said Angie. "Sometimes I feel like I was there with her."

Solo smiled. "I am sure she had many tales. Everyone brings back wild stories from Lagos!"

It was a warm night, and people had their car windows down, music blasting. *I feel good, baby I feel good all over* sang Stephanie Mills, her voice potent, then fading as a car zoomed by.

"My apartment is here on campus, just a block away," said Solo. "Would you like to come over for some tea?"

His place was small, and crammed with possessions tastefully stored. Shelves lining the walls held an array of boxes and linens and books. Clothing hung neatly from a rack in the corner, and the bookcase holding the TV and stereo also served as a desk. It was evident that nine years of living had been stuffed into a campus studio meant for transient housing. Angie looked around greedily, wondering if Ella had ever visited him here. On the one free wall hung a photograph of Solo in traditional clothing, posing with a woman, and beside that was a poster of Fela, the popular Nigerian musician, his horn thrust forward in a phallic pose.

Excited, Angie pointed to the image. "I saw him perform here last year at the Fox!"

"You were there?" asked Solo. "I was there!"

For Angie, the chance to see the same musician her sister had seen in Lagos—Africa's rock star!—felt transcendent. She'd listened over and over to his one album Ella had brought back on cassette, knew the tunes well, could recite lines from the title song: *Zombie no go go unless you tell am to go; Zombie no go stop unless you tell am to stop.* Ella had spoken with awe of Fela's activism, his allegiance with the poor of his country. Years later, playing Fela's music in her car, en route to campus, Angie felt connected to something, if only briefly. She felt aware of a larger world in a way that her classmates were not. She longed to share this with someone. The concert at the Fox had done that for her, given her a community that shared this awareness, at least for one night. The Detroit performance was part of Fela's first US tour after Amnesty International helped free him from prison. This fact, coupled with the plethora of whites and Africans in the audience, made Angie feel part of a community, possibly the same way Ella had felt. It was her twenty-first birthday that night. Fela performed for nearly three hours; even though Angie couldn't understand much of what he sang about, she could feel the pulse of the music inside her, could feel her limbs elongate, could hear small little rhythms inside the big ones. As a finale, he performed "Beast of No Nation," the song he'd written upon his release. "When I talk about beasts of no nation," he explained, "I am talking about leaders who act like animals." It was a powerful song and throughout it, he would pause from playing his sax and direct the audience to, "Say yeah, yeah!" Angie yelled back, "Yeah, yeah!" with such repeated gusto that her throat hurt for hours afterward.

"So what did you think of that show?" asked Solo.

"Amazing!" said Angie. "Just to see Fela in person was riveting! And I loved that first song! Remember? It was called 'Just Like That.'"

Solo laughed heartily. "It's true what he sings, O. In Nigeria, you can just be going about your business, reading a book or a newspaper, riding in an elevator, and they take away the power,"—Solo snapped his finger—"Just like that."

Angie laughed easily as she followed him into the compact living room. "I actually like his older songs more," she noted, loving that she could show off her Fela knowledge. "The songs from the seventies?"

"I am the same way!" said Solo. "When I was growing up, I used to go hear his band, Africa '70, at the Shrine all the time, I am telling you! And it was fun music, man! You could dance to it and all of that. Now, he is, I must say, very political. And I like it. But I miss the old music."

He headed to his stereo and put on a Fela album. Dissonant, joyous music tumbled out. Angie sat down on the worn, corduroy couch. "I'd love to go to his club some day."

"I'm afraid it's gone," said Solo.

"It's gone?" She felt a pang of loss, of having missed out on something special.

"That one, yes. It was in the courtyard of the Empire Hotel." Solo paused. "But they say he built another one, in a place we call Ikeja."

"I'd like to go there," she said wistfully. "Before that one's gone too."

"Maybe you will," offered Solo.

Angie nodded. "I remember how Ella came back talking about the Shrine, how incredible it was."

"Ah yes, I think she played Fela's music at that after-party."

"She even met him!"

"Really?" Solo whistled. "Well, take heart that in her life, your sister did something quite extraordinary. She met the great Fela Kuti."

Hearing that made Angie smile. She was comforted to think Ella's life had been spectacular in its brevity, like a meteor rushing across the sky, fast and brilliant. She swayed to the deeply sensuous music, grateful to be here, in Solo's apartment, listening to the sounds of Afrobeat. She'd once hoped college would be like this, a life full of culture and music, spent hanging out with folks from the diaspora, her universe expanding. It hadn't turned out that way. She'd gone to the University of Michigan for one semester, but ended up attending Wayne State after It happened, heeding her mother's grief-stricken request to stay close. Her days became routine: classes each morning, then to her job at Northland Mall, where she worked at Lane Bryant, and back home. By the time Ella was Angie's age, she was deep into the struggle, a dedicated Pan-Africanist, believing in something bigger than herself. Now it was 1987, and there was nothing to believe in anymore. Angie felt like a throwback to another era, like she hadn't evolved at the same rate as her classmates and friends. Oddly enough, she felt both old beyond her years, and stunted in growth.

Solo opened the cabinet of his little kitchen, and returned with two glasses and a bottle of Cointreau. "Join me?" he asked.

Angie took a glass, grateful he hadn't invited her to get high. She'd managed to get through college never having smoked marijuana. She hadn't even touched that joint hidden in her little wicker basket—so old it was surely dried out by now. She'd read in advanced psych that addictive personalities are set: once you start something, you can't stop. Ella was clearly an addictive personality. Angie never tried drugs because she didn't want to know. She worried about finding out that she *wasn't* an addictive type, which would make her fundamentally different from her big sister.

She sipped the drink Solo poured for her. She'd never had Cointreau and right away, she felt a dizzying warmth move to her head. She recalled that she'd barely eaten all day, only rice cakes and peanut butter with herbal tea.

Solo sat down next to her on the couch. "I didn't see Ella much after that party."

"She didn't see much of anybody after that party," said Angie. Ella had moved out of the house that very night.

"Yes, drugs will do that," said Solo.

Angie gave him a *how did you know* look.

He sipped his Cointreau. "Oh, I remember a lot of ganja being passed around at your sister's party. And a few other mind-altering substances."

"Yeah, I guess there were." She hated the conversation's turn. She spun it around. "But Ella went to rehab and got clean," she said. "Completely. That's why she went back to Nigeria, as a kind of celebration, a reward."

Everyone had thought it was a good idea. And for the first time in years, Angie wasn't afraid for Ella. She relaxed, hung out with her big sister the night before, waved goodbye at the airport. As Ella waved back and entered the plane, Angie panicked, just briefly. She calmed herself down. Ella had gone to Nigeria before and returned. Why wouldn't she this time?

Solo took her hand in his. "I am sorry that something so tragic for you took place in my country." He paused. "Do you know exactly what happened?"

"She got hit by a car," Angie said, her voice flat.

"Yes, I'd heard that. I just wondered if you knew any specific details."

"Not really. They say she was alone, crossing a busy road on foot, and that's when she was struck." Angie looked at Solo, eyes pleading. "You grew up in Lagos. Does that sound right?"

He nodded solemnly. "There is no word in any Nigerian language for 'pedestrian.' I'm afraid that every day people who cross main roads on foot risk their lives—so yes. The roads in Lagos are especially dangerous."

"Only, apparently no one saw her cross," said Angie. "Even though it was supposed to be a busy road."

"Do you think there is another explanation?"

"I don't know," admitted Angie. "We never got any clear information. The State Department, the embassy, they were all useless."

"Well, perhaps there's no more to know," said Solo. "The explanation you were given is quite probable."

His words saddened her. She drank more.

"You don't really look like her, you know," said Solo. "She was a big girl. You're so much thinner."

Angie felt a familiar discomfort. She wanted to seem more like her sister, not less. People who saw pictures of Ella tended to point out their dissimilarity in physique, and always with an unspoken assertion that Angie was the lucky one.

The percussive horns and relentless drums of Fela's music swelled, as Angie drained her glass, riding the top of the notes, floating along. "I'm thinking of going to Nigeria," she blurted out, overcome with a need to show just how much she and Ella actually *were* alike. "Soon."

"Is that so?" asked Solo, as if he didn't believe it.

"Yes." She felt woozy. "And maybe to a couple of other West African countries too."

He nodded. "Well, I'd say that's a perfect graduation present."

Her mother had said something similar. She'd suggested Angie take a trip this summer, encouraging her to consider Europe, or Brazil perhaps. She'd read an *Ebony* article about Bahia. There was some life insurance money—several thousand dollars—from the policy her mother took out on Ella in the early days of her addiction. A family friend, Dr. Benjamin, assisted in securing the policy by administering a lenient physical exam, given that Ella couldn't pass a drug test. Her mother wanted Angie to use the money to travel. "Get away from here for a while," she told her. But Nigeria? Her mother would never, ever approve of that, which made the fantasy more appealing.

"I have figured it out." Solo slid closer to Angie, put his finger under her chin. "What is different about you and Ella. It's not just your size. She looked like a Yoruba and you look like one of my people, a Fulani." He rubbed her cheek. "A beautiful Fulani."

He moved in to kiss her, and Angie let him. His mouth tasted like oranges. She had always wanted a Nigerian boyfriend, someone to impress with her knowledge of his country. But her only real relationship had been during her semester at U of M, where she'd fallen in love with Romare, a black American engineering student. But then, after It happened, she and Romare parted ways and there'd been no one else since. Still hopeful, she'd kept taking her birth control pills.

"Did you and Ella ever do this?" she asked Solo.

"Do this?" he repeated.

"You know, did you two ever . . . get involved?"

He smiled and his dark eyes became slits. She saw that he had dimples. "I am not the type to kiss and tell," he said, guiding her down gently onto the couch. As his tongue pushed through her mouth, she tried to feel something, but nothing moved inside her, even when she felt Solo's erection against her leg. His smooth palm slid up Ella's caftan, cold against Angie's naked thigh. She shivered as his hand moved to her panties, fingers slipping inside.

"Wait!"

"Hmm, come on," he murmured in her ear. "We are having such a good time."

She gently pushed him. "Stop, please."

He kept going, and frightened, she pushed harder. "No!"

He stopped and sat up, looking confused. "What's wrong?"

"I don't even know you."

He gave her an incredulous look. "How can you say that?" His voice rose. "I was there, with your sister in her *best* days. We share that. How many people share that with you?"

Her head hurt. It was true he was all that linked her to that dynamic time in her sister's life. She tried to think. Solo took her hesitation as approval and gently lay her back down on the couch. As he pushed up the loose dress and pulled off her panties, she told herself Ella would approve. Ella was naturally voracious—for food, for drugs, and yes, for sex—in a way Angie never managed to be. As Solo entered her, she tried to relax and enjoy it. He thrust and the slightest tinge of pleasure made its way up her groin. She squeezed shut her eyes and put her hands on Solo's back; it was smooth save for his bumpy backbone. She tried to shut off her thoughts, but her mind landed on a memory: Ella in their basement with friends, the smell of weed wafting around them, and Ella is inhaling on a joint so hard, her cheeks hollow out. Next, Ella is sprawled on the red leather couch, eating a gigantic slice of chocolate cake, icing smeared across her cheeks. Her new boyfriend, Nigel, with his soft gray eyes and widow's peak, is laughing, saying, hey leave some for me, I got the munchies too, and Ella is saying, you slow, you blow, laughing, grabbing his arm, pulling him away from the crowd, to Angie's little playroom in the back. Nigel catches Angie's eye, saying wait Ella girl, wait, that's Angie's room, but goes through the door and closes it behind them. Angie, a sixth grader, stares at the door, the plywood door on which she'd scrawled the words "My House" when she was just six. Inside, a little home—complete with Suzy Homemaker toy appliances, a toy-chest sofa, and a tiny bookshelf beside a lamp and chair—her haven after their father died, with her mother always working late and her older sisters too busy for her; the place where little Jeff Charles would come over and play house for hours. She hasn't outgrown it yet, doesn't like the idea of someone trespassing through. She worries about Nigel and Ella in there, on the other side of her closed plywood door.

She presses against the door, waiting and waiting, leaning against it, wanting them out of there, and finally the door opens. Ella bursting through, saying, move out the way, pushing Angie aside as she runs to the metal sink beside the washer and dryer. Nigel hovers over her, pulling Ella's hair out of the way while she throws up. He catches Angie's eye again as she watches, suddenly worried for her big sister, stricken.

"Girl, I told you to slow it down," Nigel says to Ella. "You gotta pace yourself!"

Just like that, Ella lifts her head from the sink, wipes her mouth; she is fine. She looks over at Angie. "What's wrong Princess?" she says. "What's wrong?"

Angie can't answer, because she doesn't know what's wrong, only that she is scared for Ella, a fear that will grip her long after the night ends. It is the same fear that had consumed her when Ella took off earlier that year for Nigeria. Angie worried that Ella wasn't coming back. But Ella did return, wearing ivory bangles and that caftan, dazzling in her newfound cultural awareness, her love of all things African.

Solo came and she lay very still until he eased himself off her, kissed her forehead. She'd never had sex with a man she'd just met, and it was like crossing over into another realm. She certainly wasn't a virgin, and yet she felt initiated into a new club, changed. Maybe now she'd be more spontaneous with her life. Angie slipped on her panties, smoothed out the dress. Fela's music raced along as Solo zipped up his pants, tucked in his shirt. She wanted to feel closer to him now, not because they'd just had sex, but because he'd known Ella and she felt they'd just consummated *that* connection.

"What do you remember most about her?" she asked him.

His face flush with a post-coital slackness, Solo seemed not to know whom she was talking about. But he caught on quick enough. "Well, she was very smart. Your sister knew a lot about Africa actually. The first black American I'd met who had real knowledge about the continent. *She* never asked me if we lived in huts, if we had running water, if we wore shoes."

She wasn't sure whether she'd known that about Ella—whether it was new information or something she'd once known. This saddened her. "I'm forgetting so many things about her," she told him. "Every day, it's like I forget another detail. It feels so cruel."

"Well, she has been gone for some years now," said Solo. "That's to be expected."

Angie stiffened. That was *not* what she wanted to hear.

"When will I see you again?" he asked.

She leaned away from him. "Hard to say." She couldn't imagine going backward, having a chaste date with this man. "I may be leaving soon."

He smiled big. "Yes, go to my country, then come back and tell me your grand impressions."

"Sure." She stood, ready to get away from his stuffed apartment, from her own deception. "I have to go."

Solo stood too. "Let me give you something."

He went to the crowded desk, grabbed a black address book, tore off a piece of that day's newspaper lying on the table, and copied something from the book. She watched, desperately wanting to leave. He moved close and handed her the scrap. "Here's my uncle's information," he said. "He's the head of mass communications at the University of Lagos. When you arrive, go see him, tell him I sent you. He'll take care of you."

She slipped the piece of paper into a side pocket of her purse, thanked him as she reached for the doorknob.

"Hey!" Solo called to her.

She turned back to face him.

"Say yeah, yeah!"

"Yeah, yeah!" she echoed, feeling self-conscious as frenetic Afrobeats followed her out the door.

As Angie walked along Second Avenue, she tried to sort out her feelings. Maybe this was fate? She got into her Ford Escort, turned the ignition. She rolled down the window, let in the night's warm breeze. She'd certainly thought about going to Nigeria when she'd been at Fela's concert last year. She'd sat in her seat at the Fox Theater, surrounded by Africa enthusiasts, looked up at the faded majestic ceiling with its blue sunburst, and imagined herself *there*. The truth was, she'd been unwittingly inching toward this moment all along. But she hadn't allowed herself to entertain the thought because her mother would strongly disapprove. Yet now was different, wasn't it? She'd done the thing her mother most wanted her to do: graduate from college. Of her three daughters, Angie's was the only college graduation her mother got to attend. So that was done. She'd been dutiful. Now, she could go. And this was the time to do it. She was the exact age Ella was when *she* first visited Nigeria.

As Angie drove home she got more excited. She'd saved all of her sister's letters from that last trip. She could retrace her steps—see what Ella saw, be with the people Ella had been with—just to know how her sister had spent her last months. Going to Nigeria would calm the achy feeling inside Angie, a feeling she couldn't shake—that Ella's soul wasn't at rest, and it was somehow her job to change that.

Ella died in Lagos on January 1, 1984. She was twenty-seven and Angie was eighteen. She died at the scene. Their mother, Nanette, refused an autopsy, so no one knew whether drugs were in Ella's system. Angie felt certain they weren't.

She had spent the three-and-a-half years since the deadly

accident in a holding pattern of denial. She couldn't, wouldn't accept that her sister had survived years of heroin addiction, and then rehab, only to die in front of a speeding car in a foreign country. The more Angie obsessed over it, the more her own life receded. Her own ambitions and desires got crowded out, no place to go. If she'd witnessed the scene, then maybe she could move on. Or if she'd sat in a hospital waiting room, filled with fragile hope until the doctor came out, said those fateful words, and she'd felt the agony, then maybe. Instead Angie found herself living in a perpetual state of anticipation mixed with dread, waiting for the thing that would provide finality, quell the feeling that Ella had disappeared into the ether. Until then, she lived as a kind of caretaker to the obsessions Ella left behind, an executor of her sister's Afrocentric politics, new age beliefs, Fela Kuti devotion. Ella died just as Angie entered college, on the precipice of forming her *own* ideas about who she wanted to be in the world. She never got to do that. Instead, Angie chose to preserve these things that mattered most to Ella, indefinitely, until . . . until . . . she didn't know when.

Their mother flew to Nigeria to bring back Ella's body. The whole ordeal had been deeply traumatizing. Angie's mother developed an allergic reaction to the pre-trip vaccinations, and spent her days in Nigeria with a swollen face. Her luggage was stolen at the airport. And as fate would have it, she'd arrived on the heels of a bloodless coup d'etat. She had to pay the Nigerian customs officials a shameful amount of cash to get Ella back home. Nanette couldn't say enough bad things about Lagos—its filth, its corruption, its horrific traffic.

They held a small service at the Unity Temple behind Palmer Park. Angie read a quote from Khalil Gibran, whom Ella loved, in a quivering voice. "For life and death are one, even as the river and the sea are one." She had chosen Ella's dress, a lace-collared navy shift. But Angie never saw the dress on her.

At the service, when it was time for the family to view the body, their mother held her sister Denise's hand as they approached the casket together. Angie didn't join them, remained seated in the front row, watching Denise's back heave up and down. Even though she needed to see her, make all this become real, she didn't want to. She thought she couldn't bear to look at Ella's face, and wished the sprays of white snapdragons, gardenias, and hydrangeas surrounding the casket would hide her profile from view. But she saw her. And still, it wasn't real.

The family hadn't heard from Nigel, Ella's boyfriend, since the funeral. A friend of Ella's told Angie that he was now a foreign correspondent.

Her childhood playroom, the words "My House" scrawled across the closed door, Nigel and Ella inside. Angie waiting, waiting, worried they'd never come out. And once they did, leaving behind turned-over kiddie furniture, smudges of chocolate on the walls, a mysterious smell.

TWO

WHENEVER ANGIE SHOPPED WITH HER SISTER DENISE, THEY silently competed, each working hard to be least impressed with the other's taste. Denise whizzed through Hudson's Department Store with her charge card and bought Coach purses and Gucci sunglasses and Liz Claiborne dresses with aplomb, wanting Angie to show how impressed she was. Angie refused to do any such thing, and would later drag Denise to a vintage store in Royal Oak to buy some floral dress or suede vest that someone else had already owned, relishing in her sister's obvious disgust.

"I could use some new suitcases," said their mother as the three of them walked through Somerset Mall. "Mine is so old, it's the one I used when we moved here from Tennessee."

"God, that's sad!" said Denise. "First up on the list today is some new luggage. Maybe we should get you some Hartmann. It'll actually still look good in twenty-five years."

The giant fountain in the center of the mall spewed water cascading like diamonds as Angie, Denise, and their mother strolled, eyeing the stores on either side. Their mother was headed to Atlanta for a few days of vacation, and to mark the occasion, her daughters were helping her shop for a few new things. In fact, Denise was treating.

At twenty-seven, Denise was a pharmaceutical rep in Atlanta, a job she snagged the week after she graduated from Spelman College. Pushing her artistic talent to the side, she'd been working for Bristol-Myers for five years. She loved to tell Angie and their mother how vital her services were to doctors, how they relied on her insights and advice on which medications worked best for which illnesses. Angie didn't trust prescription drugs, found their mysterious names and side effects scary. She leaned more toward herbal remedies and homeopathic medicine. Still, she was taken aback by how well Denise had done so quickly: a condo in a new development, the latest model Honda Accord sedan, and a closet full of shoulder-padded power suits and high-heeled pumps. Denise was now the same age that Ella was when she died, and Angie marveled at how deeply Denise had driven her stake into the ground of stability, and how immortal she seemed.

"What else is on the list?" asked Angie, already feeling tired, an effect malls had on her. They walked by a B. Dalton bookstore. She wished she could slip across its threshold, and wait out the rest of the shopping spree browsing the shelves. She wondered if there were any travel books on Nigeria. Ten days had passed since her encounter with Solo, and it didn't feel real anymore, the sex part; but what did feel real was the part about going to Africa.

"There's not that much for me to get," said their mother. "I want some new lipstick, and one or two summer dresses, maybe a pair of sandals . . ."

Denise gave her mother a knowing look. "And a nice new nightgown. Something lacy."

Their mother shook her head, but Angie could see she was smiling.

"Why do you need a new nightgown?" she asked.

"What woman doesn't?" said Denise, as she guided them into Saks Fifth Avenue.

Angie thought of her mother's simple cotton nightgowns with matching robes, how lovely she looked in them. She recalled that many years ago, her mother once wore her nightgown all day, her small girth moving easily underneath, and then changed into her armor of heavy underwear and a pretty top and pants in the evening, looking fresh when their father walked through the door. Angie remembered how he'd hug his wife, pull her to him, and plant a sloppy kiss on her lips. "Samson," she'd whisper. "You smell like them horses something awful." "Ain't that how you like me?" he'd respond, making her blush. She was so young when he died, just thirty-four. Angie knew of only one man her mother dated and cared about afterward, but he moved away and that was that. Denise set her up on dates with two former high school teachers years later, but Nanette said those men weren't her type. Since Ella's death, she'd given up dating completely, and Angie was secretly relieved.

Denise led them to the cosmetics department and promptly bought their mother La Perla face cream, Clinique cleanser, and Fashion Fair lipstick. "You need a little color in your cheeks too," suggested Denise, eyeing her mother in a makeup counter mirror. Denise looked a lot like their mother—not the same natural beauty, but the same body type, the same complexion. Both were short, with wide hips and tiny waists. Their mother was plump, her stomach round and arms fleshy; Denise was a solid size 10, maybe a size 12 during that time of the month. She kept her weight down by eating Weight Watchers frozen meals for both lunch and dinner. She looked magnificent in knit dresses, and Angie envied her big ass and shapely legs, which Denise showed off with four-inch heels and a sexy sway.

Angie watched her mother trying on some blush, silently

disapproving, convinced her simple beauty didn't need makeup. She liked her mother best when she wore her long black hair in two braids parted down the middle. Nanette had a permanent poignancy about her since Ella's death: wistfulness in her eyes, a half smile instead of the old laugh, faraway looks carrying her off. Angie found comfort in her mother's sustained grief. It was how it had to be, she thought, and it enhanced her beauty.

Denise suggested they head to the fourth floor and look at the dresses, but Angie said, "I have a better idea." She'd been saving this little surprise. "Mama can go to Lane Bryant and get a couple dresses, and I'll use my employee discount. The store has some really nice ones on sale right now, so it's like getting two for one."

"Does Somerset have a Lane Bryant?" asked their mother.

"Well no," said Angie. "I figured you could come back to Northland with me, and I can show you what I picked out."

"Their clothes are a little low end, don't you think?" said Denise. "We're here, why don't we just get her something nice right now?"

"No, they're not *low end*," said Angie. "She can get something fashionable that she knows will fit her right. What's wrong with that?"

"Did I say something was wrong with it?" Denise snapped. "Don't make such a big deal out of everything."

"I'm not the one trying to show off, acting like Mama has never had anything until you bought it for her."

"I'm just trying to be thoughtful," said Denise.

"And I'm not?"

"Girls," said their mother. "I don't want to listen to you two snapping at each other!" She sighed. "I'm going to find a ladies room, and then we can just go home."

She walked away.

"Great," said Denise. "You upset her. Happy?"

Angie stared at her sister, trying for the umpteenth time to figure out why the sibling knot between them remained so undone. "That's right, blame me," she said. "Again."

Denise sucked her teeth, impatient. "Well you *are* the one who keeps torturing her."

"What are you talking about?"

"The whole Lane Bryant thing? You know every time you bring it up, it reminds Mama of what happened."

"I work there, OK? It makes perfect sense for her do some of her shopping there. But that would take the spotlight off of you and your wonderful generosity, wouldn't it?"

"And why in the hell are you, a size 6, working in a store for fat women in the first place?" said Denise. "What woman would even trust you to wait on her?"

"I care about plus-size women looking good in their clothes. So slay me."

Denise jabbed her finger into Angie's arm. "You work there as some kind of homage, which I have to tell you, is weird. So is running to the cemetery all the time and wearing her caftan around and—"

"How do you know I had her caftan on?"

"Mama told me you wore it to some event a couple weeks ago."

"So you two *discuss* me like I'm some mental case?"

"She just mentioned it. Will you listen? I want to say this before she gets back." Denise took a deep breath. "Stop it. Stop reminding her. It's been four years, and you're not letting her get over it."

"It's only been three-and-a-half years, and how is any mother supposed to get over the death of her daughter?"

"You know what I mean! She needs to move on, Angie. She deserves to have a life."

"She's fine. We're fine."

"No you're not. You're in some perpetual mourning period, and I understand that. Really I do. But it's got to stop."

Angie stared at the escalators, at the shoppers with their bags, moving slowly upward as if to some retail heaven. "I get it," she said. "Still jealous of her, aren't you? She's gone and you're still jealous. Must you have *all* of Mama's attention?"

"What are you talking about? I don't even live here."

"Exactly. But you're trying to control what goes on here."

Denise shook her head. "It's not good for you either, you know. You should move on too. Like what's your plan, now that you've graduated? Are you gonna move out, get your own place?"

"Why would I desert Mama? Leave her all alone like that?"

"You need a plan, OK? 'Cause the way you're living now, that's not healthy."

"Who are you to tell me how to live!" Angie shouted.

"Nobody can tell you anything. That's your problem."

"I can't believe you. You waltz into town—"

Denise cut her off. "Look, Miss Deaf, Dumb, and Blind. Mama needs to get away from Dr. B. She can't do that if she's stuck in that house with you."

"But she loves her job. Why would she—"

"She loves *him*, and that's bad news because the man is never getting divorced."

Angie gave her sister a puzzled look. "What are you talking about? Are you accusing Mama of—"

"This trip is just what she needs to get over him."

Angie hated this feeling, that she'd missed something profound, something going right in front of her.

Denise saw her confusion. "You didn't know? Jesus, you do not pay attention." Before Angie could react, Denise went on,

"But get this: a high school boyfriend of Mama's tracked her down and they've been talking over the phone."

"Daddy was her high school boyfriend."

"This was *before* him," said Denise, exasperated. "Anyway, this guy lives in Atlanta, so she'll get to see him while she's there."

Angie suddenly felt duped, like she was preparing for a party she hadn't been invited to. "How long have you been planning this little scheme?" she asked.

"Shh, here she comes," whispered Denise. "Don't mention any of this to her!"

As their mother approached, Angie looked at her carefully. She was forty-nine. Angie couldn't imagine her as some *other woman*. Nor could she imagine her as one of those aging women, chasing after an old flame. Angie needed air.

"Listen, I'm going to leave now," she said. "So I won't be late for work."

"I thought you said you didn't have to be at work today until three," said Denise.

"Do you want me to ride with you, so I can look at your store's dresses?" asked their mother, clearly trying to smooth things over.

"No, Mama, it's OK," Angie said over her shoulder. "Denise has that covered. See you back at home."

She walked away, and then turned to watch as her sister and mother moved farther into Saks, suddenly wishing she had her own department store credit card, so she could charge a lot of fresh, new things she didn't need.

ANGIE SPED ALONG Telegraph Road. She resented that Denise always had a way of revealing some shocking bit of family news that Angie never saw coming. Denise accused her little sister of trying to make people be the way she wanted them to be, rather than seeing them for who they are. Angie felt she could say the same for Denise.

When their sister Ella was fourteen, she lost thirty pounds, started getting catcalls from the neighborhood boys. *Ooh girl, must be jelly 'cause jam don't shake like that!* Their father couldn't compliment her enough, gave her money to buy an entire new wardrobe from The Limited and Casual Corner, places Ella used to walk past at the mall, on her way to the chubby teens department at Lane Bryant. Their mother insisted that was too much weight dropped too quickly, and she worried that Ella was taking diet pills. Ella denied it, although anyone who bothered to notice could see she was talking faster, jittery. Denise, ever the watchdog of their mother's nerves, decided to catch Ella in a lie. She searched her elder sister's room, found the pills hidden in a top drawer inside an envelope, under her new underwire bras. They later learned she'd gotten them from a friend, whose mother had gotten them from a doctor. Amphetamines. "They're pep pills!" Ella's friend had told her. "And they really work."

Denise confronted her big sister, ceremoniously, in front of four-year-old Angie.

"These are drugs!" yelled Denise as the three of them stood in the kitchen. Ella had been making pancakes, and she held a spatula in her hand. She was wearing new eyeglasses. Denise thrust the envelope in her sister's face. "You could get addicted!"

"Oh, shut up!" Ella snatched the pills from Denise. "And stay out of my damn room!"

"Mama is worried about you!" said Denise.

Ella pointed the spatula at Denise. "Mind your own fucking business!"

"Are you gonna stop taking those?"

"I don't have to answer to you. You're just a kid."

"I'll tell Daddy," said Denise.

"You better not!" yelled Ella.

"Watch me."

"Do. Not. Tell. Him."

"I will."

Ella breathed heavily, and her pupils behind the glasses looked dilated. "If you tell him, I swear . . ."

"What?" Denise goaded her. "What can you do? Nothing." She was only ten, and yet she was a little woman, saddled with an adult's power, and worries.

"Stop riding me like I'm one of Daddy's horses!" screamed Ella.

"Stop doing bad things then!" yelled Denise. She lunged for the envelope, catching Ella off guard. Pastel-colored pills spilled out onto the checkered linoleum. Ella dropped to the floor and started grabbing the pills. Denise crushed one with her foot. Ella smacked her sister's leg with the spatula. "Stop that!" she screamed.

Denise put her hands on her hips. "I'll find them, wherever you put them. I know all your hiding places."

"Oh yeah?" Ella took the handful of pills she'd gathered and shoved them into her mouth, moved to the sink, turned on the faucet, put her head underneath, and drank. She came up, thrust her throat to the ceiling, swallowing hard. Both sisters stared, shocked.

"There," she said. "Now try to find them."

They all stood still for a moment, the kitchen clock ticking loudly, marking the seconds as the drug made its way through Ella's bloodstream. She ran upstairs to her attic room as Denise and Angie stayed frozen in place, listened as her bedroom door slammed. The stack of hot pancakes on the stove stood waiting.

Their mother wasn't home. Their father was in Muskegon

for the week, running horses. Denise followed Ella upstairs and banged on her door; Angie was right behind her. Despite the begging, Ella wouldn't come out, so Denise called their mother at work. But Angie didn't budge, rather she lay her small body down in front of Ella's door, crying softly, fearful that her big sister was quietly dying on the other side.

Their mother rushed home and when she couldn't get Ella to come out, called 911. Firemen hacked open her door, gashing it violently. Inside, Ella sat atop her bed, rocking herself back and forth, back and forth. They all went to the hospital, where doctors pumped her stomach. The girls told their mother it had been an accident, a silly truth-or-dare game gone wrong. For once, they were in solidarity. Later, their mother agreed not to tell the girls' father anything.

As she thought about that day, Angie realized that was when their roles were set: Ella was the unpredictable wild child, Denise, the cautious protector, and Angie, the baby sister forced to pick sides. As Ella walked slowly out of the hospital that day, still weak, Angie saw in her face an earned knowledge, as though she'd discovered the secret to getting her way, to being left alone. It was 1970, years before Ella made her first trek to Africa, long before she started experimenting with drugs. When she downed those diet pills, she was still a high school freshman wearing knee-length dresses to class every day, still press-and-curling her hair. That day, she wore a polyester pantsuit, fashionable but modest, given her new figure.

After the pill episode, Denise kept her distance from Ella. She still told their mother things she believed her big sister was doing wrong, but stealthily, like a household spy. She swore her mother to secrecy: *Don't let her know I said anything!* She was terrified of Ella. And Ella now seemed terrified of nothing, no one.

ANGIE DIDN'T HAVE to be at work for two more hours. She turned left onto Grand River and drove to the cemetery. As she entered the wide gates of Grand Lawn, a welcome calm came over her. The grounds were lush and green, dotted with flowers lying on individual grave sites. Angie parked alongside the quaint cobblestone office building. She found it enchanting, like a house from a Grimm's fairytale. She got out, and walked the few yards to the duck pond. It shimmered in the early afternoon sun, and she wished she'd brought Cheese Tid-Bits for the ducks. She liked the serenity and beauty of the cemetery, thought of it as the closest thing Detroit had to a botanic garden.

Her mother and Denise didn't share her attraction to Grand Lawn. They never came. She knew they disapproved of her visits here. "The body is just a vessel; her soul left it right away," her mother once said.

Angie agreed with her mother, believed Ella's soul wasn't at the cemetery, but her body was. That was certain, and she felt her sister's vessel deserved attention. So she went to her gravesite on Christmas and Ella's birthday and on the anniversary of her death. And on days she felt particularly lonely. She didn't sit there and talk to the grave. She didn't feel Ella's presence per se. She tidied the plot, brushing off old leaves or snow. Sometimes she'd rub her hands across the marker, staring at Ella's full name, the birth and death dates, and the sad words, "beloved sister and daughter," because she died before becoming anyone's mother or wife. But some days, like today, she felt satisfied to sit on a bench beside the pond and just be. She no longer told anyone that she came here; she could see in her mother's eyes that the visits worried her. And now that Denise had confirmed that concern, Angie would be extra secretive.

If Ella's bedroom still existed, things would have been different. Angie would have gone there to feel her sister's presence, would have sat among Ella's books and posters and clothes and been satiated. But when Ella moved to Ann Arbor to attend the University of Michigan, Denise immediately moved out of the room she and Angie shared and took Ella's attic bedroom. When Ella dropped out of the university, she stayed in the den, sleeping on the sofa bed. Eventually she and her boyfriend Nigel got an apartment together. The year Ella was in rehab, she lived at home again during the outpatient part; but even though Denise lived in Atlanta by then, Ella didn't move back into her old room. Instead, she again stayed in the den, folding doors with accordion blinds her only privacy.

In her own room, Angie had gathered mementos from Ella's life. On a little altar sat crystals and incense and candles that had all belonged to her big sister. Propped up beside those things was the "Free Angela" button Ella had worn throughout Angela Davis's trial, and on her wall a "Remember Soweto!" poster of two crying boys rushing toward the camera. Clippings from Ella's work as a journalist in Nigeria hung in the corners of Angie's dresser mirror, yellowing with age. If she were honest with herself, she'd admit these things conjured no strong memories of Ella. Yet they had outsize significance to Angie. They were physical proof of Ella's existence, and she needed them to offset the slippage that came with each passing year.

Below them all, propped against the dresser, was the rectangular, weathered sign that had belonged to their father. The sign once hung from a chain just above the entryway to his horses' stalls. "Samson Mackenzie Stables" it read. Ella was the one who took it down, brought it home. Funny, whenever Angie looked at that sign, she conjured her father's presence immediately. Every time.

She looked out on the sloping lawn of the cemetery. Denise was wrong, she thought. Mama and I are fine. She got up from the park bench, walked across several plots to Ella's grave. She moved her hand across the raised letters of Ella's marker. She'd always felt a gnawing sense that something happened to her sister before getting hit by that car, that she was running *from* something. But what?

She'd hoped to find her answer by researching Nigeria. She spent hours and hours in Wayne State's campus library, where she should have been working on her psychology papers; instead she dug up details about the country. She found very little beyond skeletal encyclopedic facts on population, independence, civil war, oil wealth. She found herself more drawn to accounts of the Second World Black and African Festival of Arts and Culture, or FESTAC, the festival Ella had attended the first time she'd gone to Nigeria in 1977. Angie lucked upon a *Sepia* magazine that gave a breathless account of the event, claiming that "a conspicuous ignoring of FESTAC by most of the American press could not stem the rising tide of history, could not stop the month-long homecoming for 17,000 blacks from fifty-five nations. 'FESTAC IS HERE!' trumpeted the Nigerian newspaper *Punch* in two-inch type." Angie could picture Ella there, soaking in the sub-Saharan sun alongside throngs of gorgeous black people, free.

That was the Ella she wanted to remember. Sometimes it felt like the Ella who returned to Nigeria six years later, the fragile one just out of rehab, wasn't the same person at all. Sometimes Angie wasn't sure which version of Ella she mourned. She sat back on her haunches, surveyed her surroundings. She was the only one there. A slight breeze caused a little American flag atop one of the graves to undulate, and an eerie quiet blanketed the landscape. She thought, *What's wrong with me?*

THE NORTHLAND MALL branch of the chain store was one of its busiest. Angie had gotten the job two-and-a-half years before, had worked hard to gain the managers' respect. They'd hired her out of desperation during the holiday rush, as their policy was to hire only plus-size saleswomen. What Denise said was generally true—customers preferred it that way. And she knew she probably should be working somewhere else—a manager had even offered to transfer her to The Limited, a sister company, but Angie declined. She wowed everyone with her sensitivity and knowledge about what looked good on big women, and what didn't. She was deft at measuring chest and waist sizes, and she never talked about "hiding" body parts with clothing. She had a knack for helping women play up their assets with color-blocking and good fit and the right bra or girdle. In the two years between their father's death and Ella's departure for college, Angie would perch herself in Ella's room and watch her get dressed for school each morning. Ella was a meticulous, stylish dresser and Angie learned a lot. Sometimes it was Angie's job to run to the basement and get her big sister's long-line bra and panties out of the dryer. Other times, she'd sit on the bed, watching as Ella pulled a silken slip over her head, poured baby powder down her chest, then stepped into an A-line skirt or a belted dress. Now, Angie liked the look of surprise on the women's faces when they saw her genuine interest in wanting them to look good, her total lack of condescension masking as cheerful helpfulness. The truth was, she felt more comfortable among these women than her own slim girlfriends, always in terror that she was going to mention her dead sister, or worse, snap at them for their offhanded fat-girl jokes.

Lana, her manager, borrowed her look from the women of *Dynasty*, with her pale-colored skirt suits and frosted hair. Today, she and Angie were choosing clothes for the company's upcoming plus-size fashion show for teens.

Lana nervously chatted nonstop. If this fashion show could be a success, if the girls could really look like they felt good about themselves, then their moms would buy the outfits they wore. And that would be good for business, which could prompt her promotion within the company. She was aiming for a position as buyer.

Angie sorted outfits, grateful for Lana's chatter, for the chance to busy herself. She was still bothered by the scene at the mall, by Denise's criticism of her job. She put together an outfit of leggings and an oversized T-shirt with jelly shoes and stepped back, surveyed her choices. This is what I do, she thought. This is how I make a difference. I help chubby girls and overweight women like themselves.

Lana approved of the looks, but instructed Angie to change the jelly shoes to stilettos. "Flat shoes are a no-no for our customers," she advised. She didn't like how Angie had paired a Lycra dress with a cropped bolero-style jacket either. "The model won't like that her tummy pokes out from under that short thing," she explained, handing Angie a longer, shoulder-padded jacket. "Put this one with it."

Angie adjusted the outfit, feeling annoyed with herself for not having known these truths on her own. Just how helpful was she?

When she got home from work later, she found her mother upstairs, atop her bed, surrounded by shopping bags, tissue paper lying around her like froth. She showed Angie her new purchases—a floral suitcase with wheels ("This one was prettier to me than that overpriced one Denise wanted me to get."), a pair of strappy sandals adorned with leather petals, two dresses, and two short nightgowns with lace bodices.

"I thought you preferred long nightgowns," said Angie.

"I usually do," admitted her mother. "But Denise convinced me to try something a little different."

"And where is she?" asked Angie.

"Having dinner with some of her friends from high school. It's amazing how many she's still in touch with!"

Angie had lost touch with most of her own high school friends. When Ella died, her friends were all busy with freshman year of college, and didn't really know what to say to her anyway. And she was fine with that, fine to be left alone with her own grief.

The dresses her mother had selected at Saks were lovely, one in sherbet peach, the other the color of honeydew melon, and each with its own matching, sheer cardigan.

"These are pretty," said Angie, feeling a stab of hurt. Earlier, at work, she'd taken the dresses she'd been holding for her mother in the storage room and put them back on the floor. They couldn't compare to these.

Her mother baked some chicken, and Angie opened a can of French-cut string beans, doctored them with salt and pepper and tomato juice. "How long are you going to be in Atlanta? I forgot," she lied.

"A few days," said her mother. "Not even a week. Just long enough to get a change of scenery." She hesitated. "There's a guy I went to high school with who lives there now. I plan to see him."

"Yeah, Denise told me," said Angie.

"Did she? OK." Her mother shrugged. "Denise has a few places picked out for us to go. Then, before you know it, I'll be back."

"And Dr. B. didn't object to your taking the time off?" Angie studied her mother's reaction closely. She'd been office manager for the handsome, black family doctor for fourteen years, since shortly after their father died. Her mother had run her father's horse-training business, kept his records from the start, so handling every detail in Dr. Benjamin's office came easily.

He'd become completely dependent on her to keep things running smoothly. Denise often complained that he overworked and underpaid their mother, but it was obvious she loved her job. Or at least Angie always assumed it was the job she loved.

Her mother waved her hand as if swatting a fly. "Louis would not want to object, hard as I work for that man."

Angie wanted to confront her mother, but she didn't have the heart.

After dinner, she made her mother's favorite dessert, buttery toast with strawberry jam, and took it up to her room. She turned on the TV, changed the station to channel four, and propped herself on the bed next to her mother. They'd already missed *The Cosby Show* and *Family Ties*. She was sorry she'd gotten hung up at work. The theme song for *Cheers* started, a comfort every time she heard it. Who wouldn't want to go where everybody knows your name?

"I thought it would be fun to watch *The Colbys* tonight," said her mother. "Denise says it's a pretty good show." She shrugged shyly. "Something different."

"Sure!" said Angie, a little too loud. She jumped up, changed the channel, masking her disappointment. But she felt it, a shift occurring. They always watched NBC's Thursday night lineup together: *The Cosby Show, Family Ties, Cheers, Night Court*. Dozing through *L.A. Law*. Her mother had had no taste for nighttime soap operas, was never into *Dallas* or *Dynasty*. Plus she'd shown no interest in traveling before. Now, they watched this *Dynasty* spin-off while two women, both with big hair, got into a catfight as Angie tried to pinpoint what exactly in their lives had changed.

The phone on the nightstand rang. Nanette answered it on the second ring. "Hello? Oh, hi! How are you?" From the way her mother's voice went up slightly, with an edge of formality,

Angie knew it was the Atlanta man. "Oh, no, not at all. I'm just watching TV with my daughter."

Angie rose to leave, but her mother motioned for her to stay put. She did, but she felt odd, didn't want to listen in on the courtship. She watched the commercials, including the PSA with an egg frying while the announcer intoned: *This is your brain on drugs.* Angie hated that ad. As if it was that easy to deter someone from getting high. Druggies *want* their brains fried. That's the whole point. Her mother chatted on, and didn't seem to notice when Angie switched back to channel four. She watched the rest of *Cheers.* A summer rerun, it turned out to be an episode she'd already seen, the one where Diane feels left out of the gang's activities, so Frazier plans a day at the opera for her.

Angie had looked forward to this nighttime ritual with her mother all day, and now that it wasn't what she'd hoped for, now what?

THREE

ANGIE'S EARLIEST MEMORY: SHE IS AT THE TRACK WITH her father and Ella. She is three, sitting atop a milk crate, wrapped in a warm blanket, the smell of coffee and manure and hay under her nose. She sits stock-still and watches as Ella rides a horse, Butterscotch, around the empty track, their father walking beside her, rubbing the chestnut gelding's rump. She wants to be on a horse too, and she calls out to them, "I wanna ride! I wanna ride!" but her tiny voice gets lost in the treeless wind. Either that, or they ignore her.

She tried hiding, crawling under the bleachers, determined to make them think she'd gone missing. But they didn't come looking for her and finally she left her hiding place, returned to her spot on the bleachers, and watched her big sister and daddy circle the track again and again, still hoping for a turn.

"You gotta squeeze tight," their father said to Ella. "Until you feel her heartbeat in your own legs."

Another day. More riding lessons. The giant saucer of a track stretched out in revolutions, kicked-up dust hazy in the early morning light. Butterscotch stood erect beside their father as he held the reins. The night before, the entire family had watched this horse race with elegant speed, lithe rider crouched above in a perfect arc, Butterscotch's slim ankles a blur of motion. She came in third.

"You cannot show hesitation," said their father. "You gotta show her that you trust her above all else. You trust her with your life. She's trusting you with hers."

Angie was in nursery school, too young to ride the horses. But she wanted to know that feeling her father described. Of pure trust. She watched in awe as he climbed onto the penny-colored horse and galloped off. He was the size of a jockey himself with his small frame, short stature. Angie wondered had he ever done that, raced horses rather than train them.

Just Angie, Ella and Daddy, together. Denise hated nearly everything about the racetrack. She hated the ever-shitting horses and their startling neighs, the harsh-looking grooms and exercise boys with their dirty dungarees and stinky stall smell. Their mother loved the races themselves, but beyond that didn't need to see more, not at this point thank you.

When their father returned from his lap around the track, he climbed off Butterscotch and Ella climbed on. He studied her closely as she rode around. Angie envied her sister as she watched her lean in low, chest rubbing against the horse's back. Ella hadn't discovered the diet pills yet, and her wide, strong thighs spread across the sweat-stained saddle.

"You look good up there," their father told Ella. "You look a little heavy on her, though. Gotta get some of that weight off."

His words hanging there, Ella kicked the horse's haunches and took off, bouncing up and down clumsily as Butterscotch ran around the inside track. Angie winced when Ella slapped harder at the horse's rump.

Their father shook his head as she made her way around the first bend. "She has no patience," he said. "She wants everything right away." And when Ella rode back up, he put his hand out for her to climb down, and said, "Don't try to tell her what to do. Guide her, but don't try to control her." He laughed. "You may be smart, girl, but you can't outsmart a horse."

FOR AS LONG as she could remember, Angie spent her weekend days at the raceway alongside her father and Ella. Adele, the secretary in the front office, the exercise boys, the stable-hands, the jocks, the hangers-on, everyone knew her father, each greeting him brightly as they passed by, "Hey, Mr. Mackenzie!" Angie could get whatever she wanted from the concession stand—hot chocolate and pizza and popcorn—and just say, "I'm Samson Mackenzie's daughter," and she paid for nothing. After he'd done his work, her father would walk them along the shed row, pointing out each horse's potential and peculiarities. "This one here, Whisper, she's a sweetheart." He stroked her nose. "But she needs a sugar cube every time to motivate her." And at the next stall, "Now Shadowboxer, he's a good one. Will do whatever you ask of him. Whatever." He moved on to yet another stall. "And Double or Nothing, she got the right name 'cause she been all nothing. I'm waiting on the double."

Angie held her father's rough hand, and as he rubbed the horses behind their ears and patted them between the eyes, she felt his bliss. These were as much his children as she and Ella and Denise were. Swishing tails and soft snorts punctuated the quiet, and the sweet smell from straw beds and oats engulfed her. Behind every stall's door was an enchanted little world for horse lovers. She wished her father the horseman was inside a children's book, so she could share him with her friends.

But he needed a winner. He hadn't had a horse pay a big purse since Thumbsucker. That horse was a mythical figure to Angie. He'd won the state's version of the Kentucky Derby, the Michigan Mile, years before she was born. "A horse trainer is only as good as his winners," Samson would say to Nanette, worry in his voice.

"You're one of a handful of Negro trainers in the country," Nanette would tell him. "That means something, Samson."

He'd told the girls his story: Been in the horse life since he was in short pants. Skipped school to hang around horses at the state fairgrounds. Ran away from home at thirteen to be part of that life. Took off with a horseman who gave him his first job, cleaning horseshoes, shoveling shit. He spent many a year working as an exerciser, taking the horses out on the track, letting them stretch out. He was a man of thirty and still the men he worked for called him "boy." "That there Niggra over there, now he's my exercise boy. Hard worker." Times when, running horses on southern tracks, places with no motels for coloreds, he slept in barns at night, bunching together the hay into straw pallets. Moved his family north, worked long hours at Hazel Park Raceway, got noticed for his intuition. Convinced a couple owners to trust him, got them decent wins, and finally hung out his shingle, "Samson Mackenzie Stables."

It was a hard life. Staying up nights worrying about a sick horse, ever fearful of one dropping dead, tough conversations with irate owners. And a life on the road, one that Angie came to believe cost him, the way it kept him from his wife and girls. Six months at the track in Florida every year, then six months at Detroit's track, with short stints to other tracks across the country. Keeping tabs, scouting, ever searching for the perfect Thoroughbred for his picky owners.

"You can do something else for a while," their mother said.

"Like what? Set up in some factory, putting left doors on Mustangs or Cadillacs?" said Samson. "I'd rather die first."

It was a hard life, and he would never give it up. He loved it.

Saturday morning, a sunny day not long after they'd pumped Ella's stomach. She's atop Nightshade, a dark brown horse with sandy-colored circles just above her haunches and white socks on her legs. They're done for the day and Nightshade trots slowly off the track, Angie and their father walking beside her. A man stalks toward them, obviously an owner—tall, middle-aged, white, wearing his air of privilege and presumption like a tight vest.

"Samson, you and me need to talk."

"How you doing, Mr. Jamison?" Samson asks, taking in the man's body language. "Nightshade here is looking good," he says, rubbing her nose.

"Not to me she ain't, goddammit." He nods toward the horse. "I wanna know what's up with the bitch? Coming in fourth in that last race, now what is that about? Might as well got claimed. I paid for a Thoroughbred, and you told me that's what I got. You didn't lie to me now, did you?"

"Ain't nothing to lie about," says Samson. "Only problem you got with her is you running her too much."

"Hell, what I'm gon' wait for, huh? I want my money's worth. I bought her to run her."

Their father nods. "She will do right by you if you let her rest up a bit. She don't have the same stamina as these younger ones. She's a good horse, ain't peaked yet or nothing. She needs time to recover between races is all."

"I don't know, Samson. I trusted you, didn't I? Friends say, 'What you doing with a colored as your trainer?' But I said, 'Nah, this here is 1970; I believe he can handle it.' Now I'm wondering." He pauses. "You not one of them lying niggas, are you?"

At the sound of that word, Ella abruptly turns Nightshade back toward the track and takes off, startling Mr. Jamison.

"What the—"

Nightshade and Ella glide around the half-mile track with

precision, the horse's graceful legs angled like a dancer's. Their father's look of worry shifts to elation. He whistles. "I will be damned!"

Ella takes the track with a confidence she'd never shown before. She grips the reins just so, leans in on the corners and rises up from the saddle at the stretch. Angie cheers her on in her head, *Go, Go!* One lap. *Please do it right.* Two laps. *Don't mess up!* Third lap and Ella returns, hair blown back. Nightshade gallops up to them, stops at attention, proud. *Yay!*

"Mr. Jamison," says Ella, out of breath. "You got an amazing racehorse here, and if you don't want her anymore, let me know. I can think of a few people who'd be happy to take her off your hands."

Mr. Jamison shields his eyes from the sun as he looks up at her. "I'll keep that in mind, young gal." He turns to their father. "Let's see how things go, Samson. I'm a set tight for a spell." He nods his head toward Ella. "Look like you got you a jockey in the family."

Mr. Jamison turns, walks off, his dress shoes crunching the gravel. Ella climbs off Nightshade and their father takes her into his arms, lifts her off her feet as he swings her around. He can't stop grinning. "Unbelievable!" he gushes. He whistles again.

Marveling at her father's joy, Angie is suddenly furious. Why wasn't he hugging *her*, swinging *her* around?

"You look damn good out there, girl!" He shakes his head, still grinning. "Looking like a jockey if I ever seen one!"

They lead Nightshade back to her stall, reward her with water, extra oats. But suddenly Ella grabs on to her father. "I feel like I'm gonna—"

She faints, tumbling onto the hay. Their father runs to the first aid kit he keeps in his cluttered cubbyhole office and grabs smelling salts, puts it under her nose. As she watches Ella regain consciousness, four-year-old Angie feels a fresh pang of guilt over her jealousy.

No one would know for years, but Ella had fasted for three days, living on water and a daily carrot she shared every morning with Nightshade. She was determined to keep the figure her father had praised her for.

"Wait 'til you see her!" Samson told his wife later, bedroom door flung open for all to hear. "She's got it. She's got that thing that a jockey's gotta have. I'm telling you, she can do this. Long as she don't get much taller, and she stays the same size, she can do this."

"I want her to do something respectable with her life," said Nanette. "Something clean and upstanding. I don't want her to spend her days at one dirty racetrack after another, all kinds of men lurking about. And I certainly don't want her getting run over by a horse, lose her life in some freak accident."

"Do you hear what I'm saying?" Samson was exasperated. "The girl has a gift! She could be the first colored female jockey! That's as respectable as they come."

"She's got a brilliant mind," said Nanette. "I want her to use it."

"You don't think it takes brilliance to ride a horse to victory? You don't think that requires a high level of intelligence?"

"You know what I mean, Samson. Don't try to mix up my words."

"Imagine it! She'll be in *Ebony*, a whole spread, her posing on top of a fine-looking horse, trophy in hand. Can't you see that?" He paused, looking at the imaginary magazine feature. "I see it clear as day."

"I'm just worried about you pushing her into it," said Nanette.

"That's because you haven't seen her ride! Going at it like

she got a hunger she can't satisfy. And I know all about that, how you get them horses up inside you and you just can't stay away. She loves it, Nan. She downright loves it."

"What she loves is pleasing you," said their mother. "And I'm here to tell you Samson, that's not the same thing."

ANGIE AND DENISE grew up hearing family lore about Ella: how she walked at eight months, talked in full sentences by her first birthday, and could read a book by age three. Those facts made Angie feel that whatever *she* did, she couldn't compete, could never catch up, had already blown it before she was out of toddlerhood.

When Nanette took Ella to be tested, the psychologist said she had the highest IQ he'd ever seen in a Negro girl. Each time she told the story years later, burnishing it over time, their mother shook her head, as if marveling anew at the mind of her oldest daughter. But anyone who listened knew she was really bragging. She was proud of Ella, certain she'd be a first. She'd be the first one in the family to go to college, the first to have a professional career. Maybe the first Afro-American female in Michigan to become a psychiatrist, a judge, or a US congresswoman, like Shirley Chisholm. Who could say? She'd be living proof that migrating north had been worth it, that given the opportunity, a child of two southern blacks with slight education could achieve greatness. She'd make every indignity her mother and father faced at the hands of a hostile white world worth it.

And then there were the tales of Ella's bottomless hunger, her insatiable appetite for something once she fixated on it. How she ate oatmeal every day for one year, refusing to eat anything else. How she discovered Nancy Drew mysteries in third grade, and devoured them so steadily, reading them through the night, that her mother had to talk to the librarian at the local branch, ask her not to loan any more of the series to Ella, who'd developed dark circles under her eyes. How she became obsessed with her first two-wheeler, had to ride it to school daily, threw a tantrum when their mother wouldn't let her ride it in four-feet-high snow.

The aunties, her father's sisters, had some of the best family tales about Ella. The aunties had taken care of their brother's child from the time she was five until she was seven. They called her Daughter. They'd ply her with a heaping of butter beans or fried chicken or smothered cabbage and watch her eat. Every time they dumped more food on her plate, she ate it all. "Had enough?" they'd ask, in unison. "Had enough?" And on cue Ella always said, "Not even!" which just tickled her aunties to death.

Aunt Bea loved to tell the story of Ella joining her parents in Detroit. "The day Daughter left for up North, Oh my Lord, that was some sad day. But not for her. No ma'am. She said, 'Auntie Bea, I got to go, so don't you cry. Mama and Daddy are waiting for me and I been waiting for them.' She was not afraid of riding the train alone neither. She was itching to get on it. 'I'm not gonna shut my eyes the whole ride,' she said. And you know that girl could do whatever she put her mind to. When that locomotive pulled out of the station, you talking about tears, oh I cried me a little river. But Daughter was dry eyed. I waved goodbye till I couldn't see her no more, and I thought, *She is going far in life.* That's what come to me. I could tell right then and there, she was gonna *be* something. 'Cause I'm here to tell you, that child was fearless."

Another apocryphal Ella tale: Samson letting her ride his pony, Bill, around the little inside track, and Ella always wanting to go faster, faster, until running beside them, her father couldn't keep up, let her go, and one day she lost her grip on Bill and fell off, flying before hitting the hard dirt. Ella lay there, in pain; her arm broken.

Their mother hadn't been there, had been at five-year-old Denise's birthday party, amid the cacophony of celebratory girls, already pregnant with Angie. When they walked into the house, Ella upstaging the party with her bright, white cast, their mother gasped, "What happened?"

As soon as he explained, she lit into her husband right in front of the kindergartners. "How the hell did you let that happen, Samson?"

"She kept saying, 'Faster, faster!'" he said, in defense. "And I asked her over and over, 'Had enough?' And she kept saying, 'Not even.' That's what she said, God do hear me say, she said, 'Not even!'"

"She's nine!" her mother screamed.

"But I wanted to do it," said Ella.

"You broke your arm," her mother pointed out.

"It was worth it."

ANGIE REMEMBERED SO little, really, of her father: His curly yet wild salt-and-pepper hair, those saddle-rough hands, the way he'd give her piggyback rides as he made his rounds at the horses' stalls. Those practice sessions on the track.

His smell was an intoxicating mixture of the outdoors and aftershave. Early mornings in the car, headed to the track, sun just peeling away the darkness, she'd scoot close and inhale him deeply as they sat three abreast in the front seat, cool jazz spilling from the radio.

He was on the road so much that his presence was like a holiday. Everything felt special—eating pancakes together in the morning, watching him repair things around the house, greedily eyeing him and their mother as they slipped behind the closing bedroom door. As a family, they'd go to all the races running his horses. Angie loved the crowds, the whooping yells, the starting bell, the discarded tickets scattered across the ground like oversized confetti. And when one of his horses placed—not first, but often third, sometimes second even—she loved going down to the winner's circle and standing with her sisters and parents and her father's horse. She remembered warm summer nights, cicadas singing out, the family posing as the photographer snapped, his giant cone of a flash blinding them briefly. And then her father's racetrack family would take over, crowding them out. They'd whisk him off for some post-race chatter and another hour would go by. Their mother knew the drill, like the girlfriend of a musician after the gig, so she drove her own car to the track. Angie and Denise rode with her to the Chinese restaurant where they always had dinner afterward. But Ella stayed with their father. "You want to hang out with me a bit?" he'd say to her. And she always did, even though she had to be hungry, or tired, or just ready to go. Or maybe not. Her needs or desires could never compete with his need to show her off, his daughter, the soon-to-be jockey.

Afterward, they'd all sit at a big round table at China Delight, passing plates of pepper steak and egg foo young and shrimp fried rice. Sometimes, by the time her father and Ella joined them, Angie was already asleep in her mother's lap. And sometimes Denise would try to gain her father's attention, telling him about a book report she'd done on racehorses, or a math project that determined the probability of winning. Once, she showed him a sketch she'd drawn of a horse, a pen and ink done in her art class. She'd filled it in with watercolor, giving the horse a sandy brown hue. She was clearly talented.

"Which horse is that?" asked their father.

"It's just one I made up," she said.

"See, if you'd learn to ride a horse, you'd know what one really looks like," he said, chuckling. "That there is a nice picture, but it don't look like a real horse."

Denise said nothing. *Why didn't you just draw Bill, Daddy's pony?* Angie thought. *Silly!* Throughout the rest of the meal, Denise poked at her food until the gravy on her egg foo young congealed. Later, Angie found the deft, delicate watercolor tossed in the trash. She felt sorry for Denise, but she left it there.

ANOTHER DAY IN the stalls. A chilly morning. Their father is beside himself. He failed a stress test and Dr. Benjamin has ordered him to take some time off, said otherwise he wouldn't sign off on the yearly physical exam required of all racetrack employees. "How the hell I'm gonna do that?" he complained to his girls—to Ella really, but Angie pretended he was talking to her too. "Can I tell a horse to take a break? Can I tell the races, in the middle of the season, to take a break? Can I tell these owners breathing down my back to take a break? Folks depend on me. I stop, everything stops."

He rubbed down Baby's Breath's legs and wrapped them with bandages, tenderly lifting her hoofs. This was a new horse of his, the owner new to him as well. She'd been bred from two winners and expectations were high for the pedigreed Thoroughbred. "Thing is, if I start cutting back now, I might as well admit it's all over," said her father. "And what's my legacy gonna be, huh? One big win? Just one?"

The summer before, *Jet* magazine had on its cover the picture of a black female jockey with the headline, "Cheryl White: Teenage Girl Cracks Barrier On Racetrack." Someone else had gotten there first. Ella never commented on the article, but she taped the cover photo to her wall.

Now, she stroked Baby's Breath on the nose. "This one's a winner," she said. "You can look at her and tell."

Their father rose from the stool he'd been squatting on, stood beside Ella. "Yeah, she's a beauty." He held the horse's face in his hand. "I do have high hopes for this one."

Later, they walked Baby's Breath out on the track. "She's still got a bit of wildness in her, but I'm not too bothered by that," said their father. "Gives her a winning spirit."

"Can I ride her around?" asked Ella. She'd just turned sixteen.

"Alright, but go easy. We just giving her some exercise right now."

As soon as she mounted the horse, Ella said, "Daddy, I'm your legacy," pulled the reins tight, leaned over, and took off. Fast.

"What the hell are you doing?" their father yelled. Angie, confused by her father's harsh tone, prayed that Ella would ride perfectly, impress him again, like before. Make him joyful. *Go on*, she thought. *Just get it right.* But as she watched her father's agitation, fear gripped Angie. He waved his arms as Ella flew around the track. "Slow down, slow down! She's not ready for that! She's not broken in all the way yet! Slow down!"

But Ella was too far away to hear him.

"Goddammit, that girl don't know the meaning of the word *stop*." He took off his baseball cap, threw it to the ground. "Goddammit!"

Suddenly, the horse rose up on its hind legs. Their father began running toward Ella and Baby's Breath, but they were at least a quarter mile away. He stopped. "Hold them reins tight," he whispered, as if Ella were within earshot. "Hold on, and calm her down, ride her out of it."

Terrified, Angie ran to her father and he held her in his arms, eyes on the racetrack. The horse stayed on two legs for an eternity. Angie could see Ella's blue parka, the hood flapping around as she struggled to stay on.

"Don't fall off. Hold on, just hold on," their father chanted. "Just hold on."

Miraculously, the horse brought down her front legs, and landed well, didn't snap a limb. Ella regained control, and Baby's Breath slowed to a steady gallop.

"She's OK," her father said, letting out his breath. "He patted the top of Angie's head. "She's OK."

They watched together as Ella made her way toward them. In that minute or so, Angie could feel her father tensing, the anger rising in him.

As Baby's Breath trotted up to them, he barked, "Get your ass down."

Ella knew she'd gone too far. "I don't know what made her rise up like that," she said, desperate.

"I said get down!" he yelled. Ella swung one leg over and their father didn't wait, pulled her off the horse, making her stumble. He shook her hard, both hands squeezing her arms. Ella's face froze in shock.

"What is the matter with you?" he said. "What if she'd thrown you, huh?" His eyes bucked. "What if she'd broken her leg or something, huh? Then what? Goddammit, then where would we be, huh?"

Ella winced, said nothing. Their father shook her again. "Don't you know when enough is enough? Don't you know when to stop?"

Loose tears tumbled down her face. "Not even," she said.

Their father stared at her. Seconds passed before he let out a sad chuckle and wrapped Ella into his arms, hugged her tight. "Don't you ever scare me like that again," he said, eyes moist.

Angie grabbed onto her father's leg, all she could reach. He looked down, picked her up, and the three of them stood there hugging until Baby's Breath neighed loudly, reminding them that she'd just been through an ordeal too.

That night, Ella let Angie watch as she wrote a letter to God, begging Him to allow Baby's Breath to win her big race. "In Jesus's name, I ask these things of you," wrote Ella. She signed it, "Your loving servant." She wrote it on plain loose-leaf paper, then folded it neatly and placed it between the pages of the giant family Bible that no one ever read. Angie thought God deserved prettier stationary.

A SPRING NIGHT, which turned out to be Ella's last at the stable. She and her father were prepping Baby's Breath for the next day's race, which she was favored to win. Angie sat on a stool nearby, watching them. Their father was anxious. As the horse stood in a tub of ice, he stroked her mane. "This race right here could change my luck," he said. "Turn it all around."

"She's going to win," Ella told him. "Look at her. She's perfect."

Their father nodded. "Hell, I can't believe how nervous I am. And I shouldn't be. Rodrigo Diaz, the jock, he's as good as they come."

"Wish I was the one riding her out there tomorrow," said Ella, wistful. "One day."

Her father fell silent. He hadn't done much training with her lately. "About that. You racing. Got to lose some weight if you wanna take that whole thing seriously. Look at that there girl's picture you got up on your wall. Lean as the day is long."

Each of her father's words must have felt like tiny slaps across her face. She'd gained back the weight she'd lost two years before, and then some. After she'd swallowed those diet pills, and had her stomach pumped, she left the amphetamines alone. Yes, she'd tried fasting, but couldn't keep it up. She tried making herself throw up, but that didn't work because she couldn't bear to put a finger down her throat. She stole her mother's Senokot pills for a while, but hated what laxatives did to her, so she stopped that too.

"I'm not fat," she said.

"Nah, you just not riding weight. But you can get them extra pounds off; I seen you do it before. Just push the plate away from you, that's all."

Hearing advice about willpower from her father, of all people, had to be hard. He was a lithe man who could eat whatever he wanted, never gain a pound. Angie had inherited his metabolism. Ella and Denise had inherited their mother's, setting them up for a lifetime of weight watching. It wasn't fair. She kicked over the stool she'd been sitting on, grabbed Angie's hand, and stormed out, leaving their father bewildered.

She dropped Angie off at the front office, told Adele to keep an eye on her, then wandered through the quiet track; she had to have been furious and sad and hurt and ashamed all at once. She later said that was when she ran into Jeff, one of the new exercise boys, and they went off together for a while.

When she returned to their father's stable, she found him in the barn, splayed out beneath Baby's Breath, who was licking his face. He didn't respond when she called out to him. She hovered over his body, but was afraid to touch him for fear that she would make things worse. Terrified, she ran out, yelling for help. A security guard called the ambulance.

Massive. That was how the doctors described his heart attack.

"Child, please believe me, there was nothing you could have done," implored their mother. "Doctor said he died before he hit the ground."

But Ella was inconsolable. She wept and wept, sobbing for hours at a time. "I left him alone," she kept saying. "If I had been there, I could've saved him. People survive heart attacks. He died because I wasn't there."

Baby's Breath won. First place. The racetrack owner dedicated the evening's races to "Samson Mackenzie, a trailblazing black man with a golden touch." It was heart wrenching. His family stood in the winner's circle, had their picture taken with the owner, the jockey, and Baby's Breath. The race paid a nice purse—Samson had set up a bet on the horse himself—but that didn't offer much consolation.

"Why didn't I know CPR?" Ella lamented during the ride home that evening. No one spoke as her agonized sobs filled the car. "I could've saved him. I could have."

Angie thought that she'd die herself from a heart attack, that's how much her chest hurt. And she couldn't help thinking that Ella had asked God the wrong favor.

FOUR

AFTER HE DIED, ELLA GAVE UP THE HORSES, REFUSING TO go anywhere near the racetrack. In those early weeks, she wouldn't eat and lost the very weight her father had chastised her for, that and more. She looked gaunt, sickly, too little flesh hanging onto her big-boned frame. She couldn't sleep, so Dr. Benjamin prescribed modest milligrams of Valium, which their mother initially had to force her to take. In those first weeks, Angie felt like an asthmatic, unable to catch her breath. She believed the oxygen they needed to breathe was sealed off behind Ella's closed bedroom door. Only in her absence did Angie understand what Ella's presence had brought to the household. Now she wasn't there to enliven dinner conversations with captivating stories about what Butterscotch or Whisper or Baby's Breath had done at the track that day, antics that Angie was thrilled to hear, even though she'd been right beside her when they happened. Ella was the one who gave her sisters IQ tests for fun, who showed them how to play elaborate card games with silly names—bid whist, hearts, gin rummy—who spoke French and quoted Freud and blasted classical music by black composers on the hi-fi. And Ella was the one who taught them all, their mother included, a Buddhist chant she'd discovered somewhere, *Nam myoho renge kyo*. "Say the words over and over when you can't find something or you're messed up over some situation or just plain scared, and you'll get really calm," Ella had promised. "Suddenly your mind will reveal a solution. It works like magic." They all tried it out: their mother when she misplaced her keys, Denise when she wanted a certain boy to ask her to the junior high dance, even Angie when she wanted to be chosen as a table captain at school; they decided yes, she was right, it worked.

Angie was six, old enough to feel the deep loss of Ella's dramatic infusions. She understood that now they weren't special anymore—just another average family on the block, like any other black family. No more magic. And their father was dead.

Angela Davis's trial is what finally brought Ella out of her room. The previous fall, their father had given Ella the "Free Angela" button, and she'd worn it pinned to her navy peacoat throughout winter and into spring. Samson had gotten it from one of the Nation of Islam men who stood outside Temple No. 1 on Linwood Avenue selling bean pies and copies of *Elijah Speaks*. "That girl reminds me of you," he told Ella. "Smart as a whip, putting her mind to something and sticking with it, even when she's up against hell and high water. Brave."

Ella was, like everyone, transfixed by images of the pretty, gap-toothed black girl with the big Afro, this intellectual radical who'd been on the lam, made the FBI's Most Wanted List. Ella followed the trial closely for weeks, watching the news coverage every night on the floor-model TV in the living room. She was transfixed. But Ella's obsession clearly frightened their mother. "All that book sense didn't stop that girl from buying a gun to help some thug kill a judge," she said, standing in front of the TV. Ella ignored her. Through it all, Angie thought it was wrong, simply insane that *she* was named Angela, that she'd been given that name instead of her big sister. She felt her mother had gotten it wrong.

When Angela Davis was acquitted that June, Ella went straight to the Shrine of the Black Madonna's bookstore on Livernois Avenue, where they held a celebration party. She bought a copy of Davis's book, *If They Come in the Morning*, and read it in two days. After that, Ella was at the Shrine weekly, buying books recommended by Sharif, the owner, hanging around, *getting schooled* as he called it. She read the work of Frantz Fanon and Eldridge Cleaver and Malcolm X, listened to a recording of Stokely Carmichael's 1966 speech on Black Power in Detroit, and by the end of that summer had abandoned the straightening comb, was wearing a natural that framed her face like a hair bonnet. Nanette, as a newly widowed mother of three girls, was just old enough to be frightened by the Black Power movement. "I see smart young men and women, whose parents sacrificed mightily, letting themselves get swept up in something lawless," she said to Ella. "And my years in the South have taught me they can't win," she added, "Because the white man has all the resources on his side. All of them."

Meanwhile, Angie thought her big sister was an Afro goddess.

Ella wasn't a radical who proselytized. Nor did she attend the big Black Power rallies held downtown. She was too shy, too self-conscious for that. But she did share more and more observations with her family. "Ever think about everything Daddy went through because of the Man?" she'd say. "How many years he worked his way up before they gave him a chance to train? The stress he was under every day?" Mostly she kept her head buried in Sharif's books, sometimes bringing them with her to the dinner table, oversized glasses perched on her small nose as she ignored the food in front of her.

Mimicking her sister, Angie also turned to books in those early weeks after their father's death. At first, she was content with picture books and Dr. Seuss. But then she found *Black*

Beauty on Ella's bedroom shelf, was drawn to the cover image of a beautiful ebony-colored horse. She asked Ella to read the story to her, but Ella said she was too busy; she asked Denise next, who said OK; Angie relished in the descriptions, conjuring the smells and sounds and tastes of the stables, of her father, of an accumulated loss so acute it would take years to unpack. That summer, Denise walked her again and again to the local library, where they checked out one pony book after another. Denise dutifully read them all to Angie, as they lay in their room, fan whirring, each lying across her own twin bed. "Where are the little black girls riding ponies?" Ella said one hot July day, as she passed by her sisters reading together on the living room sofa, cooled by the air conditioner. "Ignore Miss Militant," said Denise. After that, Angie still loved the pony stories but found herself nagged by the blond and raven and red-haired girls at the center of them all.

Eventually, Ella regained her appetite. She developed an obsessive love for Red Barn's chicken. Her favorite snacks were Ding Dongs and Lay's potato chips. She took to eating meals in her room, a book in one hand, fork or chicken thigh or chip in the other. Their mother made Ella's favorite desserts— banana pudding and ambrosia salad. And she sometimes bought Awrey's Boston cream pie, most of which Ella managed to eat. Nanette noticed Ella's overeating, but said nothing, acutely aware that while they all grieved for Samson, Ella naturally grieved the hardest. Food was a comfort. Why take that from her? When their mother heard Denise call Ella "a fat ass," she lashed out at her. "Who are you to talk?" she snapped. "You're no Twiggy, and never will be." After that Denise, and everyone else, knew to say nothing about Ella's weight gain.

Thinking about it now, Angie couldn't remember Ella when she was slim, only the vague outline of her that day she swallowed those pills. But she cherished the black and white photo-

graphs of Ella from her years in Nashville. In one, Ella sits at a
toy piano, poised, hands on keys, smiling softly at the camera.
In another, she stands erect, a pocketbook in the crook of her
arm. Both were taken the same day, Ella dressed in the same
Easter Sunday outfit. She is a thin girl, bright eyes looking out
from a sepia-toned universe. Angie couldn't believe this was her
sister before she herself was born, that Ella had once lived in a
different guise, in a different place, oblivious to Angie's eventual
existence.

About a year after their father's death, when Ella was a high
school senior, Sharif gave her Huey P. Newton's autobiography, *Revolutionary Suicide*. She devoured it, and was so moved by
the inspired radicalism that soon after she joined Sharif at the
Masonic Temple for her first political rally. They saw the fire-
brand political activist Coleman Young speak. His rough-side
eloquence moved her as he spoke of his bid to be Detroit's first
black mayor, and the need to rid the city of its police brutality,
as well as its "murder capital of the world" moniker.

Days later, their mother caught Ella smoking in her room,
and confronted her. "What are you doing? You could get
hooked!" she warned.

"I can stop whenever I want," said Ella.

"You don't know what you can or can't stop until it's too
late," their mother snapped back. "And you're not grown yet. I
don't want you smoking, you hear me?"

"Save your breath, Mama," said Ella. "'Cause I'm gonna do
it behind your back no matter what you say. That's just what's
happening."

Their mother's face showed the alarm, showed how hard it
was to be alone in all this, no husband as backup. "Who the
hell do you think you are?" she said, but the words had little
force behind them.

They compromised. Ella promised to only smoke light

cigarettes, which, according to the ads, were safer. And never inside the house.

Ella left for U of M the fall of 1974, just two weeks after Nixon resigned, the nation's sense of betrayal dominating the news and Angie's dreams. She watched as Ella packed a foot-locker of clothes and toiletries, and felt tinges of betrayal, as though someone had lied to her, hadn't told the *whole* story of what it means when a sister goes off to college. On the drive up, her mother was wistful, said she'd longed to attend Vanderbilt University, but had to give up that dream when she became a young wife and mother. Throughout the drive, Ella said little, in fact spent most of the trip with her head buried in a paperback edition of *Helter Skelter*, its creepy cover and splashed-on letters disturbing to eight-year-old Angie. That first semester, Angie visited Ella on campus, and was awed by the size and expanse of the university. Meanwhile, their mother was relieved to have her oldest daughter out of Detroit. "Black mayor or not, this city is out of control," she said. "You never know which way harm's coming." Angie decided that she too would one day go to the same big university in the town with the movie-star name: Ann Arbor.

Ella came home on visits saying how white students had called her a "quota baby" to her face, how they made comments in class about "some people being here just because they're black," and how her white roommate in the residence hall demanded she be given another room. Their mother said, "Stay focused on why you're there." But Ella clearly felt iso-lated, and the object of seething resentment. She found solace by joining the Black Student Union and often hung out on the lumpy sofas of the Center for Afro-American and Africa Stud-ies' windowless office.

At the end of freshman year, Ella announced that she'd be majoring in black studies. "What the hell kinda major is *that?*"

asked their mother. "You think I'm sending you to college to learn how to be *black*? I'm sending you there to learn something you don't know, something that'll help you out here in this white man's world. Black studies my ass!" And when that didn't work, her mother pulled out her trump card, "Your father would never have wanted you to do something like that. He did *not* believe in black for black's sake. You're a human being first. Race comes second. That was how he lived his life."

But even mention of her father didn't work. Ella had made up her mind; for the next three years she came home on weekends and holidays filled with newfound knowledge about black Africa and its shackles of colonialism, about all the contributions of Afro-Americans to society from "day one," and the real deal, as she called it, about slavery. Her sophomore year, Ella participated in a sit-in at the administrative building, protesting the university's paltry 7 percent black-student enrollment. She told her family of a three-day protest where students slept on the stone steps, refusing to leave. When the Soweto Uprising took place, Ella wrote the position paper for the University's Black Action Movement, insisting that U of M "had an obligation to divest from South Africa, where nearly two hundred students were killed simply for protesting the forced use of Afrikaans in their schools."

Angie found it all a bit frightening and beyond her understanding, but she loved Ella's passion, how wise she sounded, puffing her light cigarettes, bright eyes behind owl glasses, speaking through blown smoke with stark tidbits of knowing.

FIVE

ON FRIDAYS, ANGIE WORKED THE MORNING SHIFT AT THE store. She and her mother always had breakfast together at the Original House of Pancakes, a TGIF treat, as her mother called it. Dr. Benjamin's office was on Ewald Circle on Detroit's west side, in an undulating modern structure of glass block and creamy brick. Still, they ate near Northland Mall in Southfield so Angie wouldn't be late for work.

She watched her mother pour heavy cream into her coffee, stir it slowly, and noticed her mother's hands absent of jewelry.

"Where's your wedding band?" she asked.

Nanette looked up, clearly startled by the question. She stirred her coffee. "I put it away."

"Why?"

"Because it's been fifteen years since your father died, that's why."

"I mean, why all of a sudden?"

"It's not all of a sudden, Angela. There's nothing sudden about it."

The two sat through an awkward pause as Angie poured syrup on her pancakes.

"So, what are you planning for the summer?" her mother asked.

"Why, do you need me to get out of the way or something?" snapped Angie.

"What kind of question is that?"

"Denise basically said as much to me yesterday."

Her mother sighed. "She's just trying to help. She's a little worried about you, that's all."

"Why?"

"Don't get defensive, please. Because if you do, then we don't have to talk about it."

"I won't get defensive."

Her mother hesitated. "She just feels, well honestly, we both feel that you seem like you're...drifting."

"Drifting? I just fucking graduated like two minutes ago!"

"Don't curse. You know I don't like it when you curse."

"I don't know what you're talking about, really. Drifting?"

"I'd like to see you . . ." Her mother searched for the right word. "Excited about something, that's all. Not just working at that crazy store every day. You've got your psychology degree now. Maybe you want to get a master's. Or—"

"What's crazy about the store?"

"Nothing, Angela. I didn't mean anything by it, OK?"

"Yes you did."

"No I didn't. I shouldn't have said that." Her mother sighed. "Let's just eat our breakfast, how about that?"

Angie stabbed at a pancake. "Turns out, I do have a plan for the summer."

"I'm listening."

"I'm going to travel."

"You are? Well, that's something!" Her mother smiled at her. "I think it'll be good for you to get away."

It bothered Angie that her mother was so pleased. She just nodded.

"So where? Brazil?"

"No."

Her mother eyed her. "Europe?"

Angie shook her head.

"Where?"

"Don't get upset, OK?"

Her mother put her fork down. "Do not tell me you're planning to go *there*."

Angie nodded.

"Why? Of all the places in the world Angela, why?"

Angie shrugged. Suddenly she couldn't explain it, now that her mother sat across from her. "It's where I want to go."

Her mother pushed her plate away. "I don't think that's a good idea."

"Why not?"

"You *know* why not."

"Nothing is going to happen to me, Mama. I'll be very careful."

"It's not just that. It's a god-awful place, and Lord knows a lot could happen to you, but it's not just that."

"What is it then?"

Her mother leaned across the table. "There's nothing there for you to find. Believe me."

"I'm not *looking* for anything," Angie insisted. "I've always wanted to see it, ever since she came back the first time, talking about it."

Her mother sat back, folded her arms. "You want to do everything she did."

Angie looked out the picture window, watched as cars pulled into the parking lot. "That's not true."

"Isn't it?"

She turned her gaze back to her mother. "Have I tried to do drugs?"

The words hung between them, echoing back and forth. Angie regretted them but it was too late.

"No, thank God, you haven't done that," said her mother. "And I'm not accusing you of anything, it's just—"

"It feels like you are." Angie took a small bite of her flapjacks.

"Well, that's not my intention." Her mother paused. She was obviously measuring her words. "I'm just concerned that you haven't found your *own* thing that interests you."

"Going there interests me."

Her mother sighed. "That was *her* thing, Angela. She was into the whole black pride, we're-all-Africans-so-let's-unite thing. Going there, it made sense for her. But you're different."

"You don't think I care about that stuff too?"

Her mother took a sip of her coffee. Angie waited. "Not really, no."

"So I'm fake, is that what you think?"

Her mother reached out, put her hand on top of Angie's. Her touch was warm, soft. "I think there are a lot of different ways to be black in this world, and you just need to find yours."

SHE COULD BARELY concentrate at work, felt dizzied by the endless racks of clothing. When a customer entered her department, and began browsing, Angie was tempted to ignore her. The woman wore a tight V-neck sweater over palazzo pants, an outfit that didn't flatter her body at all. Angie guessed that the woman was about a size 20.

The woman eyed her, so Angie made her way over.

"I'm looking for a pretty dress to wear on a date," she said. "What can you show me?"

Angie beckoned, led the woman to a circular rack of primary-color dresses. She pulled one out for the woman to see. It was linen A-line, with a modest scoop-neck collar and a gentle flare out from the waist. "My sister bought these dresses in three different colors," said Angie. "They never go out of style. They're so flattering."

The woman scrunched up her face. "Nah, not my thing. It's a little retro, don't you think? I like to be in style, up-to-date."

"This is classic," said Angie.

The woman shook her head. "I'm gonna keep looking around."

Angie gingerly placed the dress back on the rack. She loved it, loved how Ella looked in hers, especially the purple one she wore to Angie's high school graduation. They were all together, her mother and the girls, all happy. No one mentioned Denise's missed college graduation, but that mishap underscored the day, made this one more acutely festive. The day was imbued with double triumph: Ella was drugfree, had reached her one-year anniversary, and was heading on a celebratory trip to Africa. Angie remembered how, when her name was called and she walked across the stage of Renaissance High, she couldn't see her mother in the audience, but she spotted Ella's purple dress. Just as she shook hands with the principal and gripped her diploma, she turned to see Ella waving at her, cheering her on—but to Angie, it felt like she was waving goodbye.

WHEN SHE RETURNED home from work, she found Denise and their mother sitting together, watching *Beverly Hills Cop*, the box for a new Video Cassette Recorder sitting open beside them.

"Is that what I think it is?" asked Angie.

Their mother looked up. "Can you believe it? You can watch any movie you want whenever you want." She shook her head. "Denise insisted on getting me this newfangled thing. I told her I'll never figure out how to work it."

"And I told you it's easy. Now that it's set up, all you have to do is push a couple buttons." Denise eyed her little sister. "I like that top."

"Really?" said Angie, startled by the compliment. "It's old." She'd gotten the seersucker blouse from her favorite vintage store in Royal Oak.

"Could've fooled me," said Denise. She took a swig from her Diet Coke. "Looks good on you."

"Thanks." She watched the movie for a few moments, enjoying the sight of Eddie Murphy in his Mumford High sweatshirt. "So this is a videotape we're watching now?"

"Yep," said Denise. "I bought a few more too. I got *Under the Cherry Moon* and *Soul Man* and *The Color Purple.*"

"Cool." Angie wished *she'd* been able to buy her mother a brand-new video cassette recorder. Then maybe she'd think her youngest daughter's life was on track.

"You look tired, Angela." Her mother beckoned for her to sit. "Those are some long hours you work on weekends."

"That's retail for you." She plopped down on the sofa. Together they watched the end of the movie in silence, Murphy's goofy, hip slang unfunny to her.

As the credits rolled, their mother said, "We're about to go for Chinese. Want to join us?"

Angie shook her head no. "I'm not really in the mood for Chinese food."

"Well, we could do something else," said Denise. "Just walk around Greektown, pick somewhere to eat."

"I am actually pretty tired," admitted Angie. "I'm not hungry. I'm just gonna chill out here."

"Well, you could watch another movie on video," said Denise. "There's plenty to choose from."

"Thanks," said Angie. "I might."

After Denise and their mother left, Angie popped in one

of the movies Denise had bought and watched it appear on the TV screen. She hit the fast-forward button, it whirled ahead; she hit the rewind button, and it backed up. "Wow," she said out loud. On a whim she got up, grabbed her purse and car keys, and left the house. She drove to the new Blockbuster in Southfield, signed up for a membership. She was overwhelmed by the number of films on display. She went straight to the classics section and strolled the aisle, thinking she'd rent an old black-and-white movie, or maybe one she and Ella used to watch together. Ella's two favorites were *Black Orpheus* and *Paris Blues*. But as she walked the aisle, she saw, on the "Just Released" rack, *She's Gotta Have It*. She'd seen the movie when it came out the year before, showing at the museum's art house theater. She plucked the video jacket from the shelf—its quirky colors and floating black faces calling to her—and went straight to the checkout counter.

Back at home she watched the movie while eating a dinner of cheddar cheese and crackers. She was stunned anew by it, by the verve, the fresh portrayals, the lack of stoicism, the humor. She'd forgotten how exhilarating it was to see black people in a film who resembled people she knew, and she laughed out loud at the part where Mars Blackmon got in Nola's face, begging for sex with his *Please baby please baby please*—as if she was seeing it for the first time. But as the credits rolled, she found herself sad, envious. Out there were Afro-Americans like this young guy, this Spike Lee, doing new and wondrous things. *He'd* figured out how to be black in the world. And in a modern, eighties way. What did she have but Ella's worn caftans and a vague desire to "be part of something"? What was *her* thing? Would she ever know?

She took her plate to the kitchen and placed it in the sink. As she cleared the table, a folded newspaper caught her eye, its style of typeface telling her it wasn't the *Detroit Free Press*. She picked it up, saw that it was the real estate section of *The Atlanta Journal*. Four ads were circled in the "Houses for Sale" section, listed under "downtown Atlanta neighborhoods."

She stared at the red circles, their optimistic swirl. That's what this weekend trip to Atlanta was about—house hunting. Her mother hadn't said a word to her. *What about me?* Angie wondered. She put the newspaper back on the table, hands shaking, heart punctured. *Who wants to live in fucking Georgia?* she told herself.

In her room, a paper lantern covered an overhead light, casting a reddish hue. The longer she sat on her bed, the more her resentment grew. All these years, she'd done what her mother had asked of her. While Denise had been their mother's protector, she'd been the compensator, making up for Ella's failings. She'd gotten good grades, stayed away from drugs, had responsible sex with two different men, one in high school, the other in college (Solo didn't really count). And even though she wanted desperately to return to U of M after Ella's death, her mother begged her not to, as if the university campus itself would turn her into a Black-Power-fanatic-cum-drug-addict. She'd done all of that for her mother—stayed nearby because she asked her to, because she needed her—and what had her mother done for her? Made plans behind her back to leave her, to move hundreds of miles away, near Denise. She felt tricked, her good-girl efforts mocked.

Angie leaned across the bed, grabbed the small wicker basket on her altar, removed its lid, and took out the old, pink joint she'd put there many years before. She sniffed it. It had no smell. She went to the kitchen, got a match from the box they kept below the counter, and struck it. She brought the flame to the joint, but on second thought, blew it out. She stepped out into the backyard, sat on the porch. The June night was hot-breath warm, the sky punctured with baby stars. She could hear someone gunning a car engine. She felt as though she was on the precipice of something new, still vague and out of reach, but close.

She put the joint to her mouth, feeling the importance of the act, its demarcation from old to new. She struck another match and lit it, sucked in, held the smoke in her mouth as she'd seen Ella do many times. She exhaled. She waited, but couldn't taste, smell, nor feel anything. It's too old, she thought. Part of her was relieved, and she pulled on it again, and again, content with the chance to smoke a joint and not actually get high from it. She still wasn't sure whether she had "it," that addictive personality. Out on the lawn stood the swing set her father had staked into the ground when she was a little girl. She stared at it, barely conjuring him, his strong arms, his rugged, outdoors handsomeness now a shadowy vision. She flicked the roach, ran over, and sat down on a swing, gripping the rusted chain. She pumped, taking herself higher and higher. The air rushed back at her and a gaggle of stars looked down as she pumped. When had she last done this, been a carefree girl on a swing? When she was eleven, and life was perfect.

Everything about that year at first was magical, starting with Jimmy Carter's inauguration and all the grown-ups' relief. To Angie, the world opened up. Even she, a sixth grader with a teacher excited about current events, understood the country's collective sigh to be done with Watergate and Nixon and Vietnam. "He'll pardon all those brothers and white boys who evaded the draft," said Ella. And when Carter did so, she said, "See? I told you! It's a new day." All four of them gathered eight nights in a row to watch *Roots*, Ella commenting through it all. First night: "Maybe now folks will figure out that Africa is not a country." On another night: "'Bout time this country owned up to its slavery past." Still another night: "Think black folks now will learn more Swahili than 'Watu Wazuri, use Afro Sheen'?"

Angie also remembered that year as a time of goodbyes to ubiquitous icons. Seventeen-year-old Denise sat forlorn before the TV, watching the last episode of *The Mary Tyler Moore Show.* "What am I supposed to do now on Saturday nights at eight?" she said. Their mother watched the broadcast of Diana Ross and the Supremes performing their final concert in London and lamented, "It's the end of an era." And when Elvis died, their mother said, "If the King can die, anybody can."

But Ella wasn't saying goodbye to anything, rather rushing toward more political awareness. When her Afro-American studies professor, Dr. Jordan, invited her and other favorite students to join him as part of the US delegation to FESTAC, the household was abuzz in excitement. "My baby is traveling the world!" said their mother. "All my friends can't believe it!" said Denise. Ella left for ten whole days to attend the arts festival, becoming part of the largest single group of Afro-Americans ever to return to Africa "in one body." She returned home at her apex, at the height of her brilliance and radical shimmer. She moved differently, ivory bangles clicking on her arms, regal in her new tie-dyed and indigo-swirled long dresses. She'd discovered what it meant to be the steady object of men's desire, and wallowed in Nigerians' love of her ample body, her fleshy curves. Before, she'd exclusively dated African men, but now she moved as if an entire continent of them had lusted for her.

She came back with illustrious stories, told in a rush. "One day we saw dancers performing from Cuba and the West Indies, and the next day we saw liberation fighters and revolutionaries marching through the streets! And I met the UN ambassador, Andrew Young! And then another day, Stevie Wonder performed! At the closing ceremonies, Miriam Makeba, this South

African singer? She sang. She was amazing, just amazing! And all of us from America yelled, 'We're an African people! We're an African people!'" She didn't pause, breathless with reenactment. "And Angie, we went to this place in the north, Kaduna, where they had this celebration called a Durbar, with hundreds and hundreds of men on beautiful horses and camels riding through the streets; they were just spectacular! Daddy would've loved it."

Nigeria, Ella explained, was a rich country, dripping with oil money. More than three billion dollars had been spent on FESTAC, she said. "They built a new national theater just for the festival and an entire village for the guests," she noted. "And you should see the modern expressways! Whatever you thought of Africa, you were wrong!"

Ella played those tapes of Fela's Afrobeat nonstop for weeks. And she announced that she would only refer to herself and other black people as "African Americans."

Most exciting of all for Angie: Ella came back in love. Nigel was president of the Black Student Union, a graduating senior, and part of the delegation. To Angie, he was just plain beautiful, with those light eyes and hair gathering to a tiny "V" on his forehead. "So many girls on the trip were checking him out," said Ella. "Little women with skinny legs, narrow hips. He wasn't into *any* of them, said, 'I like a woman with some thoughts in her head and some meat on her bones.'"

They became inseparable. When Nigel graduated from U of M, he boycotted the ceremony and spent the day at Belle Isle with Ella instead. That summer, while the rest of the world was listening to "Hotel California" and "Tonight's the Night," Ella and Nigel played Bob Marley's new album continuously on Ella's bedroom record player. Once, Angie caught her sister alone, swaying her hips to the music as Marley sang out, *Is this love, is this love, is this love that I'm feeling?* Seeing her sister move that way both frightened and excited Angie, because it was so sensuous and radical. She knew it had something to do with Nigel. Later, Ella explained that she was reggae dancing, and taught Angie how to do it. "Just let your body groove to the beat" she coached. Dancing like that made Angie feel older, sophisticated, more advanced than her elementary school classmates disco-dancing to Chic's "Le Freak."

A MEMORY: ANGIE awakening to a dark room. She sat up in bed, startled. Where was she? Then she remembered. Ella's room. Her big sister had let her sleep with her that night, since they were the only two at home. But Ella wasn't in bed beside her, and Angie panicked. She'd fallen asleep reading *The Amityville Horror*, and now she worried that someone, something sinister had entered their home, was coming after her. Had Ella left her alone, all by herself? She got up, crept slowly down the stairs. She smelled smoke, and terror gripped her.

"Ella?" she called out, tripping down the steps. "Ella?"

She stood very still in the middle of the living room. She felt a rumble beneath her feet, and then sounds. Music? Yes music! Coming up from the basement. She ran to the hallway door, flung it open. Smoke wafted up to her alongside the deep, baritone crooning of Barry White. Relieved that her sister was simply having another party, she ran down the steps, chasing after the booming sound of the Love Unlimited Orchestra. But she stopped abruptly on the last step, in awe of what she saw before her.

At least twenty people scattered around the room. Ella moved through the crowd, passing out pieces of paper and pens. She looked regal, her skirt and top made of beautiful, embroidered lace, head wrapped in matching fabric. Angie had never seen this outfit before. All of the partygoers' heads were bent as they scribbled on pieces of paper. To Angie, it was a fantasy classroom scene, only the students weren't at desks, rather curled up on the sofa and stretched out on the floor and writing against the wall. Lights were low, and all the brightness came from the far end of the room, where a cauldron of fire burned. The Love Unlimited Orchestra swelled in her ears.

"Ah, our youngest guest has arrived," said Nigel.

Ella turned, beckoned Angie to join her. "Hey Princess. Did we wake you up?"

Angie shook her head no. Ella took her hand, walked her closer to the mini bonfire. "Cool, huh?"

"Yeah," said Angie, enjoying the warmth of the flames, and Ella's touch.

In the corner next to the built-in bar, a guy wearing a black beret was rifling through Ella's albums. "This is some eclectic shit!" he said, cigarette burning between his fingers as he lifted Barry White's orchestral sounds from the turntable, gingerly using a surgeon's precision to replace the album with another. Right away, the wild opening chords of Parliament's "Flashlight" charged through the speakers. Ella carried Angie even closer to the fire, so that its heat danced across her arm. "We're writing down things we don't want anymore, stuff we want out of our lives, and dropping them into the fire." Ella smiled at her. "Wanna do it too?"

It was way past her bedtime, and Angie felt giddy knowing that she could stay up as long as she wanted. Their mother and Denise had taken an overnight trip to Muskegon to accept an award in their father's name. Denise had been excited about the three-hour drive, newly minted with a driver's license and thrilled to chauffeur their mother. Oddly enough, Ella hadn't wanted to go, said she'd stay behind and babysit Angie.

"OK, somebody give my little sister a piece of paper," said Ella to the crowd.

"I got her," said Nigel, waving a scrap of paper overhead. He gave the paper to Angie, led her to a spot on the sofa, plopped down beside her. "What grade are you in?" he asked. She told him. "So, what annoying things are sixth graders doing these days?"

She shrugged, shy. He handed her a pencil. "Think. Any silly boys getting on your nerves?"

There was Steven Campbell. She had a crush on him, but he only paid attention to the light-skinned girls. She'd like to get rid of him.

Angie nodded. "There is this one boy."

"OK, good. Write down his name."

"What's gonna happen to him if I do?" she asked, thinking about magic potions and spells.

Nigel put his arm around her, whispered conspiratorially. "He'll be out of your life."

She giggled. "Really?"

He looked at her with those big gray eyes, mock hurt on his face. "You don't believe me?"

"Maybe," she said. She wanted to believe him.

"I'm telling you, he'll suddenly transfer to another school, or move away." He leaned into her ear. "Or, simply be invisible to you."

Angie looked up at Nigel.

"Go ahead. Write it down. I won't look." He dramatically turned his head.

Angie wrote in block letters, "GET RID OF CRUSH ON STE-VEN CAMPBELL. HE'S MEAN TO ME." She folded up the paper as tiny as she could. The music changed again, this time to hypnotic, techno sounds beneath a woman's haunting voice moaning over and over, *It's so good, it's so good, it's soooo goood.*

Just then, a baby-faced woman in a green jumpsuit made her way to the center of the floor, and danced around, arms flailing, hips swaying. The girl kept chanting, "I love this song, I love this song, I love this song," as she danced. She looked eerie to Angie, the way she dipped her body low then threw her hands up in the air, gyrating in a circle to the heavy weight of the monotone music.

"Sheila must've gotten some good shit!" yelled one of the guys. Folks laughed.

One by one, party guests tossed their scraps of paper into the blaze, stepping around Sheila as she sang along with Donna Summer. *I feel love, I feel love, I feeel lovvve.*

Ella held up a piece of paper. "Know what I'm getting rid of? The old me." She read out loud from the Frantz Fanon quote she'd written on her own little piece of paper, "In the world through which I travel, I am endlessly creating myself!" She threw the words into the fire.

"I know that's right, sister," said the DJ from the corner.

Nigel got up from the sofa, pulled Ella to him. "To Creation!" he yelled, throwing his own piece of paper into the bonfire. The partygoers spontaneously clapped. Angie felt embraced by the applause, as though it was for her. This was how life was supposed to be.

"Your turn," said one of the girls to Angie. She wore a tube top that hugged her ample chest. Angie got up, went to the fire, tossed her paper in, watched as ashes sashayed upward.

Suddenly, Sheila unzipped her jumpsuit, exposing a hot-pink bra. She was in a trance, eyes closed, no longer moving to the beat of the music, just moving, like a robot. By now, the song was deeply hypnotic in its repetition. Sweat dripped down the sides of Sheila's face, brown in color from her makeup.

"Hey, Sheila! Girl, stop stripping!" yelled a guy wearing aviator sunglasses.

"Damn girl!" Nigel called out. "What are you on?"

She stopped, stared at him. "Why you got that bird on your head?" she asked.

"Ah shit, she's bugging out," said Nigel. He turned to the guy in shades. "Help me with her Jerome."

The two men went toward Sheila, each grabbing an arm.

"Don't touch me, don't touch me!" she screamed. Angie could see spit bubbles forming in the corners of her mouth. "FBI! FBI!" she yelled. "Get the fuck off of me! Pig!" And then she screamed.

Ella flipped on the lights, startling everyone. They led Sheila to the couch, forced her to sit. "What'd you take?" Nigel said, shaking Sheila. "What'd you take?"

Jerome took off his sunglasses. "She smoked a joint she got from Eddie," he said.

"Eddie?" said Nigel. "That nigger laces his shit with Angel Dust."

"Let it wear off, let it wear off," said Jerome, sitting beside Sheila, still holding her arm. "She just need to come down."

"I would like for you to take your damn hands off of me," said Sheila, her words slow and deliberate. She bucked her eyes. "I can't breathe, I can't breathe."

"Get her some air!" said Ella. "Walk her around."

"Anybody got a downer?" asked Nigel. "Anything that'll take the edge off?"

Someone in the crowd produced a pill, and it was passed up to the front. Ella got water from the laundry-room sink, gave the glass to Nigel.

"What's crawling on me?" asked Sheila. "What the fuck is that crawling on me?" She shivered.

"Take this, OK?" Nigel put the pill in Sheila's mouth. "Good girl. Now drink some water."

He guided the glass to her lips. She stared blankly ahead, a look that terrified Angie. Water dribbled down her mouth.

"She swallow it?" asked a tall guy wearing a mud-cloth kufi hat.

Nigel nodded. "She's gonna be OK."

"I'll stay with her," said Jerome, wrapping his arm around Sheila.

The DJ turned up the music again. He'd put on Phoebe Snow, and her sweet, soothing voice floated gently through the gigantic speakers as she sang about the poetry man. In unison everyone exhaled in relief.

"Anybody else need to drop their paper in the fire?" asked Ella. "Last call!"

A couple more partygoers tossed their papers into the flames. "OK, that's it," she said. "When I count to three, everybody yell, 'Burn Baby Burn!' OK?"

She counted to three and the crowd yelled on cue, "Burn, baby, burn!" Even Angie joined in. Ella grabbed a small fire extinguisher that sat in the corner and pumped it at the fire, which quickly died.

"We should dump the ashes outside, bury them," she said.

"Ground's still too hard," said Nigel. It was late March, wintry.

The girl with the tight tube top plopped down on the couch beside Angie. "Way I feel, I needed to burn a damn book's worth of shit." She looked over at Angie. "Fuck, am I cursing in front of a minor?"

Angie giggled, watched as her big sister carried the cauldron by its swinging handle. She wanted to follow her, but her body felt too heavy. She didn't mind, followed Ella with her eyes instead.

"Hey!" yelled Jerome, just as Ella was about to climb the stairs. "She's not breathing!"

Sheila lay against him, lifeless, on the couch. Jerome slapped her face. "Sheila? Wake the fuck up, girl! Wake up!"

Ella put down the cauldron, ran over to them. "Move!" she said to Jerome. He gently guided Sheila down onto the sofa, got up, and stepped back.

Ella dropped onto her knees beside Sheila and placed two fingers on the side of her neck.

"Feel anything?" asked Nigel, by her side.

Ella shook her head. "I don't."

She placed one hand over another and pushed into Sheila's chest over and over. It made Angie think of Ella in a horse's stall, shoveling hay, with precision and focus. Angie prayed in her head, *Please don't die, Please don't die, Please don't die.*

Ella pumped and pumped. "Come on, damn it!" she hissed. Sheila didn't move.

She pried open Sheila's mouth, pinched her nose, and placed her own mouth on Sheila's. She breathed in then out, deeply, twice. Everyone's eyes stayed riveted to Sheila's chest. It didn't move.

Ella again placed her hands between Sheila's breasts and pushed. She pushed again. And again, ten more times, counting out loud. After the tenth push, ever so slightly Sheila's chest moved up, then down. People gasped. Ella fell back on her haunches.

"Damn!" Nigel ran his hand down his face. "Where'd you learn to do that?"

"I took a class," said Ella. "Once."

Sheila opened her eyes. She moaned, and they fluttered closed again.

"Get her up out of here," said Ella. "Now."

"I got her," said Jerome. He rushed over to Sheila, gently shook her. "Come on, girl. Can you walk?"

She moaned again.

"Take her ass to the hospital," said Nigel.

"It was just a bad trip," said Jerome. "I just gotta get her home and she'll be alright."

With Nigel's help, he got Sheila to her feet, walked her slowly up the steps and out the side door.

Behind her, the other guests filed out, until just Ella and Nigel and a couple others were left. And Angie.

Ella plopped down on the couch, exhaustion hanging off of her. Angie climbed into her lap, the night's danger still under her skin.

"Anybody got a cigarette?" asked Ella.

The guy in the kufi hat held out a lit joint. "Here, you need this," he said.

Spontaneously, Angie reached for the joint.

Nigel lightly smacked her hand. "Little girl, you do not want that."

She didn't know whether she was reaching for it to keep Ella from having it or reaching for it for herself.

Ella shook her head. "I don't trust that shit at the moment. Just give me a cigarette."

Angie snuggled against Ella's chest as her life-saving big sister smoked.

LATER, WHEN THE May issue of *Ebony* came out, the cover photo boasted Africans dancing in white billowy costumes, beating drums, smiling wide, looking like exuberant, self-possessed cousins of those found in *National Geographic*. As the family sat at the kitchen table, Ella read aloud the magazine's breathless coverage: "Despite their diversity, despite their divergent lifestyles, despite their multiple languages, the very coming together of this vast congregation echoed a common desire to accept themselves as they were, to reject nonblack interpretations of them, to redefine reality in their own image, and regain control over their destiny."

And there, miraculously, was a quote from Ella herself: "Black culture," said Ella Mackenzie, a student at the University of Michigan, "is a living, organic reality."

"Let me see that!" said Denise, grabbing the magazine from Ella. She studied the page. "Wow, she really is quoted!"

"I'm going to take that to work with me," said their mother. "Make photocopies, so I can send it to folks down south."

"Can I see?" asked Angie. She leaned over Denise, awed by seeing her sister's name in print; it confirmed that Ella belonged to something bigger, was part of that scary world of current events that got discussed in serious tones by her sixth grade teacher, Miss Hanson. Angie took the *Ebony* magazine to share with the class, and the boys and girls said, "Oooh," when they saw her sister's name, read her words. Ella *was* current events for 1977.

NOW ANGIE TWIRLED herself in circles on the swing, twisting together the chain link, and then she stopped, unraveling in a whirl of dizzy circles. She did it again and again, the backyard flying past her in a blur. Finally as she let herself slow down to a halt, she planted both feet on the ground and relished the fact that she was high, as wondrously high as those sly little stars above.

SIX

THAT YEAR ENDED WITH NONE OF THE SPARKLE THAT IT began with. After Ella was quoted in *Ebony*, she decided she wasn't returning to college in the fall; their mother tried everything—reasoning, bribing, begging, and finally yelling, all to no avail.

"It's not working for me," is all Ella said by way of explanation. She would've been a senior.

When the South African activist Steve Biko died in police custody, she joined a local Pan-African group to publicize the crusade against apartheid. They passed around fliers, held meetings, and organized a rally, educating black people in America about the harsh policies of that particular majority black country.

Mostly Ella spent her free time with Nigel.

"I see *he* managed to graduate from college," their mother pointed out. "Selfish bastard." That was how it went: Nanette would make sarcastic comments, Ella would pretend to ignore them. Denise, claiming a busy, senior-in-high-school life, was at home very little and when she was, she stuck close to their mother in allegiance. Angie suffered insomnia, which made her groggy and morose all day. The harsh silence around the house got filled by the Bee Gees, whose songs spewed endlessly from household orifices—the kitchen radio, Denise's bedroom, cars speeding by the open windows, the television set. That autumn and well into the new year, "Night Fever" became an oppressive de facto anthem for Angie.

Spring arrived and Ella hosted an African Liberation Day party in their basement; the raucous affair attracted dozens of people, including Solo. That warm May night, their mother came home from an evening spent with Dr. Benjamin, and smelled the marijuana wafting upstairs. She sat quietly in the kitchen, drinking a light beer and waiting for everyone to leave. Well after midnight, Ella emerged from the basement, red eyed and hungry for munchies. Nigel followed, Angie sleeping in his arms. As Ella swung open the refrigerator door, their mother said in an even voice, "You can't live in my house and smoke that dope. I won't allow it."

Angie woke up, felt the tickle of Nigel's hairy arms. He put her down, nervously scratched his eyelid.

"OK," said Ella.

"OK, what?" said Nanette.

"OK, I'll leave. I've been thinking it's time for me to do that anyway."

"Don't think you can just come back whenever you want," warned their mother.

"I'm cool with that," said Ella.

Before dawn, she packed her things and left with Nigel. Angie had never felt such anger at her mother, and managed to go two whole days without speaking to her. Her mother didn't notice.

While Ella was "shacking up" with Nigel, as her mother called it, they knew nothing about Ella's day-to-day life. All Angie knew was that she missed her acutely. Denise left for Atlanta that June to begin a pre-freshman college program, and Angie found herself alone a lot all summer. Out of the need for something to do, she convinced her mother to let her go see *Star Wars* three times in a row with Evelyn, Ella's childhood friend.

Angie did get to see her on the fourth of July. As they all gathered in a neighbor's backyard, eating barbecued ribs and potato salad, Ella said, "I just want to say that the truly independent thing that has happened today is that Huey P. Newton returned home from Cuba." Her announcement was met with silence, and Angie glanced quickly at her mother, who shook her head at Ella, as if to say, "Not here, not now." Ella didn't meet her eye, rather took her Styrofoam plate of food to the trashcan sitting beside the grill, and tossed it in. "I will no longer eat swine," she announced. "Pigs are filthy." Then she left. "Nigel's waiting for me," she explained over her shoulder.

Angie ran after her and asked if she could please see her new home? Ella said OK, and she and Nigel arrived in his bright yellow Firebird that Saturday to pick up Angie. Ella and Nigel lived in a two-family flat on Birchcrest, on the second floor, and Angie was surprised to see a front room awash in color, as her own mother's decor was all muted tones of taupe and forest green. Here was a chunky sofa covered in a royal-blue slipcover and giant Indian-print pillows in saturated golds and purples tossed onto the floor. Satiny red curtains hung from the windows. And behind the bedroom door, Angie glimpsed a dozen or more purses piled onto the bed, their white price tags dangling seductively. She'd later learn that those designer purses funded her sister's lifestyle, as they were all shoplifted by Ella and Nigel then sold at deep discounts to bank tellers and teachers and postal workers.

Months passed. On a frigid November night, just one day after the mass suicide of Jim Jones and his followers in Guyana, Ella came back home. Angie had been watching the news about the hundreds of deaths nonstop, not sure whether she should ever drink Kool-Aid again. "You have got to use your own mind, think for yourself," her mother said as they watched the coverage together. "You can't get caught up in some man's charisma."

Ella appeared, saying that she and Nigel had broken up. Catching a glimpse of the news, she noted, "They say Jim Jones got his inspiration for starting a movement from Huey Newton's book. Sick." She explained nothing else, just disappeared up the stairs to her attic bedroom.

"At least she had the good sense to come home," said Nanette. "At least she's thinking for herself."

Angie hoped that since Ella was back home, things would return to how they'd been and they'd be a family like before. But something about Ella wasn't right. She didn't spew political rhetoric anymore, didn't keep her head buried in Black Power books, left the house at odd hours, told obvious lies. She was different. Looking back, Angie could see all the signs of Ella's heroin addiction. Mood shifts. Insomnia. Staying too long in the bathroom. Nodding out. But back then the family hadn't been to any therapy sessions at the drug-rehab clinic yet. Her mother attributed Ella's odd behavior to the breakup with Nigel and that became the official explanation. Even her obvious weight loss was no clue. Ella's size had always gone up and down. And she was still a big girl. For months, they were oblivious, months that allowed Ella's addiction to take hold and flourish.

On the night it happened, the bathroom door was closed; Ella had been in there a long time and Angie had to pee. She knocked, called her sister's name. No answer. Angie entered, found Ella slumped over the toilet seat, rubber band still tied around her arm, bloody needle and burned spoon fallen onto the tiles. Angie screamed.

The emergency medical workers struggled to lift Ella onto the stretcher. One of them used his foot to slide her down the steps. That scared Angie the most, watching Ella's large, limp body kicked down a flight of stairs. Their mother kept asking, "Is she gonna make it? Is she gonna make it?" as they carried her daughter out of the house. Nanette ran behind the stretcher, pale blue coat thrown over her nightgown, feet clad in nylon slippers. The coat was a beautiful, buttery soft leather, the color of an overcast sky, one of those impulse purchases their mother sometimes made, a symbol of a good life she believed in, worked hard to have. Their mother crawled on her hands and knees into the back of the ambulance just before it sped off, yelled at twelve-year-old Angie to go to a neighbor's house. Angie had two thoughts at that moment: Ella is going to die, and Mama is going to rip her soft, blue coat. She felt her own budding self rush away alongside the wailing ambulance.

After Ella's overdose, their mother tried to get her into rehab but she refused, claiming, "That was the first time I ever tried shooting up and I had a bad reaction, that's all. Trust me, I'm done with that."

Their mother sighed so hard her shoulders trembled. "I hope so. God do hear me say, I hope so."

Right away, things started to go missing from the house, a slow drip of thefts at first. Where was their mother's fourteen-carat chain with the pot of gold hanging from it? The silver dollars she had in a jar? The nice boom box she kept in the laundry room? Soon enough, bigger things disappeared along with Ella's excess pounds: Angie's clarinet, Denise's babysitting money, their mother's diamond-encrusted watch. In the course of a few weeks, Ella's weight dropped so dramatically, her plus-size clothes started hanging on her. One night, saying she was about to meet Nigel for a date, she begged their mother to let her borrow the soft, blue leather coat. "Mine is swallowing me and I want to look nice tonight. We might get back together. Mama, please?" Their mother finally conceded; Angie hoped

Ella and Nigel *would* get back together, believed he'd be her big sister's protector. Ella returned home two days later without the coat, claiming she'd left it at a friend's house. She didn't mention Nigel.

It broke Angie's heart to see her mother give Ella money then vow not to, then do it again in hopes of keeping her oldest daughter off the streets, free from men who might mistreat her. Vicious, sad cycle. Angie blamed Nigel for the men who came in his wake. She hated every last one of them, men who leaned to one side as they strutted with fingers grazing their palms, men who chewed on toothpicks, men who kept a cigarette behind one ear. She especially loathed a feral-looking junkie named George. Clearly Ella's life was in more peril with that awful man, who left her in places that her mother would frantically rush to get her out of. Once Ella spent a few days in jail on a shoplifting charge, left hanging by George when he ran off. Angie took her a few toiletries. In the bag were activator spray and moisturizer for her Jheri curl—which had once given Ella lovely "wash and wear" hair, turning her coarse, tightly coiled locks into glossy, loose ringlets—and a tube of Neet depilatory for her chin hairs. But the prison guards wouldn't allow Ella to have the toiletries and when she appeared in court three days later, her hair was dried out and dirty with old, crusted activator. She'd apparently borrowed someone's disposable shaver and shaved the unwanted hairs from her face; she now had a five o' clock shadow covering her chin. Angie couldn't decide which was worse—Ella's damaged hair or her stubbly face.

A year passed. And then another, and soon Angie's entire high school experience was colored by having a drug-addict sister. A missed class trip to Chicago because of that shoplifting arrest was but one example. Her mother always wanted her home after school "just in case," so she had no real social life. In a sense, she too felt addicted, as she lived like a junkie to potential tragedy—panicked by the possibility of bad news every time the phone rang, stomach knotted when it fell silent for too many days.

Middle of the night, harsh knocks at the door. Her mother goes to see who it is, peeping through the tiny window on the front door.

"I'm looking for Ella," says the man, head covered in a knit cap.

"She's not here." Angie and Ella stand beside their mother.

"Yeah? Well, she got something of mine, so tell her I'm looking for her ass." Their mother watches through the peephole as he struts back to his car.

"Who in the hell was that!" she yells at Ella.

Ella coughs. "Just some dude."

"Some dude? *Some dude?* You mean a drug dealer? You let a drug dealer know where we *live!*"

"Mama, I told you it's just some dude I was dating. Relax." Ella climbs back up the stairs to her room.

After that, their mother started sleeping with a pink-handled pistol under her pillow—Samson had given it to her half as a joke—convinced Ella's dealer was going to seek revenge and "the whole family could get wiped out on a humble," as Nanette put it.

When Denise heard about the incident, she demanded that their mother put Ella out of the house. "Mama, she's not herself," Denise reasoned through the phone. "She's a damn junkie! She could get you all killed, and then what? It's not safe to have her around."

"I don't want to put out my own daughter," said their mother, hopeless. "At least I can keep an eye on her if she's here. That's my way of thinking about it, anyway."

But Denise was relentless, calling from Atlanta daily, pressing their mother to do it. Finally, after her mink cape came up missing, their mother relented. She kicked out her firstborn.

With Ella out of sight, Angie imagined all sorts of horrific scenarios. Where was she living? And without the steady supply of money from their mother, what was she doing for cash? The possibilities terrified Angie, who couldn't accept that Ella was an addict. She kept waiting for this impostor, this intruder to leave and for her real sister to return.

"I don't understand what happened to her," she confided in her mother one day.

"She's greedy," said her mother. "She's always been greedy. Whatever it is, she can't get enough, and that's the worst thing you can say about somebody doing dope."

If Ella came by—claiming she wanted to see Angie but really to ask for money—Angie would let her in only if their mother wasn't home. "If she'll steal from her own Mama, you know she'll steal from you," warned Nanette. "Don't. Let. Her. In."

She found herself giving Ella her own money from the part-time job she had at Olga's, a restaurant at the mall. Ella always promised she'd pay it back soon. And she always took something on her way out, something small that Angie couldn't see, shoved into a giant, fake-leather purse—nothing like the buttery soft ones Ella and Nigel used to shoplift. Still, every time she let her in.

Middle of the night. Telephone's frightening trill. Their mother's friend calling to say that someone who knows someone saw Ella go inside a certain house, a known drug den, just minutes before. Angie watched as her mother got up, dressed, slipped her pink-handled pistol into her pocket, and left. Terrified both for her mother and her sister, she sat in the living room, peering out the window, chanting and waiting. An hour later, her mother came back, wordless as she put her gun on the bedroom dresser.

"What happened?" asked Angie.

"She wouldn't come," said her mother. "I tried to pull her out of there and she wouldn't come." Nanette crawled into bed, fully dressed. "I'm done," she said, staring at the wall. "I can't do this anymore."

In the last, horrible year of her addiction, Ella completely stayed away from her family. In that time their mother never called her name. Until one day, Ella showed up and banged on the side door. Angie pulled back the lace curtain, eyed her through the door's window. A car idled in the driveway, a strange man at the wheel, chewing on a toothpick. Angie imagined all her sister's possessions piled on the backseat in a large, black garbage bag.

She bent down, talked to Ella through the milk chute. "I can't risk it," she said.

"But I've got to pee," said Ella.

"I can't."

"Please, please," begged Ella. She reached into the milk chute and gripped Angie's neck, wouldn't let go. "Please, Princess. Open up."

Her fingers felt cold to the touch, dead. Angie let her in. She relished seeing Ella, and was repulsed by her. She wore polyester stretch pants that sagged, her hair was matted and her hands were so swollen they looked like flesh-colored boxing gloves. Her sweater had cigarette burns. Ella tried to be casual as they stood together in the small kitchen. "So how's it going, Princess?" Words slurred.

"OK." Angie studied the sweat beads gathering at her sister's hairline.

"Where's Mama?" Nose scratch.

"She's not here and *you* better not be here when she gets back."

"Yeah, OK." Arm scratch. "Listen. I need to borrow a little piece of change."

"No." Angie had decided she wasn't doing that anymore. "You need to get some help."

"I am, I am." Another nose scratch. Loud sniff. Sweat dripping like liquid sideburns. Ella took off her glasses, wiped her hand down her face. "I just need a little something to tide me over. For food."

"Eat here."

Ella laughed, a jagged sound. "Nah, I got a taste for Red Barn. You know how I love their chicken."

The car horn beeped. Ella moved from foot to foot. "Come on, my man's waiting outside."

"Your man?"

"Yeah, George. He'd come in but we're in a hurry."

"To get to Red Barn?"

"Look, let me have twenty dollars till Friday, OK?"

"No." She would hold firm.

"Come on."

"No!"

Ella sighed, sat down in a kitchen chair, and pulled out of her raggedy purse a bottle of Robitussin Maximum Strength Cough Suppressant. She took a long, hard swig. Angie watched Ella gulping down the cherry-flavored gunk, bottle turned up, head thrown back. She got a good look at her sister that day, the dingy sight of a ravished young woman, and her heart hardened. Such a waste, she thought.

Ella wiped her mouth with the back of her hand, stood, and pushed past her sister, down the narrow hallway to Angie's room. "I know you got it. You always keep money," she said.

Angie followed close behind. "What are you doing?"

Ella's eyes darted around the room. "Where is it?"

"You're just gonna come in here and steal my money? It's like that?"

"I told you I'd pay it back." Ella went to the top drawer of Angie's bureau and pulled it out, so aggressively that it fell to the floor with a thud, Angie's underwear tumbling out.

"Hey!" yelled Angie. "What's wrong with you?"

Ella looked at the drawer lying at her feet. "Just give me some money, OK?" The car horn blew again, long and hard.

"Tell him to stop fucking doing that!" yelled Angie.

"You tell him," said Ella.

"I will!" Angie stormed out of her room, striding toward the side door, ready to curse out this asshole that dared to lay on his horn in her driveway. But she stopped suddenly, realizing what she'd done and turned back to her bedroom, arriving in the doorway just in time to see Ella with Angie's ceramic pink piggy bank over her head.

"Don't!" she yelled just as Ella hurled it to the floor. The piggy bank smashed open, revealing gold dollar coins. Ella dropped to her knees and began grabbing them.

Angie ran over and gripped Ella's wrist. She pushed Angie hard. "Move, you little spoiled bitch!"

Angie fell back against the bed. She sat frozen, watching her sister gather one dollar coin after the other, and toss them into her giant, cheap purse, those puffed-up hands working fast. The aunties had given Angie that piggy bank, filled with gold dollar coins, when she was five, had sent five more every year since. When Ella had gathered all the money, purse sagging from the weight, she stood, eyes avoiding Angie's.

"I'll pay you back," she said, and rushed past her baby sister, moving toward the steadily blaring car horn.

Angie picked up the broken pink pieces, eyes stinging, vowing to never again give in to her sister's pleas. After that, she braced herself for another confrontation at the side door, but Ella never came back.

SHE HIT ROCK bottom on a breezy May afternoon in 1982, when Angie and her mother were on their way to Denise's college graduation in Atlanta. As they were about to leave for the airport, a man called the house. "I found your name in Ella's wallet, under emergency contact. I think you need to come get her. She's at 9278 Van Dyke." Click. Angie and her mother rushed over to a harsh flat in a rundown building hidden behind a freeway on a dead-end street, tall weeds growing in the front yard. They found Ella splayed across a naked mattress, unmoving, eyes half-opened. Angie called for an ambulance, which rushed her to the hospital. They missed their flight to Atlanta.

The doctors weren't sure she'd make it through the night. Angie and her mother kept a vigil. When she opened her eyes, Nanette cried from relief. Then she stood over Ella, placed her hand on hers and said, "I love you, I do. But I'm tired. And I got other daughters who need me. Whatever you want to do, I can't stop you. But I can make sure you don't take this family down with you."

She turned to Angie, eyes pleading.

"I'll stay," said Angie.

Her mother nodded, walked out, headed straight to the airport. But she didn't get there in time. She missed Denise's name as it was called, wasn't there when her middle child walked across the stage, something Denise would remind them of for years to come.

Left in the room, Angie sat in silence as Ella cried quietly. "I'm tired too," she said, wiping the tears away with the back of her hand. "You don't know how tired."

Only then did Angie notice that Ella's ring finger on her left hand was missing. She couldn't hide her horror. "What happened to your finger?"

Ella didn't look at Angie. "Gangrene."

She'd seen the track marks all over Ella's puffed-up hands, knew she'd been desperate for a vein that hadn't collapsed. But this was different. It hit her that the drugs could decimate Ella, that she could start losing body parts, one by one, snatched from her by the flesh-eating monkey on her back.

"I can't bear the way you're looking at me," said Ella. "You think I'm disgusting."

"I just don't want you to die."

Ella turned her face into the pillow. "I wish I'd died last night."

Ella's heart monitor beeped in her ears as Angie's eyes welled up. She hated herself for the thought that popped into her mind. *Then we'd be free.*

"Get some rest." What else could she say? "I'll be here tomorrow to take you home."

But Ella didn't leave the hospital. She signed herself into Herman Kiefer's drug abuse clinic, as an inpatient.

SEVEN

ANGIE NOW FELT WIPED OUT IN A WAY SHE NEVER HAD—
exhausted but anxious, like she'd just awakened from a ragged
sleep on a crowded train, fearful of missing her stop. She lay
across her bed, in the throes of post-high letdown. She wondered was this how Ella felt every day of her recovery?

Back then, with Denise away in Atlanta, and her mother
working long hours at Dr. B's office, Angie had been the one
who sat with Ella every day of her inpatient stay—during those
long, wretched weeks of withdrawal. Ella always said, "It's
not as bad as I look," and they'd both smile but Angie could
barely deal with the dark crescents under Ella's eyes and the
chain-smoking and the shaking hands.

She came home from six weeks in rehab just as Angie
entered twelfth grade. She was fat again, having lived off vend-
ing-machine snacks and bad food in the dining hall. At the
house, their mother stood guard: timed how long Ella stayed
in the bathroom, counted the spoons in their silverware drawer,
forbade her from staying in the attic bedroom, made her sleep
on the den sofa in full view. Angie was grateful for her senior-
year schedule, out of school each day by noon, and opting not
to work. From that September until Ella left in June, the two
were together daily. For Angie it was a poignant, sweet time.

Here was this dear person who'd been lost to her for so long, now returned. Yes Ella was different, a familiar stranger really, not unlike coming face-to-face with a distant pen pal. But it was also like falling in love again.

During those nine months Angie was Ella's willing chauffeur, taking her sister to various mandatory appointments. Ella had never learned to drive. ("I can drive a horse but not a damn car," she'd joke), so every day Angie took her first to get a dose of methadone then to her daily counseling sessions at Herman Kiefer. Wednesdays were family day and so their mother joined them. Those sessions revealed little: her mother saying "I did my best," and Ella agreeing too quickly; and when their mother did venture to ask what she'd done wrong, Ella said, "Nothing. It's not you. It's me, something I did for no good reason." And her mother's response, "You didn't have it to do."

Angie waited in the lounge during the individual and group sessions. Those were hard for Ella, she could tell, even though her sister never talked about it afterward. But she'd smoke nonstop all the way home, the butts of her Salem Lights tumbling from the car's ashtray. The weekly Narcotics Anonymous meetings were better. Angie often sat in the back of the room and listened, oddly jealous as the group members shared searing personal tidbits amid halos of smoke, some sipping fruit-flavored Hi-C and others strong coffee from their Styrofoam cups. They had a forged intimacy not unlike a fraternity of hazed members, or refugees, all the more potent for having suffered. Angie had never belonged to any group—no sororities or sports teams or after-school clubs—and she envied their common bond.

Often at the end of the day, as she and Angie hung out together in the den, Ella spoke of her dreams. She planned to go back to college, get a master's degree in social work. Then she wanted to start her own drug-rehab center, a place where patients practiced Buddhist chants and meditation and acupuncture, a place where reading rooms were filled with classic American literature and books from the movement and spiritual self-help guides. She'd encourage every patient to keep a journal, to share their thoughts on paper more, in talk therapy less.

Sometime that winter, Vincent Lowry asked Angie out. He was cute, tall, popular, and uninterested in her before. They dated for weeks and soon enough, she had sex with him. Ella helped her through the experience, even showing her how to get birth control pills from Planned Parenthood without their mother's knowledge. She felt adventurous, with Ella guiding her through the whole rite of passage. After the first, painful time, she thought she might like sex. When Vincent inevitably moved on, she wasn't sad. She'd lost her virginity before the end of high school, and that felt like a kind of achievement. And it prompted Ella to tell Angie about *her* first time, on the night their father died.

When Ella had run out of their father's barn, upset over his comments about her weight, at first she didn't see Jeff, the new exercise boy, lounging by another trainer's stall.

"You certainly seem to be in a hurry," he said.

She looked up. She had a slight crush on him, liked his muscular frame, his downy mustache. He was nineteen or twenty, and one of the less productive workers at the track. He liked to wait to be told what to do.

"Do I look fat to you?" she'd asked him.

Jeff smiled, as if he'd just won a little prize, and said, "Hardly. You look good to me."

They fooled around in Thompson Jenkins's barn, where the horses smelled different from her father's, medicinal and rank. First, she let him touch her breasts and then let his tongue touch her nipple. The feeling was so electrifying that she let him do it over and over, his mouth moving between breasts. And then they went all the way. She thought, looking back, that maybe she'd actually heard her father's low, stricken cries.

"El-la, El-la!" she imagined their father called out, with the horses frantically swishing their tails, aware something was wrong. But she didn't stop. That's the part that killed her— wondering did she actually hear him calling out to her while she was having sex? Did she ignore him?

She cried as she told the story. Angie cried too as she squeezed Ella's shaking hand, wanting to still it.

ELLA'S RECOVERY PROCESS encouraged faith in God. After some research, she decided to join Unity, a "metaphysical Christianity" church on Second Avenue. Angie thought the church itself was so pretty, with its white brick façade, and modern, windowed vestibule. During the service, no one talked of sin or God's wrath or your debt to Jesus for his sacrifice. They followed the teachings of Eric Butterworth, an affable white man with a kind face who wasn't scary, punitive, nor very preachy. He called church a "worth-ship" service and said pithy things like "God can only do for you what He can do through you." Their mother thought it was too new age; it didn't quote the Bible enough for her taste. Ella said she liked that you didn't have to use the word God at all, that you could replace it with "love" or "universe" if you wanted. "I think God is sick of hearing His name called, quite frankly," she said. Angie liked that at the end of each service congregants joined hands and sang, "Let there be peace on earth and let it begin with me. Let there be peace on Earth, the peace that was meant to be." She liked holding Ella's hand while surrounded by strangers. She felt hopeful.

That year Ella enjoyed going for long drives in the car, liked crossing the border to Windsor, Ontario, just for the change of scenery. Sometimes they had Chinese food, like in the old days with their father. Other times, she and Angie walked along its main street, licking ice cream cones, looking into the shop windows, marveling at how clean and quiet everything was in Canada. She told Angie about life in Nashville, what it was like those two years in the aunties' boarding house. "Aunt Bea had the biggest bed I've ever seen in my life," she said. "And the biggest heart to go with it. She was forever taking in some down-on-his-luck man, letting him stay in the back room. Folks forever coming and going, coming and going."

"That must have been exciting," said Angie.

Ella licked her cone. "Too exciting sometimes. One of those nasty men did some things to me he shouldn't have."

Angie hesitated. "Did he...?"

Ella nodded. "Put his fingers where they didn't belong."

Angie's ice cream dripped down her hand. "Anything else?"

Ella shook her head. "I think that was bad enough, don't you?"

Six months into her sister's sobriety, Angie made a point of saying to Ella, "You're so brave, to go through this." The counselor at the last family session had privately told Nanette they'd reached a fragile, pivotal point in Ella's recovery; the family should be alert to signs of relapse. The idea that they'd have to start all over terrified Angie. She wanted Ella on the other side of this and so she tried hard to be her cheerleader, to rah-rah her into recovery success. "You've always been brave," Angie noted. "Look how you came to Detroit all by yourself on the train. Aunt Bea said you weren't even scared."

Ella puffed on her ever-present cigarette. "I *was* scared when I got on that train, so I don't know what the hell Aunt Bea was talking about." She fell silent. "That's what recovery feels like," she finally said. "Like I'm moving toward somewhere better, but

I gotta get through this long, scary ride before I can get there."

With Denise visiting from Atlanta, one of the last things the family did together was watch the *Motown 25* TV special. Of course, the highlight was Michael Jackson performing "Billie Jean," doing his moonwalk. No one had expected his debonair style. "I was worried he wasn't gonna make that transition from child singer to adult entertainer," said Nanette. "Looks like he made it all right!" The girls loved it all—Marvin Gaye's riveting performance (which would be his last), The Temptations battling it out with The Four Tops and The Supremes gathering on the stage together one more time.

THE NIGHT BEFORE she left for Nigeria, Ella lay prone on the sofa, arm across her forehead, glasses perched low on her small nose. Nearby, Angie slouched in the matching leather chair. She imagined this was how her sister had looked in rehab during a therapy session, or maybe afterward in her shared room.

Ella got up from the sofa, headed to the den's stereo, popped in a cassette tape. In rehab, with Angie's help she'd put together a mixtape of favorite songs. The cassette case had her ID number scrawled across it on a piece of masking tape. Al Jarreau's jazzy voice floated out over them. *I hardly had a bellyful*, he sang. *Never knew a new bicycle.* The year of recovery had subdued Ella, taken away that reckless air that once had Angie both frightened and excited. Now Angie felt protective of Ella, as though she were a recently released prisoner needing to be brought up to speed on the ways life had changed on the outside.

In May Angie, Denise, and their mother had thrown a little party for Ella to celebrate her one-year anniversary. Her oldest friend Evelyn had been there, along with a smattering of friends from back in the day, people who'd faded from her life while she was lost to heroin. A middle-aged man named Joe, a new friend from rehab, also came. Nigel was there. Nigel! He'd been clean for three years to her one. Their mother made it clear she didn't like seeing him, felt Nigel was the one who brought drugs into Ella's life. But they'd gotten back together after the party, and somewhere in the span of a couple weeks, made the snap decision to go back to Nigeria. Their mother was now resigned to it, said she felt better about Ella not taking such a big trip alone. Angie knew her mother was praying that Nigel would look out for her.

Two days before Ella was to leave, she and Angie went shopping to buy new clothes for her trip. Initially, Ella didn't want to go to *that* store. "All those fat-girl dresses and old-lady stretch pants? I don't think so." But Angie knew better, had saved a little newspaper clipping about the store's takeover by the same company that owned Victoria's Secret and The Limited, how LB's clothes were now trendy. She'd hung the article on her bulletin board, alongside a treasure map of images and quotes and photos conjuring Ella's recovery. "They're really fashion forward now," she told her big sister. "Trust me." Ella walked through the store with eyes wide and mouth agape. She hadn't shopped here in six years, since her last trip to Nigeria. Together they chose flattering, peasant-style loose tops, cotton wrap dresses, and comfy but stylish jeans.

Now, Ella's bags all packed, house quiet, Angie watched her sister closely. As she lifted a cigarette to her lips and sucked hard, loose flesh hung from her arms, remnants of her weight loss and gain over the years. Angie stared at the stump where her sister's ring finger used to be. *But we got by,* sang Al Jarreau. *Lord knows we got by.* Ella looked so tired, so worn out that Angie found herself grateful for this trip, grateful for a break from having to see her sister in this "transitional" phase, as the drug counselor called it. She couldn't wait for Ella to leave so she could return transformed—rejuvenated and youthful and sensuous again, all the things a trip to the motherland had done for her before.

"What are you looking forward to the most?" Angie asked her, disrupting the fragile silence.

Ella took a final drag on her cigarette and stubbed it out in a paper plate of half-eaten Boston cream pie. "Getting back some of what I lost."

Angie realized she'd been wondering all these years if Ella actually ever did.

LYING ACROSS HER bed, still wiped out from her brief high, Angie tried to hold onto the anger she'd felt earlier, but she couldn't conjure any outrage. Rather, she felt rejected—inconsequential in the life her mother was moving toward, some shiny, fresh, southern start. She rose, went to her altar, pulled open the vanity's bottom drawer, and lifted out a bundle of letters, each written on soft blue par avion paper, each folded into its own envelope. There were seven in all and as she plopped back onto her bed and crossed her legs, she spread out the letters in front of her. She arranged them in chronological order of their postmarks, from July to December. Read together they created a rich narrative of adventure, allowing Angie to fantasize that only good things had happened to her sister in Nigeria: a successful newspaper career filled with cool people and exotic Nigerian locales. The last letter arrived after Ella's death and for a long time Angie couldn't bare to open it, fearful of what she might learn or worse, what it would fail to reveal. When finally she did open the letter, she pored over it for clues, read and re-read the last two lines:

```
Come visit during Spring Break . . . we
can just take off together, see the North
```

and maybe a few other countries on the
continent. That is, if I'm still here.

Love you,

Ella

Based on the return addresses, she could track Ella's travels in the Nigerian capital: Lagos Island, Ikeja, Surulere. Alluring names that Angie had memorized, names she'd let spill over her tongue many times over the past four years. Since her encounter with Solo, she'd felt a force beyond her control pushing her toward Nigeria and now with her mother's own plans, it was the only thing to do. Now was her chance. She kissed each letter, and hoped for the same transformation that Ella had once gone through. She wanted this trip to be a hajj of some sort, yearned to return more certain of who she was, of what she could do in the world. Figure out what type of black person to be.

And to understand Ella more, maybe solve the mystery of her death. *That is, if I'm still here.*

The trip scared her. It was a daunting proposition. Africa was so far away, with unsafe water, malaria-carrying mosquitoes, and yes, dangerous roads. What did she hope to find anyway? She was no detective, had no stomach for investigating. Besides, *which* Ella was she chasing after? The twenty-one-year-old version who went to Lagos at the height of her powers, or the one who went six years later, newly sober and chastened? The latter one was an apparition, never returned. And yet, the younger version didn't exist either, evaporated in a mist of drug-addled highs.

One thing felt certain: Detroit had changed. The passionate radicals of the seventies—themselves fueled by the city's 1967 uprising—where were they? Gone. Or addicted to crack. And those who shot up were at risk of getting the new deadly disease, the one targeting gays and needle-using addicts. Mayor

Coleman Young was mired in scandals reported with glee by an antagonistic press, and now the city had Devil's Night to cope with. She and her mother sat up half the night on Halloween Eve, guarding the house against rampaging arsonists. She had to admit, it was probably best for her mother to move away. Safer. But Detroit was home, where all the memories of her big sister were rooted. She didn't want to follow her mother to Atlanta, a place where Ella had never been. Wouldn't that completely erase her sister's life, the physical proof of her existence? That felt wrong.

But Angie didn't want to be left behind either. And so, Nigeria.

SHE AWOKE TO a dry mouth and the smell of coffee wafting toward her alongside the upbeat lyrics of "Ain't Too Proud to Beg." That meant Denise was listening to the Sunday oldies show on WJLB. Angie lay there in bed as a few more Motown songs played. Sixties music held no allure for her. But Denise was different; she loved those tunes. Angie could hear her sister's voice talking over the music, imagined Denise telling their mother a juicy story involving someone else's business; she could see her acting it out, making their mother laugh. Everyone always said Nanette and her daughter Denise were alike, and in obvious ways they were. Both were born under the zodiac sign of Taurus, both loved good gossip, both were practical minded. And they were equipped with the same moral compass. But Angie felt she'd gotten to know their mother these past few years in a way Denise couldn't appreciate, saw her chastened by grief, by a huge loss that had softened her positions, quieted her, made her more pensive. More interesting. Denise wasn't privy to this subtlety because she lived five hundred miles away. Angie and her mother had formed a bond in the absence of the other daughters. She'd gotten her mother to try new things like independent films and health food and natural hair. But when Denise was around, that side of her mother evaporated and she reverted back to Denise's mirror image. She went to see corny comedies with black actors, ate fried foods, and got her usual press-and-curl. Denise and their mother became a unit again, and Angie couldn't find a place to enter. In their presence, Angie seldom even tried to add to the conversation. The mere thought of being the third wheel made her want to lie in bed all day, hide out. But she couldn't. She had to get up, go to work. Today the store was hosting its plus-size fashion show for teens. There'd be a lot to do.

She could hear their conversation long before she got to the kitchen. Denise's voice was loud, traveled. "What I don't understand is why she has to be protected from knowing the truth?"

"I want to tell her in my own way and time, OK?" said their mother.

"Tell me what?" said Angie as she entered the kitchen.

"Nothing," said Nanette.

"Obviously, since you two were talking about me, it must be something."

"Why do you always think somebody's talking about you?" asked Denise.

"Because you are. And behind my back, yet again."

"Whatever I say, I can say to your face," Denise noted.

"So say it."

"Apparently it's not for me to say."

"That never stopped you before from blabbing your mouth."

"At least I know what's going on."

"Hey! Stop it, OK?" said their mother.

They moved, the three of them, in a clipped silence for several seconds as Angie headed to the refrigerator, grabbed the orange juice, and poured herself a glass.

"Want some coffee?" Denise asked brightly as Angie sat down. She was like that. Arguments didn't linger with Denise. She had her say—could bite your head off with her sharp tongue—and was instantly ready to move on. To her that was what sisters did.

"No, I don't want coffee," snapped Angie, still annoyed. "I gotta get to work early. Busy day."

"Do you have to work late?" asked their mother.

"Not really. I should be home by five."

"I'll fry some catfish."

Angie shrugged nonchalantly, even though they all knew she loved her mother's catfish.

WORK WAS NONSTOP all morning. The workers set up a runway and folding chairs through the middle aisles, pushing clothing racks to the side. Angie and her manager Lana and two other sales girls gathered all the models' clothing into the line of dressing rooms. Angie was assigned three teens, charged with helping them dress quickly to head onto the runway. The show, which started at noon, moved along smoothly at first, with the girls giggling nervously backstage before walking jauntily down the catwalk in their coordinated outfits. Angie was fascinated by how the white girls had each given themselves the Madonna look—bleached, platinum-blond hair cut into a curly crop, heavy, black brows, and bright red lipstick. In contrast, the two black girls had Lisa Bonet-style flowing tresses, thanks to their curly perms.

Toward the end of the show, the girl wearing the leggings and oversized T-shirt stepped down the runway too confidently in her stilettos and tripped. To a chorus of gasps, she fell face-first, quickly got up, and ran off the runway. Lana pushed the next girl out and the show continued. The fallen girl's mother rose from the audience, found her daughter crying in the dressing room, grabbed her hand, and swiftly left. The whole incident made Angie think of Ella and those diet pills, the teenage rejection of her own body. Angie was annoyed with herself: Why hadn't she stood her ground with Lana over the jelly shoes?

Afterward, as the workers broke down the runway and folded chairs, Lana said, "I think we recovered well, don't you?" She rattled on, not waiting for a response, eyes brimming with tears. "And you know, I feel good about the whole thing, I mean, you know, despite that unfortunate moment. But she was great, she got right up and I think it went well, don't you?"

Angie nodded continually, as if her bobbing head could somehow stop Lana's tears from falling.

"I hope people still order a lot of the show's pieces," said Lana. She folded her arms. "I think they will." She gave Angie a big, professional smile. "Thanks for all your help today."

Angie was still nodding as she left Lana standing there; she couldn't get out of the store fast enough, ran across the parking lot, gratefully slammed shut the door of her car, relieved to be back in her cocoon. She pushed play on the cassette player, and breathed relief as the sounds of Fela's sinewy horn and hypnotic rhythms filled her ears, soothing her throughout the drive home.

THE KITCHEN SMELLED like old times, but her mother looked new, with her freshly arched eyebrows and dewy skin, her lighthearted aura. She was playing a cassette that Denise and Angie had compiled for her last birthday. All female jazz singers. Right now, Dinah Washington sang of *this bitter earth, may not be so bitter after all* and her mother hummed along to the music as she cooked. Angie enjoyed watching her mother drop the corn-meal-covered catfish into the sizzling oil. Denise was out with friends, taking advantage of her last night in town. Her mother slid a piece of fish out of the skillet onto the awaiting plate, paper towel beneath to catch the excess oil.

"Lord, I need to pack," she said. "My flight leaves at ten tomorrow morning."

"I can help you after dinner," said Angie as she poured a Coca-Cola for herself, another for her mother. They ate together at the dinette table, Angie enjoying the fish's crispy saltiness.

Her mother stood to clear the table and Angie joined in. Together they moved to the kitchen sink, scraped plates. Her mother turned on the faucet, poured Palmolive into the water. Angie watched the soap bubbles form.

"You know, I wanted to talk to you about this Atlanta trip," said her mother.

Angie swiped at a plate. She didn't want to hear it.

The phone rang, a reprieve. Her mother dried her hands on the madras dishtowel and answered it. Angie quickly washed more plates as she listened. "Hello? Hi, what's going on? In the morning. First thing, yes. Louis, I told you about this, weeks ago. Well no, I can't, sorry. Get Jennifer to come in. In a few days. I don't know exactly. Of course, don't I always? OK. Uh-huh. Bye."

Nanette returned, took a plate from Angie. "I swear, that man acts like he's so helpless."

"Dr. B., I take it."

"Mm-hmm."

Angie washed a glass, rinsed it, handed it to her mother.

"I can't tell you what a relief it'll be to get a break from that office," said her mother. "I'm sick of it."

"I know," said Angie. She grabbed a skillet, began scrubbing.

"I'm not so sure you do. How much I'm ready for a change."

Her mother hesitated. "I feel like I've been stuck here, just stuck in one place."

Angie waited, illogically hoping that maybe she'd gotten it wrong, maybe the circled houses in the newspaper didn't mean what she thought they meant.

"This trip to Atlanta is a little more than a visit."

Angie scrubbed away, resigned. "I know."

"Do you?"

"You're planning on moving there."

"Well, I will be damned," said her mother. "How did you figure that out?"

"I just knew," she lied. "And I'm sorry you didn't think you could tell me the truth."

"To be honest, I didn't know how you'd react."

"What does it matter? Looks like you made up your mind already."

Several seconds passed as they washed and dried the remaining dishes in silence.

"Well, there's still a lot to work out. What to do with this house for one." Her mother paused. "I know you're still figuring out things yourself, but if you want to join me—"

"No, I do not." Angie shoved a pot into her mother's hands.

She could see Nanette was taken aback by her harsh tone. "OK, that's fine."

"You talk about *me* trying to be like Ella?" Angie fumed. "Look at you. Denise lives in Atlanta, so you're moving there. Whatever she thinks you should do, you do it."

"It wasn't her idea, it was mine."

"How could you even think about moving there? You hate the South! That's what you always said." Angie was worked up now. "Remember Emmett Till? You were pregnant with Ella and you made the mistake of looking at that picture of him lying in his casket? His brutally beaten, bloated face! And the sight of him upset you so much, you almost had a miscarriage."

"Yes, but—"

"And you said you vowed then that if you ever got out of the South, you were never going back."

"The South of 1956 is not the South of today," said her mother. "And Atlanta isn't exactly the *deep* South. It's thriving, with a sophisticated black mayor and new everything. When I went there for Denise's graduation—" here her mother paused, obviously still pained that she'd missed seeing her daughter walk across the stage—"I liked it. The black middle class is doing so well there. And the weather is nice."

"Is this about Dr. B.?"

Her mother looked startled and Angie felt a sick satisfaction. "Denise told me," she said.

Nanette stared at the dishwater. "That's one reason, yes." She looked back up at Angie, brazen, daring her daughter to judge her. "But that's not the only reason."

"Is it that guy from your high school days?"

"Franklin?" Her mother laughed nervously. "Oh shoot, who knows what'll come of that? I haven't seen that man in thirty years."

"Then why?" pleaded Angie. "Why?"

"Because it's something I've wanted for a long time honestly, to live somewhere else. I used to talk to your father about moving, but he didn't want to hear it. 'Leave Hazel Park Raceway?' he'd say. 'For what?' So we stayed."

"You're blaming Daddy?"

"I'm not blaming anybody, Angela, but you asked me and I'm telling you. Samson felt this was the best place for him to run horses, so this is where we moved, and this is where we stayed." She sighed. "With him, the horses always came first."

"That's not true! He put us first!"

"He was gone six months of every year. But OK, I'm not

gonna mess with your memories on that. You were so young."

"But I remember a lot. I remember him being there, holding me, playing with us." It rose suddenly in her, Angie's need to defend her father, against the man from her mother's high school days and Dr. Benjamin. "Look at how he spent all that time teaching Ella to ride."

"He did," admitted her mother. "He spent too much time on that, if you ask me. Trying to make her into a jockey."

"She loved it," said Angie.

"She loved getting his attention. And he loved the idea that he could say he, Samson Mackenzie, had a daughter who was gonna be the first black female jockey ever."

"What's so wrong with that?"

"He badgered her about her weight. I didn't like that. I tried to tell him to leave her alone. You can't do that to a girl, you got to be very careful around that subject. I know." Her mother shook her head. "I do believe that was Ella's biggest problem, him criticizing her 'cause she wasn't the perfect weight to race a horse."

Angie's fury grew at the thought of her father being blamed for Ella's problems. How could her mother be in such denial?

"That wasn't her biggest problem," said Angie. "You leaving her down South was."

Her mother looked at her. Angie could see that she'd hit a nerve.

"That was Samson's idea too," said her mother.

"But you *let* him. You followed him up here."

"Yes, I did. I had my doubts about it; it was a hard decision, but the aunts were so happy to keep her, they begged me and I thought it might be better for Ella to stay put, rather than drag her up North. Lord knows, I didn't know what to expect up here myself."

"But you left her there for two whole years!"

"It didn't do her any real harm."

"Things happened to her down there," said Angie.

"What kind of things?"

"Things."

"Did she tell you that?"

"She said the aunts didn't watch her as closely as they should have."

Realization flickered across her mother's face. She looked stricken. "Well, I didn't know anything about that. Ella never said a word." She put the dishtowel back on the door handle of the refrigerator. "And at this point, some things I don't need to know."

She walked out.

Angie felt horrendous. She followed her mother into the bedroom. "I can still help you pack, if you want."

Her mother shrugged. Angie picked up a blouse, began delicately folding it, placed it into the suitcase.

"The whole point, everything I did, was to give her a better life," explained her mother. "I hope you understand that."

Angie grabbed a nightgown, started folding. "Yes, I know Mama."

"How was I to know that she'd take that opportunity and squander it on dope?"

Angie couldn't believe her mother didn't understand, after all this time. "It wasn't her fault," she said.

"Well whose was it? Lord knows, she didn't have it to do."

"Maybe she did."

"What's that supposed to mean? You got more secrets that she revealed only to you?"

"We used to talk about a lot and—"

"I'm listening."

"Maybe she felt abandoned when you left her."

Her mother swatted her hand at the air, dismissive. "That's

nonsense. The aunties were very good to her. In fact, they spoiled her rotten. And what does that have to do with her becoming a heroin addict? Nothing."

"That's where you're wrong. I studied this stuff in school, OK? Feeling abandoned can often lead to drug addiction. It *can* happen." Her mother glared at her. "I learned that in my psych classes," Angie added, but already she regretted saying it.

"So you blame me." Her mother threw her new peach-colored dress into the suitcase.

"No. I mean, it's just—" Angie stopped mid-sentence.

Her mother threw in the other new dress. Angie felt awful. Those lovely dresses would become all wrinkled now. She wanted to say something, but could only watch as her mother threw more things into her new floral luggage.

Tears fell from Nanette's eyes. She'd seen her mother cry only twice before, and both times at funerals. Angie worried about those new dresses, worried about tear stains dropping onto the linen. She didn't know what to do.

Nanette looked over at Angie, eyes glistening. "You're right. It was my fault."

"Mama, I don't blame you," she insisted. "Really I don't."

Her mother pushed down the lid of her suitcase with final-ity, looked Angie in the eye. "But not because we left her down south. That wasn't it. It was my fault for leaving the South at all." She snapped the suitcase's locks in place, one at a time. "I never should've moved to this god-awful place, where they just throw drugs into every black neighborhood like it's Christmas candy." She pointed to her own chest. "You think it doesn't haunt me? How none of your cousins down south got hooked on dope? Well it does." Her mother sat on the bed. "I came here to make a better life for her and the place killed her."

"That's not true Mama!" Angie sat next to her mother. "That's not true. A car killed Ella. A car in Lagos—"

Her mother shook her head so hard, her face blurred. "Lagos didn't kill her. Detroit did."

She put her hand on her mother's arm. Her mother flinched. "Please, leave me alone. I'm through with it."

"Mama, I—"

Nanette turned, inches from Angie's face. "Did you hear me, damn it!? I said I'm through with it!"

She stood, a drop of spit from her mother's mouth on her nose. She watched as her mother shoved the suitcase onto the floor. It hit with a dead thud.

"Close the door behind you," said Nanette.

Angie did as she was told. Once behind her own closed door, she lay on the bed, stared at the ceiling, tears sliding sideways, face hot with shame.

EIGHT

THE NEXT MORNING, HER MOTHER STOOD BY THE FRONT door, suitcase in hand. "I'll see you when I get back," she said.

Angie nodded. She wanted to say, "I'm sorry," but the words wouldn't come.

Denise tooted her car horn in the driveway and their mother headed out. Angie went to the door, waved goodbye. Denise lowered her car window. "Don't throw any wild parties now that you got the house to yourself!"

"Don't give me ideas!" said Angie, forcing a playful tone for her mother's benefit.

Nanette got into the car. Angie waved frantically, desperate to apologize yet not wanting to do so in front of Denise, time running out.

Her mother waved back. "Be safe." She got in the passenger side. Angie watched as the car rolled out of the driveway and down the block. She waved again, knowing they couldn't see her.

As soon as she re-entered the house, she started prepping. By day's end, she'd set up an appointment for her travel shots, purchased a plane ticket on her credit card, withdrawn money from the joint account she shared with her mother—careful to take out only her portion of the insurance money—and found out where she'd have to go during a layover in New York to get a visa-stamp in her passport. The next few days were a flurry of work, preparation for her trip, work, prep. She told Lana she'd be leaving for a while. Lana promised Angie she'd try her best to hold the job for her. "You're one of my best salesgirls," she said.

When her mother called to say she'd be staying in Atlanta for another couple days, ("Just over the weekend, back by Monday"), Angie faced a dilemma. She'd selected her departure date, June 14, based on her mother being back. Now she'd be leaving before her mother returned, unless she changed her ticket. She didn't know what to do.

To calm her nerves, she reread Ella's letters. Like sacred texts, the familiar words had a restorative effect. They transported her back to those precious few months, years before, when everything had been in front of her. Ella was well and seemingly happy in Nigeria, and Angie was in college, newly in love, and thinking of visiting her sister on the continent. After a long time of worry over Ella, she'd felt the space in her world open up, came to know her own capacity for joy. She'd gotten her life back.

She dozed off and when she woke up the letters were scattered across her bed; one had fallen to the floor. As she carefully retrieved them, kissed each one, she decided not to change her travel plans.

The morning of her flight, Angie sat on the sofa and stared at her new American Tourister luggage. She'd been determined to limit herself to one bag, but it was bulging. She hadn't really known what to take, had finally settled on a few crinkly Indian skirts, jeans, tops, a nightgown, and a plethora of toiletries. Plus the gold pen and journal Ella had given her as a high school graduation present. And all of Ella's letters. It dawned on her that there'd be two long plane rides and at the last minute she threw in Toni Morrison's new novel *Beloved* and Ella's favorite novel—an old paperback copy of *One Hundred Years of Solitude*.

She picked up the phone, started to push the buttons for Denise's number, stopped. She tried again. Her sister answered on the third ring. Gospel played in the background.

"Hey!" said Denise. "Is everything OK?"

"Why wouldn't it be?"

"I'm just asking, Angie. You are there alone."

"Everything is fine," she said. "Let me speak to Mama."

"She's not here. She's out having breakfast with that guy Franklin. I think they're actually getting along really well!" Denise was obviously tickled. "Can you believe it? After all these years?"

"Wow," said Angie, oppressed by the news. "I guess you'll have to tell her bye for me." As she said it, Angie realized she preferred things this way. She hadn't known how she was going to tell her mother herself.

"What are you talking about?"

"I'm leaving for Nigeria today."

"You're what?"

"You heard me."

"Wait a minute. Does Mama know?"

"Yeah, we discussed it."

"She didn't say anything to me about this. I mean, she mentioned you talking about it, yeah, but—"

"Maybe she doesn't tell you everything after all," said Angie.

Denise sighed, exasperated. Angie had heard that sigh all her life, that you're-five-and-a-half-years-younger-than-me-and-so-immature sigh. "Look, when Mama gets back, I'll have her call and you two can discuss this."

"I can't wait until she gets back. My flight leaves at two."

"Girl, you can't just up and go across the world, to *Africa* of all places, just like that!"

"Yes I can." She paused. "Tell Mama I love her, OK?"

"Whoa, Angie. You're not even gonna say bye to her yourself?"

"You can do it for me. And tell her I'm sorry, OK?"

"For what?"

"She'll know. I gotta go."

"Listen! Call as soon as you get there!"

"Denise, the phones over there don't always work," she said, totally unsure whether this was true.

"Check in with the US embassy as soon as you arrive, you hear me? And do not let anything happen to you over there! I cannot bear the thought of delivering more bad news to Mama."

"Don't worry," she said. And then she added: "Love you, OK?"

"Angie, wait a minute—"

"Bye, Denise."

"Angie! Wait!"

She hung up. As soon as she did, the phone rang. She put her hand on the receiver, felt the vibration as the phone rang and rang. She counted fifteen rings before Denise gave up. She put her hand to her cheek; it was warm from the heat generated by the ringing phone. She kept it there as she sat on the sofa, looking around the living room, taking it in. Her eyes landed on Denise's watercolor painting that hung above the sofa, a rendering of their father's prized horse, Thumbsucker. She sat for a long time, staring at the dark beauty, at the exuberant brush strokes of swishing tail and elegant, bent legs.

Then she got up and called a taxi.

IKEJA

NINE

THE FIRST THING ANGIE NOTICED ABOUT AFRICA WAS THE
smell. The air was redolent with the scent of damp, fresh-
turned earth. Tropical, and as far away from Detroit as you
could get. She walked down the steps of the plane, her first
sight of the continent a stretch of tarmac, and beyond that
a massive glass and stone building—the gleaming, elegant
Murtala Muhammed International Airport. A crew of Nigerian workers whizzed by in a dizzying array of bold-patterned
shirts, hurling luggage from the belly of the plane onto waiting
carts. She inhaled deeply, filling her lungs with the verdant air.
Exhaling, she promised herself she'd never forget this moment.

Inside, the terminal was teeming with people of myriad
hues. Erect men stood in long dashikis beside women in matching lace head wraps and skirts; children scattered throughout, running toward outstretched hands. Two Nigerian pilots
passed by, their uniforms crisp and imposing. Angie had never
seen a black pilot in her life, certainly not two. Everywhere she
looked, behind ticket counters, at the customs desks, within
waiting areas, she saw black men and women nonchalantly in
charge. Even though she knew she was headed to an African
country, she hadn't been prepared for this, for dark-skinned
men and women moving through a public space with ease and

grace. Instantly, she understood Ella's devotion to the Pan-African movement. *This* was what it was all about—black people in charge, running their own country. She felt like a girl who'd landed in a scene from *The Wiz*, its Afro-Oz long hidden from view. And now she'd found it.

Angie was exhausted yet alert; her senses overloaded. She tried not to look confused, but the myriad lines and official-looking men in uniform daunted her. She'd never traveled internationally before, couldn't really count Canada. She gripped the new shoulder bag—at the shop in JFK Airport she'd been told it was a "reporter's bag"—and now slung it across her body. The Nigerian man she'd sat beside on the plane had warned Angie about men trying to rip her off, had told her to not let go of her passport, to hold on tight to her luggage. Her mother would have warned her of the same, yet Ella hadn't complained about such things. Only then did it dawn on Angie that Ella hadn't been a woman traveling alone. Both times, she'd been with others—a US delegation, and then Nigel. Angie had almost forgotten *she* was traveling alone, so caught up in following Ella's path, until the talkative Nigerian on the plane reminded her of that fact.

The flight had been long and she'd come to rely on the nice man's lilting voice as he regaled her with details about his "beautiful country," singing its name and making her love its four-syllable, strong-vowel lyricism: *Nigeeeria*. She'd grown attached to the cocoon of economy class, where she'd shared oxygen and movies and meals with the same people over the last seventeen hours, her family of air-travel strangers, faces grown familiar. She'd felt at home among the strewn pages of *The London Guardian*, tossed scratchy British Airways blankets and crumpled white pillows.

Yet, as the plane descended toward Lagos, she looked out her window at the archipelago of small islands jutting into the ocean, how its narrow, crowded land rushed to meet the wide arms of the Atlantic, and she felt elated.

Now she was here, in Africa.

Miraculously, a kind-faced man approached, sporting an airport badge and reminding her of Solo. He called her "sistah" and asked if she needed help. Just in the way he'd said that word "sister," she felt a belonging that had eluded her forever, it seemed. Maybe, she thought, I've found my people. He helped her get through the long queue at customs and retrieve her luggage. She tipped him a lot, still unfamiliar with the currency— lovely naira bills the color of translucent red wine, profile of a black president at their center—exchanged at Heathrow during the layover.

As Angie stepped out of the airport into the early evening, the rainy season introduced itself—a humidity that prickled her scalp and caused her cotton blouse to cling. She watched as travelers slipped into waiting Mercedes taxis; all around her men and women stood beside bulging suitcases wrapped with rope, their first-word acquisitions nearly bursting through.

"My sistah, how are you?" said a man who approached, lunging for her luggage. Awed by that word again, she almost let him take her duffel bag. Then she remembered the man from the plane's warnings, held on tight. "Wait!"

As though her voice had attracted them, a swarm of touts appeared, and jostled for the chance to grab her bag and rush her into one of many cars parked at the curb. A shoving match broke out, more startling than frightening, and she worried that her luggage would burst open in the midst of the tug-of-war. Finally the first man who'd approached yanked her bag free. And the touts, still yelling at one another, rushed on to the new arrival coming through the automatic doors, a European man in a business suit; they lunged at his suitcase, pushing one another and squawking like chickens after the last bit of corn. Angie marveled at the overt aggression.

Meanwhile, the taxi driver had rushed to a Peugeot parked at the curb, and tossed her bag into the trunk. He beckoned to Angie. "Enta!"

She quickly got into the backseat as he slid behind the wheel. He stepped on the gas, tore away from the curb. She swerved to one side and they thundered forward. The car radio blasted highlife, a drumming dance music that she'd soon hear pouring from speakers all over Lagos.

"I'm going to the Bristol Hotel, please." She gripped the door handle.

"Yes, yes, Lagos Island," said the driver. They entered a highway, passing by a skyline of high-rises and skyscrapers, some only half-built carcasses of expectation; a giant red sign lit the sky, proclaiming, "Things go Better with Coke." As the driver flew along the expressway, Angie was awed by its multi-lane expanse. This was the modernity that Ella had raved about.

Traffic clogged. The Peugeot inched forward. Horns blew incessantly—long, urgent howls sliced by short, staccato beeps—as the driver shouted back with his own horn. It was chaotic and wild and smelled strongly of gas fumes.

When the traffic finally opened up, the driver accelerated, lurching forward. Angie suddenly saw two people run across the expressway, darting past oncoming cars. She gasped, an awareness piercing her heart.

"Aren't there overpasses or something?" she asked.

"Flyovers, yes, but people don't use them."

"Why not?"

The driver shrugged. "This is Nigeria."

"Well, people shouldn't be allowed to do that," she said, incredulous. "Someone could get seriously hurt."

The driver eyed her through his rearview mirror. "So you are *akata*, eh?"

She made contact with his reflection. "A what?"

"You are a black American?"

"Yes," she said.

"Welcome to my country!" He told her his cousin drove a taxi in New York. "He is making a lot of money," he explained, and caught her eye again in the rearview mirror. "I am good driver, you see? I can be doing this in New York. Maybe you can help me get my papers to come to America, yes?"

"I'd be happy to help!" she said, wanting to make a difference in a Nigerian's life, even though she had no idea what that entailed.

"You will give me your address and I will write to you," he said. "And then you will help me."

"Sure!" She pulled out her journal from the reporter's bag, and jotted down her home address as best she could in the fast-moving car. Maybe this man and she would become pen pals, stay in touch the way Ella had stayed in touch with the people she met during her first visit here. Already, Angie felt herself expanding, blooming in sophistication and knowing.

They approached the Eko Bridge and traffic slowed again. "Ah, ah!" exclaimed the driver. "Not this *sheet!*"

Angie craned her neck, saw that up ahead, a man with a large rifle slung across his chest stood guard, halting cars. "What's going on?" she asked. She'd never bothered to check the State Department's list of hot spots. Was Nigeria on it?

"*Moto* cop," said the driver. "Don't worry sistah, I am handling it."

The cop held his hand out like a stop sign as they approached then put his head into the passenger side of the car, glared at her. "What is your business?"

"She is an American visitor," said the driver. "I have gathered her from the airport, Suh, and am depositing her at a hotel downtown."

"Your country paper!" barked the cop.

Angie didn't understand, looked desperately at the driver.

"Give him your passport," said the driver.

She quickly pulled out her passport, handed it to the cop, fear rising in her. What if he kept it? What would she do? What if he made her get out of the car, dragged her to some remote jail? When Ella was in the last, worst vestiges of her addiction, Angie and her mother often escaped to the movies; one February afternoon they saw the Jack Lemmon film *Missing*, about an American journalist who disappeared in the aftermath of the Chilean coup. It was haunting and disturbing and afterward her mother said, "So much for thinking your American passport protects you."

The moto cop looked over her passport with his flashlight for longer than he needed to. Finally he tossed it back at her.

"Open the boot!" he ordered the driver.

The driver got out and followed the cop to the taxi's trunk.

She watched through the back windshield as the cop ran his flashlight over the contents of the open trunk, then gruffly ordered the driver to close it. Again panic as she thought: What will I do if he takes him away? But they returned to the front of the car and the driver slid back behind the wheel. The cop thrust his hand into the window, palm up. It was rough, calloused.

"*Drop, drop,*" he said.

The driver pulled crumbled bills from his pocket and handed them to the officer, who calmly waved the taxi through the roadblock, his flashlight arcing across the dusk. As they left the moto cop behind, Angie stared out the back window, feeling a strange mixture of relief and disappointment. Glad to be safe, yes, but wishing she'd been bolder somehow.

"These ones with their big eye," said the driver. "Bodi dey inside cloth and they want take from me."

"What did you say?"

The driver didn't answer.

She pressed, wanting to understand. "So what was he checking for?"

The driver sucked his teeth. "Nigeria expelled many foreigners and the police are saying they are checking to make sure the undesirables do not creep back into our country."

"What do they do with these uh, these people they don't want here?" she asked.

"These Nigerian policeman, they do whatever they want, O. If they want to kill a man, they do it, just like that."

"Just like that?" she repeated, Fela's song on her mind.

He turned to face Angie. "You are having these checkpoints in America?"

"Nobody stands on the highway with a machine gun, checking cars, no."

"I will come to America," he said. But his energy zapped, he drove quietly after that, bobbing his head to the radio's highlife, with its chaotic, tossed-up sounds; its forced exuberance reminded Angie that she was indeed a visitor to a strange land.

They crossed the bridge, its ribbon of concrete looping above the Lagos Lagoon. As they passed over the harbor's black waters, Angie eyed wooden shacks built on stilts, hovering above the lagoon.

"People live down there?" she asked.

"They do," said the driver. "And when someone falls in, they are so covered in oil they are too slippery to save."

The dissonance of desperate living beneath a sprawling, modern construction disturbed Angie, fractured her senses. Plus, once off the mainland, moving through town without

the expanse of highway, the driver lurched forward, right up to
the car in front, then slammed on his brakes, lurched forward,
slammed, lurched. Angie's body jerked back and forth as she
held on tighter to the door handle; she tried to take in the
sights, but it was now dark and everything took on a shadowy,
shaky outline.

Bristol Hotel
8 Martins Street
Lagos Island, Lagos

July 6, 1983

Dear Angie,
Nigel and I have now been here a couple weeks and wow!
It's great to be back, although a lot has changed! For one,
everywhere we turn, they're playing Michael Jackson. When
I hear "Billie Jean," I think of us all gathered in front of
the TV, watching him do that moonwalk, flipping that hat.
Almost makes me miss you guys (smile).
We've been staying at this cool hotel right on Lagos
Island, in the middle of everything. I swear, Lagos has
got to be the most colorful place in the world! Everybody's
dressed in loud prints, houses are painted pink and blue
and yellow, street vendors sell big orange and red and green
fruit. My favorite sights are the ogas or "big men"—self-
important Nigerian men, girl—who wear these long, robe-
like garments in pretty pastel shades, and the most amazing
indigo blue I've ever seen. "Agbadas" they're called. As you
can see, I've learned a few words in Yoruba. This pidgin
they speak is something else—still working on that!
We've been walking around a lot, under giant umbrellas.

Everything looks magical when you see it through a sheet of constant rain. Shimmery and new. I love it!

That's all for now. Hope you're well. I'll write again soon.

Luv,
Ella

The driver screeched to a halt in front of the hotel. "You will come down here, sistah."

Angie climbed out of the backseat; she had the sensation of still moving. Her head hurt from all the slamming of brakes, and the sticky air was as thick as a steam room. He grabbed her duffel from the trunk, carried it into the hotel's lobby.

The man behind the desk knew the driver, as they greeted one another boisterously. Angie thanked the driver and paid him with the last of her wine-colored bills. She also gave him the piece of paper she'd written her address on.

"I will write to you and then I will come to your country!" he said, waving goodbye.

"OK!" she said, imagining a letter from him arriving months from now, out of the blue.

The desk clerk smiled at Angie. He had a gold front tooth. "You would like a room for how many nights, please?"

"Just one," she said. "For now."

The transistor radio on the desk was softly playing "I Wanna Dance With Somebody," Whitney Houston's powerful voice filling the small lobby. Ella and Nigel had once been in this same lobby, she thought. Maybe standing in this very spot, maybe even talking to this same guy. It amazed her.

The desk clerk was studying a sheet attached to a clipboard; he flipped a couple pages and finally looked up. "Yes, we have a single room for you. Very, very nice room. The fifth floor."

"Great!" She was amazed that she'd managed to pull this off, to get herself across the world and make it to the exact same place her sister had been. Still, she couldn't feel Ella's presence in the tight lobby.

"That will be sixty naira," said the desk clerk.

She was startled. "For one night?"

"Yes. Please pay now."

She hesitated. That didn't seem right. But at this point, she had no choice. It was dark, late. This was *the* hotel. She sighed. "Will you accept American dollars?"

He grinned. "Of course! One hundred twenty dollars please."

"One hundred and twenty *dollars*? Are you sure?"

"I am sure." His smile stayed in place.

"But the dollar is worth twice the naira, right?" She'd checked the exchange rate and was certain that was true.

"That is the exchange rate *here*," he said, holding her gaze.

Reluctantly, she pulled out her American Express travelers cheques, and handed $120 to the clerk. He handed her a key.

Angie took out a twenty-dollar bill. "Do you think you could give me naira for this?"

The clerk eyed the American money. "Yes, yes, of course." He took the twenty, pulled out a weathered, lizard-skinned wallet, picked out ten worn single naira bills, and handed them to Angie. So I'm being totally ripped off, she thought. I'm being treated like a dumb American tourist.

The desk clerk beckoned to an aged man dressed in khaki pants and shirt, sitting quietly in the corner, beside a planted tree. Angie had not noticed him when she entered.

"Help this lady with her luggage!" barked the clerk. The bellhop jumped up, grabbed Angie's bag.

"Welcome to Nigeria," said the desk clerk, gold tooth shining.

Angie headed toward the elevator, but the bellhop stopped her.

"No *nepa* today," he said.

"Excuse me?"

"Power is out," he explained.

Together they walked up the five flights. The stairwell was suffocating. Angie noticed how dusty the man's feet were inside his lizard sandals. They walked down the short hall to room 576. Angie opened the door to a modest room with a twin bed. The light came on magically, without her touching a switch. She turned to the bellhop.

"Power is back," he noted.

She handed him two naira.

"Thank you madam, thank you," he said, backing out of the room.

Angie sat on the bed. Slowly, methodically, she peeled off her shoes and clothes and dropped them into a pile on the floor as though they held her exhaustion in their fibers; she stumbled to the bathroom. When she turned the tap at the sink, brown water trickled out. She cranked the faucet all the way, but the water pressure remained weak. She ran her hands under the trickle and turned to wipe them on the hanging towel. It was used, dirty.

When she looked in the mirror, she was startled. Her hair, which had been in ringlets held together by styling gel when she embarked on her trip, was now a voluminous frizzy halo. She hadn't counted on the humidity, and now her hair was a defiant mess. She'd tame it tomorrow, somehow.

She pulled the light blanket back on the bed and found crumbled, used sheets; she stood staring at the soiled white linen, debating whether to call the desk clerk. The desire to lie down after nineteen hours of plane rides and layovers—from Detroit to New York to London to here—overrode her disgust. She clicked off the bedside lamp, threw the blanket over the sheet, and lay atop the bed. She had the distinct feeling she'd gotten something wrong. But here she was.

"I made it," she whispered into the dark before falling asleep to the muted rumble of an oncoming storm.

IN THE MORNING light, Angie noticed the hotel room's best feature: a long, white-shuttered window. Enchanted, she slid out of bed and opened the shutters, discovering a tiny balcony. She stepped out to find a bright, azure sky. Everything glistened from the night's rain, yet the sun was penetrating, lustrous. She looked down onto a narrow street bordered by tin-roofed stalls. Three men, all dressed in agbadas and matching cloth hats, stood in a circle below, talking to one another. The men's robes were in promising colors—one a rich bronze, the other lavender, and the third turquoise. The sight buoyed Angie's spirits, made her confident that she could indeed gather the clues that would help her stitch together Ella's time in Nigeria; now she could finally know her sister with an intimacy that had eluded her, a knowledge that would, in its way, bring Ella back to her. All she had to do was wait, be patient, and Ella would return—as she did back in the old days at the racetrack. Even when Angie could barely see her, a dot on the other side of the stretch, Ella always came back round, horse galloping up to where little Angie sat crouched on the bleachers, waiting.

She leaned over the railing. Each man's posture was erect, confident, pride swirling up to greet her. The sun's rays put white dots before her eyes. She closed them and let the heat warm her lids. She felt her body lifting, pulling away, and when she slowly opened her eyes and looked down, the men had moved on. A boy passed by with a small sewing machine atop his head. The soft yell of street vendors mingled with the

honk of car horns. Through the wavy air she saw the recognizable form of a big-boned woman, this one in native print, hip
swaying and casual, walking the narrow street. Angie widened
the shutters, stretching out her arms. The sun felt curative, as
though burning away the detritus of her old self. Below more
women, full of girth, strolled up the road. She closed the shutters and stepped back inside the room, anxious to start her new
life, to be out among them.

TEN

43, Broad Street
International Bank of West Africa
51 Broad Street
Lagos Island, Lagos

3 August 1983

Hey Angie,

You won't believe this, but your big sister is now officially a journalist! Cool, huh?

   Nigel and I hooked up with this friend, Chris Olapade, who we met at FESTAC. He works for this bank, but it turns out he and some friends have started a newspaper. He asked us to help out, so now we're working for the brand-new "Lagos Voice." Lots to write about too! Nigeria is about to have its first free, democratic elections. My job is to do political stories from the woman's perspective. Nigel does the Pan-African coverage. He gets to travel!

   We're staying with Chris and his wife, Brenda. She's black American too. And guess what? She went to Spelman just like Denise! She's good people. Their new home is near the airport. It's modern and big. Best thing: hot pink flowers blooming all along the front of the house. And at night, porch lights bathing everything in a lovely yellow glow. Pretty.

So you must be all packed for school by now! Write and tell me which dorm you're staying in. And please go by and say hi to Prof. Jordan for me! I really must write to him soon. He's the reason I came to Africa in the first place. It's so busy here, it's hard to find time to do anything. It takes a full day to get from point A to point B. Crazy!!

Tell Mama she's next. I'll write her soon. Promise!

Luv,
Ella

By mid-morning the streets of downtown Lagos were teeming with life. Tall buildings rose up around Angie as she moved along the hot, crowded streets. Cars, buses, and trucks crawled through one long traffic jam, horns blowing nonstop as men on motorized scooters wove in and out. Exhaust fumes drifted up, thick and smelly, yet the sun cut through the smoke, glaring off of car hoods. A rickety yellow bus filled with people, some hanging out the door, careened past her, hitting a puddle and spewing dirty water. Meanwhile men, women, and children navigated walkways bifurcated by gutters of open sewage as they hawked mangoes, coconut chunks, fabric, videocassettes, newspapers. More children, some with dangling limbs, held out begging hands as Angie gave out kobo and naira bills. Working women in traditional garb strode in high-heeled pumps, their bare ankles covered in the swirling dust, and men in three-piece suits swung their briefcases so high nothing could be inside them. Angie inhaled the chaos. So *this* is Lagos, she thought.

The desk clerk at the hotel—the same one from the night

before, now bleary eyed—had told her the International Bank of West Africa was just a few blocks away. When she found the bank, Angie hurried inside its spacious lobby, navigating around long teller lines. She approached the first man she saw sitting at a desk. "Excuse me, I'm looking for Chris Olapade," she said. "He works here, I think. I know he used to. Can you tell me where I might find him?"

"Eh, Chris? Yes, I know him, yes," said the man. He picked up his telephone and called a number. "My friend, there is a young woman here asking for you. And she looks very much like an *akata*, so I am thinking you are a lucky man. You did not tell me about your second wife, O." He laughed. "Yes, yes I will."

He hung up the phone, grinning wide. "I will show you."

Angie followed the tall, suited man to the elevator, bemused by his joke. She felt instantly accepted, liked.

"Take this to the twelfth floor and you will find him there."

"Thank you," said Angie.

"Indeed!" he said as the elevator door closed between them.

When the doors opened, he was waiting for her. A man of average height, with a thin mustache, he was dressed impeccably in a brown, silk-blend suit and a striped, cuff-linked shirt.

"I'm Chris Olapade," he said. "You're looking for me?"

She nodded, nervous. "I'm Ella's sister. Angie."

Surprise shifted his features. "Ella's sister? From Michigan?"

She nodded.

"Ah-ah, I cannot believe it!"

He moved to hug her. Unsure what to do with her own arms, she kept them at her sides.

"Come," he said, and she followed him to his office. There they both stood as he shook his head. "Wow. This is a surprise. It's a pleasure to meet you." He gestured toward a chair. "Sit, sit."

Angie sat in the chair facing his desk.

"How did you find me?" he asked, sitting behind the desk.

"Well, Ella wrote to me on bank stationery while she was here and—"

"Right!" He laughed. "I'd just gotten this job and I was giving out letterhead left and right."

"Lucky for me you did that," she said.

He stared at her. "It is very good to meet you. Very good." He paused. "Can I get you anything? Are you thirsty?"

"No, I'm fine."

He cocked his head to the side. "You don't look like her."

"I'm her sister," said Angie. "Trust me."

"I believe you." He leaned forward in his seat. "So, what brings you here?"

"I just wanted to see Lagos," she said. "I always did. Want to see it. This." She was so nervous.

He nodded. "You're traveling alone?"

"Yes."

"That's very brave."

"You think so?"

"I know so." He leaned back. "You're staying where?"

"At the Bristol Hotel."

"Ah. And how is it?"

"Well, I've just spent one night there, and it's a lot more money than I expected."

"I'm sure. This is Nigeria." He shook his head. "You'll need to get out of there."

"If you could recommend a cheaper place," she said. "That would be great."

Chris was silent for several seconds, staring at her, as if weighing the possibilities. She jumped into the silence.

"Are there youth hostels here? Or maybe a YMCA?" She felt

stupid as soon as she spoke, realized suddenly the risk of having come so far, on such an off chance.

"Of course, you'll stay with us," he said.

Angie shook her head. "I don't want to impose. I mean... I know I just showed up, unplanned. It was sort of a spur-of-the moment thing. I mean, not really, but I..." She let her voice trail off, afraid of how she must look to this man, appearing out of nowhere, needy.

"African hospitality is real," he said. "You will stay with us."

"Thank you," she said, quickly. "Just a few days."

"As long as you need." He picked up the phone and began dialing. "My wife won't believe this."

He stared at her, eyes smiling, as he spoke into the mouthpiece. "Bren! Ask me who is sitting in my office right now. Nooooo. No. Listen: Ella's little sister. Yes, *that* Ella. Angie. Yes. That is correct. Just now. She is. Undetermined." He laughed. "I doubt that. OK. We will see you shortly."

Together they left the building and walked the block to a car lot. As she stepped around rain puddles, she thought, I am walking alongside Ella's Nigerian friend. In Nigeria. Chris paid an area boy in a filthy T-shirt a few kobo and the two got into his late-model Peugeot. Chris plunged them into the maze of traffic. At one point, they idled beside a mountainous pile of garbage and she swore she could see it moving. Overhead, a billboard showed a woman spraying air freshener, its slogan beneath proclaiming, GLADE FRESHNESS INSTEAD OF BAD ODOURS. Only when Chris sped off did Angie see that the pile of garbage was covered in maggots.

They stopped by the Bristol, where she picked up her bag. Luckily the elevator worked. A different man was helming the front desk and he only looked up when she dropped off the key. Back in the car, the roadway clogged again and Chris inched his car forward, into the congestion, amid the cacophony of horns.

"Is the traffic always like this?" asked Angie.

"Ah, this is the hallmark of Lagos life," said Chris. "The *go-slow*."

"That's a great name for it," she said.

"We are a clever people," said Chris. With or without irony, she wasn't sure.

They snaked along as an industry of men and boys wove in and out, arms filled with wares. The hawkers' merchandise ranged from silver trays to Tiffany-style lamps to babies' booties. One man approached Chris's side, flashed two videocassettes of the movie *E.T.*

"Oga, Oga, for you! For you Oga!" he chanted, extraterrestrial's big eyes staring out from the video jacket. Chris shook his head just as another man appeared, holding an entire water faucet. Chris ignored him, and the hawker walked away.

"What do you think of my country so far?" he asked, his voice a tease.

She eyed a man holding a dead chicken by its limp neck, watched him thrust it into the passenger window of the car in front of them. "I don't even have the words to describe it."

Chris laughed softly. "Yeah, it's a trip. I grew up here, but Lagos has changed *a lot* since then. I lived in the States for over a decade before we came back. Hell, it's changed a lot in the time we've been back."

A hawker reached his arm into her window, showed her an array of animal-skin wallets and plastic key chains, some inscribed with the words "I love Jesus," others just big smiley faces. She shook her head and the man drew back his arm.

"What made you come back?" she asked.

"My wife and I were living in Atlanta, and we got married just as the military regime stepped down here. Suddenly Nigeria had its first civilian president and I said, 'Let's go back. I want to be part of my country's rebirth.' So here we are, eight years later."

Angie watched a hawker through her side-view mirror as he headed to the car behind them. The traffic lurched forward. "Are you glad you came back?" Based on the traffic alone, she wasn't sure *she* could live here for eight years.

"It was the thing to do," said Chris. "A lot of young Nigerians came flooding back around that time." He pushed out his chin. "With our fancy degrees from abroad stuffed in our suitcases."

"I just graduated from college," she offered, not sure why she was sharing this fact with him.

"Yeah? Then you know that feeling—I'm sure you have it now—of possibility waiting around every corner. That's how it was in Nigeria those first few years! Right away, we launched a newspaper, *The Lagos Voice*. Ella worked for it when she came here. Do you know about all that? You must."

"Yes, I knew. We all knew."

"The paper was four years old by then, and sadly at the tail end of its run." Chris shook his head. "Ah, but those last six months of its life were its best! *The Voice* was like nothing this country had ever seen! A radical newspaper that wasn't some bloody mouthpiece for the government? Ah! We were very successful, right away. People were ready for a free press." He went on, leaning into the memory. "My dear brother Jide, may he rest in peace, was editor-in-chief. The best, ah, just the best. I was political editor. Very good, if I must say so myself. And when Nigel and Ella arrived, he became the Pan-African correspondent and *she* eventually became the women's page editor."

"She wrote and told me all about it," said Angie.

Ella had composed her third letter on a manual typewriter from the newsroom, complete with strikeouts and typos. It was Angie's favorite of the seven.

c/o The Lagos Voice
PO Box 3071
72, Ranfu Williams Crescent
Surulere, Lagos

18 September 1983

Hey Ang--
Sorry I haven't written in a while, but
it's been crazy O!
    So Shenu Shagari won the election, but
it wasn't so democratic after all--a lot
of African-style vote rigging. No one's
surprised, really.
    Bigger news: Thanks to some
investigative reporting, I've uncovered
a scandal! Women here feed their babies
formula that's past its expiration date.
Western companies export it here precisely
because it would never pass inspection
in their countries (shameless!). The
piece caused some controversy and now the
editor-in-chief has written an editorial
demanding the government change its import
policies. Breaking the story got me my
very own page in the newspaper. I'm now
officially the women's page editor! Make
copies and share it with Denise and Mama,
OK?
    You should think about coming to visit
too. Maybe a post-graduation, Christmas
present?

```
Gotta go--news never takes a break
(smile!).

                              Luv,

                              Ella


P.S. I'm calling my new page Woman to
Woman. You like it?
```

The neatly folded clipping had fallen out when Angie opened the letter, pirouetting to the carpeted bedroom floor. It was a two-page spread, with UNESCO statistics and quotes from Nigerian mothers, NGO workers, and a female government official, all confirming the horrific practice. She'd read it greedily while sitting cross-legged on her bed. She was riveted by the photo—of a Nigerian woman bottle-feeding a malnourished, wide-eyed baby juxtaposed with that of a white woman breastfeeding a cherub-looking infant. And the byline—"by Ella Mackenzie"—had been circled in red ink. To think how far her sister had come, to think that just two years before, she'd been a heroin addict. Angie had done as Ella asked and shown it to her mother, then made two photocopies and sent the article to Denise in Atlanta. The other copy she'd taken to school and shared with her world history professor.

"Ella was a damn good reporter too," said Chris. "Also a fine editor. She was a natural."

Chris pulled behind a gigantic lorry loaded down with bales of some unknown substance. Angie was stunned by how rickety it was, how unstable its load, and felt certain its freight would fall off the back and crash into their windshield. He pressed his car horn. Nothing moved. Unnerved by the teetering bales in front, she closed her eyes against the sight. The smell of gas fumes was intoxicating. She imagined Ella was there, telling her to chill, roll with it.

Angie sat up, turned to Chris. "I'd like to hear more about her work on the paper, and about the whole scene, you know? What it was like, different things she did."

"I can tell you all about it," he promised.

"Good." She settled back against the headrest. If this were just a few years earlier, they'd surely all be in the car right now, Ella, Nigel, and Chris headed to the newsroom to work.

"Do you think I could see the office?" she asked suddenly.

"It's gone," he said. "We had a beautiful four-year run with *The Voice*. But we had to fold the paper after the coup."

"Oh." Regret washed over her.

He glanced at Angie. "I could take you to where it used to be. There's no business in there now, but if you just want to see the room itself, I could do that."

"Could you?"

"Sure." He paused. "Actually, I've been single-handedly trying to start up *The Voice* again, but damn if there wasn't another coup two years ago. Been hard to finance a newspaper through all this volatility, even though we need a strong press now more than ever." He leaned on his horn again. "And my wife doesn't want me to do it. I tell her, 'Change doesn't happen without risk,' but she is not hearing that. She just wants me to stay put at the bank." He swerved around the lorry, finally. "But my dreams go beyond that damn bank."

She held on as Chris sped forward. "Maybe because she's American, it's harder for her to wait," offered Angie. "Americans are used to getting what we want when we want it."

He banged his fist lightly on the steering wheel. "That is it exactly." He looked over at her. "I see you're as smart as your sister."

She smiled. That was a compliment she'd never gotten before.

"But my wife needs to understand that we're a young nation and young nations need risk-takers," continued Chris. "Just twenty-seven years ago, Nigeria was still a British colony. People want to forget that ours is a *developing* country. Hell it's developing right before our eyes." He glanced at her. "Like you. You're young, you're still developing." He smiled. "I don't mean physically. I can see that development is complete."

Chris's flirting felt nice: a friendly, harmless gesture. A way for Chris to make Ella's little sister feel welcome. "It's really good to be here," she said.

"And it's really good to have you here."

A light rain began to fall as they exited the highway. The area had large swaths of sprawling land. They passed by plots of upturned earth, homes in various stages of construction— some with walls, others with foundations laid. Hopefulness hung on the skeletal frames. He turned down a wide street, where homes of expansive size and design sat back proudly; he turned again, onto a paved road, its street sign reading, "Dukun Olapade Avenue."

Chris pulled into the driveway of a hacienda-style, two-story house. Through the moving windshield wipers she eyed the Olapades' stucco home, set back from the road, accented by cement fencing and its own car park. A palm tree sprouted its fronds beside the driveway and, sure enough, a riot of bright pink bougainvillea bloomed along the front.

"It's beautiful," said Angie. It was lovelier than she'd pictured it from Ella's simple description.

Chris beamed. "We had it built, moved in four years ago. When your sister came to stay, it was brand new; the cement had barely dried." They exited the car, he quickly gathered her bag, and together they ran through the sheet of rain to the front door. He opened it, ushered her inside, and called out, "Bren!"

Hot air rushed from the darkened hallway. His wife appeared on the stairway, slowly descended. She had shoulder-length hair, almond skin, and freckles. She wore a velour warm-up suit. She looked at Angie, squared her shoulders, then held out her arms. "Welcome!"

Angie moved into the embrace, comforted by the sweatshirt's softness against her skin.

Brenda slipped her arm into Angie's and guided her into the house. "Ella talked about you all the time," she said in what could've been a British accent.

"Did she?"

"Oh yes. 'My baby sister this, my baby sister that.'"

Angie was so moved by that revelation that she had to swallow the urge to cry as they walked through the living room, plush green carpet underfoot.

She held Brenda's arm a little tighter as she took in everything. She'd imagined the decor inside a cosmopolitan Lagos couple's home would be mud cloth and kente casually thrown over sofas and chairs—all the rage in Afrocentric homes back in Detroit. But the Olapades' living room had no dyed batiks nor native art, but rather ornate, formal furnishings, much of it velvet or gilded or both. No artfully placed African masks, no local sculpture on the coffee table.

Chris approached. "Angie, your bags are in the guest quarters out back. I have to dash. Welcome to my country!" He turned to his wife. "This meeting could run late."

"Not too late I hope," said Brenda, locking eyes with her husband's.

"Late enough," said Chris as he hurried out the front door.

Brenda stared at the closed door before turning her attention back to Angie. "Let's have a seat in the den, shall we? What can I get you, Fanta, Coke?"

"Fanta sounds good."

She followed Brenda through the dining area and simple but modern kitchen to a back room. With its golden plaid sofa, wood paneling, and shag carpet, this space was utterly different from the living room, more rec room suburbia, circa the seventies. Angie liked its time-warp quality and happily plopped onto the sofa. She took a sip of her Fanta as Brenda popped a cassette into the stereo. Roberta Flack began to sing *the closer I get to you*, a song from back then, from *that* time. She sank into the sofa as if it were a friend she hadn't seen in years. Rain beat against the windows.

"So how long are you here for?" asked Brenda.

"Just a couple days, I promise."

"No love, I mean how long are you in Nigeria?"

"For as long as it takes, I guess."

"For as long as what takes?"

Angie shrugged. "To learn things about my sister. Things I didn't know."

A wrinkle formed between Brenda's eyes, and then it disappeared. "Well, you've come to right place."

"Have I?" She couldn't hide the yearning in her voice.

"You have. Ella stayed here for a couple months. That's plenty of time to get to know somebody. Or think you know them anyway."

"Did you and she hang out a lot?"

"Sometimes, sure. She was busy with the paper, but yes, we did."

"She said you were good people."

Brenda looked surprised. "Did she?"

— 151 —

"Yes. She wrote that to me in a letter."

"Well we were close for a while there. Real close."

"What kind of things did you do together?"

Brenda smiled. "Well, we played a lot of cards! Especially during the rainy season. Like now."

"She and I used to play cards together," said Angie. "Tunk was my favorite."

"You play Tunk?"

"I do." Because it had a simple premise—the player with the lowest total amount on her cards wins—Ella had taught Angie to count that way.

Brenda rose, pulled open a drawer to the side table, and took out a deck of cards, their backs designed to resemble Ghanaian kente cloth.

Her faux British accent now mashed up with black-girl speak. "Girl, no one in this damn place knows how to bloody play cards," she said. "When she first got here, Ella and I used to sit around for hours and play. Drink our palm wine, listen to the rain, talk about the latest Nigerian craziness. It kept our minds together, you know?"

She dealt them each five cards. Angie went first, pulled a king of hearts from the deck, tossed it out. Once again, the thought of Ella doing this very thing, right here with Brenda, made her hands tremble slightly. Brenda drew next, tossed out a ten of diamonds.

"You know. I had several black American girlfriends when I first got here," said Brenda. "We banded together like war vets. That's how we felt too, like we'd gone through battle, come through it stronger, closer."

Angie pulled an ace, slipped it into her fanned-out hand. "And now?"

"And now my ass is damn near the only one left." Brenda threw out an eight of clubs. "They all went back home.

Couldn't take it here. Except for one, Lydia. Now she's something. Moved to Lagos when she was forty, went to some witch doctor who she swears helped her find a husband *and* get pregnant; now she has two kids. A whole life. And she's not the only up-in-age black woman I know who came here from the States and changed her fortunes. Got married. Started a business, whatever. You can do that in Nigeria. I will say that much for this crazy-ass place." Brenda shrugged. "Anyway, Lydia doesn't really speak to me anymore, not since Chris and I moved into this house."

"Because?"

"I'm not gonna say she's jealous. She's living all right. But not this good. That's the bargain when you give up your life back home. The deal is, you come here and sooner or later you live good. My sooner is her later and she can't take that, I guess."

Angie tossed out a seven of clubs. "Ella wrote to me about how modern this house was, but it's even nicer than I imagined."

"And if you saw where we used to live," said Brenda, "This would *really* seem like a damn palace! We used to be crowded into one room. And it was *rough*. Let me tell you, I thought with my middle-class, black-girl self I was incapable of cooking meals on a hot plate and washing my clothes in a bucket. But I did it. Lived like that for the first three years of our marriage. In my mother-in-law's compound, no less."

Brenda picked up a card, tossed it onto the discard pile. A queen of diamonds. "So yeah, I'm grateful to be in this house." She studied her hand. "But I still hate a lot of things here, like the way folks drive—" she stopped herself.

Angie studied the cards spread before her. "I don't know how they let it happen," she said. "The horrible driving."

"I'll tell you how," said Brenda. "No speed limit, no road laws."

Angie thought of that big lorry she and Chris had ridden behind, its precarious load.

"And there's absolutely no driver's-ed—you can buy a driver's license for a few naira," continued Brenda. "Plus let's not forget the rampant nepotism in the ministry of transportation and the rogue *moto* cops. That translates to total chaos on the roads."

"Still, they shouldn't let it happen," said Angie, grief taunting her like a shove. "It's wrong."

Brenda was quiet before she touched the top of Angie's hand, patted it. "Why'd you even come here girl, put yourself through this?"

"Because I wanted to see it for myself."

Brenda nodded. "I understand."

"Do you?"

"I do. Trust me, I do." Brenda paused. "It's the last place she was."

Angie sighed. "Exactly." She felt a bond gel between them. "Thank you."

Brenda touched her hand again. It felt nice. "You want a cigarette?"

Angie shook her head sadly. "I don't smoke."

"Ha! Good for you. Lord knows, I don't think I could survive this place if I didn't smoke." Brenda set down her cards, opened an ivory cigarette case sitting on the coffee table, and grabbed a cigarette. She lit it with a silver lighter lying nearby.

"Is it really that bad here?" asked Angie. "I mean, other than the driving?"

"It's exhausting." Brenda took a puff. "Back home, you don't have to think about every damn thing you do." She blew out smoke. "Here, there's always something to worry about. If it's not the constant power outages, and I could tell you stories about what I was in the middle of when NEPA shut down, it's the—"

"NEPA?" The bellhop at the hotel had used that same word. "What's that?"

"It stands for Nigerian Electrical Power Authority," explained Brenda. "But folks say it *really* stands for Never Expect Power Always."

Angie smiled. Chris was right. Nigerians were clever with language.

"Anyway, if it's not the power going out, it's the crime. Or the corruption." Brenda placed her cigarette in an ashtray. "And the filth. The damn filth is everywhere!"

She pulled up the sleeve of her velour sweatshirt, thrust her arm out, so abruptly that Angie ducked. Brenda pointed to a furry growth the size and shape of a small hot dog. "This is a fungus. A rash," she said. "I do not know how I got it. Every day I put this stinky home remedy on it that Chris's mother made for me with a bunch of herbs. It's slowly, slowly getting better. But meanwhile, *I have a fungus on my arm that's growing hairs.* I am not used to this. I grew up in a nice neighborhood in Richmond. But there you have it." She pulled down her sleeve.

Angie nodded in empathy as she held her cards aloft. "It was a brave thing for you to do, come here and live."

Brenda grabbed her cards, picked up one from the deck. "Brave or dumb? I can't decide." With her free hand, she picked up her cigarette, reminding Angie of Ella in the way she pulled on it. "On a good day, I remind myself that I'm a respected member of society. And I live in a country with a black president. Who knows what I'd be doing if I were back home, living under Reaganomics? Folks calling me a quota baby just for wanting the same things they have."

Angie thought of a white classmate of hers at the University of Michigan. "Some of us worked hard to get in here," the girl said as Angie walked by. "And some of us didn't." Angie had pretended to ignore her. But she wished she'd turned to the girl and said, "Now that they let in your dumb ass, you can try to make up for it." Ella would've done that. Fought back.

She threw out a four of spades. Her card total was low but she wasn't ready for the game to end.

Brenda grabbed the card. "So, what's your plan?"

"For what?"

"For being here."

"Oh." Angie stared at her cards. "Just to be around the people who knew Ella." She looked at Brenda. "People like you."

Brenda nodded. And then she said, "Too bad you didn't come a bit sooner. You could've seen Nigel."

Angie's cards went lax in her hand. "Nigel?"

"Yeah. You did know he was here?"

"No, I mean, not since—" she hesitated. "Not since It happened."

"Oh girl, yeah. He's been teaching at the University of Lagos for the entire session."

"But I thought he. . . I heard, we heard that he was a foreign correspondent somewhere."

"He was. Well he is. In fact, he's back in Nairobi by now. Classes ended a week or two ago, so I'm sure he's gone."

"I missed him?"

"I'm afraid so." Brenda looked down at Angie's exposed cards. "Call 'Tunk,' honey. You won."

"Tunk." She couldn't believe it. Nigel had been living in Nigeria all this time? And now he was gone? She'd missed him? By a week? Maybe I should go to Kenya, she thought.

"You must be hungry," said Brenda, taking a final drag.

Angie shrugged, still in shock.

Brenda put out her cigarette, rose. Angie followed. "Our

houseboy Godwin is off tonight," she explained as they entered the kitchen with its eat-in table and aqua appliances. She opened the oven door. "So I made pizza. In honor of our American visitor."

"Pizza sounds good," said Angie, trying to recover from the news about Nigel.

"It's one of the many things I really miss from home," said Brenda as she pulled out the pizza. "And fried chicken. This place has no real chickens, just scrawny hens, so the meat is tough. What I wouldn't give for some Kentucky Fried."

They ate at the dining room's massive mahogany table. On the wall hung an oil painting of Brenda as a bride, her hair short, traditional gown flowing. Made from flatbread, slices of American cheese, and tomato paste, the pizza had an odd, almost pizza-like flat taste.

"Your hair used to be short," Angie noted, nodding at the formal painting.

"Yeah, that was before my weave-on," said Brenda. "I love it. Makes my hair so much easier to manage. Only the part nobody can see gets nappy!"

Angie looked at Brenda's bone-straight hair. She didn't know of any black women with weaves, except for entertainers like Diana Ross and Chaka Khan. "Is that common here?" she asked.

"No, not too many women in Nigeria wear weave-ons," acknowledged Brenda. "But you'd be surprised how many wear wigs."

Angie stopped chewing her pizza. "*Wigs?* Really?"

"Yeah, in the god-awful heat too. Crazy."

"Sounds crazy." All of the *back-to-Africa* women she knew in the States wore their hair natural. It felt like a cruel joke of some sort to discover that real African women wore wigs and weave-ons. She wondered what Ella would've thought of this.

Ella who cut out her Jheri curl at the beginning of rehab, was wearing her hair in a short, fresh natural when she returned to Nigeria.

"Listen, between this rainy season's humidity and the harmattan rolling in kicking up dust, women need a hairstyle that's easy," said Brenda, as if sensing Angie's disapproval. "Otherwise I for one would be washing my hair every day, in cold water no less—'cause like I said, you can't depend on NEPA—so who knows when your hot-water tank will work."

Angie had in fact struggled with her own hair that morning at the hotel, finally adding a heap of gel to stave off the frizziness.

"If you choose to get a weave-on, let me know," said Brenda. She bit into her pizza. "There's really only one woman I trust to do it here."

"I'll keep that in mind," said Angie, clear that she had no intention of having hair sewn—or was it glued?—to her scalp. As an afterthought, she added, "Your hair looks nice."

Brenda took a swig of her Coke, burped lightly. "Chris hates it."

AFTER THEY ATE, she and Brenda sat in the den again, listening to more Roberta Flack. When Brenda caught her yawning she said, "You've gotta be jet-lagged. Come on, I'll show you to your room."

She led Angie through the kitchen and out a back door, where two cement structures, identical flat-roofed squares, sat a yard or so from the house. They entered one of the structures through a patterned curtain hanging across its doorway. Brenda flipped on the light. "These are your guest quarters."

Inside was a double bed covered in an orange chenille blanket, a nightstand, a fan sitting on the linoleum floor, and in the far corner, Angie's American Tourister duffel. The room was stuffy, yet Angie liked its cleanliness, its simplicity.

"Is this where Ella and Nigel stayed?" she asked.

"Yeah, they did stay in here," said Brenda. "I forgot about that. Do you want to stay in our guest room in the house?"

"No, no this is perfect," said Angie.

"You're sure it's not too weird for you?"

"I'm positive."

Brenda shrugged. "The loo is that little room just outside. Godwin and his wife live in the servant's quarters next door." She pulled a key from her pocket. "Use this to get into the house. You'll need to come inside to shower." She paused. "You OK?"

"I'm fine."

"OK. Get a good night's sleep. I'll see you in the morning."

After she left, Angie sat on the bed; its mattress caved in slightly. Nigel and Ella slept together in this bed, she thought. Probably had sex in this bed. Hanging from the ceiling were mosquito chasers made of small yellow boxes with pictures of mosquitoes drawn on them, large black X's slashed across the images. She could hear the nearby sound of a whirring generator. She switched the fan on, and its blades turned. Wild animals yowled in the distance. Angie leaned over, and grabbed her journal from inside her reporter's bag. It was still new, had gone unused since Ella gave it to her four years before. She'd been waiting for the right occasion to use it. She opened it, and with her gold pen, momentously wrote:

June 16, 1987

> *I'm on the African continent. Everything is so raw,*
> *without filter. And already life is an adventure. I have*
> *been stopped by a traffic cop with a gun, been cheated out*

of my American dollars, and now I'm staying alone in
servants' quarters, nothing between me and the night but a
flimsy piece of fabric. I'll have to stay alert, pay attention to
everything, and that's good. Funny thing: I'm sooooo tired,
but I feel more alive than ever.

She lay down and closed her eyes, just as the generator clunked to a halt; the room went dark, the fan stopped its whir. She lifted her hand, couldn't see it. She was drunkenly exhausted, could feel the dead weight of her own body. Soon enough, she heard the steady patter of raindrops; like white noise, the sound put her to sleep. She dreamed Ella and Nigel were in the front seat of his yellow Firebird and she was in the back, her head resting on Ella's large, black plastic bag of possessions. They were flying down a highway, men rushing across their path in flowing, pastel robes. Nigel and Ella were laughing and Ella flashed her hand, showing off a mood ring on the finger that was no longer chopped off. She turned around and leaned over, shook Angie's shoulder. She didn't know how long the hand had been there, shaking her awake. She sat up, startled to see a kerosene lantern swinging against the darkness.

"Hey, it's me," said Chris, his face an eerie chiaroscuro.

Deeply groggy, Angie couldn't remember where she was and the dream tugged at her still. "Nigel?" she whispered.

"I brought you a lantern."

"Is she with you?" She rose onto her elbows. "Is she?"

"It's me! Chris. I thought you might still be awake."

She shook her head, forcing herself to fully wake. Where was she?

"You know, you smile in your sleep," he said. The lantern's light cast elongated shadows on the cement wall.

She sat up, remembering. "What's wrong?"

"When Brenda said she forgot to put a lantern back here

for you, I said, 'The woman is not camping out in the bush! I better get her some light before she writes back home how backward we Africans are, how it's the eighties and we're here living like savages.'"

"I would never write anything like that," she said.

"I'm teasing." He put his hand atop Angie's. "Are you scared to be back here by yourself?"

"Ella stayed back here."

"Yes, but she wasn't alone."

"That's true." She was fully awake now. "But I am, so."

"No you're not." They stared at one another for a moment. "You know," said Chris, "It's amazing that you found your way to me. I was just thinking about your sister yesterday before you appeared in my office."

She didn't believe him. "Really? What a coincidence."

He looked insulted. "Africans do not believe in *coincidence.* It's fate."

The tone of his voice concerned her. But then Chris removed his hand from hers. "Soon I'll take you to the old newsroom." He was friendly again.

"I'm looking forward to that," she said.

"And I think I can even scrounge up some old copies of the paper, the ones with your sister's page."

She could hear the faint howl of those same wild animals. Were they coyotes? Wolves? "I can't thank you enough."

"I'm sure you can find a way," he said before setting down the lantern beside her bed. "Sweet dreams."

The curtain in the doorway arced as he passed through. She laid her head on the pillow, unsure whether she was going back to sleep or had been dreaming all along. She returned to the same dream, only this time Ella was driving, and they were going fast, laughing hard because of course Ella didn't know how to drive. She'd fooled the Nigerians.

A MOSQUITO BUZZED close to her ear as sun sliced through the slatted windows. She could smell wood burning. She rose, grabbed the key and pulled back the curtain. Just outside, a woman sat eating *gari* with her hands. She was heavy with child, had a toddler wrapped tight against her back. Angie walked into the small courtyard, said hello to the woman, who looked up, nodded. Angie saw that she was barely more than a girl. She headed to the house. The night's rain had left shimmering wetness on the concrete. In the kitchen, she found Godwin, the houseboy; he was short and lithe, hovering over a pot. He wore a shirt and matching pants in a swirling golden and black print, feet bare. Angie said hello. He bowed, said nothing.

"Can you tell me where to find a towel?" she asked.

"Make I get for madam," he said, putting emphasis on the second syllable, and disappeared through an archway. Within seconds, Godwin returned with the towel and washcloth and showed Angie to the bathroom. The shower felt restorative and she stayed there a long time, making up for the shower she'd avoided at the hotel, where two inches of water pooled in the stall, stagnant and dank.

She brushed her hair back into a bushy ponytail and slicked it with more gel. Back in her quarters, she dressed. As she made her way to the main house, giant flies swarmed around her head. She swatted them away, yet they followed her, persistent. Slipping into the back door, escaping the flies, she found Brenda at the kitchen table, sipping tea. She wore a flowing, embroidered caftan and silk house slippers.

"What would you like for breakfast?" she asked. "Eggs, toast, semolina?"

"Eggs and toast sounds good," said Angie.

"Tea?"

"Yes, thanks."

"I don't have any lemon, just milk," said Brenda. "I got into that habit in London."

"I'll try it with milk."

Brenda placed the Lipton tea and tin can of Pet milk in front of her. "Sleep well back there?"

Angie hesitated. "For the most part."

"Yeah, it's something to get used to. I was surprised that Chris put your bag back there, instead of in the guest room upstairs. That's where we usually have visitors stay. Especially since you're alone."

Brenda pushed the box of Domino's sugar cubes toward Angie. "If you want, you can still move to the guest room." She rose, went to the stove, grabbed a kettle, poured hot water into a cup and gave it to her.

"I don't mind it back there." Angie dipped her tea bag in and out. She wanted to stay where Ella had stayed.

"Well, see how it goes over the next few days," said Brenda. She reached for a skillet. "Guess it depends on what you prefer most, privacy or proximity." Her back to Angie, she said, "You strike me as the privacy type."

"Do I?"

Brenda ignored her as she cracked eggs into the skillet. "It's that stuff on your hair that's doing it you know, attracting flies." She scrambled. "These African flies are sensitive. They can smell the perfume in it."

"How'd you know about the flies?"

"I saw you through the kitchen door."

Angie wondered what else Brenda could see.

"If you don't want a weave-on, you could try a perm," said Brenda.

"A perm?"

"That's a big thing in Lagos right now." She stirred the eggs.

"Perms?"

"All these salons have sprung up inside little shacks on the roadside," explained Brenda. "Nigeria just discovered Ultra Sheen Permanent Relaxer, it seems. The only kind they get here is extra strong. You have to tell the girl who does your hair to leave that stuff in for just ten minutes, so all your hair doesn't fall out."

"Hmm, doesn't sound too appealing."

Brenda placed the freshly cooked eggs in front of Angie. She was famished and devoured them while Brenda watched.

"So, lucky you!" said Brenda when Angie was done eating. "I've arranged for you to meet Lola."

"Lola?"

"She was the assistant editor slash reporter under Ella. Now she covers women's issues for *The Punch*. Ella adored her, treated her like a little sister."

Angie felt a tinge of jealousy, quick as a flash. "I look forward to meeting her," she lied.

After breakfast Brenda invited Angie to join her in her bedroom. "I'll show you my newest pairs of shoes."

Angie followed her, grateful for this instant friendship. It was, she decided, the best part of travel. Within minutes, Brenda was leaning against her bed's headboard as Angie perched on the edge, holding a jelly glass of palm wine. This room was styled with off-white carpet and sleek, blond Scandinavian furniture.

"The furniture in each of your rooms is so different!" said Angie.

"That's because we can only get what somebody will ship here. That's the key to Nigerian decorating. Choose your style based on what you can get."

Earth, Wind & Fire's "Shining Star" played from the built-in speakers, their voices demanding exuberance. Brenda lifted the top off a shoebox and dug beneath the tissue paper, unearthing a two-toned, turquoise-and-cream, high-heeled pump. "This is one of my favorites," she said, balancing it in the palm of her hand. "I love shoes that show toe cleavage."

"Toe cleavage?"

Brenda kicked off a leather sandal, slipped her foot into the pump, and pointed to the baseline of her toes peeking through. "That's toe cleavage!"

Angie laughed. "OK, I get it." She sipped the palm wine. It was tangy and strong and she didn't really like the taste, but it seemed rude not to drink it.

All morning, Brenda gave her a mini trunk show. She showed off designer skirt suits and silk party dresses and high-end jogging suits, many of which still had their price tags. And then there was the myriad of shoes—all spiky heels with a few flats for driving.

Angie picked up a stray shoe from the bed. This one was fire-engine red, with a leather flower and a slender, four-inch heel.

"How do you even walk in these?" she asked. She recalled the few Nigerian women she'd seen on Lagos Island wearing heels. Their bare feet seemed stuffed into the shoes like the feet of Daisy, Donald Duck's girlfriend.

"I try not to walk much on the streets," admitted Brenda. "If I'm not driving myself, I'm with a driver. You can get caught in a thunderstorm. Or at least drenched. And in the hot months, you can get sunstroke. So this is not a place for walking."

Angie surveyed the mound of footwear on the bed. There must have been two-dozen pairs. "Boy, you do have a major shoe fetish."

"Well, it's what I do when I go to London," said Brenda. "I basically shop for shoes."

"How often do you go? Once a month?"

Brenda laughed. "No. I go twice a year. It's only a six-hour plane ride from here and a lot cheaper than a plane ticket to the States. It's my consolation prize from Chris. A reward for staying in Nigeria." She fingered a shoe. "I think Haymarket Street has the best shops I've ever seen."

Angie drank more palm wine. The pungent taste was growing on her. She picked up an open-toed pump. This one was black and tan leather with an ankle strap.

"So just where *do* you wear all these shoes?"

"To formal functions, to anniversaries, to parties. Stuff like that. Girl, Nigerians love to give themselves titles and awards and honors. There's always a reason to dress up. I'm forever heaping on the gold jewelry and lace cloths and going to some honoring ceremony." She sipped her wine. "I'm co-chair of the Ikeja Women's Auxiliary for Prenatal Care. We have dinner-dance fund-raisers twice a year." She leaped off the bed. "I'll show you my absolute favorite party shoes, the ones I wore to the dance last year."

Brenda slipped into her closet, came out seconds later modeling a pair of royal blue, sequined stilettos. Draped in front of her body, still on its hanger, was a matching, sequined dress with a jagged hemline, Wilma Flintstone-style. The shoes showed off Brenda's shapely legs to great effect and the sequins sparkled in the afternoon light pouring in from the slatted windows. Standing there like that, she reminded Angie of Denise—those same strong-calved legs—even though she couldn't imagine her middle sister in such an extravagant dress. Brenda twirled around a couple times before she slipped back into the closet.

"I taught secondary school when we first got here," she said from inside the closet. She reappeared holding a shoebox. Looking down, she studied her own feet, still sporting the sequined pumps. "I sat behind my desk a lot on that job, so the heels were OK."

"And now you don't teach anymore?" asked Angie.

"No." Brenda slipped out of the dressy pumps and gently placed them back into their box. "Now my job is trying to have a baby." She carefully covered the shoes with the tissue paper. Angie kept quiet, unsure what to say.

"Chris is freaking out that it hasn't happened yet, to put it mildly. They say a man without children is a child himself." Brenda put the lid back onto the box. "That's what the trips to London are mainly for. They have this procedure there that helps women get pregnant."

"But how old are you?"

"Twenty-nine and counting. So close to thirty, it ain't funny."

Just a year younger than Ella would've been. "You've still got plenty of time."

"No I don't. This is Africa."

"Oh." Angie paused. "I'm sure it'll work out."

Brenda lifted her jelly glass to Angie's and they clinked. "Hope so."

On the anniversary of what would've been Ella's thirtieth birthday, she'd gone to the gravesite and released thirty balloons in different colors. She was often sad about the things Ella would never get to do, but funny how having a baby wasn't one of them. Sure, she knew her sister had that option, like most women, but she never envisioned Ella as a mother. It was strange to her that any of Ella's friends here in Nigeria could be parents. She'd mentally frozen everyone in time—kept each stuck at New Year's Day 1984.

Shining star for you to see, sang Earth, Wind & Fire. *What your life can truly be.*

Brenda placed her shoebox back into the closet, returned to the bed, plopped down, and arranged the pillows behind her head. The song was over. They drained their glasses of wine.

"So what *do* you think you'll do with your hair while you're here?" Brenda asked.

Back home Angie used a mild relaxer, a *texturizer*, which worked well enough in Detroit's weather. Not so in this humidity.

The wine made her feel impulsive. "Maybe I'll cut it off, wear a short Afro."

"Or get it braided. Ella's braids were so pretty."

Angie was startled. "She had braids?"

"She did," said Brenda. "She got them right after she came. I can't remember whether she kept them the whole time but she had them."

"I never knew that." She hated that tidbits about Ella that had escaped her could never be fully retrieved, like loose pearls from a broken necklace rolling in every direction across the floor.

"I may have some pictures somewhere of her," said Brenda. "I'll look."

"Could you?"

"Sure I will."

"And can you help me get my hair braided too?"

"That's easy," said Brenda. "I can set it up for tomorrow if you want."

"By the same woman who did Ella's?" She knew as soon as she said it, how desperate it sounded.

"It doesn't work like that," explained Brenda. "The Fulani gypsies do it. They don't stay around. You just catch one where she sets up."

"I see." Angie gathered together her courage. "Brenda, can I ask you something?"

"OK?"

"What was it about my sister that you really liked?"

"What kind of question is that?"

"I just want to learn as much as I can."

Brenda's eyes flashed understanding. "Well, I liked that we

had a lot in common. Both black American women in Nigeria, the same age. She was from the South, so was I."

Angie corrected her. "She was born in the South but she grew up in Detroit."

"Oh I know all about her migration," said Brenda. "She told me the story of taking that train ride up north."

"Did she?" It felt odd, talking about a piece of Ella's life that was before her own time. Still, there was comfort in it too. "That was a big story for my Aunt Bea," she said. "She loved to tell how brave Ella was, even though Ella once told me she was scared as hell."

"Well yeah, considering what happened on that train, of course she was."

"What do you mean?"

"The thing that happened."

Angie's body tightened, preparing itself for a blow. "What happened?"

"She never told you?"

"Told me what?"

Brenda's finger traced the rim of her jelly glass. "Maybe you don't want to know; I mean if she never told you—"

"I want to know!" Angie said, louder than she intended.

"OK, OK. I get it . . . She said she was only like eight or nine and—"

"She was seven."

"OK, seven. Anyway she was scared. That was a long ride to take for a little girl all by herself. Nobody looking out for her." She paused. "This white man on the train took her in the little bathroom and made her touch his thing." She looked over at Angie.

"Go on." Angie tried not to react, even though a hand was squeezing her heart.

"There's nothing else to tell, really."

"If she gave you details, I'd like to know."

Brenda sat up, and a pillow fell to the floor. "Well, she said what she remembered most was the movement of the train along the tracks, how it felt like it was moving in her hand, how he got off on that, on the way her hand jerked up and down. He put his own hand on top of hers and he was pushing her little head down toward it when somebody banged on the door. First he ignored it, said to her 'Go on, go on', but she was so terrified she froze and he pushed it up in her face."

Angie gasped, hand reflexively covering her mouth.

"Yeah." Brenda looked over at Angie. "Do you want me to go on?"

Angie nodded.

"OK." Brenda breathed in deeply and her words rushed out with the exhalation. "She said it was so hard and ugly and stiff it hit her in the eye and it wet her eyelid and the banging got harder and harder and finally he opened up. It turns out an old black woman had seen him take her in there and told the conductor." Here she stopped for air. "All the conductor said was, 'This here gal with you, sir?' And the woman said, 'She by herself,' and the nasty old white man said nothing so the conductor said, 'Go back to your seat, gal. I don't want no more trouble outta you.'" Brenda's head shook in disgust. "She wanted to move to a different seat, but of course all of the colored people were crowded into the back of the train. She could've sat up front after they crossed the Mason-Dixon Line, but that was before the Civil Rights Act, so nobody knew to tell her she could do that. That's the fucking land of the free, home of the brave for you." Brenda shook her head again. "I swear, Nigerians may be crazy and they may be running their country into the damn ground, but at least it's *their* country to run into the ground, you know what I mean?"

Angie didn't want to hear political commentary. "What happened after that? Did she tell you?"

"Um . . ." Brenda frowned, working to pull up the memory. "After that the old woman had Ella sit next to her, but she didn't say anything, didn't ask how she was doing or what exactly happened in the bathroom. She just fed her some cold fried chicken. Ella said it was delicious and comforting, that food. She said she felt the wetness on her eyelid for miles as the train rolled along; said she was afraid to wipe it off, because she didn't want to confront any proof that what had happened had happened. She just ate one drumstick after the other."

Angie felt both sad and betrayed.

"Why didn't she ever tell me?"

"Maybe she wanted to spare you. Which is why I didn't really want to tell you."

She cut her eyes at Brenda. "You certainly didn't spare any details," she said, wanting to slay the messenger.

"Well forgive me for trying to—" Brenda stopped midsentence, began furiously clearing her bed of the endless shoes, as if *that* had brought Angie's umbrage. "I really don't know what to say to you right now."

Brenda violently flung shoes into boxes with their awaiting mates as Angie watched.

"I'm sorry," Angie said, devastated. She began gathering shoes from the bed. "It's just that I didn't know. I'm in a little bit of shock."

Brenda's eyes glistened. "Me too."

THAT EVENING, LOLA arrived. She sashayed into the house, a petite young Igbo woman with thick, cascading ropes of braided hair and big red lips. She kissed Angie on both cheeks.

"I can tell you're Ella's sister," she announced. "It's the eyes. Behind her glasses, she had those same eyes."

Having never heard that before, Angie absorbed the compliment with gratitude. She hadn't expected to like Lola.

Godwin put out the food on the dining room table—bowls of chicken stew steeped in palm oil with white yams.

"How is your wife, Godwin?" asked Lola.

"She is good, madam," he said. "God willing, the baby will be here very soon."

"I will pray for the baby's safe arrival and for your wife," said Lola.

"Thank you." Godwin padded away, feet silent on the carpeted floor.

Brenda grabbed a bowl, passed it around. "Poor thing," she said. "The baby's late and she's miserable, barely able to walk. Godwin took her to the midwife yesterday and the woman gave her some kind of herb tea but still, nothing yet."

They passed around the food. It was Angie's first real Nigerian meal and she was eager to taste it. "This is delicious," she announced after the first forkful.

"I told Godwin to pull back on the pepper," said Brenda. She pronounced it *pep-pay*. "It was a fight, O!"

"He should insist that his wife go to hospital," said Lola. "*That's* what you need to fight with him about. Really, these village women have *got* to stop having babies in their quarters!" She wagged a manicured finger at her friend. "And another thing, after the baby is born, Brenda you must encourage her to breastfeed. Here they are, giving their babies formula because they think it's modern and the formula is absolutely no good, bloody rotten."

"That's the story Ella broke, right?" asked Angie.

"An exclusive!" said Lola. "Four years ago Ella wrote about

this and still these companies are selling expired formula to our mothers."

"The problem is that nobody has written about it *since* Ella," said Chris.

Lola rolled her eyes at him.

"I will encourage Theresa to breastfeed," promised Brenda. "Whether or not she'll listen to me is another story. Her first challenge is to have a healthy baby and not die in the process."

"Tell me more about Ella's work on the paper," said Angie to Lola.

"It was so bold and new!" exclaimed Lola. "Before her, the women's pages were filled with advice on how to keep your man happy, how to avoid gossiping. Fashion, cooking. What they called traditional women's issues. Rubbage, you know? And then Ella came and transformed the whole concept of a woman's page. She showed that family planning, health care, working conditions—these were all women's issues. And more to the point, all these serious matters were vital to Nigeria's development." Lola smiled from the memory. "Really brilliant reporting. I was graduating university and I saw what she was doing and just begged her to let me work for her. I became her reporter-in-training." She smiled wide. "Ah! A great page, O!"

"And not without controversy," added Chris.

"Yes, so true," chimed in Brenda. She turned toward Angie. "Nigerians were furious that the job had gone to an American."

"Then Jide, brave boy that he was," added Chris, "gave the *Daily Times* a quote saying he simply wanted the most qualified person for the job and he did not care whether it was a Nigerian or an American or a Brit. In this case, he said, the best person was Ella."

Angie felt a jolt each time she heard Ella's name.

"Ah, but she could speak for herself!" Now Lola turned to

Angie. "She wrote a bruising letter to the editor of the *Daily Times*, and they actually published it. 'Dear Nigeria, I am an African American' she said. Who had ever heard such a term! 'And I have every right to bring my Western-world expertise to bear on your so-called third world problems. I am your link, Africa's most populous nation, to your becoming the beacon of the continent that you so ardently proclaim your intention to be'. Something brilliant like that."

Angie put down her fork, too excited to finish her meal. *Here* was the Ella she'd always imagined in Nigeria. Really, she should be here right now, telling her own story. The pure injustice of it all was almost too much for Angie. Why did all the rest of them get to be here? Who was more deserving than Ella?

"Was she always like that, your sister? So brave?" Lola asked her.

Angie nodded, remembering Ella taking off on their father's wild horses. Saving that girl's life at the basement party. Moving in with Nigel, against their mother's protestations. "Yes, always," she said. She thought too of Ella's political work. "And she wasn't afraid to fight for what was right."

Suddenly, the others broke into laughter.

"What?" Angie's eyes darted from face to face. "What's so funny?"

"We know that your sister was a fighter," said Chris. "With good fists, O!"

Everyone howled.

"Tell her," said Brenda. "Go on, Lola."

"What?" Angie couldn't take it. "Tell me!"

"It *is* a bloody good story," said Lola. She took a sip of water, swallowed hard. "So. I used to be engaged to a man named Tunde," she began. "And let's just say Ella helped me when I got into a little situation with him."

"A situation?" echoed Angie.

"Well, I asked Ella to join me to visit him at his flat one evening."

"A visit that was born of suspicion," added Chris.

"Who is telling the story here?" asked Lola.

Chris smirked. "Go on."

Lola continued. She and Ella showed up to her fiancé's flat, but no one answered the door.

"We were about to leave when I noticed that the curtain to his bedroom window was blowing. The fan was on. I got close to the window and could see his watch sitting on the ledge. He never left home without his watch."

"Uh-oh," said Angie, riveted.

"So. I called out, 'Tunde, Tunde, are you in there? Come open the door!' At this point Ella says to me, 'Let's just go, Lola,' but I had no intention of going anywhere."

"Indeed, this was what she'd come for," said Chris as he shoved food into his mouth.

"Stop with the commentary," said Brenda. "Let the girl tell the story."

"I took off my shoe." Here, Lola took off her black, four-inch stiletto pump. "And I banged it against the bedroom window like this." She demonstrated with shoe in hand. "Glass shattered everywhere. It was so loud, like a gunshot! Ella yelled at me I think, but I'm not sure."

After that, they saw a shadow hurry past the bedroom window and seconds later the front door swung open. Tunde stepped out, wearing trousers and no shirt, eyes bloodshot. Lola pushed past him, one shoe on, one off.

"Wha?" Tunde had mumbled, looking half-asleep.

Ella followed Lola to the bedroom. Tunde ran after them, tried to pull Lola back. As they stood at the bedroom entrance, they saw a woman crouched in the corner, half-naked, scurrying into her clothes. Tunde closed the bedroom door, stood guard in front.

"I screamed, 'How could you?'" said Lola, arms out, manicured fingers splayed, in total performance mode. "'After all I've done for you! After what my mother has done for you! Treated you like a son!'"

Ella begged her to just leave. But to no avail.

"I lunged at him. Beat him with my fists." Lola smiled at the memory. "I was like a very annoying fly to him. As big as he was, as little as I am."

Just then, said Lola, the bedroom door swung open and the woman, now dressed, pushed past all three of them and ran out the front door.

"She was one of those *acada* girls," said Lola. "I recognized her from the telly."

Brenda filled in Angie. "She means one of these women who are kept by big men in Nigeria. Government men who give them on-air jobs at Nigerian national TV in return for certain favors."

Angie, engrossed, couldn't believe the others were eating. Even Lola had taken a break in her storytelling to finish her dinner. "Go on!" she urged.

Lola quickly chewed, swallowed. "So I am sobbing and crying and saying how his father told me I was worth any bride price a family could name, blah, blah, blah. And he is saying to me, 'Why did you just show up without warning?' As if *that's* the real issue. This is when I pull off my engagement ring and hurl it at him."

"And the bastard thought enough to pick it up and put it in his pocket," said Brenda.

"A diamond costs a lot of naira," said Chris. "Of course he picked it up."

Brenda cut her eyes at Chris.

"And then." Lola pushed back from the table, stood up for effect. Her arms acted out the story. "Out of no where, the little *agaracha* returns, with a big healthy woman at her side, O! And her hands are like this." Lola held up clenched fists.

Angie gasped.

"She said to the girl, 'Which one did it?' And the whore points to Ella!"

"What?" yelled Angie.

Lola nodded. She placed her hands on her hips. "This hefty woman says to Ella, 'You ripped off my sister's clothes?' And that's when we notice that, bloody hell!"—Lola makes a ripping motion—"The whore's top is actually torn and hanging from her shoulder blades! Tattered! I yell, 'Nobody touched her! That *agaracha* was with my man!'"

"It gets really good now," said Brenda.

"American soap opera style," added Chris.

Lola affected a deep voice. "'She said you ripped off her clothes,' growls Hefty to Ella. And then, Oh Lord, she charged at Ella! I screamed, right? But Ella balled her fists, and punched her in the face!"

Angie's mouth flew open. "No!"

Lola nodded. "Hefty didn't expect that. She stepped back, ready to plunge at Ella like a wrestler. I am still screaming and—"

"Meanwhile Tunde is just watching the show," said Brenda. "Can you believe that pussy of a man?"

"Don't speak of him that way," said Chris. "That's a nasty word."

"He is a nasty man," said Brenda.

Angie couldn't bear marital bickering getting in the way of Lola's tale. "Shhh!" she said.

Lola whispered for effect. "And suddenly, mercifully, a very handsome and muscular man appeared out of nowhere and stepped between Ella and Hefty." Lola shifted her voice to imitate the man. "'Zainab, come on home girl,' he said. And he pulled her away. 'You know ain't nobody hurt Sade. Why you dig am out?' And Hefty says, 'She hit me in the eye!' And Ella says, 'I'll hit you in the other one too, bitch!' And just like that, this man pushed Hefty out the door."

Lola plopped back down, performance done.

"Wow," said Angie. "Ella did not mention *that* in any of her letters!"

Lola laughed. "It was insane. Really something."

"And when Ella got back here," Brenda chimed in, "She said the part that galled her the most was—"

"Brenda, really?" pleaded Lola. "Do you need to?"

"Yesssss," said Brenda. "It's all water under the bridge anyway." She leaned toward Angie. "Ella said the part that galled her the most was that at the end of the night, Tunde and Lola were holding hands."

Angie met Lola's eyes. "Really?" The whole story was so juicy, the kind Denise and their mother would greedily share at the kitchen table. Only *this* one involved Ella as heroine. Fighting back!

Lola sucked her teeth, loudly. "You must understand," she said to Angie. "I was feeling the pressure to marry." She smirked. "Now my family has given up on me, and I'm a free woman."

"Tell that to Yomi," said Chris.

"Yomi?" asked Angie.

"My new boyfriend," explained Lola. "He still lives with his mother so I have nothing to worry about there."

Angie laughed, warm blood rushing through her limbs. "Lucky you!"

Lola stood. "Let's move to the den. I, for one, could use a

spot of Cointreau. Talk of my own humiliation makes me very thirsty."

Everyone rose, filed into the cozy den, draping themselves over the sofa and chairs. Brenda opened the liquor cabinet, served brandy to Chris, Cointreau to Lola and Angie and herself.

Lola held up her glass. "To our dear departed brother Jide, who died for the struggle." She turned toward Angie. "And to our dear departed sister Ella, who changed lives everywhere she went."

"Here, here," said Brenda, glass aloft.

"To our beautiful brother and sister," echoed Chris.

Angie raised her glass too. "To Ella. And Jide." She took a sip of the liqueur. The drink's orangey, sweet taste reminded her of that day with Solo. This was what she'd wanted and she'd gotten it. To be here, among Ella's friends. Had she ever gotten what she wanted before?

"I am grateful that I can continue Ella's work with my own women's page," said Lola. "I call it Woman to Woman, in honor of her."

"I'd love to see it," said Angie.

"It's a very good page," noted Brenda. "And I love the new picture of you, Lola."

"Too bad *Punch* is an organ of propaganda for the government," said Chris.

Lola shrugged. "Sometimes, you have to work within the system. I'm trying to do the most with what we have."

"You can't work within a system that is fundamentally corrupt," said Chris. "We have to create organs of change or what is the point?"

"Here we go," said Brenda.

"Listen, I loved *The Voice* as much as anyone, but you are

fooling yourself if you think we'll ever go back to how it was," said Lola. "Those golden days of democratic votes and all of that. The heyday of the Second Republic." She shrugged. "I'm afraid that's over. Military rule is here to stay."

"That's a view I reject," said Chris. "And I, for one, refuse to work for a newspaper where some *oga* arrives in the newsroom with a suitcase of money and poof! Suddenly a flattering profile of him appears in the paper, dominated by a photo of his smiling white teeth and giant belly."

"Jide had the same uncompromising position and you see what happened to him," said Lola. "We have to be cautious."

"What exactly happened to him?" asked Angie. She'd wanted to ask that question for some time.

"*The Lagos Voice*'s office was raided," explained Chris. "And since he was our editor-in-chief, they arrested Jide, claiming the paper was treasonous against the government. He died in police custody."

"Where was Ella when that happened?" asked Angie. Only now did she realize that working for a newspaper in Lagos had put Ella at risk.

"She wasn't there at the time, thank God," said Chris. "None of the rest of the staff was there. We would have all been arrested, for sure. And worse."

"And that was *before* military rule," said Lola. "Now, with Ibrahim Babangida as president, imagine one's fate for such a thing. Executed on Bar Beach like in the old days."

"All I know is that these last four years in Nigeria have been nothing like the first four," said Brenda. "Night and day." She took a huge gulp of Cointreau. "I don't think I can live here much longer under these conditions."

"Things will improve," said Chris.

"They better," said Brenda. "Because if they don't soon, it's time to return home."

"I am home," said Chris.

Brenda eyed her husband, who threw his head back, drained his glass, then rose to get another drink.

Lola stepped into the tense silence. "So Angie, do you plan to follow in your sister's footsteps? Become a journalist too?"

"I might," she said. "I'm not sure. I haven't decided."

"It's not burning inside you," said Lola. "You're different from Ella in that way. I can tell."

Angie felt a hot flash of jealousy. Lola couldn't be more than three or four years older than her, and already she was a women's page editor, Angie's own sister's protégé. She tried not to think about the vast nothingness of career plans that awaited her back home.

"She's not so different," offered Chris. "I totally could see Angie staying in Lagos, doing what her sister did."

Angie smiled at Chris with gratitude.

He smiled back. "She might even come work for *The Voice* when I get it back up and running."

"Lord, I hope not," said Brenda. She looked over quickly at Angie. "No offense. I mean, I hope you guys don't start up that newspaper again."

"You needn't worry Brenda," said Lola. "It'll never happen."

Chris lifted his drink and murmured, "I'll remind you later that you said that," before taking a loud sip.

"Everything doesn't have to be about writing for a newspaper, you know," said Brenda. "There are other ways Angie can honor her sister's memory."

Angie sensed the others waiting for her to say something. She was amazed how quickly her balloon of happiness had deflated. "I'm still trying to figure out what that means, exactly," she said quietly. "Honoring her memory."

"It'll become clear soon enough," said Chris.

Angie nodded, drained the glass of Cointreau, all eyes on her.

"You want another drink?" asked Brenda.

"No thanks," said Angie. She just wanted to escape to her quarters, be alone. "I've actually had enough."

THAT NIGHT, CHRIS stood in the doorway whispering, "Psst, Psst, Psst," until she woke up. He entered, this time holding a flashlight.

She sat up abruptly. "Please don't just appear like that," she pleaded. "It scares the shit out of me."

"Now you're sounding like Ella. Feisty!"

"When you come to my room in the middle of the night, Brenda has to know that you're gone."

"I am a night crawler. She knows this about me."

"Why are you here?"

"To ask you a question."

"Is it urgent?"

"Let's just say it's personal."

She braced herself. "OK?"

"He put his flashlight on the little nightstand. "Did Ella write to you about us?"

"No." Angie paused. "What *about* you and her?"

He sat on the bed beside her. "We had something."

His words made no sense to Angie. "She and Nigel were together."

"Oh, those two. They broke up every month."

"I don't believe that."

"Ask Brenda. She'll tell you."

"Should I ask her about you and Ella too?"

"She knows."

"What exactly does she know?"

"She knows that if Ella had lived, we would've been together."

"As a couple?"

"Yes."

"What about Brenda?"

"In our culture a man can have more than one wife."

Angie shook her head, as if *this* were a dream. "I'm sorry, this is a bit much. You're telling me that Ella would've become your, like, second wife?"

"I'm surprised you find that so hard to believe. Or did you really know your sister?"

Angie's body stiffened. "Why are you telling me this?"

"You were talking about honoring her memory, her legacy if you will. I am part of that."

"In what way?"

"I just told you."

"I'm confused. What are you suggesting?"

Chris put his hand near her thigh, atop the thin chenille blanket. "I would've been a big part of her life, and now I can be a big part of yours. It's the African way." Chris rose. "I'm sure you agree with me."

Before she could respond, he grabbed his flashlight, turned and moved through the doorway, fluttering the curtain.

Angie lay awake for hours, trying to figure out her next move.

For the next two days, she hung out with Brenda, trying to find the right moment. It wasn't when they shopped together in the market for the Asian hair she needed for her braids, nor when they drove to the school where Brenda volunteered; and it wasn't en route to a meeting of the Ikeja Women's Auxiliary. Finally, as they were bringing groceries into the house on the third morning, Angie asked, as nonchalantly as she could, "Did Nigel and Ella break up a lot?"

Brenda turned to her. "Where did you hear that?"

"I was just wondering. That's all."

She locked eyes with Angie. "He loved her. She loved him. That's what you should know. That's the main thing. And that's everything."

SATURDAY MORNING, GODWIN'S teenage wife Theresa led Angie along a muddy road. Theresa carried her baby high on her back, while her unborn child strained against the cloth wrapped tautly around her. Angie held the ponytail of hair that Brenda had helped her buy. The sun was high; Brenda had predicted they had about three hours before the rains returned.

Theresa offered to walk her to meet the hair-braider, felt the walk would do her good, help the baby to come. Angie had a flash of terror that Theresa might go into labor while on this walk. She hated that she wasn't like Ella in that way, couldn't imagine saving a life.

They walked slowly as Theresa was so big she could just manage to waddle forward. They passed plots of land where houses were under construction. Mounds of wet, red earth piled high next to hills of gravel. A backhoe stood idle. They arrived at a construction site where the entire frame of a house had been built, standing naked in the hot sun. A slab of concrete had been poured around the base. In the middle of the concrete—what would one day be the house's front porch perhaps—sat a tin-roofed shanty. Theresa took twenty naira from Angie and moved toward the lean-to. Angie followed, but at its threshold Theresa stopped her with a raised hand. "Come out," she said.

Angie waited as Theresa entered. Two minutes later Godwin's wife stepped back outside, transaction complete. She waved goodbye, slowly began to waddle away. Angie hoped she'd make it back home safely.

Suddenly a woman stepped out of the shanty, shrouded in a sheer fabric covering her head, and a faded wrapper tied across her waist. She moved toward Angie. Her face was all but hidden, a thin scar snaking across her forehead and a tiny ruby sparkling in her aquiline nose. The shrouded woman stared at her with startled almond eyes and let out a high-pitched scream. Angie dropped the Asian hair.

"Ah! Ah! Come back!" the woman called out to Theresa. "Too much, too much!"

Angie's hair, no longer wrangled into a gel-slicked ponytail, had been washed and air-dried into its true self—thick, kinky, unruly. She was used to this woman's reaction, had seen it at high-end salons and basement shops alike: women who insisted that her hair was too much to handle. Hair-washers who begged not to be given the task of combing it out. Stylists who charged extra for the added labor. Shop owners who closed down while a poor hairdresser worked on her hair until long after darkness fell. She, tipping extravagantly by way of apology.

Theresa turned around. "Aunty. Abeg." Her baby started to cry.

The woman glared at Theresa, so swollen, bulbous. Finally, she nodded.

"It is fine," said Theresa, who again turned to leave. Angie bent down and picked up the fallen hair.

The woman entered her shanty, came out carrying a straw mat, pillows, scissors, a comb, and a jar. She placed the mat in one corner of the yard, put a pillow on it, and instructed Angie to sit. She did, noticing the beauty of the mat and wishing she could have one as a souvenir. The woman took a plastic can, flipped it over, placed the other pillow on top and sat hovering over Angie. An Afro pick lay idly in the dirt nearby and beside it a jagged piece of mirror. The woman investigated Angie's hair with her fingers, as if searching through tall grass for a precious object.

She showed Angie how to pull apart small sections of the bought hair and hand them to her. She parted Angie's hair with the fine-toothed comb, gathered a section, braided it, gathered another, braided it. The woman's hands conveyed competence, experience—knuckles bumping against scalp, fingers pulling hair from root. She gave the woman a mental name: *Missy*.

As they worked, she eyed Missy's bare feet, which stuck out on either side of her in full view. They were small, dirty, cracked. Yet they looked strong as shoes. As Angie handed her sections of hair, Missy sometimes told her *too big* or *small-small* and she'd adjust a piece of hair before handing it back. The sun sat high overhead, heating her face and arms. She closed her eyes and concentrated on the rhythm of her slightly bobbing head as it moved back and forth under the guidance of the woman's push and pull. She liked the feel of hands in her hair. Missy and Angie worked together for an hour in silence. Angie mastered her task of handing hair to Missy, anticipating when she'd need the next piece. Missy paused from braiding to dip a fingertip into the jar of coconut oil, run it down the exposed parts. The lubrication was startling and cool and sensual. Angie could feel her scalp drinking it in, refreshed against the beating sun.

When a gust of wind blew across and the hair flew from Angie's lap, Missy ran to get it. Within minutes, it blew away again. Angie held on tighter this time, but the wind was harsh.

"Too much," said Missy, who got up and moved the materials to the opposite side of the yard. Angie helped carry the mat and pillows. "Quick-quick" said the woman. "Rain soon."

They set up shop again and just as they'd settled back into a rhythm, Angie heard someone approaching from behind. Her back was to the shanty, so she couldn't see who it was. But she noted the softness in Missy's voice as she spoke. She twisted around to see a skinny little sandy-haired girl rubbing sleep from her eyes. She approached Missy, who spoke to her in a lilting language as she wiped the child's face clean with her hand. She was dressed in a mini version of her mother's attire—a wrapper tied at the chest, sun-beaten shroud covering her head, locks of hair sticking out. Angie also gave the girl a name in her head: Red.

Red and her mother spoke in more loving tones before the girl ducked back into the shanty. When she returned she was carrying a piece of cardboard, a nail and a rope. She jabbed holes in the cardboard with the nail and pulled the rope through the holes, busying herself with this game for several minutes as she played in the penumbra of her mother's gaze. Red ducked into the shanty again and came out carrying a boxy tape recorder and a cassette. She popped in the tape and pushed a button and music dominated by flutes and horns poured out of the little built-in speaker. Red and her mother sang together to the music, as light and airy as the Hausa language they spoke. The sun hummed behind overcast clouds. Near Angie's foot, a lizard nibbled on a corncob. The minutes peeled away. When Red ran off to play, Missy noticed tiny red mosquito bites covering Angie's arms. She put her finger on one spot. "Sorry-O!" she said softly, then put her finger on another. "Sorry-O." And yet another: "Sorry-O."

Red returned with a bottle cap filled with water. Gingerly, she held it out to Angie. "Tea?" she asked.

Her mother laughed. It was a waterfall of a laugh, clarion and cascading. Angie smiled and the girl skipped away.

Just as the clouds gathered with ominous weight, nearly four hours after she'd arrived, Angie felt the final tug of Missy's strong fingers. She glided more coconut oil down Angie's scalp, then with scissors in hand, cut the bottom of the braids, one at a time. Angie had a panicky thought: Does she know where the extensions end and my own hair begins? Missy gave her the jagged mirror and Angie took in the extensions, which fell to her chest. It felt odd to have hair longer than her own. Is this how Ella had worn hers? She doubted it. "Too long," she said, pointing to the braids.

"Ah, Ah! Not too long. Is good!" Missy's ruby nose ring sparkled. Thunder cracked. "Is very good!"

"OK, OK," said Angie, both tired out from the sun, and afraid of getting caught in the approaching storm.

Just then a high-toned voice sang out, "Ahooooooh!" and a woman came toward them, her head covered in a faded sheer fabric. She was taller and perhaps thinner than Missy, with kohl-rimmed eyes. She and Missy greeted one another and the woman plopped down on the ground, talking easily with Missy. Missy soon called out to Red, who appeared with a candle and matches, handed them to her mother. She lit the candle and began burning the ends of Angie's braids. The smell of candle wax mixed with burning hair, coupled with the women's chatter, conjured a memory. When she was in ninth grade, Angie joined her mother on her biweekly visits to see Mabel, the woman who did hair in her basement. There, Mabel would wash then press her mother's hair with a hot comb. Angie could remember waiting her turn as she sat on a nearby couch, head bowed over a worn paperback of *Flowers in the Attic*. Back then, she carried Ella's copy of *One Hundred Years of Solitude* in her purse everywhere—feeling she *should* read it but not doing so. Ella was never in any shape to discuss books with her, besides. In a way, she carried Marquez's novel as a talisman against Ella's further decline. *One day we'll talk about it.* Meanwhile, fourteen-year-old Angie enjoyed the distraction of children held captive by a notoriously abusive grandmother. The smell of frying hair aloft, she'd listen to the women talk as they ignored her presence. Those were some of her favorite memories, witnessing her mother forget briefly that she had a daughter on drugs, chatting about money and men and making a way. Angie soaked in the ease and casualness in her mother's voice—such a rare sound. Out here in this open-air beauty shop on a concrete patch in Lagos, listening to the lilting inflections of these women's voices was like hearing the instrumental version of a song whose lyrics she knew by heart.

Seeing Angie's completed hair, Missy's friend lowered her headscarf and showed off her own fat, brown plaits hanging down her back. The woman's hair looked like hers—the same texture and volume and soft kinkiness. In fact, Angie resembled both of these women. Casually, the woman picked up the abandoned Afro pick, examined it for dirt, and raked it through one of her braids before re-plaiting her hair. Angie had put little stock in coming to Africa to find her roots; it hadn't been her goal. She secretly feared there was little African left in her. She resembled no one in her family—not her father nor her mother nor Denise nor Ella. Not even the aunties or the photos of grandparents. When she dressed up for Heritage Day in fifth grade, she'd worn an American Indian costume—complete with fringed moccasins and a feathered headband. Her mother had said that her great grandmother had "a bit of Indian blood" in her, and she felt a child's pride in being related to the people who showed the pilgrims how to prepare the first Thanksgiving dinner. Angie won the Heritage Day award for best costume that day, and ever since she'd secretly harbored the desire to see her face on someone else, someone with "a bit of Indian blood" perhaps. It surprised yet pleased her to find here in Nigeria, nomadic gypsy women with both her features and her hair. Solo had told the truth; *she could be Fulani.*

When Angie got back to the Olapades', Brenda was waiting for her. "It looks good, O!" she exclaimed.

Missy had given her an intricate pattern, with the tiniest

of cornrows running across her crown and braids tumbling down.

"Now you're dangerous," declared Brenda.

"Dangerous?" repeated Angie.

"You look like a Nigerian woman but you have the cachet of being a Western one," explained Brenda. "The men will be all over you."

Brenda's words drifted past Angie. She felt strange—exhausted from running all the way back; she'd gotten caught in the rain, had barely made it inside before a torrential downpour. Her head ached from the tight braids. Brenda's face floated in front of her.

"Could you excuse me?" she said, and stumbled to her guest quarters, fell across the bed.

Later, Angie awoke to the sound of plaintive cries. She sat up, blanketed in darkness, fear encroaching. More raw-throat moans. What was it? Suddenly the flimsy curtain separating her from the outside world was a joke. She hugged her knees, tried to discern whether the sounds were growing closer. Should she get up, look? Stay put? She listened hard. After several moments, the desperate screams grew less human and more guttural. She wondered was a wild animal attacking another? She got up her nerve, rose, pulled back the curtain as it hung demurely across the doorway, and stepped outside. The full moon hovered just above, watchful. A wet lizard ran across her foot, startling her, and Angie scurried back inside.

She sat on the edge of her bed as the screams persisted, several short ones in succession, each growling, aggressive, evolving into low wails. Now she was less fearful, more curious. Minutes passed and the screaming shifted, sounded defeated, exhausted, dying out. Angie climbed back into bed and curled up. Moans now replaced the screams; then whimpering; then silence. She lay there, disturbed by the wild night, certain an animal had lost its battle. Suddenly, the curtain fluttered and Chris appeared in the doorway. She felt a rush of relief.

"Hey!" She sat up straight. "What's going on out there?"

He came toward her. "Don't be afraid," he whispered.

"I'm not afraid," she said, as if saying so made it true.

"Good." He sat beside her, reached for one of her braids, fingered it in his hands. "I like it. Makes you look like you belong here."

She said nothing, didn't want to encourage him.

"So, you've thought about what we talked about the other night?"

"No."

He smiled. "You can't deny that we have a special connection, you and I."

She hesitated, not sure what to say. She needed a place to stay.

He leaned in to kiss her lips.

She pulled back. "Chris, please don't."

"So you are not attracted to me, eh?"

She wanted to say *in fact, that's it exactly*. "I like Brenda. I don't want to betray her friendship."

"Brenda is the one who *betrays*. If Ella were alive, she could tell you that."

Hearing him speak of her sister pained Angie. "Please don't mention her name."

He nodded. "Listen. It's obvious, we want each other. And I understand you don't want to hurt Brenda. She'll never know. I promise."

He put his hand on her thigh, and grabbed her around the neck, pulling her face to his. He pressed his lips against hers. She pushed him away.

"Oh you like to play that game?" he said, smiling. He pushed her hard enough so that she fell back against the headboard. He pulled her legs down, climbed on top of her and held her arms back, straddling her.

"Stop!" she yelled. "Chris, please stop!"

"Shhh!" he whispered. "We're just having fun."

As he pried open her legs with his knee she screamed, her own cry as desperate as those she'd just heard outside.

He slapped her. So hard, her face pulsated.

"You cannot fucking yell!" he growled. "She might hear you!"

He climbed off of her and as he moved toward the doorway, she begged, "Please don't hurt me! Please." She felt as doomed as whatever animal lay out there, another beast's prey. I'm about to be raped, she told herself. Okay. Okay. Just get through it.

Chris pulled back the curtain, looked out. She gasped in short, frightened breaths, hugged her knees to her chest.

Certain no one had heard her scream, he returned, hovered over the bed, a hard glint in his eyes.

She winced. "Please don't hurt me," she repeated.

"I want you out of here by morning."

Angie looked up at him. "Leave?"

"The best thing is for you to go. Before she suspects something. Or before I tell her you tried to come on to me."

He hit the doorway curtain and it froze in midair for a brief, terrifying moment. He held it back as he turned to her. "Ella understood how things work. And here I thought you were smart like her. You may wear the same hair, but you're nothing like her. Not even close."

He stalked out.

Once Angie's breath returned to normal, once the throbbing across her face subsided, once it was clear Chris wasn't returning, she lay awake and contemplated her fate. Where would she go? She chided herself for naively landing in the midst of people living messy lives and not being prepared for that fact. She could just go back home. She was already near the airport. She rose, grabbed her gold pen and a sheet of thin, blue par avion paper from her bag—paper she'd purchased for long, detailed letters home that she'd failed so far to write. She quickly scribbled:

Dear Brenda,
Thank you for everything. I've decided to move on. I'll never forget your hospitality and the friendship you extended to me. Be well.

Love,
Angie

She lay still and waited until the sun slid through the slatted windows; on cue, she rose, packed her bag. When she stepped outside, Godwin was there, tossing a jerrican of water onto the concrete inside his doorway. His newborn baby's cries sliced into the silence with hiccups of ferocity. She watched as the houseboy tossed another and another, washing away the after-birth and blood stains seeping into the cement floor. *Waa, Waa, Waaaaa.* Understanding now, she walked up to Godwin, hugged him. "I wish the best for you and your family." He looked stunned. "Thank you, madam."

"And make sure Theresa breastfeeds," she said, as she passed by to slip Brenda's note under the back door, along with the key. Then she quietly made her way to the front of the house, toward Olapade Road.

Only while zooming along the highway in a taxi did she realize she'd never gotten to see Brenda and Chris's house at night, totally missed the pretty, yellow porch lights casting their soft, hazy glow.

SURULERE

ELEVEN

28, Onibu Ore
Surulere, Lagos

30 November 1983

Hey Angie,
More news: I'm now staying with a real
Nigerian woman! Nigel is not with me--we
decided to cool it, do our own thing for
a while. C'est la vie. Quite frankly, I'm
relieved.
   Her name is Funke Akinlolu and she's
amazing! I met her while reporting
a story on Lagos businesswomen. She
works as an executive secretary for the
assistant commissioner of the ministry
of transportation, and THEN on weekends
she runs a kiosk in the market, where
she sells beauty and hygiene products.
AND she takes in foreign travelers as a
host. She's a true feminist, like so many
Nigerian women--working day jobs, being

entrepreneurs and community activists and
wives. Her husband is an asst. minister of
forestry and he's never home, always in
Abuja. Oh yeah, and she's pregnant with
her first child! I got the best quote from
her for the profile. She said, "Most women
are too easygoing. They sit back lazily
and allow themselves to be tossed about
by men like helpless pieces of corn in a
river."

I used that as my pull quote!
Fantastic--and VERY shocking to everyone
that she dare speak the truth.

I'm learning so much from Funke. She's
already taught me how to cook a few
Nigerian dishes. The other day, we went to
the market and bought some gorgeous indigo
fabric (I'm just loving that color!)
and she taught me how to tie a "rappa"
and a "gele," the matching head-wrap. I
look very authentic! I'd send a picture
but getting them developed here is crazy
expensive, so I'll show you when I return.

The area she lives in, Surulere,
is my favorite in Lagos. It's largely
residential--the whole district was
built for civil servants--with a kiosk
here or there. I love all the flat-topped
structures with their stone lattices built
into the walls. It's like looking at
fences made of lace. Very practical too--
lets the cool air in (whatever that is).
And the place is so manageable compared to

Lagos Island! Besides, it's much closer to
The Voice office.

    Anyway, write me back soon. Glad you're
liking U of M. Join the Black Action
Movement--if the damn thing still exists.
And yes, come to Nigeria for Winter Break!
I miss you.

                      Luv,

                      Ella

"This is Surulere," said the taxi driver.

Angie stared into a gutter that snaked alongside the narrow road, skim of algae glistening green and viscous in the Sunday morning drizzle. A small group of women dressed in white walked just up ahead, carrying Bibles. She wondered whether they were headed back from baptisms. She'd once read that Nigerians called baptism "the water god." Where would the preacher have dunked them? In the oil-slick lagoon, with its beckoning dark presence beneath the city's bridges? She'd decided to go home. But then she thought of her mother, their argument, how she'd left so abruptly, and she couldn't bring herself to return. Not yet. The thought of Denise's *I told you so* was enough to make her stay.

The driver turned onto Onibu Ore Road. They passed a church, a square cinder block building with a neon sign proclaiming, YE MUST BE BORN AGAIN. The women must be headed here. She had the urge to stop, go inside the little church, sit among the simple pews and raised altar. Surrender and declare herself born-again.

She was so relieved to have escaped Chris's clutches that this felt like a fresh start. She didn't need to be in the middle of Chris and Brenda's domestic drama. She was headed to a better place, a place that Ella had loved—with an authentic Nigerian woman. She hoped Funke was still accepting foreign travelers, hoped she'd be pleased to see Ella's little sister.

Just past the church, makeshift tin-roofed shacks clustered alongside the road. Many sat atop cinder blocks, some were lean-tos held by poles, others squatted low behind open gutters, planks of wood set up as walkways. She eyed a woman stooped over, sweeping an area with a low broom, a naked girl at her side. Abruptly, the woman whacked the girl with her broom and the child wailed. Cooking fires simmered outside the shanties, creating clouds of black smoke. Chickens ran amok. Angie wondered how a woman who lived in a shanty-town could offer her home to a foreign traveler. She wondered too why Ella hadn't mentioned this fact in her letter.

Then she noticed the houses on the opposite side of the road. These were solid, closely built wooden homes with gravel yards and clumps of foliage out front. Painted in lollipop colors of pink, yellow, and blue, with their rough charm they looked like crude images drawn by a child's hand. Number twenty-eight was faded orange and had a front porch with a white railing. She exited the taxi, grabbed her bag, walked up to the house and knocked. Within seconds, a young man opened the door. He was angular save the horizontal tribal marks gouged into his face. He wore a soiled dress shirt opened to his navel, exposing a smooth, frail chest. The shirt hung over black trousers, which were shiny from too much ironing. His hair was in a Jheri curl. He ground a chewing stick as he studied her.

"I'm here to see Funke Akinlolu," she said.

"Funke no dey."

"She knew my sister, Ella?"

"Wetin be yua name?"

"Angela."

"Ah, this name no sabi."

"I'm visiting from America," said Angie. "Please."

He chewed on his stick. "Enta," he said at last, stepping out of the doorway.

The room was dimly lit, and her eyes took a while to adjust. A string of Christmas cards hung across the room, dipping below the ceiling. Dust covered the cards and the three chairs and end tables that comprised the room's furniture. A small TV with rabbit ears sat atop one of the little tables. Books and papers were stacked high in the corners. The room smelled of mold, and looked all but abandoned. Angie thought of Godwin, ever dusting and cleaning at the Olapades' sprawling home. She set down her bag, certain this young man was Funke's houseboy and these were his quarters. Angie scanned the space. Four doors lined the length of the hallway.

"You know Michael Jackson?" asked the young man.

"What?"

"Michael Jackson."

"No," she said. Her throat was parched.

"No?"

"Well, everyone knows of him," she explained. "But I've never *met* him."

He chewed on his stick, as a horse might chew a carrot, digesting her answer. He stood there.

"Do you have anything to drink?" she asked.

"I get minerals," he said, walking out the open front door.

Angie sat down in one of the chairs and peered into the kitchen. A large, white refrigerator stood beside another smaller one and a tiny cooker sat atop a large modern stove. The kitchen wall was lined with shelves filled with an array of blue jerricans, tin basins, straw baskets, wooden bowls, metal pots, yellow plastic buckets, assorted rags—a still life of color.

When the young man returned, he handed her a cold Fanta and watched as she drank.

"I am Andrew," he said, pointing to himself.

She held up the Fanta. "Nice to meet you Andrew."

"I am a singer."

"Oh?" She held the bottle to her cheek. The room was muggy and stifling.

"*Beat it!!!! Beat it, beat it, beat it, beat it!*" he sang, snapping his fingers and spinning around for effect. His voice was warbled, straining high.

Caught off guard, she laughed.

He smiled, his teeth small and ecru. "I will go to United States and become a singer like Michael Jackson. A black can be big, big in America."

"He's not just any black," she said.

It was then she noticed that the young man's hands and face were much lighter than his chest. In fact, his face had the anemic, washed-out complexion of Nigerian women she'd seen on Lagos Island who obviously bleached their skin. Too bad, she thought, he was trying to look like a 1983 Michael Jackson, when the 1987 one had moved on to a new look and even lighter skin.

Andrew did another spin and a woman burst through the door, a little boy at her side. She was short and wide, a market bag in her hand. Her sideways cornrows gave her a girl-like quality. When she saw Angie, she stood stock-still, stared. The young man filled her in, speaking rapidly in Yoruba. She took in the suitcase on the floor, turned to Angie. "Who are you, please?"

Angie saw that she was pregnant.

"I'm Ella's sister," she said. "She stayed with you, here, four years ago?"

Recognition lit the woman's face. "Ah-ah, the black American girl who ran in the street and died?"

Angie nodded, undone by her description.

"And you are her sister."

"Yes."

"And you have come, why?" said the woman, rubbing her belly.

Both Chris and Brenda had asked the same question. "Just to visit. Meet you." She wished she could come up with a better answer. "I hope this wasn't a bad time to come?"

"That depends," said the woman. "I am Funke." She nodded her head toward the young man. "And so you have met my nephew, Andrew."

"Yes." She realized her presumption; he most certainly wasn't a houseboy. "If this is not a good time—?"

"Ope!" yelled Funke. The little boy had teetered his way to a pile of papers in the corner and was pulling them down. Funke scooped him up, parking him on her hip. She walked over and thrust the boy at Angie. "Here, take him please, thank you."

She disappeared behind one of the doors as the boy squirmed in Angie's arms. This must be the boy Funke was expecting when Ella visited. Angie's only experience with children came when she was fourteen and got her first job working for a nursery school a few blocks from home. Timbuktu it was called, and the director spent much of his time telling her about the great kingdom for which his place was named. She didn't like the toddlers' high-pitch screams, found their neediness exhausting. When he left her alone with the children one day, he returned to find her napping alongside them. He fired her.

Ope slapped Angie in the face with his pudgy hand. Flashing back to Chris's violence, she grabbed the boy's hand and squeezed it. He yelped and she let go, held him at arm's length. He squirmed, about to fall from her grasp.

"Please, take him!" she said to Andrew, who laughed, grabbed Ope, and sat him on the floor. He took a pan from the kitchen and handed it to the boy, who gurgled in delight. Funke reappeared in a bright wrapper tied around her waist and a T-shirt with a Coca-Cola logo. She turned toward the kitchen.

Angie, feeling awkward, followed her. "Can I help?"

"You can make draw soup?" asked Funke.

"No."

"Then you will watch."

Angie stood close as Funke pulled an onion, tomato paste, dried shrimp, okra, and dried red peppers from her bag. She grabbed the small gas burner from atop the huge stove, placed it on the floor, and lit it with a match. She then placed a huge pot on the flame, squatting as she poured palm oil inside. "I had no warning of your arrival, so there is no meat stew."

"That's fine," said Angie, watching as Funke chopped the onion and dropped it into the hot oil, along with the other ingredients and a Maggi bullion cube.

Angie reached for something to say. "Ella wrote to me that you're an executive secretary?"

"Yes, that is true."

Angie tried again. "And on weekends, you run a kiosk?"

"And what else did your sister tell you about me?"

"That she really enjoyed staying with you."

Funke smiled. Angie relaxed. They sat in silence for a while. Funke removed the soup and placed another pot on the flame. Once the water boiled, she added a cup of cassava grain. As she stirred she said proudly, "We are building a house in Lagos."

These new appliances, she explained, would be put into the new home. "Light never stays on here," she said. "So why would I even plug them into the wall?"

Angie nodded in understanding, having had her own experiences with the city's erratic power system.

Funke took the cassava mixture, which looked to Angie like mashed potatoes with lumps, and placed it in a wooden bowl, which she sat on the kitchen table. She put the pot of soup on the table as well and they all sat. Funke and Andrew scooped up fat pieces of the mixture, rolled them in their hands, dipped them into the soup. The glob of thick, sticky-looking grain mocked Angie. "Do you have a fork?" she asked.

"You cannot be eating *eba* with a fork," said Funke. "Grab it with your hand O."

Angie broke off a small piece and dropped it into her soup, which was green and slimy. She picked up the piece of *eba*, placed it tentatively into her mouth. Andrew laughed. It was gummy and hard to swallow, sticking to her throat. Andrew rose, handed her a dusty spoon. She dipped it into the soup, took a sip, coughed. It was so hot, her cheeks salivated.

"You must get your tongue used to draw soup," said Funke. "If you are shy with it, it will always be too much for you."

Funke fed Ope, who ate greedily. Andrew cupped soup with his *eba* and pushed it into his mouth. Strings of okra hung onto his chin.

Angie tried again. The soup was tasteless beyond its scorching spice. She wanted water, but feared she would insult Funke if she asked whether it had been boiled first. She'd read somewhere not to drink the water in third world countries; now she longed for the purified pitcher of water that beckoned in the Olapades' ever-humming refrigerator. Her stomach growled in reaction to the heat. The others stared at her. She forced herself to eat much of what was in her bowl, out of respect and hunger. Her insides burned bright.

Funke grabbed Ope and tied him to her back, began clearing the table as Andrew disappeared out the front door. Angie helped Funke with the dishes, washed with a sudsy sponge then plunged into a bucket of cold water.

"Where were you staying before you came to me?" asked Funke.

"With a Nigerian man and his wife," said Angie.

"And what does this man do?"

"He works for the International Bank of West Africa."

"And where does he live, this banker?"

"In Ikeja."

"Ah-ah? In a new house?"

"Yes, he said it's only about four years old."

"This is where our house is being built, O! Right by the airport in a new development!" Funke grabbed Angie's hand, sat her down at the table. "Tell me about this big man's house."

Funke had Angie describe how each room looked, how it was furnished, where the washer and dryer were located, how loud the generator hummed.

"And does it have two floors?"

"Yes," said Angie. "The bedrooms are upstairs."

"Ours will be like this!" shouted Funke. "And the boy's quarters, were they out back?"

"Yes, I stayed in one."

"Eyyyy! In the boy's quarters?"

"It was set up like a guest room."

Funke sucked her teeth. "And did you bring her a gift, this madam who put you in the boy's quarters?"

"No." Angie wondered, had Brenda noticed? "Ella stayed back there too, before she came to stay with you."

Funke stood, returned to the kitchen. "I don't remember that a-tall."

Angie watched Funke clean her pots. "How long did my sister stay here?" she asked. She couldn't really tell from Ella's letters.

"A long time," said Funke. "Many weeks."

"Was there anything she told you that you could tell me?"

"What do you mean?"

"I don't know. Just . . . anything."

Funke shrugged. "She told me everything. We were very close."

Angie felt both heartened and envious. "Maybe you can share some memories with me."

"Yes." Funke stood. "But now, I must get my rest. I am doing many jobs you know."

"Of course." Angie also rose. "We can talk tomorrow."

"Let me show you where you'll sleep," said Funke.

"Is it the same room where Ella stayed?"

Funke looked at her, dark eyeliner exaggerating her big eyes. "That room is very cluttered."

"I don't mind."

She eyed Angie for a bit longer. "Very well. Come."

The room was dust laden and mildewy. Three cots filled the tight space, alongside several boxes and basins and wide-open drums of grain. Left alone, Angie took off her clothes, and rifled through her suitcase until she found her gown and slipped into it. She lay across the cot, which had neither a pillow nor a sheet, just a bare mattress. She tried to conjure the feeling that had escaped her in the back quarters at the Olapades', that sense that Ella's presence lingered in the room. Nothing came. Exhausted by her disappointment, she fell asleep, hoping to dream about her sister. But she didn't.

Some time before dawn, her bowels awakened her. She couldn't remember where she was. Her need for a bathroom forced her out of bed; she fumbled down the dark hallway. She thought she might be having a waking dream and opened one door, which turned out to be a storage room, closed it, stumbled to the next, where she could make out a body curled atop a mat on the floor. A snake slithered downward inside her. The next room *seemed* to be a bathroom, but she couldn't be certain. She held her stomach in desperation as her eyes adjusted. The room had a cement floor and a sink whose bowl was filled with corrosion. Buckets and basins of water were everywhere, along with barrels of unknowable objects. She could see a shower-head in the corner but no space existed to stand beneath it. She finally spotted a toilet, a basin of water on top of its closed lid. She lunged for the water basin; it was heavy and she lugged it carefully from the toilet to the floor; when she raised the lid, she was assaulted by the smell and the sight of human waste. Desperate, she climbed atop the seat-less toilet, hovering, and let her bowels go. She knew before she tried that the toilet wouldn't flush and so she closed its lid, returned the basin of water atop and stumbled in the darkness back to bed, her own body's smell pungent as a trapped animal's.

IN THE DAYLIGHT the washroom was less ominous but no less overwhelming for its clutter, its vast array of water containers, its lingering odor. With Ope wrapped snug against her back, Funke pointed to two covered jerricans on the floor.

"These are for cooking and drinking," she explained. She pointed to other buckets. "The wide-mouthed ones are for bathing and washing clothes. And you must use that basin on top of the toilet for pouring water into the commode after you have relieved yourself."

"I actually have to relieve myself right now," said Angie.

"Come outside when you are done," said Funke as she walked away.

Afterward, Angie found her on the front porch, holding a large metal pole. "Follow me," she said. Sticky heat clung as they walked to the side of the house, stopping before a small water pump.

"My husband and I had our own borehole built," Funke said proudly. "It's sixty feet deep."

She turned on the curved, rusting spigot; water gushed from the tap. She quickly turned it off. The neighbors, she explained, were allowed to fill their buckets after they gave her twenty-five kobo each.

"They pay you for the water?" asked Angie.

"We have spent big-big money for this!" said Funke. "We pay and so they must pay."

"But shouldn't the water department supply the water?"

Funke sighed. "If you live on Vic or Ikoyi Island or maybe with your ay-leet friends in Ikeja, you have running water. Here, we have a borehole. We are lucky to have it."

Angie thought of all the times she had brushed her teeth, mindlessly letting the water run. The thought loosened her bowels again.

"I'll be back," she said, running off.

When Angie returned, Funke was waiting with more rules. "Whenever you use water, replace it from the pump," she said. "Sometimes the well dries up and the day goes by without a drop."

She slid the elongated metal rod down a circular hole. "You lock the pipes like this." She turned the key clockwise. "To unlock it, turn the other way." She let go of the key. "You try."

Angie gripped the metal, felt it catch against a lever.

"Never leave the water pump on when you are gone!" said Funke. "A-tall!"

Back inside the house, Funke grabbed a satchel, noticeably flat. She turned to Angie. "You have *running stomach*," she said.

Angie nodded. The name was so clearly accurate.

"You must make your way to the chemist. It's just up the road, straight, and there in the Gbaja Market you will find the kiosk. Tell them what you have and they will give you pills to make it go away." Funke opened the front door. "Lock this when you leave."

Once Funke and Ope left, the house quiet, Angie went back to bed and slept. Her diarrhea had awakened her so early that she could feel her tiredness hanging from her, pulling her down, as a swimmer feels the weight of water after climbing out of a pool. Three hours later she awoke, was instantly reminded of her delicate stomach and headed back to the washroom. Afterward, she took off the lid of a covered jerrican, found a cup bobbing in the water. She dipped the cup, barely skimming the water's surface, and used that to wash her face and brush her teeth. She spit the toothpaste onto the cement floor, as she couldn't figure out another way. Next she filled a large, idle bowl with water from the bathing bucket. She was afraid to use too much, too intimidated to refill the bucket at the tap outside. Nor did she dare venture to boil the water on the gas burner. She grabbed a giant bar of black soap sitting on the ledge of the rusting sink, stripped out of her nightgown, dunked the soap into the dipping bowl and washed under her arms. She quickly rinsed, the water so cold, her body broke into tiny goose bumps. Water dribbled down her legs to the cement floor, where dirty suds lathered in a pool, slowly swirling toward an unseen drain. She thought: something here is not right.

Lacking a towel, she dried off with her nightgown.

After she'd dressed in jeans and a tank top, Angie headed out the front door in search of a chemist. Humid air engulfed her as chickens and roosters ran across her path. At a wide intersection, a cluster of school children passed by, pealing with chatter and laughter. Dressed in uniforms—the boys in tan cotton shorts and matching shirts, the girls in tan dresses— they carried books on straps slung across their backs. The dust created knee-high stockings on their legs. Each girl's hair was braided in an elaborate design. They waved at Angie. She waved back.

Feeling weak, she moved slowly up the road. She'd made little progress when she spotted a bus stop, where a cluster of people crowded around a yellow *danfo*, one of the rickety minibuses she'd seen barreling around Lagos Island that first day. On impulse, she decided to take it. At the doorway, a throng of people pushed themselves onto the bus. Angie stood beside a woman carrying a box on her head cushioned by a ring of cloth; she asked her whether this bus went to Gbaja Market? The woman nodded and Angie let herself be carried along with the throb of bodies. Hands reached out to a boy in the front collecting kobo from outstretched palms. Someone stepped on her sandaled foot but she couldn't move and swallowed the pain. The seats were all taken, one by an old man carrying a cage of cackling chickens. The *danfo* took off and she freed her own arm enough to hold onto the back of a seat. Her nose was under a man's armpit, forcing her to inhale the sweet stank of his body funk. The driver zoomed down the road, swerving around a corner so sharply that the van rode on two wheels. Three boys hung from the doorway. A sign over the driver's head said, I TRUST IN GOD FOR SAFE JOURNEY. YOU SHOULD HOLD ON.

As soon as they reached Gbaja, she descended with the others in one mass exodus and made her way through the market, which was actually more of a shopping complex. She walked through the outdoor mall for several minutes before spotting the chemist kiosk, its hand-painted sign askew. A boy of eight or nine was manning the shop. Angie asked him for the tablets that help with *running stomach*. He turned, grabbed a jar of huge white pills on the shelf behind, opened it, put his hand inside, and scooped up a handful.

"How much?" he asked.

She wondered where was the packaged carton of tablets

with instructions and an expiration date, the protective seal? And these did not look like "over-the-counter" pills, rather something you get with a prescription.

"Please, do you have any in a box, still sealed?" she asked.

"No, aunty," said the boy. "How much?"

She looked at the pills, picked a number. "Six."

He counted out the six pills methodically and placed them inside a scrap of nearby paper, which he then crunched, and handed to her.

"Twelve naira, Aunty."

Angie handed him the money, and moved through the market until she found a boy selling baggies of water from a pan he carried on his head. She bought a baggie and swallowed two of the pills, washing them down. They caught in her throat.

SHE GOT LOST on her way back, cursing herself for not taking a taxi. Still it gave her a chance to explore Surulere, see the latticed fences Ella had described as stone lace. Eventually, she asked directions back to Funke's street from a man carrying a gigantic boom box on a shoulder strap, highlife blaring. He turned off the music, and using her gold pen and a page from her journal, drew a little map. She entered Funke's street just as darkness encroached; cooking fires burned all along Onibu Ore Road—ribbons of smoke undulating upward, rimming the sky. Women on the lean-to side of Funke's street called out a greeting to her, "You are welcome!" they said. "You are welcome!"

When the four of them sat for dinner later, Angie didn't dare eat. Tonight's meal was more soup and more starch for scooping it up, this time *fufu*. Funke and Andrew each pulled off a piece of the fermented cassava, rolled it into a ball, pushed a thumb into it, then scooped up soup in the *fufu's* little reservoir. They popped these into their mouths and swallowed without chewing. Andrew shoved the bowl of *fufu* at Angie. "You try," he said.

"I don't think so—"

"Try!"

"OK!" She hated yelling. She picked up a small piece, and emulating what she'd seen, dipped the ball of *fufu* into her bowl of soup, placed it in her mouth.

"No, no!" yelled Andrew. "You cannot chew it. That is bad luck O! Just swallow it."

Angie gulped it down, nearly choking. "I've had enough."

Andrew grinned. "You will do me a favor."

"What's that?"

"You will help me find work in America."

"What type of work would you like?" she asked.

"I want to be in movies in Hollywood."

She sighed. "It's not that easy."

"I can do it! I am into your acting and singing."

"You cannot even finish your O-levels," noted Funke. "They do not let lazy men into Hollywood just because they have the curly look, O."

Andrew ignored his aunt. "I will come to America and you will help me," he said to Angie. "You will help me become an actor in Hollywood."

"Call me when you arrive," she said, tired of him. Her stomach *still* hurt.

Satisfied, Andrew broke off a giant piece of *fufu*, rolled it with one hand, scooped it into his soup, shoved it into his mouth, and swallowed. His Adam's apple came alive.

Funke said, "My water is very low. You are drinking a lot of it today?" she asked Andrew.

"Nah! I don't drink water. Never! Me, I only drink Coca-Cola."

Funke turned to Angie. "It was you."

"I only used water this morning to bathe," said Angie.

"Then you used my drinking water for your bathing," said Funke as she rubbed her protruding belly.

"No, I made sure I dipped water from the big, wide bucket—"

"You must *not* use my drinking water for your bath."

"But I didn't use the drinking water, I'm sure of it."

"I'm sure that you did."

"Here in Naija, it's all about the water," said Andrew, grinning wide.

"But I swear, I didn't—"

"Ah, this one is kicking hard!" They all paused. "Again!" exclaimed Funke. "God willing, it will be another boy." She rubbed her belly. "I will name him Yele."

"What does Yele mean?" asked Angie, relieved to change the subject.

Funke rubbed in circles. She looked right at Angie. "It means *I am grateful.*"

After dinner, Angie was extra careful to wash each plate and bowl and fork with the soapy sponge before dunking it into the bucket of cold, this-is-for-washing-dishes water. She wanted to show her gratitude. Throughout that night, she ran back and forth to the toilet. Funke woke her at 4:30 in the morning.

"You are pouring water down the toilet when you pee," she said.

Angie lifted up, neck stiff from a pillowless sleep. "I thought you said to use the basin of water on top of the toilet for that."

"Not for pee, O! You just swat on the floor and it's done."

Groggy, Angie apologized, willed her tummy to calm down, and tried to fall back asleep.

Later that morning, Funke suggested a chemist on Lagos Island. "No little boy this time!" she warned before leaving for work.

Angie spent the next two hours in a taxi trapped in traffic as it crept along Apapa Road, passing by the National Stadium, which looked to her like a giant hole opening up from the ground. Finally they crossed Eko Bridge onto the island. Nigeria's tallest building—the forty-story Nigerian External Communications headquarters—loomed over other skyscrapers, and a billboard proclaiming "New York Before Breakfast" with an image of a Nigeria Airways plane taking off made her instantly homesick. She fixated on the image as the taxi sped by.

The congested streets of downtown Lagos were teeming with a frenzy of bodies and vehicles, all trying to share the same finite space. Gleaming skyscrapers towered above as the stench of close living wafted toward her open window.

Once she got out of the taxi, she navigated crowded, narrow pathways, almost colliding with a man rolling an overstuffed wheelbarrow through the street, its pile of bricks nearly falling out. She spotted a chemist's shack nestled between two tall buildings, its sign more professional than the one in Surulere. A woman in an indigo head-wrap sat behind the counter. Angie decided the dark blue gele was a good sign.

After Angie explained her ailment, the woman said, "I am a trained pharmacist. Listen. You are not doing the right thing to get rid of this situation. You must do what I say: do not drink the water unless it is boiled, stay away from soda drinks—too much acid—and do not eat anything with *pep-pay*. Do not, in fact, eat anything that looks strange to you."

The woman grabbed off the shelf a small bottle filled with white liquid, handed it to Angie. "Drink this."

Angie downed the liquid, thinking of Alice in Wonderland. It tasted like chalky licorice. Would she shrink? She thanked the woman, paid her, and left. Back on the road, sticky heat rushed at her. She was famished. But afraid to eat. Clouds hung heavy in the clingy air. She hailed a taxi. As they lumbered through the center of Lagos, the elongated island appeared as one massive collection of junk sculptures punctuated by palm trees. Abandoned tires dotted the landscape, piled high in pyramid-like mounds and bordering cesspools of dirty water. Dead and deserted cars, their collapsed metal like grotesque figurines, stretched for miles. Glints of saturated color peeked out from the discarded debris, lone jewels half-buried in the endless rubbish. A road sign demanded without irony, "Keep Lagos Clean."

Finally back over the bridge and onto the causeway, they crept past a giant billboard boasting "Phillips Black & White TVs—The Only Ones That Think Like Color" and passed the National Arts Theatre, its windowed, jaunty exterior shaped like a sombrero. The juxtaposition of sophisticated modern architecture and unbelievable disorder shocked her anew. She marveled at how Ella had been part of this crude, modern life-style; had she made the daily commute to her newspaper job, perhaps in a *danfo* or on foot even, rushing there in bare-legged high heels, along roadways with no sidewalks? Angie tried to picture her sister this way, but she couldn't.

GIVEN THE TRAFFIC'S usual snarl, it took hours for Angie to make it back to Funke's house. The lights were out and she banged with the side of her fist. Mosquitoes swarmed in an orbit around her, floating drunkenly in the moist air. Still no answer. She scratched at a bite on her arm, another on her neck, and plopped down on Funke's small porch, swatting away the bugs. Candlelight flickered in a few shanties across the street, glowing through cut-out windows. She watched as one by one, the lights went out, and fire embers smoldered. Most people went to bed early here, to rest for the next day's struggles. She felt her own fatigue, and by the time Funke returned waddling up the unlit street, Angie had dozed off, head on chest.

"Why are you sitting here?" asked Funke, waking her. Ope was asleep on his mother's back.

"I can't get in," said Angie, her own back aching from sleeping hunched over.

"But where is Andrew?"

"I haven't seen him."

"Ah-ah! This one will kill me, O!" Funke's eyes widened. "What is the use of a man if he is never doing a man's job? All he cares about is smoking his Indian hemp and lazing about and acting like a big man!" She sucked her teeth. "He's nothing but a useless chewing stick!"

She unlocked the front door as Angie followed her into the dark house; Funke made her way to the kerosene lamp, and lit it.

"I spit on NEPA!" Her face in silhouette, she set the lamp on the table, its shadow crawling up the wall and across the ceiling. She went to the back bedroom, lay Ope on his raffia mat, returned.

"Have you eaten?" she asked Angie.

"I can't eat."

"Still you have the running stomach?"

"It's better, but—"

"You are afraid of food now. That is expected." Funke sat down wearily. Angie sat beside her. Maybe now they could talk.

"Could you tell me about Ella, about her time with you?"

"Later," said Funke. "I am very tired." She took another lamp from a shelf, and lit it. This one brightened the room. "I have been at our construction site since I left my kiosk," she explained. "It is not going well."

"What's the trouble?" asked Angie.

"Ah-ah! What is *always* the trouble with Nigeria?" said Funke. "Thieves everywhere! The contractor is saying we must pay more, must give *drop drop* to port inspectors to get building materials through customs. Do they think that I am a bank? My husband will blame me, O." She rubbed her belly in a vicious circle. "And nothing done for two weeks, it turns out. No work. Two weeks! And now, gypsies have moved into my house. I am just fearing that they will not leave. Once these people drag their dirty possessions inside and put up a curtain, you can never get them out. And my husband is not even here to take care of it, to be the man."

She put her face in her hands. Angie sensed that Funke's life had been somehow easier before, when Ella was here. Or perhaps Ella had been a bigger help. She reached out, touched her back. Funke flinched.

"You are thinking this is too much for me, eh?" said Funke. "You are thinking I should just settle for this little life, forget this whole business of a new house. That is what you are thinking."

"I was thinking maybe this stress you're under is not good for the baby," said Angie.

"Wha?" Funke looked incredulous. "I am doing this *for* him, you silly girl. This baby understands. He is Yele. He is grateful."

In that moment, Funke reminded Angie of her own mother, certain that her girls would appreciate how hard she and their father worked to give them a better life, a good education. And so hurt when one didn't take full advantage of that.

Angie feared Funke would never talk to her about Ella. Did she even remember her? Was this even the right woman? "Please, tell me about my sister," said Angie. "Anything. Anything at all. I don't care how small it is."

Funke pressed her thumb and forefinger against her tear ducts. "Tomorrow." She rose. "Please, abeg, blow out the lamps before you go to bed."

Funke trudged out of the room. Angie surveyed the place, with its chaotic clutter, its layers of dust, its unplugged new appliances sitting idle. These two days with Funke had forced her to see life stripped down to bodily function and sustenance, the fragile dance between the two. She was light-headed from lack of food, from dehydration. She felt literally emptied out, transparent, like a ghost. She sat still for some time. Then she blew out the lamp, throwing herself into darkness, disappearing.

That night, as a rainstorm raged outside, she dreamed that the bins of grain piled on the other bed in her room spilled over and she barely managed to escape the avalanche, fleeing for home; there she found no one, only running water every-where—coming out of faucets, pouring into tall, shapely glasses of ice, swirling like mini tornadoes down flushed toilets, sloshing inside her mother's washing machine.

Angie stayed in bed the next day, listening to rain march on the corrugated roof as she read *One Hundred Years of Solitude*, Ella's paperback copy that she'd carried around in her purse as a teen. Its pages were coming loose from the binding. She read it hungrily, relieved to hide out from Funke and be among the Buendia family and their South American city of mirrors.

The following day, she got up and watched a bit of televi-sion with Andrew, waiting as he fiddled with the small TV's rabbit-eared antennae. At first they watched a pretty young woman with a short, curly Afro and heavy makeup read the news. She spoke about a mandate passed by the newly formed National Committee on Ethical Revolution. "The committee strongly suggests that businessmen, messengers, and traffic men alike refrain from demanding kickbacks for all transactions," she read from the paper before her, looking up intermittently to gaze wide eyed at the camera. Andrew laughed. "Nigerians and their stupid committees!"

After the news, the theme song for *Good Times* began, the

screen filling with the familiar oil painting of a long-limbed black family. *Keeping your head above water, making a wave when you can. Temporary layoffs* . . . It fascinated Angie to see a show airing in Nigeria that had been off the air for years in the States. Andrew sang along, and when J.J. appeared in all his lanky, big-nosed glory, Andrew jumped up and imitated his "dy-no-mite" routine. "That cat is cool!" he said. "No jive!"

When she was growing up, Angie seldom watched *Good Times.* Her mother forbade it once J.J.'s character became more buffoonish. Besides, it came on opposite *The Waltons* and she'd felt more affinity for the Depression-era white family in rural Virginia, longed to be in a household where everyone was safe and in bed as darkness fell, calling goodnight to one another. But now she felt endeared to J.J. and his family, as if they were fellow travelers, recognizable faces in an off-kilter world.

Later that evening, she watched as Funke shook Omo detergent into a bucket of water and dropped in several garments, squatted, knees spread, and began scrubbing.

"How can I help?" asked Angie. She hoped Funke would talk to her now, share stories of Ella while they washed clothes together. But Funke observed Angie's feeble attempts at scrubbing a blouse and ordered her to "have some tea and bread and go back to bed, thank you." Angie was actually relieved and did just that, hungrily devouring the rest of Marquez's novel.

Her last morning in Surulere, she awoke to a rooster's crow and lay there unmoving, waiting. Lightning crackled. The chalky medicine had finally worked. She rose and dressed. The house was quiet. On a bold whim, she boiled a pot of water on the little burner, mixed it with cold water and used that to take a warm bucket shower. Afterward, she made a cup of tea with sugar and pet milk and sat at the kitchen table. She could hear Funke getting out of bed. Rain poured down in sheets. Out of nowhere, the fan in the main room came on and the mini refrigerator hummed—a magical burst of electrical current running through the house. That gave her resolve. When Funke walked into the room, Angie said, "Tell me what you know about Ella."

Funke rubbed her eyes. "Later," she said, yawning.

"No. Now."

Funke looked at her. "Do you want the truth?"

"Yes." Angie cupped her tea, bracing.

Funke moved around in the kitchen, making Ope's breakfast as she spoke. "This sister of yours came to my kiosk and started looking at all of the jars and bottles. Reading them closely, telling me this one has an old date on it and so does that one and you should not sell this to anyone. Telling me not to sell my Venus de Milo cream—my skin brightener—to women. My best seller! That is what I remember about your sister. Telling me what *not* to do. Like a preacher on Sunday."

"What else did she tell you?" asked Angie. "I'm sure you two talked about lots of things."

"Talk, talk, talk. That is what she made me do. And then she was putting words in my mouth and into that radical newspaper. Why did she do that, eh? It made my husband very angry when he read my name next to those words."

"I'm sure she was trying to help," said Angie. "You know, improve women's conditions."

Funke set Ope's food on the table, ignoring her.

Angie pressed. "Please, tell me something I can take with me."

"I *have* told you something," said Funke. "Now. You tell me something: Do you have a gift for me?"

"A gift?"

"From America. A gift."

"Oh, I'm sorry, I don't," she said.

Funke sucked her teeth and headed for the washroom.

Angie drank her tea and waited. She'd just keep asking, wear Funke down if need be. She wanted *stories.*

Funke returned with fists balled. "You have used all the water!" she yelled.

"I just made myself tea and—"

"Just filling many buckets like we have our own river!" She thrust out her hands and shook them. "What if the well is dry and we must go through this day with no water?!" She slapped her hands against one another, rubbed them back and forth. "Not a drop."

"I only used one bucket of water," Angie insisted. "For a shower. That's it."

"But you did not *replace* it." Funke threw her hands up. "You must replace water when you use it! You must never, never leave a bucket empty. I am telling you this over and over!"

Angie stood. "I really am sorry."

Ope stumbled out of the bedroom, grabbed onto Angie's leg.

"I cannot use your sorry to give my son drinking water, to bathe him, to cook for him, can I?"

"The well will fill up again soon, won't it?" She tried to gently shake off Ope.

"What is *soon?* Who can be without water even one day? And you are talking this foolishness about soon? You and your American thinking."

"Well, I am American," said Angie, defensive.

Funke bucked her eyes. "Are you sure? I have had many Americans stay with me and I have seen these Americans on telly and in movies. You are not like them a-tall! You come to my country with your clothes from some *bend-down boutique,* bearing no gifts for your hostess in those bags of yours. What type of American are you?"

Angie picked up Ope and handed him to Funke, as if he

were a piece of luggage she'd borrowed. "Apparently not the type you were expecting."

"Look at you with that nose and that skin. Those braids in your hair. You are Fulani! But do you know how to wash a baby or cook a dinner or fill a bucket? Eh-eh! You are an African woman but you don't know how to act like one. Not like your sister, O. She was a *real* African woman."

Angie stepped backward, as if pushed. Funke turned and moved into the kitchen. Angie watched her back for several seconds, before retreating to the bedroom. She sat on the hard bed. It's true, she thought. I'm no good at this. This is all wrong. On impulse, she quickly packed her bag, exited the room.

She stood before Funke. "I'm leaving."

Funke didn't look up from the stove, where she was stirring something in a saucepan, Ope at her feet.

"I appreciate your letting me stay here," continued Angie. "But it's obviously not working out."

"Silly girl, do whatever," said Funke. "I don't know what you mean by this 'working out.' Is it like that American actress Jane Fonda and her exercise videos, this working out?"

Furious at being mocked, Angie turned with such force her gold pen flew out of the front pocket of her reporter's bag and hit the floor.

Funke quickly moved to pick it up, examined it. "I will keep this," she announced.

"No! Ella gave me that pen."

Funke wrapped her hand around it. "It is mine now. My gift from America."

"Give that to me!" screamed Angie, lunging for the pen.

Funke wouldn't let go, holding her arm with the pen above her head. Ope cried, "Mum! Mum!"

"It is mine now!" Funke laughed, mouth wide open.

Angie tried again, reaching up to grab the pen, but to no

avail. She gave up. She couldn't wrestle with a pregnant woman. The unfairness of it overwhelmed her and suddenly Angie was sobbing. Harsh, messy tears. Funke's eyes flashed with concern. She gently pulled out a chair for Angie.

"Sit," she ordered.

Angie did, hiccuping through her sobs. She cried until her head ached. Funke waited until she stopped. When all was quiet save her sniffles, Funke made florid, wide gestures in the air with Angie's gold pen. "I will use it to write you from my new home," she announced.

"I just want my pen back," whimpered Angie. She felt like a child taunted on a playground.

"You are American. You can have many pens such as this," said Funke.

Recognizing defeat, Angie stood, picked up her duffel bag, headed for the door.

"Wait!"

Angie whipped around, held her hand out, ready to receive the pen.

But Funke was grabbing one of the pieces of paper piled high in the corner. She thrust it at Angie. "Give me your address."

"No." She never wanted to hear from this woman again.

Funke thrust the paper at her again. "I will write to you about your sister."

Angie eyed Funke for several seconds before dropping her bags and scrawling her Michigan address; she handed back the paper and Ope reached his arms up to Angie. She ignored the boy as she turned, slowly walked out of Funke's house.

SHE MADE HER way up the road to the taxi park, where the sun now shone on lingering puddles from the morning's heavy rain. She climbed in the back of a waiting car and directed the driver to take her to the airport. What else was there to do? Angie felt deflated, as though she'd failed a test, blown a once-in-a-lifetime opportunity. She didn't want to be here anymore, a lone woman chasing after a ghost in a harsh, lonely place.

Traffic stalled. As cars inched along the road, she saw that it was not the normal go-slow causing the logjam: it looked like a bundle fallen from a rickety lorry but as the driver got closer, Angie realized what it was: a body splayed out, lying in the slow lane of traffic. Cars were swerving around it. It was a woman, a foot still holding its thong sandal, head in a grotesque twist. Angie screamed, "Stop!"

The driver turned around. "What is it, please?"

She pointed to the woman's body, struggling for words. "Right there. Her."

"Ah. Yes, it is an unfortunate part of Nigerian life." He maneuvered around the corpse, behind other cars. "I am afraid you get used to it."

Suddenly, Angie pushed the driver in his back. "You have to help her!" She pushed him again, so hard his chin hit the steering wheel. "Do something!"

He turned to face her. "Ah, ah! You *bee-tch!* What is your fucking problem!?"

"You have to do something," she repeated.

The driver drove on in angry silence. She turned around, eyeing the dead woman through the rear window. "Please do something," she begged, heart racing.

He ignored her, drove past the logjam, and once the traffic opened up, he pulled over to the edge of the road and hit the brakes. "Get out," he said. "Come down," he ordered her. "Get out of my fucking taxi!"

"What?" Angie felt confused.

He pushed her against the back door. "I am telling you! Come down!"

"I didn't mean to—"

The driver got out, grabbed Angie's arm. She screamed as he pulled her from the back, throwing her bag behind. Grabbing her duffel, she stumbled onto the narrow shoulder as he got back in the taxi, slammed his door and screeched away. Cars whizzed by. Four lanes of traffic stood between her and the exit on the opposite side. Desperate, she waved her hands in hopes that someone would stop. But the cars were flying too fast, as if grateful to be past the inconvenient roadkill, speeding to make up for lost time.

Angie stood on the highway's edge. Gravel flew up, hitting her legs and arms. She could be stuck here for hours. Forever. Her chest throbbed with panic as she began walking along the shoulder. The sun pricked her skin. Was this what happened to Ella? Was she caught on a road like this, desperate? She thought of Denise's admonition. *Do not let anything happen to you over there. I cannot bear the thought of delivering more bad news to Mama.* Please God, Angie thought. Please. I do not want to die like Ella.

Against the sun's glare, she thought she saw tiny figures making their way toward her. She stopped, stood still. The figures grew larger and as they got closer she could see that yes, it was a man, a woman, and a boy. They walked in single file along the edge, closer and closer, approaching.

"Please!" she yelled against the traffic's steady roar. "How do you get off this highway?"

"There is no flyover," yelled the man. "You must cross." He nodded toward the traffic. "We will cross with you."

"But there must be an exit on this side!" she yelled back.

"Miles away. This is best, to just cross here." All three of them were without shoes. The man gently nudged the boy's back. "Go," he said; the boy, who couldn't have been older than ten, looked up at Angie with saucer eyes, then ran onto the highway. Angie gasped as the boy deftly dodged oncoming cars. When he made it across, he waved at them.

"My God," she said. "I can't do that."

The man turned to Angie. His narrow face was all hard angles but his eyes were sympathetic.

"You must make your mind blank and just go," he offered. "I will show you." He created a rhythmic momentum with his shoulder blades, like a girl entering a double dutch jump rope game, then darted into the fray. Aghast, Angie watched as he wove between zooming cars before making it to the other side. He waved wildly at her, or perhaps at the other woman, who stood beside her, staring straight ahead. Cars flew by. The boy and the man both waved. The man cupped his hands to his mouth and yelled something that got lost to the wind. Cars passed and the boy and man disappeared, reappeared. The man gestured for them to *come, come*. Cars flew by. *Come, come*.

The woman, uttering no words, dashed across the highway. Her wrapper flapped in the breeze as a van barely missed her; she moved adroitly between oncoming traffic and leaped gracefully onto the embankment, like a modern dancer. Once across, the woman too beckoned for Angie to come. The sun was like a laser aimed at Angie's face. The man, woman, and child appeared and reappeared between the whoosh of traffic and the relentless heat mingled with her terror, making her light-headed. Angie could no longer be sure: Was it Ella prodding her on? Was her sister telling her to come? Did she want Angie to join her? More cars flew by. *Come, come*. She looked straight ahead at the disappearing, reappearing woman. White dots floated across her vision. Yes, it was Ella! If she made it across, there her sister would be. The Buddhist chant Ella had taught her came to her. *Nam myoho renge kyo*. Angie threw her bags to the side of the road. She moved her shoulders in rhythm with *nam myoho renge kyo, nam myoho renge kyo.* Staring ahead, focused on Ella's face, she yelled: "I'm coming! I'm coming!" She counted: one, two, three . . .

Suddenly, a car swerved at her, so close spewing gravel hit her face with force. She jumped back. More cars passed at breakneck speed. She tried again, moving her shoulders in rhythm, but the chant in her head disappeared. The moment had died. She couldn't do it.

She waved to the others. They beckoned from across the highway, all three of them. She shook her head no, hoped they could see her gesture, knew they couldn't. She waved goodbye again. Exhausted from the effort, her legs untrustworthy, she sat on the highway's edge. Her face hurt. She hugged her knees. Soon enough the man and woman and boy moved on, shrinking figures making their way up the exit ramp. She thought the boy waved at her one last time.

She regretted her own fear. Yet the terror sat with her, an unmovable force as the sun loomed overhead. Parched, she longed for water. How long could she sit here before someone stopped to help? Even though it was barely midday, the thought of darkness forced her to rise. She grabbed her bags and ran along the road as traffic whipped past, and flying debris attacked her limbs. When she tired, she walked for several minutes, gravel crunching underfoot, duffel heavy. She ran again. And then she walked for an hour, more, another hour, resting briefly at intervals. The sun was a penetrating heat lamp. Her throat felt glued shut. She didn't know how much farther she could go. She looked out onto the oncoming traffic but terror kept her on the highway's edge, one foot in front of the other. Her hands dripped with sweat and the handle of her duffel kept sliding from her grip. Walk, rest. Walk, rest. Walk, rest.

Mercifully, she glimpsed a sign for the next exit. She hurried on, feeling blood drip down her legs and a welt forming on her face. Minutes later she was making her way clumsily up the exit ramp, its incline a small mountain under the weight of her bags.

She trudged to the first building she saw, a post office. She walked inside, the interior's dark coolness a relief. She headed straight for a nearby bench and collapsed. She closed her eyes and waited for her heartbeats to slow. In time she opened her eyes and searched until she spotted it; she stood and dragged her bag across the floor.

"I want to call the United States," she said to a young woman perched behind a desk. The woman had drawn-in, dramatic eyebrows. She handed Angie a scrap of paper and instructed her to write down the number she wanted to call. She pointed to a row of phone booths without doors and told Angie to enter number four. Inside was a large, gray telephone with no dials. Angie sat on the little wooden seat jutting out from the wall and watched as the woman attempted to make the connection from her main switchboard. Moments passed. The little booth was hot, stuffy. Finally, the woman arched her exaggerated eyebrows, nodded her head and said, "You can pick up now."

She picked up the receiver. "Hello, Mama?"

She could hear her words echoing back. There was a delay in the transmission, a beat before she heard her mother say, in a formal voice, "You have reached the Mackenzie residence. No one is in to take your call right now. Please leave a message after the beep."

When had her mother gotten an answering machine? A gift from Denise, no doubt. *Beeeeep!* The sound felt like an affront, jarring and discordant. Feeling the pressure, Angie opened her mouth to speak but nothing came out.

She hung up.

YABA

TWELVE

ANGIE WALKED THROUGH THE MAIN ENTRANCE OF THE UNIversity of Lagos, reporter's bag slung across her body, luggage heavy in her hand. Now she realized how little she'd known when she left home. Travelers to foreign lands carry backpacks, not American Tourister duffel bags. Large puddles were everywhere and it was hard to avoid them with her cumbersome load. She stood, surveyed the campus, grateful to be in a place with protective gates around it. She checked for the third time to make sure she had the piece of scrap paper on which Solo had written his uncle's name. She'd kept it tucked inside her journal. Yes, she still had it. "Dr. Aliko Diallo."

After her aborted call home, she'd sat inside the Ikeja post office for some time before this idea occurred to her. As she'd wiped away the blood from her legs and arms and nursed the face welt caused by flying gravel, she knew she lacked the energy to get herself back home. Traveling that far right now felt too overwhelming, like walking another three miles to an exit. Besides, she worried that her mother would be gone, literally moved on, and she'd find herself alone in an empty house. But she'd run out of places to follow Ella's path, and that hadn't worked out so well anyway. This was her last option, a place to just be, to rest before returning to Detroit.

She watched a plethora of African students strolling the walkways. This must be what it's like on a black college campus, she thought. Not just relegated to one table in the cafeteria, or the corridors of a Harambee House. Two tall young men passed by, clad in jeans, holding books.

"Excuse me!" She called out to them. "Can you tell me where the mass communications building is?"

"That is the building, sistah," said one of the young men, pointing to a wide structure yards away. "You are a new student?" he asked.

"Not quite," she said, rising slowly, gathering her bags, feeling the ache in her limbs.

"I am waiting for your admission, O!"

She smiled and made her way along a cobblestone path, hoping for the kindness of another stranger as she climbed the front steps of the building.

"Excuse me," she said to a young woman sitting at a front desk. "I'm looking for Professor Diallo."

"He's not here," said the young woman.

Disappointed, she dropped her heavy bag. "Do you know when he'll be back?"

"He is on holiday."

"Holiday?" Angie's voice rose slightly. "You mean he's on vacation?"

The young woman looked at Angie's bruised cheek, wild hair. "Who are you, please?"

"I'm a friend of his nephew's, from America."

"So you will come back."

"When?"

"In two weeks."

"Two weeks?" Every part of her body hurt. "I can't wait until then."

The young woman, clearly seeing her desperation, said,

"There is an American mass communications professor in his office. Maybe he can help you reach Dr. Diallo."

Angie blinked. "Yes, please."

The secretary nodded her head toward a long hall. "The second door on the left," she said. "Knock first."

As Angie approached the door, she wiped her face, tried to smooth her wayward hair. She knocked.

"Enter!" said a male voice.

She opened the door. He sat behind a spacious, cluttered desk, head bent over something he was writing. "Be with you in a second," he said, not looking up.

She put her bag down and waited, could see the top of the man's head. The office was sparse, with a few papers push-pinned to a corkboard and little else.

After several seconds he looked up. Their eyes locked. He rose so quickly his chair fell over. He picked it up without taking his eyes off her. "Angie?"

"I can't believe it's you," she said.

As soon as she spoke, Nigel moved out from behind his desk, toward her. They hugged. His strong arms felt as they had back when she was a little girl, and he'd scooped her up. Strong and reassuring.

He held her at arm's length. "Wow. Talk about a surprise."

He looked the same—those soft gray eyes and widow's peak. His hair was shorter now, but nothing else about him had changed in four years.

"I can't believe it's you," she said again.

He closed the door and gestured for her to sit. He sat on his desk, hands clasped between his legs. Now that he was so close she could feel him staring at the welt on her face. She braced herself but he didn't ask about that. Instead he asked, "What in the hell are you doing *here*?"

"Here?" She repeated. She had the sensation of watching

herself from outside her body and it made her mind go blank.

"Here! Nigeria!"

"Oh. I just wanted to come," she said. She fell back in the chair. "I graduated from college in May, so I thought, you know, I'd do this for myself."

He leaned back. "Riiiight! You would be coming out of college about now. U of M too, yes?"

"No. I transferred to Wayne State."

He nodded quickly. She didn't need to say why. "So how did you make your way to UNILAG?" he asked.

"I ran into this guy back in Detroit, Solo? Remember him?"

"Ah, yeah, of course. How is brother Solo?"

"He's fine. He told me to look up his uncle when I got here, so—"

"And you didn't even know I was teaching here?"

"Not until Brenda told me."

"You've met Brenda?"

"I stayed with her and Chris for a few days; I met Lola too."

He shook his head. "Wow, so you've met the old gang. OK."

"Brenda told me your semester was over and you were gone already, so I didn't expect—"

"Yeah, I'm headed back to Kenya soon."

"You look the same," she said.

"You've grown up," he said, grinning. "Little Angie!"

"You think?" She felt acutely aware of how she looked, wished she'd ducked into a restroom before.

"Tell me, how's your mom?" he asked.

"She's OK. Thinking of moving to Atlanta, actually."

"Really? Wow, that's a big change."

"That's what I thought too."

"Well, change is good."

She shrugged. "I guess."

He folded his arms. "So does she still hate me?"

Angie frowned. "Is that what you think?"

"If she does, I don't blame her."

She felt odd, as though she needed to defend her mother, and at the same time, reassure Nigel. "She never mentions you, actually."

He nodded, as if to say, *That's fitting.* "And Denise? How's she doing?"

"She already lives in Atlanta," said Angie. "She sells pharmaceuticals. Seems to love it."

"I can totally see that! She was always a go-getter." He paused. "So yeah, that makes sense your mom would wanna move there. And you? You joining them?"

"Never." She shivered from the thought. "I don't like the South."

He leaned back as if the velocity of her response had struck him. "I hear you."

"So tell me about you," she said. She swept her arm across the air. "How'd you end up doing this?"

He told her that after *The Voice* folded—she noticed he was careful not to mention Ella's name—he became a freelance reporter for the *International Herald Tribune,* filing stories from different African countries. "I did that nonstop for nearly three years," he said. "And then this job offer came and I figured it might be nice to sit still for a minute, do the academic thing. And to, uh, do something a little more lasting."

That word *lasting* stung. When they'd heard he was "traveling around the world as a foreign correspondent" she assumed that he was off living a carefree, jet-setting life. Of course that would include women. Still, it was hard to hear it from him directly, the obvious fact that he'd moved on. "So you're married?" she blurted out. "With kids?"

"No, no, no," he said. "Not that."

He pulled a pack of cigarettes from his shirt's breast pocket.

Benson & Hedges. He offered her one. She shook her head. "Good," he said. "Don't start."

She waited.

He lit his cigarette, pulled on it, exhaled. "I've started a fellowship in Ella's name."

Angie leaned back in her chair. The ache she felt just from hearing him say her name was astonishing. "A fellowship?"

He nodded. "Yeah. 'The Ella Mackenzie Fellowship for Black American Female Journalists.' It's funded by the university, and allows a black woman to come here from the States, work for Nigerian media, cover women's issues. All expenses paid."

Hearing Ella's name in the title of an award felt long lasting, yet so finite. She didn't know whether to feel pride or sadness. "How come you didn't tell us about it?"

"I was going to, believe me. I was. I thought I should tell you guys in person, you know? We just awarded our first fellow this year. I'd planned to come home for Christmas, figured I'd tell you guys then."

"Can I meet her? The fellow?"

"You will."

"Thank you for doing that Nigel."

"Please don't thank me." He ran his hand down his face, and she remembered the gesture from back in the day. "It was the least I could do," he said. "She was, well I don't have to tell you, she was Ella, you know?"

She nodded. She did know.

"What no one could've known is what a damn good journalist she was."

"So I heard." She hated that she'd missed out completely on Ella's brief, brilliant life's work, except for a newspaper clipping or two. It was a cruel fact.

Nigel leaned over, touched her face gingerly. "What happened?"

His finger felt cool, comforting, and she closed her eyes, put her own hand over his. "Minor accident," she said.

"I'm sorry for your accident," he said, "But I'm glad it was minor."

THEY WALKED THE short distance to his campus flat, Nigel carrying her heavy bag as a light drizzle fell. His building was a modern wonder, not unlike a waffle, with its weave of tan columns crossing against white ledges. They climbed three flights and when he swung open his door, she liked what greeted her. It was small and cozy, a cross between a college dorm room and an expat's home. A two-room flat with a small kitchenette, the space had two posters on the wall—one of W.E.B. Du Bois, another an iconic image of Stokely Carmichael. A hand-woven prayer blanket lay across the back of a wooden rocking chair, and two big, colorful wicker baskets sat in the corner. The back wall had one large window that framed a lovely view of the Lagos Lagoon.

"Nice!" She went to the window, looked past the raindrops to a small park below, tucked behind the administrative building, just where the campus ended.

"University sits on the edge of the lagoon," explained Nigel, coming up behind her. "They call that area the lagoon front. Best thing about UNILAG."

She stumbled as she made her way to the sofa, plopped down.

"You OK?" he asked.

"Tired. It's been quite a journey to get here."

"Did you come here straight from Chris and Brenda's?"

She shook her head. "I was staying with this woman, Funke, who—"

"The Funke Ella stayed with? In Surulere?"

"Yes."

From his expression, she couldn't tell whether he felt sorry for her or freaked out by her itinerary.

"Rest," he said finally. "In this place, you learn to do one big thing a day. I can tell you've done yours."

"And then some."

"Well, you're here now. You can chill." He moved toward the door. "I've got to get back to the office, handle a few things, and then we'll go have some lunch, OK? Make yourself at home." He turned back. "It's so good to see you, Angie."

After he'd left, she took a long shower, dabbing at her leg and arm wounds. She couldn't believe her luck. She'd found Nigel. Now, everything she'd been through—her back-to-back ordeals—felt worth it. Right away, a bone-deep exhaustion took over, as if finally able to exert itself now that she didn't have to fend for herself every second. Now she could collapse. And when she lay across Nigel's bed, she fell with abandon into a hard sleep.

She awoke to darkness. She had that eerily familiar feeling of not knowing where she was. Snippets came back to her; she wondered how much had been a dream, how much was real. She got up, opened the bedroom door. Nigel was sitting at the little table, smoking. It hadn't been a dream. Thank God.

"Hello Sleeping Beauty," he said, grinning.

She smiled, ecstatic.

"I see Lagos has worn out your ass." He chuckled. "Welcome to Eko!"

She laughed, happier than she'd been since she'd arrived in Lagos. Since before that, even. She couldn't even remember when.

AS THEY TOOK the short ride from Yaba to Ebute-Metta, she could feel him stealing glances at her in the backseat of the taxi. She could've caught him with her eyes, but didn't. She sensed him conjuring fragments of a past that included her and she didn't want to break the spell.

Stepping into the Mainland Hotel lobby was like entering a sanctuary—with its hushed sound of feet against shiny tiled floors and cool, air-conditioned interior. No sun, no bugs, no humidity.

Apart from the waitstaff and some Nigerian businessmen huddled at the bar, Nigel and she were the only blacks in the room. Men glanced their way. The waiters wore white shirts with white towels draped across their arms as they carried around pitchers of water, refilling glasses. It reminded Angie of an upscale restaurant in midtown Atlanta that Denise once told her about. The Mansion was an actual former plantation house, and Denise said you felt odd the whole time you ate there, watching black servants tend to white customers. And you.

Nigel ordered fish stew with boiled yams and greens for both of them. And lager. When the drinks arrived, Nigel raised his glass. "To the wonders of coincidence!"

"Maybe it's our karma," she said, giddy with gratitude. She took a big gulp of the lager. It was bitter; she frowned from the taste.

"Uh-oh, too strong?"

"Just different," said Angie. "I'll get used to it."

His face broke into a wide smile. "This is exactly how I remember you. So game, so willing to hang."

"Yeah?" Angie loved hearing that. Their food arrived and with it a cosmopolitan feeling that had escaped her throughout this trip. I am here with Nigel, she told herself. Having yams and fish stew in a nice restaurant in Lagos.

"Seriously. I have such vivid memories of you at those base-ment parties," continued Nigel. "You were so young, how old? Like eleven? Twelve? You could've been a tattletale, you know? Or whiny. Or scared. But you weren't. You were such a little trooper. And you saw a lot." He cut into his fish. "Too much maybe."

"I don't think of it that way," she said. "I'm glad I had that time with you guys. With her."

He touched her hand. "I'm sorry I said that. It's just, well—"

"It's OK." She thought of the last time she'd seen Ella, of her waving goodbye from the boarding gate. How healthy and assured she looked. And how nervous Angie was, praying silently for a safe flight. Her relief when she got Ella's first letter.

They ate in silence. The yams were delicious and the lager was improving. She sipped from her beer. It gave her courage. More silence as they ate. Suddenly, she put down her fork. "Nigel, tell me about that night."

"That night?"

"You know. When It happened."

Pain moved across his face, the look Angie had seen when their eyes met at the funeral, before he disappeared. He took a huge gulp of his lager. "I was away when it happened. In Guinea, interviewing Kwame Ture."

"You mean Stokely Carmichael?" The name conjured images of Ella back in the day, listening to his recorded speeches as she rolled her hair with twisted pieces of a brown-paper bag, attempting to get the right amount of Afro curl.

He seemed grateful for the interruption. "Yeah. Cool, right? I knew he was living in exile there, and since I was the cross-cultural correspondent of *The Voice*, I decided to do this profile of him. He'd married a Guinean, had a new son, so I thought it would make for a great piece." He took more swigs, grimaced as though the beer gave him heartburn. "As soon as I got back to Lagos, I heard she'd been hit by a car." He paused, avoided Angie's eyes. "I called your mother, took care of things."

"When did you get back?" asked Angie.

He drained his beer mug, put it down with a thud, wiped his mouth with the back of his hand. He was sweating. "The day after. January second."

"What I don't understand, what I've always wondered, is why didn't you spend New Year's Eve with her?"

Angie had spent that very night hearing jazz at Baker's Keyboard Lounge with her new boyfriend Romare. He was from Grand Rapids, and she was a woman in love. He knew everything about jazz, kept reminding her that Baker's was the oldest jazz club in the world. He knew all the major acts that had performed there. The club was celebrating its fiftieth anniversary and its house pianist, Claude Black, was phenomenal. That night, as free champagne flowed, she decided with an eighteen-year-old's devotion that she'd become a jazz lover too. She saw their lives together, in clubs, at festivals, on plush sofas with faded LPs spread out at their feet. After they got the news, she called Romare, told him; he was kind in that formal way people are when a loved one dies. Said, "Wow, I'm sorry for your loss." But he didn't come to the funeral, and when next they spoke he said, "I hope you're not going to become really needy now that your sister is dead." After that, she avoided his calls. Soon enough, he stopped calling. She abandoned jazz too, because it reminded her too much of frivolity, as if the intricate music itself had distracted her, caused her to lose focus, be off guard, let the unthinkable happen.

"I wanted to be with her on New Year's Eve, but it was complicated," said Nigel.

Angie studied his face closely. She took a final sip of lager. "Did you have a fight?"

"What made you ask that?"

"In one of her letters, she said you two were cooling it, doing your own thing. That's how she put it."

"That was true."

"And then Chris told me that you two broke up all the time."

"Oh yeah? What the fuck does he know?" Nigel pulled out a cigarette, lit it, took a hard pull, exhaled. It came back to her now, the memory of how he pursed his lips as smoke passed through. "That Nigerian nigger don't know shit."

She wanted to tell him what Chris had done to her, but something stopped her.

She pushed the wilted greens around on her plate. "So that's not true?" she pressed. "You and Ella didn't split up a lot?"

"No. Like I said, we were planning to spend New Year's together. It just didn't work out."

"Why not?"

"Because of the coup."

"The coup?"

He stopped mid-puff. "You do know there was a coup that New Year's Eve?"

"Chris did mention that." Details she'd suppressed came back. "And I remember my mother saying it got in the way of her handling arrangements when she came. But I didn't think Ella was affected by it. Not as an American. And it was bloodless, right? Doesn't that mean basically a change of government?"

"For one, it wasn't completely bloodless," said Nigel. "And we were *all* affected. The military imposed a curfew for a few days. You couldn't move around freely."

"So you two couldn't get to each other?"

"It was hard." He sucked on his cigarette as though it gave him strength. "Everything was hard."

Angie could tell she was exhausting him, but she couldn't

stop. "Why didn't you say anything to me at the funeral? Why'd you just leave?"

"I apologize for that. It's just . . . I don't know, the look your mother gave me . . . I couldn't bear to face you guys afterward. I just had to get out of there."

"And you never called, to check on us or anything."

"I called once."

"You did? I never knew that."

He nodded. "Your mom thanked me for helping her out when she came here to . . . to get Ella. But I could tell she didn't want to hear from me any more after all that. And that was just as well." He paused. "I really went through a rough time."

She dropped her fork and it clanked against the plate. "*You* went through a rough time? How do you think we were doing?"

He tapped cigarette ashes into his plate of half-eaten food. "I can't imagine."

It was days and then weeks and then months of loneliness. That's what she remembered most, being lonely. And assaulted by memories. She couldn't go anywhere without a reminder. In a desperate move to escape, she'd returned to the University of Michigan against her mother's wishes, determined to finish college there. But that first day back, she'd gone to visit Ella's Afro-American studies professor, Dr. Jordan, and he'd said, "I've taken care of everything; your transcripts have been sent to Wayne State. Of course you'd want to be close to home right now." She'd felt a deep dread as she made her way back to the city that very night, a failed fugitive from grief.

"Why are you really here?" asked Nigel.

She pushed away her plate. "*Why* does everyone keep asking me that?"

"I guess because coming to Nigeria just seems like a painful, almost cruel thing to do to yourself."

"I'm here because I feel cheated." As soon as she said it, she realized it was true. "I nursed her back to health for a whole year and then when she was doing better, she left me." Angie looked up at Nigel. "Came here with you. I never got to be with her at her best, never got to be with the new and improved Ella." She realized for the first time that she was angry at Ella. And Nigel. "That wasn't fair. I want to know what I missed."

Nigel touched the top of her hand. To steady it? She was shaking slightly. "Know this. She thrived working for *The Voice*. The paper gave her a purpose in life, and she thrived."

Angie felt herself sliding quickly from anger into an alcohol-induced sadness, unconvinced by Nigel's claim. "Yeah, but was she *happy?*"

"Believe that she was, Angie." He put out his cigarette, squashing it so hard that pieces of loose tobacco fell onto his plate. "That's what I tell myself."

She stared at Nigel and he met her gaze. A connective thread pulled taut between them.

Later, just as they pulled up to Nigel's waffle-style flat, the sky opened and a torrential rain came down. He gave her his jacket and she threw it over her head as they ran into the building, the raindrops like salve against her tender limbs.

THIRTEEN

THEY MADE THEIR WAY WITH RELATIVE EASE THROUGH THE Saturday morning traffic. Nigel had decided Angie should see some of the city's attractions, tourist-style. "Not that there's any such thing as a damn tourist in Lagos," he noted.

Angie felt good—rested and content. Nigel had given her his bed and he'd slept on the futon in the living room. She'd had the best sleep of her entire trip. Now she was wearing her favorite crinkly Indian skirt, and the wind from the open window whipped through her new braids. The desperate, lonely traveler of the past twelve days, the young woman who got herself into dangerous situations, was gone. Today she felt experienced, more self-assured. She'd gotten what she came for without even knowing what she was looking for: she'd found Nigel.

She studied his profile openly now. She'd been afraid before, as if staring at him too closely would make him disappear. He was as handsome as she remembered, with his strong chin and long, little-boy lashes. But she could see halos of darkness beneath his light eyes, and hard parentheses at the corners of his mouth that hadn't been there before.

They crossed the bridge and rode alongside the Lagos Lagoon. Victoria Island's skyline of sculptured high-rises greeted them. Lush greenery framed gray buildings and twin fountains sprayed water into an overcast sky. A large puzzle piece of a park sat in the center. The taxi cruised along the coastline; Angie inhaled the husky aromas of the Atlantic Ocean as palm trees swayed along its wide avenue, huge sign announcing its name, "Ahmadu Bello Way." Mansions stood facing the water.

"It's almost like we're not in Lagos anymore," she said. "It's so pretty."

"This is where all the *ogas*, all the big men, live," explained Nigel. "They rob the country's coffers, then build mansions on the water. But the coastline is eroding and one day, these houses are all gonna fall into the ocean." He looked out at the line of massive homes. "And it serves those motherfuckers right."

Angie turned from the window to look at him. "That's harsh."

"When you've seen as much poverty and disease and starvation as I have, you get like this," he said. "The corruption, the goddamn greed, drives me nuts."

She could imagine Ella's outrage matching his, could see them both appalled, bound by their sense of injustice.

He pointed to a formidable building, the US Embassy. Its American flag whipped around in the breezes coming off the water and Angie was comforted by it, which surprised her because she never put her hand over her heart when she said the Pledge of Allegiance in school. Ella had taught her that tiny protest. She suddenly remembered that Denise had insisted she register her presence here. She didn't need to now.

Near the embassy stood sleek, tall apartment buildings. "Most foreigners—your diplomats and UN workers and journalists—stay out here," said Nigel. "Of course Vic Island has the finest restaurants and hotels and clubs. There's a whole expat scene, just waiting for you."

It did seem inviting. She fantasized about staying in Nigeria for a while, maybe even a year. What was waiting for her back at home? She hadn't applied to graduate school, hadn't interviewed for any jobs, hadn't figured out what she wanted to do. As graduation day approached, it had gnawed at her, that lack of knowing, the lack of any real passion. She realized she'd hoped that coming here would somehow define that passion for her. Detroit itself, her old life, seemed like a remote place from a former existence. If she stayed here, she could work at the UN. Or the embassy. Or teach, like Brenda once did. Or yes, report for a Western newspaper, like Nigel. She could do this. Live on Vic Island, be an expat.

She turned to say these things to Nigel, found him staring at her, brazen. "What?"

"Did you know she had her hair braided like that?"

Angie nodded. "Do you like it?" She instantly regretted the question.

"It's nice." He turned from her and looked out his window.

The driver dropped them along an embankment and they crossed a walkway to Bar Beach. The sun hid behind clouds and yet the ocean still sparkled. The beach was nearly deserted, except for small clusters of foreign beachgoers. They hovered on their blankets, these white men and women, skin sunburned bright red. Their body language had none of the matter-of-fact entitlement Angie was used to. It was quite the opposite, as if they didn't want to occupy too much space. In contrast, Nigerian men strolled confidently along the sand, their arms filled with wares—baskets and ivory and batiks. Raffia huts sat back, away from the beach's edge.

They plopped down in a spot close to the shoreline. Nigel spread out his long legs, leaning back on his arms. Angie did the same. She watched the froth rise up off the ocean, curdling like a giant foaming mouth before it tumbled backward, only to rise again.

She slipped off her sandals, crossed her legs at the ankle. "This is nice."

Nigel nodded, eyes distant. He looked unmoored, as though he were drifting away with the tide. She wanted to bring him back. "I could see why you and Ella wanted to come here, to Nigeria I mean."

Nigel's neck muscles jumped. "We didn't really choose Nigeria," he said. "Not at first, anyway. This is where FESTAC took place, so this is where we came."

"Tell me about the festival," she said. "Of course, Ella told us about it when she got back, and I read a little bit about it too, but—" Angie paused, told the truth. "I just want to hear you talk about it."

He smiled. "It was amazing. Just to think, celebrations went on for twenty-nine days! We were only here for about ten of them, but we did *a lot*. You really couldn't choose between the films and art exhibits and the music and the theater performances. It was insane! We'd be out all day, then return to FESTAC village and party all night." He laughed. "You have never seen so many platform shoes in your life." Nigel said the best part for him was the Colloquium. "Every day, the leading black scholars from all over the world got together and read papers, then got into hot debates over a range of shit—religion, literature, history. That was my kind of scene. I loved it."

"And for the closing ceremonies, you guys saw Miriam Makeba perform, right?"

He nodded vigorously. "Yeah, I'm so glad we got to see her. That woman's voice is crazy powerful and just, hmph, gives you chills." He shook his head. "We almost missed it too, because by day four or five, we decided to break off from all the official shit on the agenda, get away from that fake village, and just go off on our own."

"Where'd you go?"

"Everyone was talking about the country's most popular musician, Fela, how he was boycotting FESTAC, refused to be part of a corrupt government-sponsored festival, right? Turns out, he was having his own counter-festival at his club. Ella was like 'I want to go there!' She kept saying it, 'I want to go there.' Seeing how determined she was to check out Fela turned me on, I ain't gonna lie. Other folks in our little group, they were scared to travel on their own. You know, dangerous roads and all that. But she was game! Got me to climb into one of those *danfos*—I remember the damn thing rode on two wheels all the way there."

"I rode in one of those things!" Angie interjected. "Crazy."

"Yeah?" He paused. "Well, somehow we found the Shrine. Ah man! It was the shit! You have never seen anything like it. We went back every night."

Angie thought of Fela's frenetic, hypnotic music racing out at her as she drove around in her car. "I saw him perform you know."

Nigel turned to her. "Where? In Detroit?"

"Yep." She was so proud of herself. "At the Fox. Last November. He was amazing!"

Nigel whistled. "A lot has changed in Detroit, I guess."

"Not really," said Angie. She wished she hadn't interrupted. "Go on, tell me more about the Shrine."

"Well, it was a cool scene. We got to meet Fela, in between all the celebrities and dignitaries who came through. On that last night we were there, damned if Stevie Wonder didn't show up! And Sun Ra! They were in Lagos for the official festival but they wanted to check out Fela too, man. Everybody did." Nigel threw his head back. "Shit was mind blowing."

Angie tried to picture the scene. Instead, her mind landed on a memory of herself, her mother, and Denise hanging onto every word as Ella gave them a blow-by-blow account of her trip, the dining room radiator hissing in the background.

"I want to go to the Shrine," she announced.

"That old one is gone," said Nigel. "It was in a hotel courtyard but—"

"I know. I heard. But Fela built a new one, right?"

His shoulders rose and fell in a sigh. "Yeah, he had to. Government burned down the first one. And not only that, a week after FESTAC, soldiers raided his compound and raped the women, destroyed his master recordings, and threw his mother out a window. His mother died from her injuries."

"My God," whispered Angie.

"Yeah. And it was clearly retaliation because he refused to perform at *their* festival. They say that really changed Fela. I've been to the new Shrine many times, and the vibe is different now believe me. Not like back in '77."

Angie uncrossed her legs, sat up. "So, I missed that great moment too?"

"What great moment?"

She threw her arms out. "All of it. The festival, Fela's original Shrine, Stokely. I mean Kwame Ture . . ." She dropped her arms. "I feel like I was born too late."

"Everyone feels that way," offered Nigel. "When I sat there listening to Brother Kwame, hearing about the intensity of the sixties, I felt like I was born too late. But then again, look at Kwame. He's dying."

"What?"

"Prostate cancer. And he'll tell you straight up—living through the movement, always up against the Man, all that stress, fearing for his life, forced to live in exile? He says that's what put disease in his body."

"But he got to do what he believed in," said Angie.

"But was it worth the price?"

"Maybe it was."

"I don't think he feels that way."

"Anyway, I never even got to make that decision."

Nigel's voice was kind. "This is a cliché, but it's true: you've got your whole life ahead of you."

"I just wish I'd been at that festival," she said, wistful. "All those black people from all those different countries, from the *diaspora*," she sang the word—"all in one place. For the first time! I just wish I'd seen it."

"It was great. But it was also a mess," he said. "People died at the festival's opening ceremonies."

"I never read that." Angie was skeptical.

Nigel nodded, lips pressed together. "Yup. Nigeria built this massive arts theatre just for the festival. I'm sure you've passed it on the bridge coming from the mainland. Shaped like a big military hat?"

She did remember, the sombrero building.

"Well, it could only seat sixty thousand people. More than one hundred thousand tried to get in. Folks got stampeded to death. You can believe that choice fact didn't make it into all those gushing news stories."

She could see what he was trying to do, refused to allow him. "That was an unfortunate accident, but that doesn't mean—"

"That was poor planning, pure and simple."

She wasn't going to let him ruin it for her. "And still, admit it. Being at the festival changed your life."

He thought about it. "It opened up my world."

"Then it changed your life."

He chuckled. "Good point."

"I remember that time so clearly," said Angie, triumphant. "When you guys got back, you two were inseparable. You were so in love."

He kept his eyes on the water. "We were. Young and in love."

"Meeting like that at the festival, that had to be romantic in itself."

"Oh that's not how we met. I had a class with her."

"Really? I never knew that."

"Yeah."

She waited, but Nigel didn't go on.

"So, tell me!" she insisted.

"I had an anthro class with her," he began. "I'd noticed her before then at a couple student protests, but she was so quiet, shy even, that I hadn't really paid her much attention." On the day of the midterm in anthro, he'd come rushing up to the building, late, and saw her standing outside smoking. With no coat on. And he thought that was the oddest sight, because it was one of those windy-cold October days in Ann Arbor. She was just casually puffing away, yet shivering, and he had this sudden urge to take off his leather jacket and give it to her. He asked her why she wasn't inside taking the exam.

"I want to see if I can do the test in the last twenty minutes," she said.

That blew him away. As he went inside to take the test himself, he kept anticipating her coming through the door. Sure enough, twenty minutes left, she entered. After he finished his exam, he waited, and when she turned hers in, he followed her out. She walked fast but he caught up and asked her how she thought she did on the midterm.

Ella shrugged. "I finished it," she said, like *that* was the important thing.

"Hey, would she like to go for a drive?" Ella shrugged, said "OK." They walked to his car and left campus, cruising along the cutesy shops on the town's main street. She smoked and so did he. With the heat blasting and the windows up, the car turned into a warm, foggy capsule. "This place bores me," she announced.

He asked her where she wanted to go. She said to the racetrack. He wasn't expecting *that* and he laughed. She cut her eyes at him, asked what was so funny? He said it was just that he never had a girl tell him she wanted to go bet on horses. And she said she didn't *bet* on the racehorses; she rode them. And Nigel said, "You?" She asked him what was so hard to believe about that? And he said that well for one thing jockeys are men aren't they? And aren't they like, small?

"Are you suggesting I'm too big to be a jockey?" she asked.

No, no he insisted. He didn't mean anything by it.

But she told him, "I'll prove it. Take me to Hazel Park Raceway right now."

All the way in Detroit? He asked her. She said yes. So he decided what the hell? He drove the forty-five miles and when they got there, the front-gate guard actually knew Ella, said how good it was to see her again. He let them in even though the track was closed and she walked him along the barns. The air smelled like Vicks VapoRub. She turned, walked down a row of stalls, stopped in front of one, and said, "This is where my father dropped dead."

She told him how she and her father had been prepping Baby's Breath, his prize horse and how hopeful he was that the horse would win, how he had a heart attack after she'd stepped away for a while, how she found him there, dead, when she returned.

Angie felt a chill from the ocean's breeze. She kept quiet.

When he heard that story, he wanted to get out of there, felt that was not a good place for them to be, but Ella suddenly asked if he wanted to ride one of the horses. He said 'Can you do that?" and the look on her face was so tragic that he quickly said sure, let's do it, even though he'd never been on a horse in his life. He watched her go up to one, a dark horse, pet his nose.

"You're a good boy, I can tell," she said.

She led the horse out of the stall, saddled him, and slowly guided him out of the barn. Nigel followed as she walked the horse to the large, silent racetrack. The sight both awed and frightened Nigel. It was so quiet and, with the overhead lights off, eerily dark. She stuck her foot in the stirrup, hopped up, swung her other leg around, and mounted the horse. She held her hand out to him and even though Nigel was terrified— how could the horse see a damn thing?—he got on behind her. The animal stumbled, perhaps from all the weight and he envisioned the worst: the horse would break a leg, they'd be stuck out here, the police would find them, arrest them for stealing and hell, worse, causing the death of the damn thing. Plus, it was cold! But Ella crouched low and kept talking to the horse and before he knew it, they were gliding around the track. He held her around the waist and felt the air rushing past him, the exhilaration of the animal's muscles moving beneath his thighs. They went around halfway, not too fast. And then she sped up the horse and they galloped around the rest of the track. It felt liberating.

Ella led the horse back to the barn, where they dismounted and she quietly returned him to his stall. She gave the horse water to drink and a few oats and kissed him between his ears.

"Thank you, whatever your name is," she said.

And right there, Nigel moved in and kissed her. She kissed him back and everything about her, about this moment, excited him. They fell back in the hay and kissed some more. Finally, he took her hand and pulled her up. "Should we go back to campus?" he asked as they walked to his car.

"Not tonight," she said.

He asked if she wanted to go home and she said absolutely not.

"What do you want to do?" he asked.

"Get a room."

She told him how to drive to Woodward Avenue at Six Mile, and they checked into a motel, returned to Ann Arbor the next morning.

Waves made their way lazily up to the shore. "So you were already together when you went to the festival," Angie said quietly. She was hurt that Ella hadn't ever told her that story—especially the part about being on a horse again. "She never even mentioned you until she got back from her trip."

"We liked being a secret," explained Nigel. "I had a girlfriend at the time, and there was a little overlap there for a minute; I admit that. But once we went on the trip, hell, it was clear to me this was the woman I wanted to be with." He paused, smiling. "And we had a nice run there, me and Ella. For about a year or so, it was good. It was damn good."

She wished the story stopped there; but she pushed herself to probe, to get him to tell the ugly part. "So what happened with you two?"

"I think you know what happened."

"What?" she insisted.

Nigel stared at the ocean. "Drugs happened."

"You got her into all that, didn't you?"

He turned to her. "Is that what you think?"

"Didn't you?"

He turned his attention back to the shore, its groggy waves. "We got each other into all that."

"Then you dumped her and that was when it all got worse," insisted Angie. "I remember. That was when she overdosed."

"I didn't dump her."

Angie studied Nigel as he sat up, pushed his hand into the sand, let it pour through his fingers. "I think you did," she said.

"Believe what you want, but I'm telling you that's not what happened."

"Then what *did* happen?"

Nigel shook his head. "We were fine until we stared snorting smack up our noses. Suddenly we had to feed our habit and shit got crazy. We got wilder with the shoplifting and all kinds of illegal shit—busting scripts, forging checks, boosting."

Angie remembered that back room in Nigel and Ella's apartment, all those supple leather purses piled on the bed, price tags still attached.

"It all got to be too much," continued Nigel. "I made her go home. We lost our place, anyway. I think we both were trying not to drown, you know?" He hesitated. "We didn't talk to each other for a couple months. I figured she was still snorting. When I heard she'd overdosed, I couldn't believe it. We never shot up, that was our rule, so I was really shocked. I called just to check on her, you know? We decided to hook up, see each other again, go from there."

"I remember that," said Angie. "She wore my mother's blue leather coat on a so-called date with you."

He winced. "I helped her pawn that coat."

"My mother said that's what happened."

The sun had pushed through the clouds, now shone across Nigel's face. "That was when I learned that yeah, she was shooting up. And she made it sound incredible. I'll be honest. We did it together that night." He squinted against the sun. Or the memory. "It was a bad scene though. She got sick, I got sick. I think we had some bad shit. The next day, I begged her to go to Herman Kiefer, see a doctor. She wouldn't. But that was it for me. It scared my ass. I grew up around junkies. I quickly lost all romantic notions about shooting up. I stopped everything after that. Cold turkey. No more snorting shit. But Ella, she loved getting high. She told me, 'I'd rather die than stop.' That really fucked with me." He shook his head. "She was so greedy for it."

"You make her sound pathetic."

He shielded his eyes with his hand as he turned to her. "Come on, you know how she was."

"I just know that she spent the next three years hooked on heroin," said Angie. "And you didn't, apparently. But how would we know? Because you never even bothered to come back around."

Nigel kept his gaze on her, hand over his eyes like a salute. "What do you want me to say?"

Sweat tingled Angie's armpits. "I want you to say, 'I'm sorry I was able to kick the habit and she wasn't.' I want you to say, 'I'm sorry I got to go on with my life and she didn't.'"

He dropped his hand, squinted. "I can say I'm sorry, and believe me I am, but it's not gonna bring her back."

"That's mean." Angie suddenly rose, stalked up the beach; but her angry strides were hard to maintain in the sinking sand. The clouds had disappeared and the day's dose of sun bore down on her. She could feel the few beachgoers staring as she passed by. Wet beads rolled down her sides. She didn't know whether Nigel was behind her or not. She refused to turn around and look, kept going, sand hot and hard against her feet.

Nigel caught up with her, held her elbow. "Come on Angie, let's go back. It's getting too hot out here."

She wanted to stay angry but the heat was zapping her resolve. She wobbled a little.

He gripped her more tightly. "Let's get something to drink."

He guided her toward a vendor set up on the beach. The smell of something fried wafted toward them, carried by the ocean's breeze, making her hungry. Nigel bought them each a *puff-puff* and she tore gingerly into the doughy bun as they made their way back to their spot on the sand. Eating helped her mood. As she looked out onto the ocean, she breathed in its beauty: how the sun swooned over the water, creating dia-monds of shimmer. She'd never seen the Atlantic Ocean before. It stunned her anew that she was in Africa.

Once, at Wayne State's library, Angie had spread out an atlas and stared at the continent for a long time, country upon country sprawled before her, each in its own alluring, sinuous shape, each carrying an exotic name: Burkina Faso, Gabon, Mauritania, Sudan. She had no idea there were so many, and counted an astonishing fifty-four countries, including seven tiny islands dotting the waters around the continent. Hovering over that map, she traced her finger along the North African border, then along the eastern, Indian Ocean shoreline before running it across the continent to the western coast. Her finger paused. She traced Nigeria, so angular and large in comparison to the countries it bordered. Its shape reminded her of a rough-hewn heart. And now here she sat.

She stared out at the horizon. It pained her to confront that Africans had been pushed off from these very shores, made to travel like cargo in slave ships across the vast endlessness of the ocean. During the plane ride over, she'd read several chapters of *Beloved* and those haunting images of Sethe and her torture perched inside her mind, tenacious and unrelenting. "Can you even imagine the horrors of slavery?" she said.

"Yes and no. I've been to both Gorée Island and the slave pens in Ghana," said Nigel. "Seen the hovels they kept all those Africans in before they dragged them onboard."

"What were you thinking when you saw that?" she asked.

"Thank God our ancestors got on those fucking ships."

Angie frowned, incredulous. "How could you say that? That's horrible."

He kept his eyes on the ocean. "It's no more horrible than what Africans do to their own people."

"Nothing compares to hundreds of years of slavery, Nigel."

"Hmph. Who knows?" He squinted as if spotting one of those very slave ships making its way to shore. The waves rolled in, rolled out. Nigel nodded at the water. "This is where the military used to execute prisoners."

"Lola talked about that."

"Once a month on Sundays, they'd bring them out here, and while a crowd watched, they'd shoot them. They say their bodies would fall back with a thud onto the sand."

Angie imagined she could hear the "pop, pop" sound, dark men in prison attire dropping to their knees.

"It was a popular event too," said Nigel. "And they say that sometimes, you might sit here as we're doing, days later, enjoying the view, la dee da, and a body would wash up to the shore."

Angie closed her eyes against the image but it persisted, conflated with that of the dead woman she'd seen on the side of the highway.

"Do you think their souls are at peace?" she asked. "With their bodies floating out there?"

"I guess as much as those poor souls sold off by their own people, then thrown overboard during the Middle Passage."

She couldn't bear the image. "You're relentless, you know that?" she said. "I don't remember you being so jaded before."

"You were a child back then."

"So?"

"So, I was young too. We all were."

A hawker approached them, holding up a batik, his skinny arms stretched wide to accommodate its width. The batik was a series of monkeys—soft pink against a saturated indigo background. Each monkey was engaged in a different activity, one playing a horn, one drumming, one carrying a basket of fruit, one dancing. Each had the same eyes, pink dots of vivid expression.

"That's beautiful," she said.

"You want it?"

She'd given no thought to souvenirs. What would be her proof that she'd even come here? What would she have to prove it to herself? "Yes."

Nigel haggled with the man, got him down from the fifty naira he demanded to the twenty naira he reluctantly accepted. The hawker snatched the money, and then carefully folded the batik into a perfect square, handed it to Angie. "For you madam." He walked away quickly, in search of the next customer.

Angie opened up the batik, stared at the monkey playing the horn, ran her finger over the waxy image. "I'm going to Fela's club tonight," she announced.

"Oh no you're not," said Nigel. "That area's too dangerous."

"I don't care."

"Well, I care."

"I'm going," said Angie. "Tonight."

Clouds had rolled back in. "I haven't been there in years," said Nigel.

"I'll let you know how it is."

He looked at her, head tilted askew, as if unsure what to make of her. The clouds cast his face in half-shadow. "Are you a mirage?"

"I'm real," she answered.

His gaze held. She knew that he was seeing her anew, this brave young woman he'd once known as a little girl back in Detroit, traveling alone in Nigeria, finding him. She saw the admiration in his eyes.

"We shouldn't leave too late," he said.

FOURTEEN

IT WAS LATE AFTERNOON BY THE TIME THEY INCHED BACK to campus in bumper-to-bumper traffic.

"We'll come down here," Nigel told the taxi driver. "No way we'll get any closer to the entrance tonight."

As the two walked alongside the high fence guarding the university, they passed a line of Mercedes and Volvos and army jeeps snaking their way up to the main gates. Every car stereo seemed to be blasting Whitney Houston's "I Wanna Dance With Somebody." Angie watched as young women spilled out from the dormitories, overnight bags slung across their bodies, and ran to the idling vehicles. Girl inside, each made a dramatic U-turn, and headed off campus into the sun-setting twilight.

"*Acada* girls," said Nigel.

"Brenda told me about them," said Angie.

"*Ogas* whisking away their kept women for the weekend." Nigel nodded his head in that direction. "Notice all the god-damn government vehicles."

Angie watched the girls, thinking of the chances she'd missed to be whisked away from campus, of her commuter-college routine, its extended high-school feel. It made her want to remain at the University of Lagos for a while, to grasp at a life that had eluded her. She wished *she* could be the recipient of the "Ella Mackenzie Fellowship for Black American Female Journalists."

They made their way across campus to Nigel's flat. Angie walked behind him as they climbed the stairs. When he opened his front door, he stood still for a second. "Oh, hey!" he said. "I didn't know you'd be here."

"Surprise," said a woman's voice.

Angie approached the doorway. The woman sat at the little kitchenette table, a mug in front of her. Angie quickly took in her dark skin, short-cropped frizzy hair, and wide-spaced eyes. She smiled at Angie, revealing a gap between her front teeth. The smell of something sweet and banana-like permeated the air.

"This is Regina," said Nigel. Angie saw it in his face. His girlfriend. "Regina, Angie."

She and Nigel entered the flat as Regina stood. She was tall, and wore a West African-print crop top and jeans that Angie had sold a million times to curvy women, the kind Ella had brought with her to Nigeria. Angie felt her breaths becoming shallow.

"It's so great to finally meet you!" Regina said to her. "How was Bar Beach?"

"Good," said Angie, her voice cracking slightly. "Interesting."

"Filled with pathetic white folks trying to make the best of it," said Nigel, closing the door behind them, and stealthily moving away from the women.

"Come, sit," said Regina. She thrust her arm toward the table, like a tour guide. "Tea?"

Angie nodded, sat in one of the café-style chairs.

"I've been thinking of doing a piece on Bar Beach," continued Regina as she placed a kettle on the stove. "I want to focus on how it's all these different things, you know?" She used her fingers to count. "A place of commerce, a respite for foreigners, a hangout for the locals. And of course, a former execution spot."

Nigel had darted over to the tiny stereo set up on a snack tray; Angie followed him with her eyes. Why had he told her nothing? Not only did he have a girlfriend but she was a journalist *and* black American. *And* tall. *And* big boned. Really, Nigel? He rifled through cassette tapes piled into a woven basket. When he scratched his eyelid, another gesture she remembered from back then, she knew he was nervous and that made *her* feel strangely guilty.

"I got us some *dodo* from that little buka near campus," said Regina. "Have you had *dodo* yet?"

"No, not yet," said Angie.

"Oh, you're gonna love it! But it's only good if you eat it while it's hot, so I've been warming some in the oven." She lifted her chin toward the living room. "Baby, come on. Help me with this."

"Coming." Crouched in front of the cassette deck, he pushed a button, rose, and joined Regina in the little kitchen. Al Jarreau's jazz-tinged, soulful voice sang *I hardly had a bellyful* and sliced at Angie's heart. *Never knew a new bicycle.* Ella had played the same song that last night at home.

They stood side by side, their backs to Angie, arms touching. Unable to bear it, Angie got up, walked over to the room's big picture window, and looked down at the lagoon front. A few students lay sprawled alongside its tiny shore. It wasn't that she expected Nigel to stop living; she'd known for years that he'd gone on with his life. It was that she was being forced to bear witness to it, to see what could have been, *should* have been his life with Ella.

"We're all set," said Regina. Angie turned from the window and joined the other two at the small table with its three mugs, tea bags hanging out. In the center sat the diagonal slices of plantain, nestled on top of old newsprint. She could still make out the newspaper's name. *The Punch.* Lola's paper. The food's sweet aroma was strong. "Looks good," she said. What else could she say?

"Oh my God, it's *so* good!" said Regina. "The best thing about traveling is discovering yummy local food!"

Regina's enthusiasm oppressed Angie, reminded her of the young black women at Wayne State who stood before hallway bulletin boards, jotting down contact info for opportunities they planned to take full advantage of.

Nigel stuck his hand in to grab a plantain, and Regina lightly slapped it. "Wait for our guest!"

Nigel feigned embarrassment, placed a hand over his chest. "Sorry, no home training." He gestured toward Angie. "Please."

Angie sorrowfully speared a piece with her fork.

"Blow on it first before you bite into it," advised Regina. "It holds heat."

Angie blew as instructed, then bit into the *dodo*; the crunch of the outside contrasted perfectly with the soft sweet inside. "It is delicious," she offered.

"See?" said Regina. "I told you!"

"I'll take some fried plantain over all that pounded yam and *fufu* any day," said Nigel.

Angie kept quiet. She said nothing about the local food at Funke's that hadn't agreed with her. She'd planned to tell Nigel everything that had happened to her in Lagos, including Chris's assault and the harrowing walk along the expressway. Not anymore.

Regina poured hot water into their mugs, holding the top of the pot with her index finger. Angie noticed how long her fingers were, felt a rush of relief that the third one on her left hand, the finger Ella had lost, was devoid of a ring. As they ate, Regina asked Angie about her time in Nigeria. Angie told her about staying with Funke, prompting a peppering of Regina's reporter questions: What kind of home did she have? What food did she cook? Did she seem to have a hard life?

"And before that you stayed with Chris and Brenda Olapade," said Regina.

Did she want Angie to know that *she* knew? "Yes, I did."

"I've met Chris," said Regina. "In passing."

Nigel cut his eyes at Regina. She met his gaze. "What?"

"Yeah," said Angie. "Chris told me all about how Ella and Nigel worked with him at *The Voice.*" There, she'd put Ella's name in the room.

"She was amazing," said Regina. She paused. "I heard she was amazing."

Nigel looked at Angie for the first time since they'd arrived at the flat. His sad eyes flickered, the color of wet granite.

Regina quickly looked back and forth between Nigel and Angie. She put her hand atop Angie's. Her fingertips pressed down, warm from her mug. "I'm really sorry about your sister."

Angie felt a sudden melancholy, the same feeling she had when people in Detroit came up to her and offered condolences, as if her very being showcased loss. It made her feel exposed and disheartened that this most private of things in the world, her personal grief, couldn't be felt without public scrutiny. She always wished she could keep it a secret from others. She felt that way now. But of course Regina knew. Everyone knew. Ella's death was, Angie understood, the thing that defined her. *That girl who died in Africa? That's her little sister.*

They carried their mugs over to the small living room. Al Jarreau sang on. *But we got by, Lord knows we got by.* Regina and Angie sat on the sofa, Nigel in the rocking chair.

"So what's next on your agenda?" asked Regina, curling her feet up under her body. "What else do you plan to see?"

Angie cradled her mug in both hands. "I'm going to Fela's club tonight."

Regina's eyes widened. "Not alone, I hope!"

"If I need to, I will."

"There's no way in hell I'd let you do that," said Nigel.

"Nigel's totally right," said Regina. "We'll go with you." She sipped her tea.

"You'll come?" Nigel asked, incredulous.

Regina looked at him from over her mug. "Is that a problem?"

"I'm just surprised, since you hate his music."

"I do, but I think it'll make a great feature story. I'm sure I could sell it to *Ebony*."

"Hmph, I doubt that," said Nigel. "Black folks don't care about nothing African unless it's got something to do with their"—here he used his fingers to mimic quotation marks—"roots."

"That's not true," insisted Regina.

"No? You had no trouble selling that piece on the little black girl who joined a Maasai tribe, initiation mutilations and all, but you couldn't get a single publication interested in that profile on Doyin Abiola." Nigel blew air from his lips, making a half-whistle sound. "Nobody cared about Nigeria's first woman newspaper publisher."

"You're being cynical again," said Regina. "Not a good look, Nigel."

"I'm just telling it like it is." He took a gulp from his mug. "In fact, the American press wants to read one thing about Africa—stories of untold suffering. Preferably told through the eyes of one person—a boy soldier, a woman raped by an entire rebel force, a child prostitute supporting her family, a man who's seen his wife and kids hacked to death by tribal enemies. Those stories get sold."

"I'm ignoring you." Regina turned away from Nigel, faced Angie. "You don't mind if I come to see Fela, do you?"

Angie was startled by the question. Regina didn't need her approval. Girlfriends don't need approval. "Why would I mind?"

Regina patted Angie's thigh. "So it's settled. We'll all hang out at the Shrine tonight!"

Nigel said nothing, pulled out a cigarette. The music shifted to Steely Dan. A mixtape, Angie thought. All his favorite songs.

"You know," Regina said, "I've been admiring your hair since you walked in."

She touched her new braids. She sometimes forgot she had them. "Thanks."

"Did you get it done here?"

She told Regina about the Fulani woman running her impromptu hair shop in the open air beside her squatters' home.

"Wow, I'd love to do something like that," said Regina. "Have an authentic Nigeria experience."

"You make it sound like you've been holed up in a fancy hotel on Vic Island," said Nigel. "This campus is authentic you know. It's not a movie set."

"That's not what I mean. I want to get to the real stories that matter, that show Nigerians in the full range of their humanity." Regina turned to Angie. "I want to do right by your sister, really take seriously the honor of this fellowship. It is in her name after all."

Nigel leaned forward and quickly stubbed out his cigarette as Angie turned to him, mouth slightly agape. He wouldn't look at her.

Regina's eyes moved rapidly between them. No one spoke. "You didn't know," she finally said.

Angie, eyes still on Nigel, slowly shook her head.

"Nigel?" Regina's entire face was a question mark.

He looked at Angie, brow furrowed, widow's peak inching down his forehead. Still he said nothing.

"How could you *not* tell her that I was awarded the fellowship?" Hurt bunched up Regina's words.

"I planned to," he finally said. "I just hadn't gotten the chance."

"You spent *the whole day* with her at the beach." Regina spoke this fact with new awareness, her voice devoid of its former benefit-of-the-doubt gaiety. She stared at Nigel so long her eyes seemed to move even farther apart.

Angie felt a tight fury. How flagrant could Nigel be in his replacement of Ella, using this younger version to usurp her sister's memory? He *was* the selfish bastard her mother had said he was. Angie was sorry she didn't have her own room on campus. She was trapped and could do nothing but endure.

"I just don't understand why you didn't tell her," insisted Regina.

"Neither do I," Angie echoed.

Nigel raised his palms to the sky, looked at Angie. "What do you want me to say?"

Regina narrowed her eyes. "Is this why you made us wait and not go back to Kenya?"

"What are you talking about?"

"So you could meet up with Angie, here?"

"You know I can't go back to Kenya until I get my grades in," he said. "And I told you, she walked into my office that day out of nowhere. She just appeared."

"I know that's what you told me, but—"

"It's true," said Angie. "I just appeared."

Regina looked at Angie as if seeing her for the first time. "Really?"

"Yes, really." Now Angie was getting an attitude.

"And by the way," said Nigel. "You were *thrilled* to finally leave Kenya, so don't act like you were rushing to get back."

"No! Get it right." Regina placed her mug onto the coffee table with a dull thud. "I didn't have a problem with Kenya per se. I just didn't like those men you were hanging out with. Especially Harry!"

"I told you then, I'm telling you now," said Nigel. "You're paranoid."

She turned to Angie. "It's like a little club of foreign correspondents, all white men of course, except for Nigel. All from Europe and Australia, all thinking they're on some kind of native-watching safari."

"Regina doesn't like my friends in the press corps because they're not all touchy-feely."

"I don't like them because they're racist beasts."

Nigel sighed. "Here we go."

"They are *so* condescending to the Africans." Regina paused. "Even though they don't mind sleeping with the local women."

"I don't see those women complaining," said Nigel.

She cut her eyes at him. "Are you trying to tell me something, Nigel?"

"Stop it. Angie does not want to hear this."

Actually, she did. Angie felt immense satisfaction in the fact that these two were not blissfully in love.

Regina was on a course now, hurdling forward, unable to stop. "From the day we hooked up in Kenya, everybody treated us like we were some freak couple," she said to Angie. "Because we're both black American,"

"That's how *you* saw it," he chimed in. "Not me."

Regina ignored him. "They basically told Nigel he was crazy not to sleep with the pretty Kenyan and Somalian girls, or better yet, the wild white girls who hang around all the time. You know, the peace corps backpacking types who finally get to have their black-man adventure."

"OK Regina, enough."

"I'm just telling it like it is, as you love to say."

"Then tell it like it *really* is," said Nigel. "You don't like those guys in the press corps because they call it the way they see it."

"Funny how everybody ends up seeing the same thing," said Regina. "And how does that happen?" She counted on her fingers, held aloft. "You hang around each other, you share the same sources, the same drivers. And I'm sure you're all sharing the same women. I guess you *do* come to the same conclusions."

Nigel glared at her. "*That* was unnecessary."

"Oh come on, Nigel! You think I didn't know?"

"Shut up, Regina."

"Just admit it!"

Nigel fell back hard in the chair; it rocked wildly. "You're just pissed that I refuse to write a goddamn human-interest story about some middle-class black girl who decides she wants to join a Kenyan tribe. I'm covering disease and war and famine in one desperate country after another. I'm covering resistance and mass murder. So I can't see out of those rose-colored glasses you wear. Shit is foggy as a motherfucker when I put them on."

"My profile of that girl was a very good piece!" yelled Regina.

Angie couldn't believe she was witnessing this. Was there no escaping folks' domestic dysfunction in Lagos?

"Like I said, editors want to hear one story out of Africa." Nigel smirked. "And that sure as hell ain't it."

Regina plopped back onto the sofa, arms folded. "Well, that's the story I want to tell."

"And thank God you're traveling on my dime, 'cause otherwise you wouldn't be able to survive on those cute little feature articles that you wanna tell."

"Is that what you think of them?" Regina's face crumbled.

"They're cute?" Abruptly, she stood. "If you'll excuse me." She stalked toward the bedroom.

"Regina," he said to her back. "It's not personal."

She looked back at him over her shoulder. "Fuck you."

She closed the door gently behind her. Nigel rubbed his hand down his face.

"Nothing like a rich and trusting relationship," said Angie.

He looked at her through his fingers. "I don't remember you as sarcastic."

"And I don't remember you as so deceptive."

"It's not how it looks."

He glanced at the closed door, rose slowly, like a reluctant escort. "I'll be back."

He entered. She could hear their muffled voices but couldn't make out what they were saying. She got up, turned down Steely Dan, tip-toed closer, put her ear to the door. She heard a sob. Soon enough, she couldn't hear anything, so she moved over to the window and waited. The lagoon front had thinned out and she imagined clusters of Nigerian students gathered in the campus cafeteria, shoving jollof rice into their mouths, all talking at once, carefree. She waited for the door to open, her anxiousness growing as she pictured Nigel and Regina in each other's arms, turned on by the thrill of make-up sex with her just outside. She thought of her childhood playroom and its closed door, of turned-over furniture, smudges of chocolate on the walls, that smell.

She left.

FIFTEEN

NIGEL FOUND HER SEVERAL MINUTES LATER. ALONG THE shore, a tree trunk had defiantly climbed out of the earth, reaching for escape, its branches dangling so low bottom leaves tickled the lagoon's surface. The day had peeled back to dusk.

He sat beside her on the water's edge. "I'm sorry I didn't tell you."

"That must have been some pick-up line," she said. "'You look like a girl who could use a fellowship and baby, I got one for you.'"

"It wasn't like that. She came before the fellowship. And she really is deserving. Despite her cutesy articles."

"Save it," snapped Angie.

From an open window somewhere came Whitney's faint vocals. *Didn't we almost have it all? When love was all we had worth giving.*

"I take it she's not going to Fela's club tonight."

"No, she is not. But I'm still going with you."

"Do you love her?" asked Angie.

Nigel shifted uncomfortably. "I don't know. I think so, yeah."

"Why?"

"What kind of question is that?"

"Why do you love her?" she repeated.

He pulled out the pack of cigarettes from his shirt's breast pocket. "She's loyal. I like that."

"Are you loyal?"

"I'm trying to be."

"Do you love her more than you loved Ella?"

He thumped the bottom of the pack. "There's no comparison."

Angie needed to hear this right now. "Go on."

"You were there." He pulled out a cigarette, worried it between his fingers. "You saw us."

In fact, the last time Angie had seen them together was at Ella's one-year anniversary party. She thought about her sister's giddiness that day, how Nigel kept leaning over, whispering in her ear. How everyone watched them while pretending not to. She told Nigel about her memory. "What was it like to see her again, after all that time?"

"Amazing." Nigel pulled out his lighter. "She looked good, you know? I hadn't seen her in four years! I was so happy that she'd gotten herself together. I couldn't *wait* for the party to be over so we could jump in my car, be alone."

"I remember that." She also remembered her mother's concern.

Nigel cupped his hand around the fledging flame as he lit his cigarette. He took a puff, blew out. "We were hungry for each other. I never felt so much desire in my life. We did it right there in the car."

He pulled on the cigarette again, as if extracting memories from it. "We just rode around, ended up in Greektown, sat at one of those all-night diners and started reminiscing about the Lagos trip, how extraordinary it was, how much fun we had, how we both missed that, that energy of the continent. She told me she'd stayed in touch with this couple we met at

FESTAC—Brenda and Chris. How they'd gotten married after graduation, and moved back to Nigeria. She said Brenda told her about all the new opportunities there, what with a civilian president and all. She said black Americans were moving there, taking advantage of opportunities they didn't have in the US. It sounded exciting." He took another puff, made a little whistle sound as he exhaled through pursed lips. "It sounded like back in the day, you know? When all these black folks moved to Ghana in droves, nation-building with Nkrumah, kicking it with Du Bois and shit. I always wished I could've been part of something like that. This felt like my chance. And it sure as hell sounded better than staying in Detroit. Detroit was dead."

"What do you mean 'dead?'" asked Angie. What had she been too young to notice? What had she missed?

"I mean nothing was happening there except for Reaganomics and racist talk about welfare queens; plus crack thrown up in our neighborhoods, and with it a shit-load of gang violence. Meanwhile, black folks who had something going on? Seemed like all they wanted to do was become motherfuckin' black yuppies. Buppies. Depressing shit."

The Black Power movement, Nigel said, which had limped along in the seventies, was nonexistent. All the big brothers and sisters they'd admired? In the ground, locked up, or fucked up. Huey Newton was a drug addict, Eldridge Cleaver was a Republican. Bobby Seale was denouncing guns and wearing three-piece suits. And Assata Shakur was still hiding out in Cuba. Killer cops were on a rampage in the city's ghettos. And with Reagan in office, white supremacist groups flourished. Life for black folks in America was hazardous, pure and simple.

"We were sitting in that diner eating our Greek salads, and Ella said, 'I cannot stay here and stay clean. I have to leave. I'm going back to Nigeria.' I was like, 'How you gonna do that?' She said she had this insurance money from your father and suddenly it was a real possibility. I sure as hell didn't have nothing going on. I was working at WJLB, doing programming, not really digging it." He took another drag. "I looked at Ella across that table and she looked, I don't know, beautiful. I wanted to be with her again, so badly. I told her, 'I'll come with you.'"

He looked over at Angie. "She said she wanted to go to your high school graduation; after that we could split. But not before she saw her baby sister graduate."

A flutter of emotion flew around her chest like a little bird trapped inside a closet. After the ceremony, Ella had scrawled a note in Angie's yearbook. "The world will be hearing great things from you one day soon."

"We left on June 21," continued Nigel. "She liked that date, said it always felt like New Year's Day to her, because it was the first day of summer, the longest day of the year. Solstice. And we both decided it meant something symbolic, this day of new beginnings." He paused, shook his head. "When I think back, it sounds crazy. We didn't *really* know anybody in Lagos and we didn't really know each other that well, not after all those years apart. But we had once shared something special and we wanted it back. We wanted to be part of something magical again."

When he fell quiet, Angie gently prodded him. "Go on," she whispered.

He nodded. "Within a couple weeks, we were staying with Chris and Brenda." He flicked his cigarette into the lagoon. "They'd just moved into this nice big house, so they had plenty of room. Chris was working for a bank by day and for *The Lagos Voice* by night, and on weekends. You could see *The Voice* was different—new and radical. We both got involved with it, and that placed us in this whole scene of progressive folks—writers and artists and journalists, cool expats. Here was a genuine Pan-African movement." Nigel smiled. "And we were up in it!

Ella was really proud of that, that we'd found our tribe so to speak. That we'd gotten it right."

"It meant a lot to her, getting things right," Angie said, as she thought of those endless hours Ella spent on top of racehorses, practicing over and over, their father pushing her to do even better.

"Yeah, she said her dad inspired her to be that way," Nigel noted, as if reading Angie's thoughts. "She was so determined to do what he'd done. To find this thing to do with her life that she loved the way he loved training horses. She said to me once, 'While all those other black men in Detroit were busy putting left doors on Chryslers? My father was out on the track, making winners.' That's what she wanted to do, be distinctive, leave her mark, be a dynamic force in the world."

Angie wondered again what that meant for her, what it was *she* could make.

"The paper was just a few months old when we got here," continued Nigel. "And scrappy. They had this little office in Surulere, these manual Portuguese typewriters, one telephone line. But ah, man! They'd already caused a stir, 'cause for the first time here was a truly independent press, produced by all these well-educated Nigerians, with Western models of what a newspaper could be. Folks who'd been reading the *Guardian* and the *New York Times*. Plus it looked good. Completely distinguished itself from those other Lagos dailies with their crooked, hysterical typeface and giant tabloid headlines and typos galore. *The Voice* had clean lines, Helvetica type, a sophisticated blue banner."

"I could see that from the clippings she sent me," said Angie. She wanted to be part of the story.

"It was the journalism that really distinguished it though," Nigel pointed out. "No silly stories about standing fans being

stolen from some government office, no Page Six girls in biki-
nis. Here were brave folks doing serious, risky stories, willing
to call out corrupt leaders. I started doing what we called diaspora stories, pieces that really linked the struggle across different African countries. And Ella? She'd never even thought
about journalism before, but she found she had a knack for it.
Interviews were her specialty. She could get Nigerian women
to open up, really talk to her. " He glanced at Angie. "Do you
know about her baby-formula exposé?"

"Yes. But tell me more."

"Well, that story caused a serious little brouhaha. She'd
been talking to all these different Nigerian mothers about
their lives, and noticed that every one of them was feeding
their babies Similac. OK, that was strange. In Africa? She
just happened to pick up one of the cans, started reading it.
Shit was expired. That led her to all the kiosks in the markets
around town, and damned if all of them weren't expired. She
faxed a letter to UNESCO, found out the shit was banned in
Europe and the US. From there, she wrote a killer investigative
piece."

Nigel moved his hand across the air. "Jide ran it on the
front page." Angie could see the headline. "And that itself was
revolutionary, to put a woman's issue on the front of a Nigerian
newspaper? And a scandalous one? Showing government culpa-
bility? Jide was like 'You'll be our women's issues reporter' and
Ella was like, 'You know what? Let's take this to a new level:
Give me an entire page.' And he did."

"Woman to Woman," said Angie, proud of that knowledge.

Nigel's eyes flashed with remembrance. "Yep! Holy shit,
she was off and running then. She took it *so* seriously, like
every article she wrote was gonna prepare Nigerian women for
nation-building. She'd spend hours in that damn newsroom.

I'd try to pull her out to go eat or whatever, but she wouldn't come. She'd sleep in there some nights, curled up on a lumpy sofa in the back." He smiled. "But she loved it. She was so into it, I swear she glowed."

Angie hugged her knees to her chest. "The way you describe her, that's just how I imagined her life here."

"Oh, she was totally in her element," he said. "The wild thing is, you really couldn't' tell Ella wasn't Nigerian either, especially after she got her hair braided. She liked to wear tops and skirts made out of native fabric, right? So she looked more authentic than a lot of the educated Nigerian women, like Lola, who did the whole Western thing. Somebody was always asking her whether she was Igbo or Yoruba. She loved that."

"Do you have a picture of her?" Angie ached for an image. "Did you take any?"

"Funny thing, we didn't really stop to do that. We were so busy! We arrived just weeks before the country's first free elections. The first time Shagari had gotten into office, the whole thing had been handled by the military and they used some convoluted vote-counting system that no one could figure out. Court ended up deciding who won the election. Can you imagine that shit happening in the US? Judges deciding who gets to be president? Anyway, this time it was gonna be through a truly democratic process. "

"Oh." She couldn't understand how no one stopped to snap *one* picture.

Nigel kept talking. "There was this electricity in the air! It's hard to explain what it felt like to be part of something big, where so much was genuinely at stake. Not like the presidential elections in the States, where one privileged white man replaces another. Same ol', same ol'. We were totally caught up in the excitement of it! To me and Ella, it felt like this rare and precious gift, seeing a black man elected president. We were part of a whole milieu of folks, part of this—" He paused for a moment, searching for the right word. "This *intelligencia,* helping a fledgling African country develop into greatness." He grinned. "And since Nigerians know how to party, we did a lot of that! Mostly highlife parties, where they had multicolored lights strewn across back roads, giant speakers blaring, food and liquor galore. We danced our butts off! Everybody accepted us, and *that's* what Ella loved. She said to me, 'Here, I'm not just some big, tall, dark, black girl too smart for her own good. Here, I'm just me.' She couldn't get enough of the whole scene. That's when we became regulars at Fela's club too, hanging out there until three, four in the morning."

"Sounds like you barely slept," said Angie, envious.

"You got that right! On the day the paper came out? Wednesdays? Shit, we *did* stay up all night, waiting 'til the delivery guy dropped the papers at the door, sometimes at like five in the morning, just so we could see Jide's latest editorial. He never showed it to anyone beforehand."

"Why not?"

"Because the shit was so hot! Searing! He wrote scathing editorials about the country's so-called leaders. That brother was relentless. He did not share our optimism. He hadn't gone abroad to be educated; he'd been in Nigeria the whole damn time and he'd seen *a lot.* He and the older, wiser cats knew the election was rigged from the start."

"Shagari won, right?" she asked. "Ella wrote and told me that."

"Yeah, voting took place that August, but nobody liked how it went down, nobody believed it had been fair. A lot of ballot tampering. Plus Shagari imposed these austerity measures and kicked out all the foreigners who supposedly were taking jobs from Nigerians. Half a million Ghanaians got deported. Crazy shit like that."

Yes, that taxi driver had said as much on Angie's first day in Lagos. That felt like eons ago. Light years.

Nigel's voice sped up in excitement. "So Jide is writing about all this, taking no prisoners. Chris is railing on the economic front, writing these follow-the-dollar stories about all the cash the government has hoarded, how after all that oil money, the country was crying broke. And about the insanity of millions living in harsh poverty despite Nigeria's natural resources, right? Such a fucking irony. Ella was railing against poor prenatal care for mothers, high infant mortality, no malaria nets, that kind of stuff. And I was doing stories about armed struggle in the countries on the continent." He shrugged, his shoulders frozen upward before falling back down. "Eventually *The Voice* came under attack, mainly from the city's other newspapers. They were all mouthpieces of the government, and they didn't like how we were showing them up."

Nigel squinted at the water. "One day, we were all in the office, working, when somebody threw a smoke bomb through the window."

"Oh my God!" said Angie. "Did anyone get hurt?" She had an irrational thought: maybe this was the *real* way Ella died. She had another, guilty thought: she wished it had been. Being hit by a car wasn't heroic in the same way.

"We were all OK," said Nigel. "But after that, shit wasn't fun anymore. The whole city felt, I don't know, stressed out. Folks grumbling, services not working, blatant government thievery, and this sense that, just like Achebe wrote back in the day, things were falling apart. Big time."

"Jide must have known it wasn't safe anymore," said Angie.

"He knew. But that brother was committed, God rest his soul. Brother Jide. No one like him."

"What did you and Ella do after that, after the smoke bomb?"

"Me, I wanted to pull back from the whole political thing. Just relax, see the sights, chill out. It had been hot and heavy since the day we arrived, and after a few months of that intensity, after the disappointment of the elections, I was tired of the whole thing. I felt like, what's the point? Ella and I argued about it. I told her I couldn't be in that same little newsroom day after day, every day; but that didn't bother her. She said she'd spent nearly every weekend of her life at the track with her father, for *years*, sometimes hours in one barn, so she was used to being in a confined space. I was not.

"Plus," said Nigel, "Ella really believed in what she was doing, believed in holding Nigerians to a higher standard so the country could live up to its potential, really become a beacon of Africa, a genuine second-world country instead of a third-world one.

"It was noble, but fucking exhausting." He stared at the rivulets weaving between the shoreline rocks. Angie stared at him. "Things with me and Ella started getting really out of whack," he said. "For one thing, we handled being black American in Nigeria *very* differently. I wanted to hang out with other expats, really get into *that* scene, 'cause folks from all over the world were living in Nigeria—you know, diplomats, UN folks, NGO workers, peace corps volunteers—and I found that interesting. She hated that scene. She just wanted to be with Nigerians. She felt it was more authentic."

Angie's crossed legs felt stiff, so she stretched them out in front of her. Nigel did the same.

"Things really blew up when we went to this party in Surulere, the three of us, me, Ella, and Jide," he said. "I had shifted my tastes, tended not to like Nigerian house parties anymore. My choice was to hang out in some diplomat's nice apartment, where they gave very fine parties. One dude had this huge space with a sweet view of the Gulf of New Guinea. You could just stand there for hours, drink in hand, watch the waves frothing up to the edge of Ikoyi Island." He paused. "But Ella didn't care about any of that. She preferred the locals, hands down. We'd go to these things and she'd be all dressed in her outfits made from native cloth and she'd make all these observations. 'Have you ever noticed that no one in Lagos ever slouches?' she said to me once. 'Everyone has erect posture.'" He shook his head softly. "That's how she was."

Nigel became quiet, drifting in his own thoughts. Angie felt she had to keep him focused on the tale. "So, the party in Surulere," she said.

"So the party in Surulere," he repeated. "This one was a little different 'cause it was at a nice house, with a *megadi* guarding the gate and a sweet little courtyard out front with flowers blooming. And folks were dressed in modern, Western clothes. Barely a native fabric in sight. "Beat It" was blasting through giant speakers. Everybody was dancing, enjoying themselves. The kitchen was well-stocked with liquor. I was digging the whole thing. Ella was just standing around talking about newspaper shit with Jide. Me, I decided to have a good time, so I grab this pretty girl I'd seen on national TV, and I'm doing my best Michael Jackson imitation on the dance floor, pretending not to watch Ella watch me out of the corner of her eye."

"You doing a Michael Jackson imitation?" Angie interjected. "I cannot see that!"

"Yeah, you didn't want to see it."

She laughed, grateful for the excuse. She could feel the story was headed in a not-so-funny direction.

At one point during the party, Jide approached the DJ. "Can you please play some Nigerian piece for a change?" he asked.

"Wha?" said the DJ.

"Some Nigerian music!" Jide yelled over the din.

The DJ's eyes opened wide. "Are you kidding?" he said. "You wanna spoil the party?"

A guy standing nearby heard the exchange and burst out laughing.

Jide screamed, "What's so goddamn funny?"

By now others had gathered around.

"I been doing this for three years and I ain't never heard such shit," said the DJ. "What century have you returned from?"

"You're telling me it would hurt the party for you to play just one Nigerian record?" asked Jide.

"I'm telling you this ain't the Dark Ages!" said the DJ. "I haven't got one single Nigerian record here."

"How can you call yourself a DJ!" yelled Jide.

Ella, who'd been at Jide's side throughout, chimed in. "Yeah, how *could* you?"

Nigel moved toward them, grabbed Ella's arm to pull her back, but she shrugged him off, stayed next to Jide. Now the music had stopped completely and everyone was staring at them. Nigel was pissed.

"Not one?" pressed Jide, incredulous. "No Oyelana, no Oriental Brothers, Mbarga? No Fela?"

Suddenly, the hostess, Pat, walked up to the small group gathered around the DJ. A young, modern Nigerian woman, she wore a sleek black dress with padded shoulders and a dropped back. She said to Jide, "It's not that kind of party."

"What kind of party does it have to be to play Nigerian records?" said Jide. "Isn't it bad enough that our airports and bars and radio all play American music, eh? What's wrong with you people?"

Pat moved in, inches from Jide's face, and yelled, "It's my party, you hear!" She stepped back, looked him up and down. "Who invited you anyway, old man?"

The DJ dropped "Billie Jean" onto the turntable, and the TV girl took Nigel's hand and pulled him back on the dance floor. Jide and Ella came over to them and Jide, fuming, said, "Let's go, my brother. Let's get out of here."

Nigel kept dancing, thinking, *Why should he tell me when to leave a fucking party?* "I'm not going," he said.

"Well I am," said Ella.

Nigel stopped dancing. He reached for Ella. "Stay here with me."

"Just come with us," she insisted.

"OK, after this dance."

Ella rolled her eyes, stalked off with Jide. Nigel resumed dancing, could see Ella consoling Jide, trying to calm him down as he complained loudly to no one in particular, her hand on his arm. The TV girl said, "I'm thirsty."

Nigel didn't like how buddy-buddy those two were. He followed TV Girl to the kitchen, drank two lagers fast as she drank one. He was thinking *Ella saw me, she'll come in here,* but she didn't come, didn't come, and he worried about that a bit, but he was a little drunk, and the next thing he knew, he and TV Girl were upstairs in one of the bedrooms.

When Nigel came back down, Ella and Jide were gone.

IT WAS DARK now, only light coming from office windows of the administrative building. Nigel stood. "My butt's sore. Let's get off the ground."

They moved over to a large stone bench.

"So did you go after her?" asked Angie. "After you fooled around with TV Girl?"

Nigel winced. "No, I didn't. I figured I'd see her back at Chris and Brenda's, but when I got there, she wasn't there. I wasn't really worried. We'd had fights before and we always got through it." He paused. "But she didn't return for two days."

His face was in profile, barely visible in the dark. "Go on," said Angie.

"Turns out," he said, "Ella had stayed at Jide's that whole time. We argued about it. I accused her of having some kinda Daddy fixation, because Jide was older than us, like forty. Not even that old, but it seemed old at the time. I told her Jide had turned us into sitting ducks, and the best thing we could do was just cut out of Nigeria, go back home. 'Go if you want to,' she said. 'I'm staying.'"

"You would never have left her here," said Angie. "Would you?"

"Of course not. But I *did* start taking these small trips to places like Togo and Ghana and Benin. Started traveling with this group of foreign correspondents covering West Africa. I liked it, liked the idea of doing stories about Africa for the Western press. Busting myths that way. Mostly, it was just good to get out of Lagos. I kept trying to get Ella to come with me, but she wouldn't."

Angie was trying to connect Nigel's story to the letters Ella wrote her, but she couldn't follow the timeline.

"Then Nigeria had its Independence Day celebration," continued Nigel. "And it was a big overwrought extravaganza in Tafawa Balewa Square. The whole staff went, ostensibly to cover it, to be critical. But we enjoyed it more than we expected and standing there, watching the whole thing felt nice, almost like the closing ceremony at FESTAC. And there were lots of horses, which mesmerized Ella of course. I turned to her and said, 'Hey, whatever grand democratic experiment Nigeria tried has failed. Let's make *this* our last memory of the country and just go home.' But she said she wasn't leaving yet. I said, 'Give me a date, because my ass is ready to go.' 'You know, I want to see the North,' she said. 'Where they dye those beautiful cloths from indigo.' She'd heard the pits were over five hundred years old, that they still dyed fabric the traditional way, and that got her all jazzed. 'I want to see old Africa, the way it was *before* the colonizers arrived,' she said. 'I want to see something on this continent that's centuries old. Then we can go home.' I didn't really want to bother, but she pointed out that everyone had been telling us you hadn't seen Nigeria until you'd seen the North. So I said, 'OK, we'll go.'"

Nigel spread his arms across the back of the bench. Angie leaned back, and he let his fingers rest on her shoulder.

"That changed things between us, just having an exit plan. She even went to some expat stuff with me, enjoyed herself. We stopped talking about politics, and she let herself miss a few days in the newsroom. We found out from folks that Kano was the place to see, that the best dye pits were there; we booked our flight. We were getting out of Lagos! I was so fucking relieved."

"She mentioned those dye pits in one of her letters to me," said Angie, grateful for the touchstone.

Nigel shook his head as if the next memory was hard to fathom. "But then one day we're sitting at Museum Café, and she's reading the *International Herald Tribune*. We're having coffee and I'm digging the whole scene, right? It feels continental. The weather is nice, it's actually not raining for a change. This is how our lives here should be, I'm thinking. But all of a sudden she goes, "Wow" and then she's silent. Like, radio silence. I'm thinking she's reading about some famous person who died. But then she reads out loud to me, 'Cheryl White, the first Afro-American female jockey, just became the first female jockey to win five Thoroughbred races in one day at a major track.' She looks up and I see this look on her face I've never seen before. Like deep regret or something. She says, 'That was supposed to be me.'"

Angie could see the *Jet* magazine in her mind's eye, its cover photo of the teenage Cheryl White taped to Ella's bedroom wall.

"After that, she got obsessive again," said Nigel. "Went right back to staying long crazy hours in the newsroom, sleeping there again; so I started hanging out more and more on Vic Island, crashing for nights on end at folks' cribs."

"Did you ever get to Kano?"

"She wouldn't even talk about the trip to Kano."

Angie felt acute disappointment, as if *she'd* missed seeing the North.

"Anyway, as the weeks passed, I was getting more and more homesick," said Nigel. "I stopped going to the newsroom altogether, just out of resentment really. I was convinced that Jide and Ella were involved, and my pride was bruised pretty badly. I didn't want to see their asses together. I guess I felt abandoned by her, I don't know." His chest heaved. "I started spending more time with Brenda. Her ass was lonely too, and she liked being able to talk to someone from the States. We sat around, complaining together—about the shitty food and the shitty roads and the shitty TV." Here, Nigel started talking faster. "Then she started confiding in me, started telling me how Chris was having an affair with some woman, how there wasn't a damn thing she could do about it, it was just the Nigerian way, how it was an open secret, how they didn't like her anyway because she was black American; she said his people told him he should've married a white woman. Preferably British. She even told me she'd caught him looking at Ella."

Angie closed her eyes against what was coming.

"One night Brenda and I are sitting around and we realize it's Thanksgiving Day, right? She says she never gets to celebrate the holiday because it means nothing to Chris; and so we go in the kitchen and start cooking some pathetic little scrawny chicken and try to dress it up like a turkey and she makes yams and greens and we're having fun and drinking a lot of brandy; and at some point after we eat, she confides in me that she's never been with a black American man, that Chris had been her first, that she'd gotten with him her freshman year, and she really regrets what she missed."

Angie put her hands to her ears.

"I don't know how it happened," said Nigel. "It just did. She started crying, saying how she was homesick for Virginia, how Chris demanded that she have a baby but she wasn't ready, how she felt pressure from his family; she talked about the whole cultural-difference thing, his haughty attitude toward black Americans, blah, blah, blah. She's crying, I'm consoling her and one thing leads to another." He paused. "It happened. One time."

Angie felt hurt, on Ella's behalf. "So you and Brenda betrayed her too. She couldn't trust anyone."

Nigel frowned. "We decide not to tell anybody. Just act like it never happened." He sighed. "But a couple weeks later, Brenda tells Chris. She wants to get back at him, make him jealous I guess. Of course all hell breaks loose, and Chris kicks my ass out of the house. Ella is equally pissed, doesn't want to have anything to do with Brenda. She leaves too."

"Chris tried to force himself on me," said Angie.

Nigel jumped up from the bench. "What? I will fuck up that motherfucker!"

"I'm OK now," said Angie.

"Is that what happened to your face? And all those marks on your arms and legs?"

"No." The scars had all but healed. "That was something else."

"Something else? Something *else*?" He sat back down. "I'm gonna shut up now, and let you talk. Start from the beginning."

She told Nigel about Chris's visits to her guest quarters, his advances, the slap.

"I have a mind to go to Ikeja right now, and kick his punk ass," said Nigel. "I *never* liked that motherfucker!"

Angie basked for a moment in his chivalry. "He claimed he had a relationship with Ella," she continued. "That they were planning for her to become his second wife."

"That lying son of a bitch! He and Ella didn't have no damn relationship! And what black woman you know is gonna be some man's second wife? That's some bullshit!"

Angie was glad to hear it. She couldn't imagine her sister would ever choose Chris over Nigel. Regardless. "So that's when Ella left and went to Funke's?" she asked.

"Yeah, she went to stay with her for a minute."

"I had a weird time there," Angie admitted.

"Pretty basic standard of living, right?"

She nodded, choosing not to tell him about her harrowing experience on the highway.

"I begged Ella to come with me to Vic Island and stay in a decent place with running water," said Nigel. "She refused. She was angry, said she needed to get away from me."

Nigel and I are cooling it.

"That was the worse thing," said Nigel. "Because at the Ola-pades', we'd go our separate ways but we'd always end up back in those servant's quarters together."

"Did you even try to get her back?" asked Angie.

"Hell yeah! I showed up at Funke's a few times, but that crazy-ass woman wouldn't let me in. So I started going back to the newsroom just to see Ella. And by then, shit was getting deep. You could feel the coup in the air. No one knew when it would come, or how, but everyone felt it coming. Would it be bloody or not? That was the only real question."

"You should've made her leave," Angie insisted. She hated that this part of the story was where one different choice would've changed everything. Her chest tightened, gripped by that fact.

"Believe me, I was begging her to leave," said Nigel. "She would not go. And you couldn't *make* Ella do anything. But I wasn't returning to the States without her."

That must have been around the time she'd written the last letter.

16 December 1983

Dear Angie,

I'm missing you guys so much, wish I could be there for Christmas! God, what I wouldn't do for Mama's oyster dressing and homemade rolls and some collard greens. Nigerians are good at a lot of things, but cooking is not one of them!

Romare sounds great. Good to hear my little sister is in love! My advice: go slow. It's better that way, because then you'll know if it's the real deal.

I'll write a long letter after the New Year. This is a very busy time at the paper. So many troubles with this place, believe me, there's a whole lot to report on! It's endless.

Maybe you should wait and come visit during Spring Break. They say March is a nice month in Lagos--Harmattan winds have calmed down, and the rainy season's not quite in full swing. When you come, we can just take off together, see the North

& maybe a few other countries on the
continent. That is, if I'm still here.

                    Merry Xmas!

                    Love you,

                    Ella

December 25 came fast. "A lot of expats had gone home for the holidays, or headed off to some fabulous vacation spot," Nigel remembered. "I've always been a sucker for Christmas, and the idea of spending it alone was something I couldn't fathom. I wanted to be with her. Plus, I had a plan."

This time when he showed up at her place, he was prepared to push Funke out of the way and barge in if he had to. But she wasn't home. Ella was there with Funke's mother, who was visiting from her home village. But the woman was old and feeble, stayed in the back room. Ella let him in. She looked exhausted, spent. She'd lost weight. He was worried about her.

Angie again thought of that summer when Ella was fourteen and dropped a lot of weight with the help of speed, remembered how terrifying it was when she swallowed all those pep pills, silencing Denise's protests.

ELLA AND NIGEL sat on the bed next to one another. "Wow, this is soft," he said.

"It's filled with feathers," explained Ella. "Funke gave me her nicest bed."

He held her hand. "Aren't you tired of all this?"

She opened her mouth, but nothing came out.

He cocked his head, reaching for eye contact. "Aren't you?"

"I'm worn out," she admitted. "Doing the page is hard work." She shrugged. "But it's my responsibility to—"

"It's not your goddamn responsibility!" He couldn't take it, this way she'd become so engrossed in other people's struggles. "Nigeria is not your problem," he said. "You have to take care of yourself, for Christ's sake."

She looked up at him. He saw fear in her eyes.

"What?" he said, squeezing her hand. "What is it?"

"I'm afraid of letting somebody down." She sounded chastened, like a scolded child. "A lot of people are depending on me."

He guided her head to his shoulder. "Still, you said it yourself Ella, you're tired."

He could feel her nodding. "I'm a little scared too. We keep getting threatening phone calls at the newsroom."

He gingerly lifted her head, put her chin in the crook of his finger. "Listen to me. It's time to go. We're leaving."

She shook her face free from his touch. "I'm not going back to Detroit yet, Nigel. Not yet."

He held her by both arms. "I didn't say go home. I have a better idea."

"What?" Her eyes were distrusting.

"Go with me to Guinea tomorrow. I'm interviewing Kwame Ture."

She brightened. "Stokely Carmichael?"

"Yep."

She smiled big and he saw glimmers of the old Ella. "That is so damn cool!"

"So you'll come?"

She hesitated.

"I already got you a ticket."

"You did?" She looked at him as if it were the kindest thing anyone had ever done for her. "I'll come."

They hugged. "Merry Christmas, Baby," he said, kissing her as they fell back on the soft feather bed. With Funke's mother in the next room, separated only by a beaded curtain, they made love quietly. But that didn't damper his desire. He'd been aching for Ella, and he had to muffle his cries in the crook of her neck. Afterward, they sang Christmas carols to each other, not caring whether they woke up the old woman. Ella sang "Oh Holy Night" in a surprising vibrato. Nigel sang, *Hang all the mistletoe, I'm gonna get to know you betterrrrr,* in a funny Donny Hathaway imitation: *This Christmas, fireside's blazing bright, and we're caroling through the niiiiiight!* She laughed out loud.

As she drifted off in his arms, she said, "I missed you." He held her all night, so in love he couldn't sleep. He never heard Funke return, and the mother never made a sound. He finally dozed off.

He awoke from the movement of Ella rising to get out of bed. Morning sun barely filled the room. She was putting on her clothes. He yawned, rubbed his eyes. "The flight's not until late in the day," he told her. "We can just chill."

She didn't look at him as she slipped on a simple shift in a purple print. "I'm going to the newsroom."

He sat up. "It's Boxing Day! Nobody's going to no damn office today."

She didn't say anything, just kept dressing.

He didn't want to argue, knew how tenuous their makeup was. "So listen. Pack your bag now. I'll take it with me, then swing by the newsroom later, pick you up on the way to the airport."

She put on one sandal before she said, "I can't go to Guinea." She busied herself with buckling it. "So many staffers have abandoned Jide already. He needs me."

"Are you serious?" Nigel couldn't believe she was choosing Jide over him. Again.

"He says this coup could jump off at any moment, and we need to make sure folks understand what's up, what to do, where to go."

"But we had a plan."

She held the other sandal aloft. He could see her weighing her decision. "I'm sorry," she said finally, slipping it onto her foot. "Try to understand."

Nigel threw off the bed's thin blanket with such violence it landed on the floor in a defeated hump. He swung his feet around, sat on the edge. Ella moved slowly toward him, leaned in between his legs and wrapped her arms around his neck. She kissed him. It was a long, passionate kiss.

"Listen, when you get back, we'll go to Kano," she told him. "We can spend New Year's Eve there. Promise."

He liked hearing that. "OK. I'll be back by the thirtieth."

"Perfect."

"I'll get our tickets while I'm at the airport today."

"Sounds good."

She waited while he dressed, and the two left together. He hugged her before she walked off, toward *The Voice* office. After he lost sight of her, he got into a taxi, and headed to Ikeja.

NIGEL AND ANGIE sat in the darkness and watched the defiant tree's shadowy low leaves skim the water's surface.

"I let her go," he said. "I will always regret that I let her go."

"And that was the last time you saw her," said Angie.

Nigel was silent.

"And then what happened?" She hated his silence. As long as he talked, Ella was still alive.

"You know the rest, Angie."

"Tell me."

He spoke in a robotic voice. "I was in Guinea with Ture for a few days. Like I said, he'd just had a son the year before and he was in good spirits. We hung out, I did my interview, it went well." Here his voice shifted, became shallow. "But the whole time, I had this nagging, bad feeling. I couldn't shake it. Turns out it was actually a premonition, because that was exactly when the police raided *The Voice* newsroom and dragged Jide out of there."

"He died in police custody," said Angie. "Chris told me that."

Nigel nodded. "Ella barely escaped arrest. She went to hide out at Kalakuta, Fela's compound. And two days later, New Year's Eve, the coup finally did jump off. And then—"

"Wait a minute," interrupted Angie. "Fela's *compound*? The others didn't tell me anything about that."

"The others don't know everything," said Nigel.

"How do you know that's where she was?"

He didn't answer at first. "I heard."

"But why would she go there?"

"Because Fela's wives adored her."

"His wives?"

"Yeah. He married twenty-seven women all at once, back in '78. He wanted to make a statement about Yoruba tradition, whatever. Anyway, one of the extraordinary things Ella did with Woman to Woman was a huge profile on the wives. She interviewed a lot of them, then did a feature spread with pull quotes, gorgeous photos, the whole nine. They loved her for that, because it legitimized them, gave them a chance to tell their stories." He smirked. "The elite class *hates* Fela and they call his wives prostitutes." He paused. "The piece was controversial as hell. But it endeared those women to her. When she needed a place to hide out, they took her in. Took good care of her for those few days."

"I can't believe the things I didn't know," said Angie.

"How would you know?"

She shrugged, helpless. "I just—"

"You want me to stop?"

She shook her head hard. "Go on."

"OK," he said nervously. "The next day she was on Agege Motor Road in Ikeja, right by Kalakuta." He hesitated. "That's where the accident happened."

There was a pause.

"That's it?" she wasn't ready for the story to end, not ready for it to be over.

"That's it."

"But, where *were* you? You promised her you'd be back for New Year's Eve." She was beside herself. If only he'd kept his word. "So where were you?"

His jaw muscles hardened. "You don't think I was *trying* to get back to her? The coup made that difficult, Angie."

"Oh." She thought for a moment. "So Fela and his wives were the last people to see her alive."

Nigel said nothing, seemed spent, incapable of uttering another word.

Angie couldn't believe her luck! Here, she'd been thinking the Shrine was simply some iconic place that Ella had experienced and enjoyed, when in fact it was so much more than that. So much more! Thank God she hadn't gone there first without understanding that fact. She stood abruptly, excited. "Let's go."

Nigel looked up at her. "Where?"

"To Fela's club."

"*Now?*"

"Now."

"It's late, Angie. Let's do this another night."

"You and Regina can do this another night." She turned, started walking away from Nigel. "I'm going now."

SIXTEEN

THE NIGHT WAS BLACK CRUSHED VELVET, DEVOID OF STREET-lights. Their driver turned down a slim road and barreled forward, headlights slicing the dark. When he suddenly slammed the brakes, both Nigel and Angie slammed against the front seat.

"What the fuck man!" yelled Nigel.

"Bandits," said the driver. He nodded his head toward what he saw. Yards ahead, two men pointed guns at a small group of people clustered around a Mercedes, it's four doors flung open.

Angie gripped Nigel's arm. "Oh my God," she whispered. He put his hand on hers as the driver slowly eased the car in reverse and drove backward to the corner. He turned the car around as gunshots pierced the air. Angie screamed. Nigel shoved her head down into his lap and covered her body with his. The driver sped up and swerved, turning down a bumpy road.

Nam myoho renge kyo. Nam myoho renge kyo Angie chanted. Eyes squeezed shut, she repeated it over and over, unable to stop as the moments passed.

"We're here," Nigel whispered into her ear. "We're here."

She sat up, could just make out the road's crooked sign,

"Pepple Street." The driver pulled up to the brightly lit club, where a crowd milled around out front.

As they climbed out, gunshot sounds echoed in her ears. She turned to Nigel. "We almost—" she started.

He gathered her into his arms, holding her with a protectiveness laced in fear. It surprised her. "If something had happened to you . . ." He kissed her forehead—as he used to do when she was a child—before he let go. "We're here. We're safe. That's all that matters."

She nodded, still feeling his lips on her skin.

As they moved closer to the club, he grabbed her hand. "Stay close to me, OK?"

She nodded, stunned by the warmth of his hand in hers, by how long it had been since she'd been touched. When had she last done this simple thing, held a man's hand in her own?

They made their way to the front entrance and Nigel nodded his head in greeting to a couple of men hanging out by the door. "Suh, how are you?" said the bouncer to a man dressed in the uniform of *moto* cops, his orange shirt aglow from the neon sign flashing, AFRICA SHRINE. The officer nodded, silently entered.

"So policemen are here?" asked Angie, still unnerved by the highway robbery.

"A lot of government workers come to the Shrine," said Nigel. "They know the president despises Fela, still they show up. Even some of his cabinet members have been spotted here, in dark glasses."

They pushed through the entrance into a vestibule where a chubby, chapped-lipped man sat at a long table, a giant boom box blasting Fela's music. On his long table sat Fela albums, with vibrant, pop art covers and beside them an array of books—*The Autobiography of Malcolm X*, Frantz Fanon's *Black Skin, White Masks*,

How Europe Underdeveloped Africa. Ella once had those same books on her bedroom shelf. The chubby man busily rolled a gigantic joint of marijuana. Others sat piled at his elbow, looking like swollen, misshapen cigars.

"Krishna, my man!" said Nigel. "Haven't seen you in years!" The man stood, gave Nigel a bear hug. "This is the hippest Ghanian you will ever meet!" Nigel said to Angie.

"Buy something from me tonight, Brother," said Krishna. "Help the cause!"

Nigel reached into his pant pocket, pulled out a small wad of naira, handed it to Krishna.

"Have a joint, on me, my brother!" said Krishna as he sat back down.

"Nah man, that's not my scene," said Nigel.

Angie thought of that pink joint she'd smoked. She'd enjoyed her high. Part of her was tempted to take Krishna up on his offer. What would it be like to get high with Nigel? But he pulled her along and the moment passed.

The main concert hall was cavernous and dark; its walls were covered in psychedelic posters illuminated by black lights. Strings of red bulbs swept across the ceiling. The sweet aroma of many lit joints thickened the air.

Fela's band, Egypt 80, was performing, its thirty members squeezed on stage, blaring horns and banging pianos and beating drums. Back at the Fox in Detroit, the band had been much smaller. Still, the music was the same—aggressive, polyrhythmic sounds racing after and colliding with one another, driving and hardcore, somehow both exuberant and sensual. Above the stage hung a huge sign proclaiming, BLACKISM IS A FORCE OF THE MIND.

Dozens of people sat on benches while others crowded near the stage. Gone was the hard-eyed, set-mouth look she'd grown accustomed to seeing on the faces of Nigerians. People looked enthralled. She marveled too that this crowd was so diverse— student hip, dreadlocked, uniform crisp, dashiki clad.

I'm here, she thought. I'm at Fela's Shrine.

There was so much to take in: Atop the stage and below it, young women danced in cages lit by big white bulbs. She'd never seen anything like this in her life. Sure, Fela had a few women with him at the Detroit concert, his "backing singers" he called them. But this! These dancers' faces were adorned with colorful dots and swirling stripes that traveled across their noses and cheeks. Their eyes were heavy with black shadow, thick mouths glistening wine red. These women were both ample and svelte, their perfect bodies accentuated by halter bikini tops and micro-mini skirts skimming thick thighs; some had squares of leather climbing their legs like gladiator's sandals. One was bare chested. They were, she thought, a cross between sixties style go-go dancers and mythical African bush women—the kind of images that might be found in a hip version of *National Geographic*. Of course Ella would have admired them. They were mesmerizing, beautiful, stone faced, and trancelike even as they bent and gyrated and undulated their hips in deep rhythm with the blaring bass lines. Angie was transfixed, watching each dancer thrust her pelvis just so, flat belly circling, legs strong, knees bent akimbo.

"Those are all Fela's wives," said Nigel, leaning into her ear. "His quote unquote queens."

She wondered: Which ones took care of Ella?

As Fela walked onto the stage, several backup singers behind him, the crowd roared. Nigel grabbed Angie's hand and pulled her to the front. Dressed in matching white pants and shirt adorned with Adinkra symbols, Fela stood spread eagle on stage and puffed a fat joint between his fingers before handing it to a dancer. Oddly, he looked smaller than he had when she saw him perform at the Fox.

He grabbed a bottle of Gordon's and poured some onto the stage floor. He turned to face the crowd, held out both arms. "I am the chief priest, the chosen one!" he yelled. As a dancer took away the gin bottle, Fela gripped his sax and blew. Behind him, the horn section blew in unison as the backup singers leaned into their mikes and sang along. But the music wasn't what Angie had anticipated. She'd expected the wonderful call-and-response songs she'd heard at the Fox, was ready to say "Yeah, Yeah" following Fela's instruction. Instead, he played "Beast of No Nation," the song he'd performed for his finale at the Detroit concert, and kept interrupting himself to describe his prison experience.

"I mean, they beat the shit out of me, man," Fela was saying. "But you see, they cannot hurt me, dis Fela sef. I am the chosen one, I am telling you."

He played only the one song, stopping to talk about the abuse, blowing his horn, talking about the abuse, blowing his horn. To Angie it was so harrowing and funereal. It upset her. When a giant blunt passing around made its way to her, she took it gratefully, put it to her lips, wanting to enter another, heightened zone, feel something profound in this Africa Shrine.

Nigel snatched the joint from her. "What the hell is wrong with you?! You don't know what's in that shit!" He passed the marijuana to a guy standing nearby.

His vehemence startled her. "You don't have to scream," she said.

"I'm sorry." He spoke over the music. "It's just that Fela is known for lacing his weed with shit! Bad shit!" He glared at her, accusatory. "And I had no idea you get high."

"I don't. Not really," she said sheepishly.

"Well I don't want you starting on my watch," snapped Nigel.

Her mind flashed back to their basement, her child's hand reaching for a joint offered to Ella, Nigel's big hand coming in, slapping hers, him saying, *little girl, you do not want that.*

"So you don't ever get high anymore?" she asked Nigel.

"No."

"How can you be around all this and not be tempted?"

"Because. I'm done with all that."

It moved her, his resolve, and she saw him as a protective barrier against herself and bad choices. She felt stunned yet again that she'd found him. As bodies squeezed in around them, making it hard to move, she leaned hers against his.

"Yo, I need some air!" he yelled. "Let's get something to drink!"

She'd liked the feeling of their bodies touching, but it was over now as she followed him through the crowd; they made their way to the makeshift bar in the back of the club, where bottles sat in a small refrigerator. Nigel got a lager and Angie decided to try a Shandy. She drank it fast.

"Hey, slow down. That thing is only half lemonade," warned Nigel. "The other half is beer."

"Whatever, it's delicious!"

"You hungry?" he asked.

It seemed so long ago that she and Regina and Nigel had eaten the *dodo.* "Starving."

He led Angie over to a table where thin slices of meat sat on skewers under a heat lamp. He bought three from the vendor, gave her one of the little kabob-like sticks.

"This is *suya,*" he said. "As the Nigerians say, let's chop-chop!"

She tore into the meat, which was deliciously spiced and sweet at the same time. He handed her another one and she ate that one with gusto too, finishing her Shandy before they returned to the main room, just as Fela paused from playing. He raised his hand to stop the music. "I am here to speak truth to you," he told the crowd. "You must learn to hear the truth."

He told the audience how he'd just returned from a trip to Burkina Faso, how that country's president had been the only leader in all of Africa to embrace him and his music.

"IBB with his zombie men, he cannot stop me, O!" he roared. "I am Fela, one who is great. I am Anikulapo, he who carries death in his pouch. I am Kuti, one who cannot be killed by man."

He suddenly ripped open his shirt and revealed a chest full of lesions, each one a red or festering or scabbed sore. Everyone gasped in unified shock.

"Shit!" yelled Nigel.

Angie didn't want to look, didn't want to see Fela that way. Yet, she couldn't stop herself from staring.

"You are hearing rumors about me, and I am telling you my brodas and sistahs, I am becoming a new man!" he roared. "I am changing skin. That is what you see. The spiritual guides have assured me that I am transforming with the help of my Yoruba gods. Do not worry, O! I am Kuti, the one who cannot be killed by man!"

He left his shirt open, stood spread eagle, and smiled, so beguiling that the crowd roared with love. "And so my brodas and sistahs, I must tell it to you like it is," he said. "I must sing it to you plain."

With that, he launched into an old song with renewed force. *Zombie-O, Zombie no go go, unless you tell am to go,* he sang. *Zombie no go stop, unless you tell am to stop.* Here was the song she knew well from Ella's cassette tapes and yet why didn't it satisfy her to hear it sung in Lagos, at the Shrine? The dancers kept grinding, the band kept playing, Fela kept singing, the backup girls kept harmonizing, and the smoke kept rising; but Angie couldn't absorb any of it. This had gone all wrong. She'd wanted to feel Ella's presence here, be transformed by this experience, and instead she felt just horrible. She'd wanted to see this man 'live' at his own club, this man who'd been so larger-than-life to Ella, whose wives had nursed and protected her in her final days. But he looked frail to Angie, vulnerable. And crazy. Her head spun from the Shandy. The sight of his crusted-over lesions was too deeply disturbing. Why didn't he just close his damn shirt?

"I have to get out of here," she said to Nigel. "Now."

IN THE TAXI, she held Nigel's hand until they'd left the dark, scary roads of Ikeja and had made it back to the gated campus in Yaba. As they walked up the stairs to his flat, she became convinced of her own misjudgment. She'd been going places Ella had been, when in fact she needed to go where her sister *hadn't gotten a chance to go*, to carry out Ella's last wishes.

They entered Nigel's flat. "I'm leaving," she said.

"You mean Lagos?"

She nodded.

"Yeah, maybe it's time for you to go home."

"No, I mean I'm leaving to go to Kano."

He didn't say anything, just sighed heavily.

"I want to see those dye pits."

"I guess I should've known that was coming."

"I'm not asking you to come with me."

Nigel shook his head, smiling. "And you know I'm not letting your ass go there alone."

KANO

SEVENTEEN

AT THE DEPARTURE GATE, THEY WAITED FOR THE SAME PLANE that had just left for Kano to return, deplane passengers, refuel, and get cleaned in order to fly back to Kano. "*Danfo* in the sky!" said a kufi-wearing man sitting next to Nigel and Angie. Nigel chuckled. "Yeah, the Nigerian factor."

When they'd returned the night before, Nigel had given Angie his flat and gone to be with Regina in her dorm room, where she'd waved her open return ticket in Nigel's face and assured him that if he stayed too long in Kano, she'd be back in Baltimore by the time he returned.

"Are you worried?" Angie now asked Nigel.

"Not yet."

"She doesn't think there's something between us, does she?"

Nigel shrugged. "She doesn't know what to think. I tried to explain, but it's not like all this makes a lot of sense."

"She had to know what Ella meant to you." Angie wanted to say, *She has you. Ella is dead. What's she worried about?*

"I'm not going to Kano with Ella."

Embarrassed, Angie turned her face away from his. She stared out the massive picture window at the airbus humming on the tarmac, gleaming green letters on its side spelling out Nigeria Airways. She hadn't slept much the night before. Lying in Nigel's bed, alone, as the hours of insomnia piled up, she'd become more and more anxious. With this trip, she'd get to complete a goal Ella had wanted to accomplish. But why was she so nervous? Wasn't that what her whole life had been about these past four years?

She turned back to face him. "Do you think about what might've happened if you and Ella had gotten to go to Kano together, like you planned?"

He looked out the giant window as if searching for words on the runway. "I like to think I would've convinced her to come back home with me." He looked over at Angie. "But who knows?"

"I think you would have," she said. "I think you two would still be together right now."

Nigel smiled. "It's a nice thought."

Angie was relieved to see him smile. It was so rare.

When a voice over the PA system finally announced boarding, in a scratchy and unclear garble, everyone rose and ran in a stampede to the departure door.

"Why are they running?" she asked.

Nigel rose. "To get seats on the plane."

She rose too. "There are no seat assignments?"

"First come, first served." He grabbed their bags. "I usually fly British Airways when I travel in Africa, but intra-country travel usually means flying on the national airline." He took her hand. "Needless to say, this one is run like the rest of Nigerian government."

They ran and made their way through the thicket of people clogging the entryway, and onto the tarmac. The throng of bodies pushed them along and up the metal stairs of the plane. Inside the cabin, people shoved giant bags and tied-up boxes into the overhead compartment. Several seats were saved with passengers' possessions, staked out for travel companions. They walked toward the back of the plane, found two seats together. He offered her the window.

As the plane lifted off and roared through the sky, Angie felt she was finally honoring her sister's memory in a real way. She looked over at Nigel and a new wave of gratitude engulfed her.

When the plane reached a cruising altitude, a few passengers pulled out their own food, making the cabin smell like a meat parlor. The flight attendants, stylish young Nigerian women in chic green skirts and white blouses, served drinks. A veiled woman reached out, grabbed a flight attendant's arm. "Heat up this soup for me now, dearie," said the woman as she handed over a greasy paper bag. Angie thought about the difference between now and just two weeks ago, when she was on the plane en route to Nigeria. It was astonishing how different everything was now, how different *she* was. It had only been fourteen days and yet she felt she'd outrun that old Angie, finally left her behind for good back in Lagos. That Angie was lost to her.

When turbulence hit, she squeezed Nigel's arm and he patted her thigh reassuringly. The pilot spoke to the control tower, his voice caught on the loudspeaker, "I have one hundred and twelve souls on board, including six crew," he said. The choppiness subsided and right away, Angie relaxed. Try as she might she couldn't keep her eyes open. As she nodded out, bobbing and catching herself, Nigel gently guided her head to his shoulder, and she slept for the rest of the flight. When the plane made its harsh landing—a hard, bumpy touchdown, she abruptly awoke to a brief shock of desire between her legs, which startled her. Everyone was clapping loudly. "Thanks be to Allah!" yelled one man.

"Thanks be to the goddamn pilot," said Nigel.

Angie laughed. It felt so good to open her mouth wide and do that.

AN HOUR LATER, Nigel sat beside Angie in a battered Datsun as the driver cruised along a major road of modern Kano, with its numerous banks and low-slung businesses. As they approached the Old City, before them stood a tall, reddish-brown wall winding its way in a circular path, stretching for miles. It reached so high that when Angie craned her neck to look up, she couldn't see the top from her backseat view.

Nigel whistled. "Brother, how tall is that wall?"

"Twelve miles long and more that fifty feet high," said the driver. His name was Emeka, their de facto tour guide. "In the local language, we call it the *badala*."

As they got closer to the wall, it dominated the view from their windows. Angie felt slightly claustrophobic, as though moving through an endless tunnel.

"How old is it?" she asked.

"This wall was built in the fifteenth century," said Emeka. "But the original one was built in the twelfth century. Inside is the Old City of Kano."

She stared at the structure, couldn't fathom anything that old still standing. "What was the whole purpose of the wall?" she asked. "I mean, why build an entire wall around a city?"

"To protect the people of Kano from invaders of course."

"Ah, the first gated communities," said Nigel. "Who knew?"

"People are supposed to protect you," said Angie. "Not walls."

"It is not so much for protection now," explained Emeka. "It's now where the majority of Hausa Muslims live. And the southern Christians mostly live in the Sabon Gari, the new city."

As they drove ahead, a mountain came into view, framing the sky like a huge humpbacked camel, its tan beauty stark in contrast to the dark, crumbling wall.

"That's Dala Hill," noted Emeka.

"Is it hard to climb?" she asked.

"Not at all. There are steps. And at the top, quite a view."

"Wow, I'd love to climb it!" said Angie, excited to be a tourist.

"We can do that in the morning," said Nigel. The driver turned to navigate a tiny alleyway, causing the mountainous hill to disappear. Soon they pulled up to the small hotel he'd suggested. The late-afternoon heat hit Angie with force as she stepped out of the car. "Feels like it's a hundred degrees," she said.

"You are coming from Lagos," said Emeka. "We are much closer to the Sahara here, so the weather is hotter. But you've come at a good time. The rain helps. Just this morning we had thunderstorms."

Out front, a man sat atop a gold Vespa moped. Nigel began chatting with him about the motorbike, kept saying how cool it was.

"You can rent it, my broda," said the man. "I am Bola. I will give you a good price."

"I just might do that," said Nigel. "Later, man."

Angie's room was sparse, but charming. She had a low-lying bed on a wood frame, a porcelain sink with its own mirror and to her delight, a tiny balcony. She opened the shutters and was greeted with a distant call to prayer. She leaned out and saw a few people walking along a street, the women veiled. A motorcycle taxi with two men riding together sped by. Gone was the frenetic pace of Lagos. She liked the contrast.

Angie lay across her bed. Her body hummed. The shock of desire she'd experienced on the plane was back. She'd never felt this before, a kind of rogue turn-on. She'd had only one real boyfriend in her life, and sex had been pretty good. With Romare hovering above, she could rouse desire, sure, but this was something else, like a little beast in her belly, coiled and waiting, making her restless, sweaty.

She undressed, stepped into the white rectangular tub and turned on the shower nozzle. She was grateful for the cold water. As she soaped her body, she ran her hands over her hips and belly, her breasts. She'd hoped to fill out by coming to Nigeria, had hoped that all the rice and stews would have their way with her, and she'd add a few well-placed pounds. She'd always longed for more voluptuousness, always wished she'd been a "brick house," like the woman The Commodores sang about. But her sick days at Funke's had thwarted that plan.

She put on the tie-dyed caftan that had been Ella's and headed to the slim lobby, waited for Nigel.

He stopped when he saw her, a flicker of recognition in his eyes. "You look nice."

"Thank you," she whispered, the coiled beast heavy inside.

They walked to a Lebanese restaurant just up the road. The place was charming, with a giant thatched roof supported by bamboo poles and wooden tables adorned with coconut shells holding bougainvillea flowers. Straw covered the floor, except for a large, shiny square set aside for dancing, its disco ball glowing overhead. A DJ played highlife music. The place was filled with many foreign businessmen and southern Nigerians, their broad noses distinguishing them from the long-nosed northerners and Lebanese waiters.

She and Nigel ordered their meals from clever menus pasted to sticks. The place made her think of an episode of *Gilligan's Island*—when the crew members transformed a portion of the island into a nightclub for Thurston and Lovey. The waiter brought Nigel stout and her, palm wine. She found herself liking the tangy wine right away, not like back in Brenda's bedroom. She sipped slowly. Thinking of Brenda made her feel jealous that *she'd* gotten to have a fling with Nigel, and the animal inside uncoiled, rose up a bit, its seductive tongue licking her nerve endings, teasing her with longing. She was ashamed of herself and drank more, hoping to drown the beast. Nigel ordered. "Give us a smorgasbord," he told the waiter. "A little bit of everything."

He took a swig of lager. "So tell me what things are like back home. What's the big D up to these days?"

Angie shifted in her seat, feeling she'd been asked a trick question. Did he want to know what *she'd* been up to? How do you say, *not a damn thing*?

"It's different from back in the day, that's for sure," she offered.

"Oh, I could see that when I left," he said. "Crack killing off our young brothers. That shit is *nothing* like what we were dealing with."

"And now, the whole AIDS thing." She shook her head. "I mean, never mind Rock Hudson. All those folks who shot up? Now they have to worry about getting the virus."

Neither of them said the obvious—that *that* could've been Ella's fate had she lived.

"It's on the continent too, unfortunately," said Nigel. He took another swig. "Mostly in East African countries. Uganda is getting hit hard. They call it the 'slim' disease. And back in Nairobi, damn near every prostitute is infected, which makes Regina's charges absurd. Like I'd even touch one of those women."

Angie looked out at the couples on the dance floor. She didn't want to hear Regina's name.

"It's wild, isn't it, that one disease can reach across continents?" continued Nigel. He burped lightly. "When I got back to Africa four years ago, nobody was talking about AIDS. It was all secrecy and denial. Now, the World Health Organization is trying to play catch-up."

Angie turned up her glass of palm wine, finished it off. "Let's not talk about death and dying right now, OK?"

Nigel nodded his understanding, followed her gaze to the dance floor as music blared from the speakers. Angie twisted her torso as the DJ shifted to a new tune.

"Sonny Ade! I love him!" Nigel rose and held out his hand to her.

"I can't dance like that," she insisted as he pulled her onto the shiny square. They joined others and right away Nigel started doing the highlife—hip-swinging, rhythmic moves, hands out in front, palms spread.

"I can't do it," she said to Nigel.

"I'll show you," he said, gyrating just so—slow and sensuous. She mimicked him, pushing her butt out and rocking it up and down.

"That's it," Nigel whispered in her ear. A chill tumbled down her neck. She had a memory flash of Ella dancing to Bob Marley, recalled the thrill of seeing her sister move like that.

"That's it!" he repeated. "You got it."

They danced through two songs, and the whole time she watched the muscles in his neck move, the way his chest pushed against his shirt, straining the buttons, the way he threw back his head and chuckled. When they returned to their table, exhausted and thirsty, both gulped down fresh drinks waiting for them. She was tipsy by the time their food arrived—an array of exotic Middle Eastern choices that reminded her of the food in East Seven Mile eateries back home: grilled shish kabobs, garlic-laced salad, creamy hummus, baba ganouje, and spicy cabbage leaves. She ate greedily, thrilled to be away from the extreme choices of Nigerian cuisine—bland and gooey or searing hot and tasteless. They dipped their pita breads into each other's plates, fed one another forkfuls of spicy delicious chicken, licked their fingers. Their empty plates were whisked away and the two shared diamond-shaped baklavas, the attar syrup a delight to Angie's sweet tooth. They followed dessert with cups of dark, strong Lebanese coffee, looking on as the dance floor swelled with bodies.

Afterward, Nigel leaned back, lit a cigarette; she watched his cheeks suck in, then balloon out, watched his eyes squint. She was full, but not satiated. She watched him more, transfixed. She felt her desire rising, tried to calm herself with deep breaths. At last he tossed the butt to the straw floor and mashed it with his foot.

"We should get back," he said. "The guy at the front desk said it's best to see Dala Hill early, before the sun gets treacherous. Or before it rains. You never know what to expect."

They walked side by side, Nigel's strong arm around her; the feel of his lightly damp skin against her arm was almost unbearable. I'm out of my mind, she thought.

At the hotel, they made their way down the hall. She was so full and leaned her weight against him; he guided her to her room. After she opened the door, she grabbed his arm and tried to pull him inside. He resisted, and the force of his resistance pushed her closer, so close she stood on tiptoe and landed a kiss on his lips. A quick one, a dusting. She felt his hesitation, felt him freeze before he gently pushed her away, held her at arm's length.

"Whoa, girl! What are you doing?"

She wasn't listening, tried to move in again, kiss him. Just one kiss she thought. Just one.

He gripped her wrists. "Angie, no. We can't. Hear me? We absolutely cannot. No."

"Don't say no to me."

He looked at her with those hazy eyes. "Listen, you've had too much to drink. Get some sleep, OK?"

He turned, walked back down the dark hall. She watched him leave, then slammed her door, grabbed the loose dress with both hands and pulled it over her head, flung it across the room. She peeled out of her underwear and lay across the bed, breeze from the open window blowing across her naked body. She imagined Nigel undressing, crawling into his own hotel bed. She shoved the pillow between her legs and gripped tight. A mere brush of her fingers against her nipples, and she was crying out in release. Right away, she fell into a drunken slumber.

EIGHTEEN

NIGEL BANGED ON HER HOTEL ROOM DOOR THE NEXT morning, waking her. She had to pull the bed sheet around her body as she stumbled toward his knocks.

He looked her up and down before he said, "Come on, get dressed. Dala Hill awaits."

At first, as she hurriedly pulled herself together, she tried to recall what had happened, couldn't remember beyond the failed goodnight kiss. And then she realized it was still there, the desire, lying in wait. She found Nigel in the lobby, sipping coffee. He'd gotten one for her too from somewhere, but she waved it off. She needed water, already perspiring. The hotel manager got her a bottled water, and she drank it down in a series of continuous gulps.

"You OK?" asked Nigel, looking at her with eyes that asked, *Are we OK?*

She nodded, bobbing her head nonstop.

"OK, let's go."

When they stepped outside the hotel, Nigel climbed onto the Vespa parked in front.

"You rented it?"

He smiled like a kid. "Hop on."

"You sure you know how to ride this thing?"

"Don't you trust me by now?" Light flickered in his eyes.

She climbed on behind him and held tight, grateful for this legitimate reason to grip Nigel's body, press her own against his. The streets were moderately busy and the sky cut-glass blue as Nigel guided the motorbike through traffic. The wind created a billowy arc of her top, refreshed her wet skin. They traveled a few miles through the city, passing an array of buildings with Arabic signs, some with schoolchildren filing into them. Approaching the old wall, Nigel guided the bike through a large opening.

"The guy who loaned me the bike, Bola? He told me these passageways are called *kofars*, gates," said Nigel, his words rushing back to her, carried on the wind. "Gates like this are all around the wall, and each one has its own special name. They used them once to control people's movement in and out of the city."

She tried to imagine what that was like—controlling people with a giant wall and many gates. Her head ached. As they sped along, Angie found the Old City otherworldly, like a sepia-toned photograph overlaid with jewel tones created by Muslim women's vibrant head shrouds. The Jakara River ran alongside, chasing them, and she buried her face in Nigel's back for the rest of the ride, to still the buzz in her head. When they reached the Old City's far end, Dala Hill rose before them in grandeur, an endless staircase carved zigzag style, from the base up to its crest. Nigel skidded to a stop.

"It really is more like a mountain," she said.

"Bola says it's seventeen hundred feet high. Maybe even higher." Nigel threw down the kickstand. "Hop off."

She stood looking up at the hill, felt her equilibrium upset by the moped ride, and his presence. A gatekeeper sat cross-legged at the base of the hill, which was scattered with debris. Angie thought it looked neglected as she watched Nigel give the man a few kobo. No one else was around.

"Let's see how far up we can get," he said.

"How many steps do you think there are?"

"According to Bola, exactly 999."

"Shit!" she said. "That's a lot!"

"You curse?" he joked, grabbing her hand. "Come on, we've gotta get to the top so we can see the view."

They climbed slowly as the morning sun bore down on them. They climbed higher and higher, an hour passing, until finally they reached the top landing. Below them stood a sea of flat, brown rooftops and conical thatched ones, palm trees sprouting between them. A maze of roadways cut through the haphazard cluster of buildings, tiny figures walking the sinewy roads in between buses and cars.

"This is beautiful," said Angie. "Imagine it at sunrise."

They sat there for a long time, looking down on the ancient city, so contained in comparison to the push-and-shove and sprawl of wild, rambunctious Lagos. Nigel leaned forward, brushing his arm against hers; she still wanted him, wanted to open herself up to him right here on the top of this hill, right here in its soft earth. She was disgusted by her own desire, couldn't be near him.

She stood. "I have to go."

He looked up at her, squinting from the sun. "Go where?"

"Anywhere. Away from you."

He grabbed her hand. "Angie, look, about last night, it was just something that happened." He was still squinting. "We stopped it, that's the important thing."

She jerked away, freeing herself. "I'm leaving." She turned, ran to the steps, began making her way down.

His voice hit her back. "Angie, stop it! Come back here!"

She ignored him, and trying to get away, stumbled and nearly fell.

"Hey!" he yelled. "Slow down!" But she kept running. The stairs were mere clay carved into the earth, and they softened under her feet, making her slide down.

"Angela!!!" he screamed, terror in his voice. He caught up with her, gripped his hand around her arm.

"Let go!" she yelled. "You're hurting me!"

"Wait! Just wait, for Christ's sake!"

"I have to get away from you!" she yelled, convinced this torturous feeling was all his fault. He'd caused it somehow, was making it happen. "Let go!"

But he didn't let go, and for the rest of their descent, he held fast to her arm. They made their way down in silence, her need to flee subsiding with each step. If only he'd take his hands off of her, stop touching her. Once they were at the base of the hill, he looked at her and she saw it—desire in his own eyes.

In silence, they mounted the Vespa and took off, flying through the street, rushing against the wind. He was going so fast she wrapped her arms around him as tight as she could, desperate to hold on. She could feel the muscles in his body tensing, felt his urgency as he guided the bike through the Old City's streets, dipping low at corners, terrifying her, the terror mixing with her aching lust. He passed the Jakara River, tore through an opening, and roared back through the Sabon Gari, flying past the Arabic schools and banks and mosques.

Once back at the hotel, they didn't look at each other. He returned the Vespa to Bola and walked straight inside, to the back. She followed behind, slightly running to keep up. She thought about that Woodward Avenue motel Nigel and Ella had gone to, for their first time. She pushed the thought from her mind, forced herself not to think at all.

Standing outside her room, Nigel took her face into his

hand and kissed her. She could taste the nicotine on his lips. He planted tiny kisses on her neck and she whimpered, collapsed against the door.

"Come on," he whispered, and she fumbled with the key, until the lock clicked. Her room suddenly looked unfamiliar, as though she hadn't spent a night there already. The shutters remained flung open and the calls to prayer wafted upward from nearby loudspeakers.

Wordlessly, he closed the shutters, darkening the room; he undressed her, took off his own clothes. He led her to the bed and they fell into one another, ravenous, starving animals. Afterward, both lay flung out, on separate ends of the bed. Afternoon car horns filled the room. A picture came to mind, of her ten-year-old self, on his lap, arms around his neck. She turned over, her back to him.

He touched her arm. "Hey, you alright?"

"No."

He spoke to her back. "It was just one of those things that happened."

She turned to face him. "Like you and Brenda?"

He looked taken aback. "Why do you have to go there?"

She felt on the verge of tears, shame and regret converging. "I don't know."

"Look at it this way," he said. "It was hanging there and we took care of it, so now its lost its power, we can get on with things."

Even as he said it, she could see his erection. They stared at one another. "OK" she said, and they both slid down into sleeping positions. He turned over, hugged the one pillow. His back was the most beautiful sight, its vertebrae an elegant stepladder to the broad expanse of his shoulders. She reached out, gingerly, touched him. He turned, abruptly pulled her to him and their bodies tangled together, sheet sliding to the floor.

NINETEEN

ANGIE FELT LIKE AN AIRPLANE PASSENGER, TRAPPED ON A transatlantic flight both never ending and unmoving. She and Nigel didn't leave her room for two days. When hunger crept over them, Nigel brought back random items from the *buka* nearby—sliced mangoes, peanuts, boiled eggs. Once, he found *dodo* from somewhere and Angie ate the sweet, crispy-soft plantain with a yearning she'd never felt for food. They'd eat atop the bed, naked, and once done push the greasy paper to the floor, crawl toward each other.

She'd never understood what women meant when they said, "I couldn't get enough of him," or "the brother just did something to me." Now she got it. Nothing else mattered, other than being with Nigel. She felt a kind of insanity, and while it frightened her, it was liberating. She'd never known what it meant to let go completely. And it wasn't just that she'd had her first orgasm with Nigel, it was her lack of self-consciousness, her full-out passion. That was new. Often, afterward, they'd lay there spent, and she'd be certain they couldn't possibly do it again; but then her foot would brush against his leg and he'd move his hand up her thigh and she'd turn and violently throw her body atop his. He'd moan and laugh and grip her ass and she could tell from his kiss that he was as stunned and grateful as she was. Curled up in Nigel's arms in a post-coital exhaustion, Angie could feel his heartbeats as she listened to yet another call to prayer outside the thrown-open window.

Finally, they decided to get out, see the sights. Neither dared mention the dye pits. Instead, Nigel suggested they go back into the Old City, and so they sought out their driver Emeka and climbed into his battered Datsun. In the back, they held hands as he drove right alongside the ancient wall, thick at its base. "As wide as eight people lying head to foot," noted Emeka. They rode so close to the wall that Angie could see crumbling pock-holes of disrepair in the clay. The sight of its disintegration saddened her, and she felt a pang of longing for Nigel, as though what they had was already gone, already a poignant memory she'd look back on, a beautiful relic of another time and place in her life.

"So what's this gate called?" asked Nigel as Emeka drove through a narrow opening.

"The *kofar nasawara*, the white man's gate," said Emeka. "They call it that because it used to lead to the colonial residence."

"Oh, I like busting through this one," said Nigel. "Feels gangster!"

Angie laughed. He was so funny.

Inside the gate, the Old City hummed. Hawkers and goats and children and head-covered women walked languidly along the sandy roads. Motorbikes sprinted by. Low buildings in reddish-brown ochre were everywhere. Funny how now that this thing had happened between them, she could really *see*, could focus on the city's sights.

"They look like mud houses," said Nigel. "Like some adobe-type thing in Mexico."

"The city has all of these lowland pools and borrow pits that create mud during the rainy season, like right now," said

Emeka, adding that they used the mud to build Sudanese-style structures.

Angie pointed to an aqua-blue dome jutting into the horizon, brightening the cloudy sky. Emeka stopped and they stepped out for a moment to admire the dome and its majestic white-stoned structure beneath.

"That is the central mosque, Nigeria's biggest," said Emeka, coming up behind them. "It's of course not very old. Thirty-five years old or so. But it's a very important part of people's lives."

Angie was awed by the reverence it evoked. "How long has Islam been practiced here?" she asked.

"In Kano? Since the sixteenth century," said Emeka. "It's the foundation of who we are, our love of Allah."

She wished she'd had a love like that, a deep and penetrating faith. Apart from her visits to Unity Temple, she'd had so little experience with religion. At her father's funeral, Aunt Bea had yelled out, "Get up Samson. Get on up from there!" and six-year-old Angie had waited for him to do so; she stared hard at his dead body, willing him to rise; when he didn't and they closed the casket, she felt she'd failed him. She'd conflated church with death and failed resurrection ever since.

Back in the taxi, Nigel kissed her and she was grateful that desire could push away death. She moved her hand over Nigel's crotch and he groaned lightly.

"You know what?" Nigel said to Emeka. "We'll just go back to the hotel."

THE NEXT DAY, they tried again. "This time, keep your hands off of me," said Nigel, only half-joking.

"I'm not going to even stand near you," she promised, as they climbed back into Emeka's car.

"Today I will take you to Kurmi Market," said Emeka. "It's one of the largest and oldest in Africa."

They entered the walled city through a different gate and made their way toward the market, the Jakara River shimmering alongside it; soon enough they came upon a thicket of people, making it impossible to go farther.

"You will want to get out and walk around now," advised Emeka.

The market was choked with hawkers, cloths hanging from their arms, five different objects in hand. It dwarfed Gbaja Market in Lagos. It was endless, massive. Sinewy main arteries bordered by gutters turned off into tributaries of slim alleyways. They strolled through what was essentially a giant maze, meandering down one dark corridor after another. Nigel abruptly pulled her into one of the darkened corners, and with vendors eyeing them, kissed her passionately. She'd never kissed in public before and the exhibitionism excited her. Now she was holding on as he pulled her through an alley with its dizzying array of wooden carvings and large calabashes. She ached with longing, felt she'd burst if they didn't get back to the room soon. They went down another alleyway, this one filled with brass and bronze and beaded jewelry in a blur of shapes and colors. Stall vendors called out to the couple. She followed Nigel along yet another corridor, where sheets of leather hung, their smell of wild beasts driving her to distraction.

They were running now, lost in the maze, desperate to get out, get back to the room. Vendors kept calling out to them: "Enta," they chanted. "Enta."

Together they ran like escaped prisoners, navigating through the labyrinth, bumping into people, until they turned down a row of stalls with vendors selling cloths. Women stood against a backdrop of traditional prints, pastel laces, and textiles of deep, brooding hues and saturated colors. Angie recognized the women's faces—the elongated noses and gently brown skin, the high cheekbones. Women like Missy, who'd braided her hair. They called out to her as she and Nigel ran by: "Sistah, come, come Sistah. You are welcome! Sistah, come!" She kept her gaze on the women as long as she could as she and Nigel ran by.

Finally, mercifully, they found Emeka leaning against the battered Datsun, eating peanuts and tossing the shells onto the ground. They crawled into the backseat, humidity another passenger in the car. Angie and Nigel both instinctively sat on opposite ends, straining against the car doors, not daring to touch one another. After an eternity, Emeka pulled up to the hotel. Like children admonished not to run in the hallways at school, she and Nigel speed-walked in single file back to her room.

Once inside, Nigel pushed her against the door, pulled up her skirt and entered her right there.

"God, I love you," she whispered, her legs wrapped around his waist. "I love you so much."

Everything about this felt right. Sacred. As their hands interlaced, she understood why African women married their dead husbands' brothers.

They tried again the following day, this time determined to get through a few hours of sightseeing without rushing back. But when they looked for Emeka in the lobby, they couldn't find him. In fact, the entire hotel was all but deserted.

"What happened?" asked Angie. She had the sinking feeling that a coup had occurred while they were sequestered away, having nonstop sex.

"It is Friday," explained Bola, the Vespa owner. "Everyone is headed to afternoon prayers. Except for me because I am a Christian!" He smiled at them both. "Anyway, you will not be able to get around. The streets are blocked."

As if on cue, a call-to-prayer issued forth over the ubiquitous loudspeaker, prompting Angie and Nigel to head outside. There they saw dozens and dozens of men in neat rows along the main boulevard in front of the hotel, each on an individual prayer rug, each prone and facing the West, all praying aloud in Arabic. Their unified voices rang out, creating a vibrating chorus. The spiritual surrender en masse made Angie step backward, made her feel silly for her own Buddhist chant selfishly recited when she was in need or in fear.

They turned silently and returned to the room.

For three more days, they went nowhere, distrusting themselves, afraid of "getting caught out there" as Nigel described it. He gathered their rations from the same *buka*, bringing back an array of bottled pop and chunks of coconut and cans of potted meat and loaves of bread. She laughed with glee when she saw his hands filled with food. It was as though they were fugitives, hiding underground. "I could be her, *that* Angela, on the lam," She thought. "Only I get to have my man with me."

They didn't bother with clothes. She lost track of time again, could only tell when night became day from the shuttered window and the sunlight slipping away, moonlight taking its place. On the second night, there were thunderstorms and lightening, the booming torrent itself a turn-on. In the middle of the third night, Nigel said, "Let's change it up," and he led her to the tiny balcony, where he entered her from behind and made love to her in full view of whomever might think to look up from the street below. She could see a man riding a rickshaw watching her and her small cries drifted onto the night wind as she came.

None of it was real, and that was what Angie liked, that surreal quality of their lives together. Their future was a fuzzy outline, but that was OK. They had time to work out everything; she didn't try to think beyond the moment. It wasn't hard to do that, as the past four years had been like that anyway: she hadn't known what was next, hadn't thought beyond the days in front of her. This felt, in its way, normal.

ON THE FOURTH night, she felt feverish. She found herself clinging to Nigel in bed just for the relief of his cool skin against hers.

"You need some salt-water air," he announced, gently moving her hot body away from his. "And we both need the power of the ocean to break this spell."

It was true. She felt as though all the sex had drained away her color. She was like a convalescing woman, longed for the sun on her skin. In the morning, they sought out Emeka once again to take them to the Old City. He dropped them off on the bank of the Jakara River and promised to wait for them in that very spot.

The horizon stretched above the water, white and taut as vanilla taffy. Angie took off her sandals, walked closer to the shore, her feet sinking into the cool sand. She waded in, letting the water lap at her ankles. The breeze helped her to feel a bit better. Overhead, seagulls swooshed across the blank sky, their rhythmic *caw caw* like an impromptu wake-up call. She watched as one seagull swooped down, dipped its head into the river water, rose with its prize, and flew off. Nigel came up beside her.

"What do you suppose this all means?" she asked, looking out at the horizon.

"This what?"

"This! You and me connecting like this."

"I think it was a fantastic coincidence."

"I don't think it was that," she insisted. "Really, what are the odds that we'd run into each other?"

"Well, if you think about it, the odds were pretty good," he said. "You stayed with people in Lagos that I had a connection to, so it's not *that* strange."

"I can't believe you don't think it was more than that," she said, hurt obvious in her voice.

He turned toward her. "Why are you getting upset?"

"Because." She didn't really know why, only that she wanted him to be as awed by their reconnection, their togetherness, as she was. Otherwise, it felt like just any affair, only more sordid. "Chris told me that Africans don't believe in coincidence. Everything happens for a reason. Everything is fate."

"Chris would've said anything to fuck you."

She turned to face him. "Do you have to be so crude?"

"Hey, I'm not the one who tried to rape you."

Her head pounded. "Are you saying this is nothing, what we have?"

"I didn't know we were still talking about us."

The throbbing was relentless, pushed against her forehead. "You're ready to go back to Regina, aren't you?" she said. "Just say it!"

He looked out on the water. "I'd be lying if I told you I'd forgotten all about her."

"So go be with her!" She moved farther into the river. She had the urge to jump in, just dive, swim away. She remembered what that taxi driver had said about the Lagos Lagoon, how when someone falls in, they're so covered in oil they're too slippery to save. She kept wading farther in. The water rose to her waist. She kept going.

The water was at her chest when Nigel gripped her arm; she was secretly relieved, and said a quick prayer of gratitude before she turned to face him. His eyes said he still wanted her. She moved into his arms, the water lapping around them, and they kissed for a long, desperate time, as if their lips were charged with reassuring one another nothing had changed. She was the one who pulled him out of the water, toward the raffia hut up a ways on the shore. They crawled inside and she lifted her Indian skirt, slipped off her panties. The sand crunched under her ass, and through the woven straw of the hut she could see clouds, a vast cluster of them. She was shivery cold yet feverish, thought she might faint as his rough jeans chafed against her thigh. She kept her eyes on the piece of sky, which spun before her in a tumble of white clouds, and when he shuddered, she held on tight, dizziness pressing down on her alongside the weight of his satiated body. "I love you," he whispered, out of breath. "I do love you."

She held him as though she might fall off a cliff. In fact, she felt a kind of vertigo, and didn't free him from her embrace until it passed in a wave. Eventually, they crawled out of the raffia hut and Angie fell onto the cool sand, just lay there. Something ripped loose in her, some kind of band that had been holding together her limbs. She spread across the sand like a rag doll, limp and weak. She could feel herself fading.

"Angie, you OK?" he yelled from a great distance. She thought she nodded. Or shook her head.

Nigel tried to pull her up, but she felt too slippery to save. He lifted her into his arms and carried her back to the awaiting taxi. Emeka and he exchanged words, the car moved. Behind her closed eyes, firecrackers of light exploded, and then all went dark. Again, crackling luminescence, then darkness.

She awoke hours later to a drenched bed. At first, she was comforted by the wetness; assumed she was lying in a damp cocoon of their lovemaking. But Nigel's head swam above her, a disembodied face. He looked stricken. He'd gotten hot liquid from somewhere, tried to get her to drink. He placed a cool compress on her forehead. His hands, cold against her flaming skin, pushed thumbs against her pressure points, forced open her eyes. He wouldn't leave her alone, kept poking her, and she hated him. He kept barking questions at her: Did she know where she was? Was she taking the pills every day? Could she walk? She lay there, unable to respond, drifted back to her netherworld, to the place of popping sparkle and dark beauty.

Bare hands lifted her and the blanket she was in, carried her out. Soon, morning's air chafed her skin and its sun sealed close her eyelids. Now she was in a moving car, stretched across the backseat, joints aching from the rough motion; all stopped and hands slid beneath her, scooped her out into the dark sun again, carried her inside somewhere, lowered her into a chair, where she slumped over. Her chest hurt. She was cold, so cold. Someone said the word "American" and her eyes opened. Nigel was there, helped her up, led her past a crowded waiting room, down a hallway, behind a door, blanket bunched at her feet. Inside stood a stark metal examining table and a stark black man in a spotless white lab coat.

"Hello," he said, mouth hidden beneath a bushy mustache. Fear made her wobble.

"On the table," he ordered.

Nigel helped her onto the metal table. She was freezing. The doctor put her chin in his hand, looked in her eyes. "You don't feel so good, eh?"

She shook her head slowly.

"You are feeling like you have the flu, only worse?"

She nodded.

"Perhaps you were a little sick like this a couple days ago but got better?"

She shrugged, didn't remember.

"Don't worry my sistah, you will be fine."

"I'm pretty sure she was taking those anti-malarial drugs every day, Doc," said Nigel.

The doctor smiled. "Those pills don't work so well with the mosquitoes in Nigeria. They call that lunch."

He left, and Nigel coaxed the blanket from around her, draped it on his arm.

"What are they going to do to me?" she asked. It felt odd to speak, to hear her own voice.

"Give you medicine to make you better, just as the good doctor said."

"What kind of medicine?"

Before he could answer, a nurse walked into the room, unsmiling. She wore a long wig but no uniform. "Stand up," she ordered Angie.

"Why?"

"Arm or hip?" asked the nurse.

"What?"

"Do you want the injection in your arm or hip?"

Only then did Angie see the long needle in the woman's dangling hand. "You're not shooting me up!" she yelled.

"This is why you have come here, no?" asked the nurse, nonchalant.

"It's OK," Nigel said, standing beside her. He rubbed her arm.

She slapped his hand away. "Don't talk to me like I'm a child!"

"Arm or hip?" repeated the nurse.

"Don't you fucking come near me!" Angie screamed.

The nurse sucked her teeth. "I do not have all day!" she snapped. "Plenty-plenty people are waiting. Sick-sick people, O!"

Angie could not fathom that needle sliding under her skin. Even as a child, she was in terror of needles. She'd always been afraid of them, even before she found Ella slumped over the bathroom toilet, syringe inside the crook of her arm, needle jabbed into a vein. She endured shots when she had to, like her vaccines to travel, but this needle, she was convinced, was unclean and deadly. And gigantic.

She got off the table, and squatted, in an ugly and pathetic crouch. "If you come near me, I'll kill you," she said. Nigel gingerly lifted her upright. Sighing, as if to say *you American girls really are spoiled babies*, the nurse barked, "Lift your skirt, please."

"No," she whimpered.

Nigel grabbed her arms just as the doctor stepped back in. He helped to hold her as Angie screamed. The nurse lifted her skirt, yanked down her panties and jabbed her in the buttock. Pain shot through her entire leg, a pain so acute no sound escaped when she cried out. The nurse threw the needle into a trashcan and walked out. The room spun around her. A million ants danced on her nerve endings. She went limp.

"Oh shit." Nigel caught her before she hit the floor. "Is she gonna be alright?"

"She'll feel like new in a few hours," said the doctor. "Except for the bruises on her arms." He hovered over her. "Next time, my sistah, you must let us help you, not fight."

"Fuck you," she said.

The doctor flinched. "You can get her out of here now," he said brusquely as he left the room.

Nigel helped Angie sit back on the examining table, held her wrists, looked into her eyes.

"You OK?"

With the energy she had, she shook her head. "No. That shit hurt."

He sighed relief. "I had to do it Angie. You weren't getting better on your own."

Her leg ached. Badly. A searing burn dripped from her hip to her ankle. "I think I'm paralyzed."

Panic moved across his face like a shadow. She felt a sick satisfaction in the thought that he blamed himself. It made her feel they were in this together.

"Come on, try to walk." He helped her down, led her out and past the crowd of sufferers, many of them children with runny noses and drooping faces. Sick eyes staring at her as she passed. Nigel led her to a Volkswagen Beetle, gingerly helped her into the backseat and slid in the front. She lay across the space, achy leg stretched out before her.

"Whose car is this?" she asked.

"Bola's. He lent it to me."

Nigel tried to start the car, but it wouldn't ignite. He tried again. And again. Nothing. He leaned his head on the steering wheel. Angie studied the back of his neck for several seconds. Her mouth was glue. "I've never been this thirsty in my life," she said.

"Yeah?" He opened the car door. "Wait here."

He jogged across the road to a kiosk. She watched him buying a pop, parched throat oppressive, and a memory came rushing at her: In the backyard with Ella. She is six, maybe seven. It's the middle of a harsh Michigan winter and the yard is covered in fresh, crunchy snow. Ella is helping her fill a bowl with it. She wears mittens; Ella's hands are bare. "There's nothing in the world better than snow ice-cream," Ella says as she leads Angie into the house. She tells her to close your eyes and count to twenty. When Angie opens them, there before her is white, glistening ice cream. "Go ahead, Princess," says Ella. "Eat up." It was delicious, that sweetness against the cold. She was awed by her big sister's magical powers, thrilled to be shown something wondrous in the world, something she might never have known existed without Ella. Angie realized she hadn't thought about Ella these past several days; yet she had always been there, hovering, waiting.

Nigel returned with an opened bottle of orange Fanta. "It's warm but it's wet," he said, handing it to her through the window. She took a long swig, burped softly.

"Now how does it feel?" he asked.

"What?"

"Your leg!"

Miraculously, the pain in her leg was gone, as was the overall achiness. Her hip was a tender bruise, but still.

Nigel blew out air. "The power of chloroquine. A miracle drug costing pennies, and still millions of people here die from fucking malaria." He turned the ignition. "One more shameful example of callous greed," he mumbled as the car refused to start. He turned again and the engine stayed silent. He pounded the steering wheel. "Fuck!" He tried to light a cigarette, but his hands were shaking; he placed the unlit cigarette in the ashtray. "You scared the shit out of me."

She leaned forward, touched him lightly. "I'm OK now."

When he looked back at her, she could actually see the fear, like tiny crouching animals, just behind his eyes. He laid his head against the headrest, stared at the car's interior. "Thank God."

He lifted his head and she studied his profile, the shamefully long eyelashes, the rise and fall of his adam's apple. "Nigel?"

"Yeah?"

"I want to see those dye pits."

He caught her eye in the rearview mirror. "I think you need to just rest, Angie. Heal completely."

"I'm healed," she insisted. And she did feel new, as though the malaria had stripped away the final vestiges of an old, tentative self.

He turned around to face her. "I guess that *is* why we came here."

This time, when he turned the ignition, the engine purred.

SHE SLEPT THE rest of that day and through the night, and the following morning she felt fine, and so before noon they were back in the banged-up Datsun, moving through yet another opening into the Old City. "The Emir's wives and concubines used to pass through this gate to the palace," explained Emeka, ever the tour guide. "That was how it got its name, *kofar mata*, women's gate."

"You'd think they'd have separate entrances," said Angie.

Emeka navigated the car expertly. "Legend has it that the Emir loved all his women with the same intensity."

"I hear that," said Nigel, and he gave Angie a goofy smile as she looked over at him. She smiled back. We can joke like this because we're lovers, she thought, a real couple. She scooted closer, cuddled against him. She felt no desire, nothing, as though the malaria had stripped her of that too. She decided that was OK, felt right somehow. She and Nigel had been tested, been pushed past lust, and they'd survived.

They followed a narrow road that curved and curved, until they came upon another entryway. Emeka said they should come down here. A gatekeeper stood before the entrance, and Nigel dashed him a couple naira. They entered, the only visitors, save a German family with two small blond-haired boys. The wide-open area was dominated by vast cement holes in the ground, their darkness accentuating the sub-Saharan red earth. Men squatted before the deep vats, some dipping in white cloths, some stirring with dyed sticks, some pulling out long poles, these draped with dripping-wet, inky-blue fabric.

They watched as each man bent over his vat of dye, hard at work. She had an urge to dip her toe into those deep, shimmering pools of darkness. Sheets of fabrics hung across rope lines, drying, each in a varied shade of blue: cerulean, azure, indigo. The sun hit the hanging sheets, bathing them in light. She had seen these colors together before: in the negligee Ella had worn as she posed for pictures Angie took of her with a Polaroid, pictures Ella sent to Nigel, who'd been caught on a shoplifting charge, was serving a month upstate. The gown, she now remembered, was voluminous in accordion pleats, fanning out in gradations of blue, from the palest sky to the darkest navy. Angie, all of eleven, had snapped and snapped with her child's hands until there were half a dozen photos developing before them, each of Ella in a slightly different pose, lying across the carpet, soft pleats rising seductively up her ample thighs. Angie wondered was Nigel having the same memory right now, of that graduated blue nightie, of those Polaroids arriving in the prison mail, and she hoped so, hoped they were honoring Ella, silently together.

Angie kept staring at the dyers, wanting to feel something beyond a memory, something present and timeless. Here was the place Ella had so wanted to see. Angie waited, her mind straining. Nothing came, and she felt disappointed in herself.

"We should be going," said Nigel, finally.

Back in the car, they followed a circular path around the perimeter of the wall, passing back through the *kofar mata*. "These gates are all securely locked at night," said Emeka. "And manned by armed guards."

"What happens if someone needs to get in after the gates are locked?" she asked.

"No one goes in or out after sunset," Emeka answered.

She looked behind her at the wall rising into the skyline, formidable and protective. It looked like a giant womb. No, she thought, it looks like a giant tomb.

Kano, its Old City, its wall, its dye pits even, was just a place. The wrong place, Angie realized, because Ella had never been here. They moved along the modern streets, again passing by low-slung houses and Koranic schools and myriad banks.

She turned to Nigel. "I want to go to that road."

"What road?"

"The one where It happened."

His look became grave. "I don't see the point of that. In fact, I'd say that's a bad idea."

"I want to see it."

"What do you think you'll see? It's just a road, Angie."

"Just a road?"

"What I mean is that it's . . ." Nigel struggled for the right words. "I mean there's no, there's nothing there that would suggest anything . . . that anything happened."

"But something did happen." She folded her arms, resolved and ready to be out of this banged-up car for good.

"What is it you're looking for?" he asked.

She didn't hesitate. "A feeling."

At first she thought she couldn't feel her presence because Ella had died so far away. Then she thought it was because she needed to see her body. Then she thought it was because she needed to go to the places Ella had gone. Then she thought it was because she needed to go where Ella had longed to go. But still it hadn't come, that certain feeling.

"I need to go to the last place she was alive."

Nigel tried, futility lacing his words. "I wish you wouldn't."

She stared at Emeka's back. "I'm going with or without you."

Nigel rubbed his hand down his face, held it over his mouth for a moment, as if stopping himself from saying something he'd regret—or to hold back nausea. Finally he uncovered his mouth. "I know you are, Angie." He sounded defeated. "I know you are."

They agreed to return to Lagos in the morning.

That last night in Kano, they both fell into a deep, draggy sleep as soon as their bodies hit the bed, the decision itself having utterly exhausted them both.

DURING THE TWO-hour flight back to Lagos, she held Nigel's hand the entire time. He was fidgety, kept glancing out the window, tapping his foot, smoking nonstop. But she was calm. To Angie, it felt right to be on this leg of the journey together, to be sharing this act of homage alongside one another.

As the plane made its descent, she watched the aircraft teeter above the tarmac, its left wing wobbling; she listened to the wheels whine, and as they dropped down, her thoughts stayed on the spinning wheels, on their yearning reach for solid ground before the aircraft bounced against land, and zoomed along the runway. Nigel gently let go of her hand, unbuckled his seat belt, and said grimly: "We're already in Ikeja. Let's just get this over with."

TWENTY

AS THEY STOOD OUTSIDE THE LAGOS AIRPORT, ANGIE thought of all that had transpired since she'd last stood in this very spot, upon arriving a month ago. Now she was about to retrace Ella's last steps, and she was nervously excited, certain this, ultimately, was what she'd come here to do: to bear witness, to honor a sacred place, and with it a life. Her sister's life. And create a marker to leave behind.

The go-slow was not so bad—Sunday morning, explained Nigel—and for the most part they moved smoothly along Airport Road. When the taxi turned onto Agege Motor Road, she took in the passing sights, looking for significance in each billboard sign, each petrol station, each roadside vendor. When she spotted a Chevron station up ahead, she recognized it, recognized the cluster of roadside shacks beside it. They whizzed by and she craned her neck to look again as they passed, to be sure.

"I've been on this road before."

"You have," said Nigel. "It's the road to Fela's club."

"Why didn't you tell me when we were on it before?" she asked, words tinged with hurt.

"It's a major road, Angie. People use it all day long."

She looked out her taxi window, straining to find something

significant to hold on to, but the images collided together and she feared that some day, in a future that loomed, she'd have trouble recalling this place at all, its acute details a blur.

"We'll come down here," Nigel told the taxi driver.

"Here, suh?" asked the driver.

"Right here."

The driver pulled over and Nigel offered his hand, helped Angie out, his backpack dangling from one shoulder, her duffel from the other. Cars whizzed by.

"Where are we?" She hugged the reporter's bag to her chest.

"We're near where Fela's compound used to be. He built a new one somewhere else. But this is where it was back then."

"How far away? Like a block?" She needed to get the logistics right in her head.

"A few blocks."

Angie stood very still, watching the indifferent rush of traffic. An overpass stood a few yards away. "I don't believe it happened here," she said.

"It did, trust me," said Nigel. His voice was deadpan.

"No way she'd run across a road this busy. For no reason? That would be suicide."

"It wasn't busy." He sounded annoyed. "It was late at night and the most dangerous road in Lagos. People knew *not* to be on it."

"Then why would she be out here?"

Nigel wouldn't look at her. "She had her reasons."

Angie shook her head vigorously. "No, I don't believe that's what happened. Maybe that's what people *claimed* happened, and maybe the truth is still out there."

"That's what happened."

"How do *you* know?" she snapped. "You weren't here. You were off doing your fabulous interview. You left her alone on New Year's Eve, so how would—"

"I was here," said Nigel. His words hit her like bales of loose cargo. "I did not leave her alone on New Year's Eve. I was here."

Angie couldn't piece together the implications of what he was saying. Slowly, she started to comprehend. "You saw it happen?"

Nigel looked at her, eyes brimming. He nodded slowly.

A car got too close as it flew by, rustling their clothes, and both instinctively backed away. Angie kept stepping backward until she stumbled and fell. She stayed down, and Nigel sat down heavily beside her.

"You said you were in Guinea when it happened." She was shaking slightly.

"I lied about when I got back."

OK, she told herself. He lied. OK.

"I got back the morning of New Year's Eve. She'd left me a note, telling me she'd gone to Kalakuta. I tried to come straight here and get her. But the coup jumped off, and they imposed a curfew. I couldn't get to her until late the next day, New Year's Day."

"So you *saw* it?"

"She ran across," he said, voice raspy. "And—"

"And you saw it."

"I saw it."

Angie turned on him. "What did you do to make her run?" She reached and gripped his shirt. "What did you do?"

Nigel placed his hand on Angie's. It was heavy. "She wasn't upset with me. It wasn't me."

She let go. "Then what was it?"

"It was . . . she was upset with herself."

"Why?"

"Are you sure you want to know?"

Angie put her hands to her head. "Please, Nigel just tell me! Just fucking tell me!"

"OK." He swallowed. More cars zoomed by. "When I got to her, she was high."

"High?"

"She'd smoked a lot of weed at Fela's compound."

"So she had a relapse?"

"Yes."

"And so?"

"And so everyone knows Fela laces his marijuana with all kinds of hallucinogens. She was very high."

Pain shot through her chest. "This is what we all wanted to know, and you didn't tell us?"

"She made me promise, Angie. She definitely didn't want you guys to know."

"Are you telling me she killed herself?" This thought forced her up onto her feet. She hovered over him. He was shaking his head. "That she couldn't bare the thought of a relapse, so she—"

"No!" yelled Nigel. He looked up at her. "Do not say that! I told you, it was an accident."

"But what made her run into the street? Was she hallucinating?"

"No. Something else happened that I didn't tell you about."

Angie braced herself. "I'm listening."

"Sit down," he told her.

She kept standing. "I'm listening."

Nigel took in air. "She saw Jide get killed."

"In jail?"

"He never made it to jail. When the police barged into *The Voice* newsroom, they put him in a chokehold and he died on the spot."

Angie felt the full weight of Nigel's words. "And, and she saw it?"

Nigel nodded. Her legs weak, Angie plopped back down.

She hugged her knees, buried her face in them. For a while, she and Nigel sat in silence, nothing but the sound of lorries and *danfos* and cars whishing by. The sun was a hot wall against her back. She lifted her head too quickly and black dots appeared. She closed her eyes to steady herself. "Listen, I have to know," she said. "Did she do it on purpose?"

"I swear to you, she did not."

Angie wanted for him to be right. Still. "But how can you be so sure? She had to be distraught."

"She was distraught. About Jide, her own relapse, about us. Like I said, she was high as a kite—"

Angie opened her eyes, shielded them from the sun with her hand. "So then she might have—"

"No. The last thing she said to me was, 'I need to come down.' Before I knew it, she bolted out into the road. I called after her but she didn't stop."

"So what you're telling me is that she didn't run into traffic?" Angie felt the need to be explicit. She didn't trust her own understanding.

"The road was empty, OK? It was late at night, the curfew was still in effect, and no one wanted to be out anyway. I told you, this is the most dangerous road in Lagos. She ran into an empty street. She leaped for the curb—I'm never gonna forget that sight—just as an Army jeep came barreling out of nowhere and hit her. It was all so fast."

"An army jeep?"

Nigel nodded. "Didn't even stop. A fraction of a second later and she would've been safe."

Angie refused to follow his gaze, yet hungrily imagined her sister leaping to safety, triumphant and alive.

"She didn't look back at me," said Nigel. "If she was trying to take her own life, she would've looked back at me. She would have. I know it."

Angie nodded. That made sense. "So then what?"

Tears suddenly slid down Nigel's face. "I ran to her and called her name over and over. I checked for a pulse, a heartbeat, but she didn't respond. I—I tried to give her mouth-to-mouth. She just lay there, eyes closed, unmoving. No blood. I think she hit her head on the pavement." He shook his head slowly. "I held her hand and, and—" Nigel was crying full on now, his voice a growl, face covered in tears.

No one came. That was how it was in Nigeria, after a coup. So he held her there, in his lap, and waited for daybreak. He didn't leave her, and finally someone, a woman walking up the road saw them. He told her that his American girlfriend had been hit by a car, and could she please go get help? He held her in his lap and cried. More time went by, morning traffic appeared and he began to think the worse thoughts—that she'd lie in the sun too long before anyone got there.

But finally a van came, and a man helped him place her body inside. Nigel rode with her to the morgue. From there, he went to the US Embassy, used their phone to call her mother. It was three in the morning Detroit time. January 2.

Her mother hadn't awakened her, had waited until Angie was out of bed. She remembered that right before she got the news, she'd been thinking of Romare, and how sweet he'd been to her on New Year's Eve, how she'd slipped him into the basement after they'd left Baker's Keyboard Lounge. She'd led him to her old playroom, where a lumpy sofa had replaced her childhood furniture. Angie had planned to write her big sister a long letter that day, before she saw her mother's stricken face.

"Lord, Nigel," she whispered. "How did you survive that?"

"*I* thought about suicide." He sniffled. " But I was in terror of your mom's arrival, and that gave me a purpose, you know? I decided my job was to handle all the details once she got here, make the whole thing a tiny bit more bearable for her. But I was wracked with guilt and she knew it. And she didn't try to appease me." He wiped his nose with the back of his hand. "I don't blame her either."

"Did she ask you anything?"

He held up his index finger. "One thing. She wanted to know if drugs had been involved. And I said no." He made an ugly face, fighting back more tears. His voice was low, quivering. "To protect your mom, I guess, but really to keep my promise to Ella."

That was the first time her sister's name had been uttered since before they'd boarded the plane to Kano, and his speaking it brought finality. To everything. Angie understood for the first time, fully and completely, that Ella was dead.

But Nigel kept talking. "I dreaded the plane ride back. Because I feared your mother would get the truth out of me. But, it wasn't like that. She didn't ask any more questions. She didn't talk, really. There's something about planes. You're in this limbo state, up in the sky, suspended from a reality that's waiting at the gate. I saw this kind of, don't get me wrong, *calm* come over her. This thing she'd feared for all those years had happened and it couldn't control her life anymore."

A shock wave of homesickness sliced through her, so swift it made Angie keel over slightly. She wondered how her mother had endured that trip to Nigeria. How had she endured at all? What was she doing right now? Was she OK?

"The funeral was much harder for me," continued Nigel. "Seeing you and Denise, all Ella's friends. I couldn't face it. I felt like I was responsible for keeping her safe and I failed all of you. She died on my watch. Literally." He looked out at the road. "And I still feel that way."

How strange that of all of those who loved her big sister, Nigel had suffered the most since her death. The very person she always imagined had moved on and lived a rich post-Ella life. She rummaged through her bag for a tissue, handed it to Nigel.

He blew his nose. "I left Detroit right after that, crashed with some of my family in Chicago. I gave thought to working for a newspaper in the States, but I didn't have the stomach for starting over."

"You mean without her?"

He hesitated. "Yes. But I also didn't want to pay my dues all over again. Covering school board meetings and city hall and parades and other local bullshit."

Nigel became his old self again as he talked about his career. It helped her too, the diversion. She could look at him rather than the road.

"Then on to state politics," he said. "And if I was lucky, on to a national correspondent's beat, where I'd get to run around to Podunk towns on tiny planes in whatever state they decided I should live in, hoping for a major disaster so I could get some attention. Then hoping for a shot as a foreign reporter, if, of course, Joe White Boy didn't want it first. Plus, you know I had that brief jail stint. Didn't want *that* to get out."

Angie had to ask: "But what brought you back to Africa? To Nigeria? There are *so many* other places in the world."

"Because, honestly I didn't know what else to do with myself. It was what I knew."

She could imagine Nigel back then, heavy with guilt, filled with recurring nightmares, desperate for somewhere to go, to outrun the grief.

"Plus I felt this obligation to continue what Ella and I had started at *The Voice*," he said. "I mean, not necessarily in Nigeria. At first I went back to Guinea, and hung out with Ture and his Pan-African crew, that whole scene. But it felt, I don't know, like I was out of sync with those old cats. So I went to South

Africa, and when I got there, the whole anti-apartheid thing consumed me. Just *consumed* me."

Angie thought of her sister's outrage over of Steve Biko's death, of the "Remember Soweto!" poster that still hung on her own bedroom wall. She'd read in *The Detroit Free Press* that students at U of M held a candlelight march and vigil on the tenth anniversary of Soweto's uprising. There'd been no such events at Wayne State. The news story had made her feel, once again, that she'd missed out on something big.

"I stayed in South Africa about a year and a half," continued Nigel. "And that was thrilling! Covering this massive resistance movement led by the ANC, all the boycotts and strikes and marches. I was reporting and writing and filing stories nonstop, trying to explain to readers the courage of these black folks against constant violent attacks. I went to too many funerals. So many, it started to feel normal." He caught his breath. "When they started the daily protests in front of the South African embassy in DC? I was the one sending dispatches from Joburg straight to Ron Dellums at the Congressional Black Caucus, to keep him in the loop."

She'd watched the protests on the nightly news, seen a who's who of famous actors and politicians getting obligatorily arrested, never imagined Nigel had a role in any of that.

"With the international community putting pressure on South Africa, even *US banks* pulling out"—he put his hands out to mimic its size—"it was a *great big* global story. Still is, especially now that Congress finally passed that anti-apartheid bill, thanks to Brother Dellums. The story of the century, really." He peered over at Angie. "And what's amazing is that it made a difference, you know? We can see the effects of our efforts. We're winning! Apartheid is collapsing."

"You think so?" she asked, as if their fate were somehow tied to its collapse.

"I know so. They just repealed South Africa's pass laws a few months ago. That's huge."

Angie hated that Ella had missed this, missed the story of the century, didn't get to be part of something so big, so important. Wasn't that what Ella set out to do? Dismantling apartheid had been *her* passion long before it became in vogue.

"Anyway, I pretty much burned myself out," said Nigel. "I needed a break. So I went to Kenya for a bit, ended up staying there a year. It's a good base for covering East and Southern Africa. Well-run airport, UN headquarters, relative calm."

"And that's where you met Regina."

"Yes." He waited, to see if she'd say more, and when she didn't, he continued. "Lo and behold, I landed in another gigantic news story. Uganda's civil war had just ended, and with that out of the way, the country started promoting safe sex, of all things. They were facing a real AIDS epidemic there. The president of Zambia even announced that his son had died of AIDS. That was *huge.* So I was flying all around the region, covering *that* story."

"You've had an exciting career," she said, not bothering to hide the sarcasm.

Nigel didn't look at her. "It's less glamorous than it sounds." He was quiet for a few seconds. "I'll be honest. After a while, I felt like I was running on empty. That's why when Dr. Diallo contacted me, saying he needed a guest lecturer, I jumped at it."

"Still," she pressed, "Why come back *here*, to Lagos, to where it happened?"

He closed his eyes for so long, Angie thought he'd slipped into a meditative state. "I decided that I should leave something behind," he said finally. "I wanted to. That's what the scholarship in Ella's name was about." He shrugged. "A half-ass attempt, I know. I see that now."

She wanted to say something to make him feel better, but

what was there to say? Angie stood and stepped away from Nigel. She walked closer to the edge of the road and, bracing herself, peered down its path. Traffic was thick now. Horns honked, exhaust rose. She'd come here, been led to this spot, hoping to finally feel her sister's presence, her spirit. But instead she felt an overwhelming sadness. She's dead, Angie thought, and her sadness for Ella expanded. Ella had spent her life being down for the cause and up for anything. Angie could see it now, in its starkness: Ella always the one to stand up for the race, to do the right thing, make her people proud. With her insatiable appetite, that capacity to push herself to the limits, and everyone egging her on, Ella had rushed to be brave, to be first, to be the best. It was an exhausting life.

Angie stared out at Agege Motor Road. There was no sign, no indicator, nothing. It looked like every crazed highway in Lagos. There'd be more deaths on this road for sure, and they'd leave no traces either. Try as she might, she felt nothing. Suddenly, she longed for the peace of Grand Lawn Cemetery with its sloping hills, white ducks, waiting benches, quiet dignity. She longed for a real resting place, a place with a clear marker.

She turned back to Nigel. "I'm ready to go."

HOME, AGAIN

TWENTY-ONE

HER MOTHER DIDN'T DRIVE ON EXPRESSWAYS, ALWAYS MADE that clear to visitors—they were on their own getting from the airport. When Angie had called from Nigeria to say she'd be home the next day, her mother had sounded genuinely pleased to hear from her, and apologetic that she couldn't meet her at the arrival gate. Angie assured her it was fine.

Still, as the driver drove along I-94, she noted the oddity of taxis in Detroit: in a place called the Motor City, everyone owned a car. Taxis were reserved for visitors. She'd never been inside a local car service before that day in June when she'd left; now as the driver pulled up to the curb of her childhood home, she felt like a visitor. Having just spent a month in the backseat of taxis, this experience gave her the odd sensation of feeling both out of place and familiar.

Her mother swung open the door, watching as Angie made her way up the walkway with her luggage. She embraced her mother, taking in the comforting smell of Jean Nate bath oil.

"You've lost weight!" her mother said.

"Yeah, the food didn't always agree with me."

And right on time, she followed her mother into the small yellow kitchen, where fried catfish sat piled high on the stove. Still hot.

Angie ate with gusto, moreso to show her appreciation than out of hunger. The thing she'd said to her mom before leaving came rushing back at her—accusing her of abandoning Ella as a child—and she felt ashamed; she gobbled down her mother's cooking as a form of apology.

Nanette watched her eat, didn't comment on her braids. Angie stuffed more catfish into her mouth.

"So, how was it?" her mother finally asked.

"Different."

"I could've told you that."

"I guess I needed to see it for myself." The food lodged in her throat.

"Apparently."

"It was worth it," said Angie.

"Good for you, because I was worried sick."

"I told you not to worry!"

Her mother pressed her lips into a downward smirk that said, "You can't be serious." She got up and poured a glass of lemonade, handed it to Angie.

She thought about telling her mother everything she'd learned about Ella, as proof of just how worth it the trip had been. But she couldn't bring herself to do it. Not yet. She ate the rest of her fish and macaroni and greens without either of them speaking another word.

UNABLE TO SLEEP thanks to jet lag, Angie lay awake that first night in a panic: she had no plans. She admonished herself for not applying to graduate school as so many of her classmates had. But she hadn't seen the point of it back then, and once she decided to go to Nigeria, she thought that would somehow arrange a path for her future. It clearly had not. She got up, flipped on her light, and stared at the little altar. Everything was just as she'd left it—the crystals and incense, candles, the "Free Angela" button. These things had always given her succor, kept her feeling close to Ella until she could *really* honor her sister somehow. Now, these mementos had lost their power, insignificant against all that Angie had learned. Childish. She shoved everything into a drawer and took two Excedrin PM's, determined to thwart her insomnia.

Throughout those first days back, she and her mother were cordial with one another. She had moments when she almost told her what happened in Nigeria. But it offended Angie that her mother wasn't the least bit curious, didn't ask a single question. This, coupled with the fact that Detroit was just as she'd left it, made her feel the Nigeria trip was somehow not real. Her mother had, it turned out, quit her job at Dr. Benjamin's office and was now home all day; for the first time ever, the modest house felt too small for the two of them, for their strained conversations. Angie took to the attic bedroom, which she noted had been converted into a storage room, boxes shoved all around the bed. Her mother's move to Atlanta was going forward, and her goal, she told Angie, was to be living there by New Year's.

SHE AND NIGEL had left that spot on Agege Motor Road and returned to his campus flat. A note was waiting for him under the door, and Angie saw his neck muscles tense before he bent down to pick it up. Turned out, it was from Dr. Diallo, who was back in town and wanting to get together. They met him for dinner that evening at a meat parlor near campus.

It was a muggy night, a rare pause in the rain. The moon was laden, low. As they entered, Angie took in the deep smells of meat trapped inside the tiny restaurant; she watched with respect as the proprietress moved back and forth between the kitchen, both cooking the food and waiting on customers. Ella surely would've written about this woman, a female entrepreneur. As Nigel and Dr. Diallo downed their dark stout, Angie drank a light beer, and studied her lover. The tension in Nigel's face was gone, his widow's peak pointing down to a relaxed mouth. He laughed heartily at something Dr. Diallo was saying, and she could see he'd been liberated; the boulder of a deep, painful secret lifted from his chest. She'd done that for him. He caught her eye and winked, a kind of thank you. Suddenly she wondered what it would look like, their lives together? Where would they live? Nigeria? Kenya? Detroit? She wanted to picture it, but she couldn't.

That night, they entered his darkened flat and he immediately took her into his arms, kissed her; but she didn't kiss back. He stopped and stared at her, then silently turned, sat down at the small café table. She sat too and in the darkness, neither spoke. Finally, he offered her his hand. She took it, and they stood, entered the bedroom, undressing in silence, slowly removing their clothes as though the garments weighed too much. They lay down. He pulled her toward him and she curled into a ball, feeling small in his embrace. He moved his hands slowly over her stomach and then her arms, then her face— as though the capacity for memory lay within his fingertips. She felt herself waning, felt his grip anchoring her body so she wouldn't disappear. But it was too late. She was already gone.

The next morning when she announced, "I'm going home," he simply nodded, gray eyes dotted with flecks of sadness.

But as he helped her enter a Lagos taxi for the last time, she panicked. "I don't know what I'm going back to," she said.

"Your new life," he told her. "It's waiting for you."

It was the nicest thing anyone had ever said to her. She hugged him hard and when she finally let go, he kissed her forehead, like back then.

"I'll write to you," he promised.

"No you won't."

He chuckled softly. "We'll see."

She slipped into the taxi and they waved to one another as the driver sped off.

On the ride to the airport, she forgot that she was traveling along Agege Motor Road, didn't notice when they passed the same spot where It happened. So consumed with thoughts of home, she'd missed it.

ONE MONTH AFTER she returned, a letter arrived from Nigel. She was stunned. It bore a stamp with an image of four tall, orange cylinders rising within the blue walls of a factory as light flooded its windows, the word "Bophuthatswana" printed below. The letter was brief.

July 24, 1987

Dear Angie,
I'm in South Africa. This story is just too big to ignore.
The ANC is fighting back strong! Plus Nelson Mandela
is approaching his seventieth birthday, so the clock's ticking.
And I ain't gonna lie: Joburg is a welcome change from
Lagos. No go-slow! (smile)

   Look for a special item in the September 10 edition of
The Michigan Chronicle. I think you'll be pleased.
   You take care of yourself.

                              Always,
                              Nigel

When that issue of Detroit's weekly black newspaper came out—distinguished by its green newsprint—she brought it home and stood in the living room, scanning headlines until she found the small article on page twelve. It announced the "Ella Mackenzie Fellowship for Black American Female Journalists: In memory of Detroit native Ella Mackenzie, for her trailblazing work as a journalist in Africa." A photograph accompanied the piece. There she was! Ella sitting at her desk. She was beaming. Long braids framed her face, then cascaded down to her shoulders. She looked radiant. Angie touched the photo, and then her own lips. Suddenly, standing there beside the picture window, staring at the image, sunrays warming her face, she felt her sister's presence. Like a current moving through the air, she felt her. Right there. She felt Ella in the room.

When she showed the announcement to her mother, Nanette's face rearranged itself from a protective wall to a poignant smile. "Well, I'll be," she said. "That's really something."

"I learned all about her work while I was there," said Angie. "She did extraordinary things."

Her mother's smile pushed out as she pressed her lips together. "We'll have to get this laminated."

"Mama?"

Her mother looked up from the newspaper.

She could tell her now. Right now. But what exactly? About Nigel seeing the accident? About Jide? About the drugs? To what end? Her mother already knew how Ella died. "I'm sorry I did that to you," she said finally. "Went to Nigeria, and then didn't get in touch. Made you worry."

Her mother's eyes were watery as she returned her gaze to the newspaper. "I'm just glad you're back home, safe and sound," she said. "That's all that matters to me."

Angie moved toward her mother, into her soft arms, *The Michigan Chronicle* falling and landing softly onto the carpet.

Later, in her room, Angie slipped the green clipping into the mirror over her dresser. Then she sat down and unbraided her hair. It took many hours. The next morning, on a whim, she pulled the "Free Angela" button from the drawer and took it to her car, where she pinned it to her graduation tassels hanging from the rear-view mirror. Next she drove to the main library downtown; this building had always been a favorite of hers and as she rushed up the marble staircase, her footsteps echoed, and the sound made her happy. She went into the cool stacks and pulled out a variety of college and university catalogs. Just as she'd once spread an atlas of Africa before her, she now spread out the various booklets with their alluring photos of attractive students in perpetual autumn settings, and read through them. She had a while to decide—applications weren't due until January—and so she indulged a host of possibilities: cultural anthropology, film school, twentieth-century American literature, International Studies. Before, her lack of focus, lack of passion for one thing over all else, had been a liability; now it felt like an asset. It signaled openness to her vast array of options.

With the last bit of money left from her trip, she bought a personal computer, a Leading Edge. The guy at the computer store assured her it was simple to operate, and showed her how to use the word processing program he'd installed. She set it up in her room alongside a new dot matrix printer and while she was a little intimidated by these modern machines, their very presence beckoned with the promise of intellectual pursuit. She kept them plugged in, humming.

THAT OCTOBER, SHE and her mother were informed that Hazel Park Raceway would be honoring the fifteenth anniversary of Samson Mackenzie's death with a ceremony. A wing of the track was to be named in his honor, and a blown-up photo of him would be hung in the lobby beside the betting windows. Angie and her mother had to choose the photo, and so on a rainy day, they stood before the dining room table where dozens of black and white photographs spread before them, all taken of her father in the winner's circle. They were a hodgepodge of pictures, most for small wins, a few for the big ones. Many of the photos included Ella.

"You choose," said her mother, obviously overwhelmed.

Angie favored one photo where Ella, no more than eleven or twelve, stood beside her father, who was glancing at her; Ella's head was turned toward the horse. The notation on the photo said the horse was named Good and Plenty.

"This one," said Angie. "I like how they're both looking at what they love."

Her mother agreed, and they shoved the other photographs back into big manila envelopes.

Over Christmas holiday, Denise came home, and in the privacy of her Ford Escort's front seat, Angie told her sister: Ella had witnessed yet another man's death, was distraught and guilt-ridden when the accident took place. Denise said, "She suffered *before* she was hit?" and broke into sobs. Angie handed her sister a stream of Kleenex from the car's glove compartment. Denise kept shaking her head, fresh grief stunning her. She looked up suddenly, terror in her eyes. "Don't tell Mama!"

"Never," said Angie.

Afterward, they drove to a florist's shop, purchased a festive holiday arrangement. At the cemetery, they dug their bare hands into the freshly fallen snow, brushing it aside before placing a wreath of poinsettias and ivy atop her grave. They crunched together through the creamy snow back to the car, holding each other's cold hand all the way.

AT THE FIRST hint of spring Angie headed to Belle Isle. Having replaced the ubiquitous Fela tape in her car's cassette player with Michael Jackson's new album, she sang along to "The Way You Make Me Feel" and "Man In the Mirror" as she drove along Jefferson Avenue. She parked in front of the Detroit River. She'd decided on a master's in international studies—her time in Nigeria a plus on her applications—and had received acceptances from four schools: Johns Hopkins, University of California Berkeley, Duke, and Carnegie Mellon. She'd have to make a decision soon.

Looking out onto the Canadian skyline, she felt a rightness that had for so long eluded her. She still wanted to be part of something big, but now she trusted that whichever path she took, she'd settle into her own way of being black in the world.

When she thought of Ella now, she thought of her as one of many vital foot soldiers, idealistic young men and women who fanned out to far reaches of the country and yes, the continent, to agitate for change. She admired her with a ferociousness totally lacking in envy; and she understood that to honor her sister was to take advantage of every opportunity Ella and all those other protesting black activists made possible. And of course, to never forget, to wear the marker on her heart.

As she stood on the river's edge, Angie's mind drifted back to a day at the racetrack. A morning where, barely four, she'd hid under the bleachers for so long that she stumbled out to find herself alone, left behind. Right at the onset of her fear, Ella rode up on their pony Bill and in one smooth motion reached down and swooped up Angie, plopping her atop the saddle. Ella gave her the reins, whispering reassurances as she guided Bill toward the stables. Angie felt a trust mixed with joy, certain it would always be this way, that whenever she was afraid or lonely Ella would be there holding out her hand, waiting for Angie to grab on and climb up, so together they could take off.

ACKNOWLEDGMENTS

IN MY MIND, THIS BOOK TOOK FOREVER. HAD IT NOT BEEN for the support of those who helped me get here, it might've taken forever and a day.

I am grateful to the writer friends who encouraged me in those early years, when this story was a rough idea lusting after more: Lizzy Streitz, Danzy Senna, Roslyn Bernstein, and Amanda Insall assured me I was on to something. Eisa Nefertari Ulen's joyous affirmation of the work made me take it seriously.

When along the way I doubted the story's value, Tonya Hegamin and Samantha Thornhill sang its praises in two-part harmony (yay, Mahogany Mavens!). And when I was lost in a sea of overwritten pages, Tayari Jones appeared bearing gifts of encouragement, brilliant insights, and an outstretched hand to help me find my way.

Many thanks to the sister-friends who cheered me on through the years as I toiled away at my "Nigeria novel": Farai, Linda V., Angie D., and especially my BFFs—Diane, Steph, and Karen. Thanks to Audrey Siegel, for careful listening. And a special thank you to Natalie Peart, for both the friendship and the introduction.

To the members of Tom Jenks's 2003 NYC writing workshop, thanks for being the first to offer encouraging words long before I knew what I was doing.

I'm especially grateful to the Thomas J. Watson Foundation, whose travel fellowship allowed me to experience 1980s Nigeria; and for the support given by Baruch College and its Weissman School of Arts and Sciences; research and travel grants provided by PSC-CUNY; and a wondrous ten days at Virginia Center for the Creative Arts, where I was able to write and think without interruption. And I'm lucky to be part of the Buffalo Colony, where this book took shape amid spectacular mountain views. Thanks to 3B, the downtown Brooklyn bed and breakfast, where in a whirlwind, overnight stay I finished the final chapter. Equal thanks to the Brooklyn Ladies' Text-Based Salon for my first reading from this work, and the confidence boost it gave me.

Special thanks to my agent Neil Olson, who read multiple drafts with gracious patience; to my editor Amy Scholder, who believed in this book from day one and has never wavered; to Jeanann Pannasch, whose subtle yet brilliant edits left the novel better than she found it; and to the entire Feminist Press staff and community: thanks for the open arms.

I am deeply grateful to my uncle, horse trainer extraordinaire John Drumwright, for letting his young niece tag along to the racetrack, and witness firsthand what it looks like to love what you do.

I will be forever thankful to my family here and gone on, who encouraged me to travel far then sent me letters and telegrams and their love across the ocean the whole time I was away. And a special thank you to the men and women I met and whose hospitality I enjoyed during my stay in Nigeria lo, those many years ago.

Also, I'm indebted to those African authors whose stories

inspired me as a young writer, from Buchi Emecheta to Chinua Achebe to Ama Ata Aidoo to Florence Nwapa to Tsitsi Dangaremba; and those who inspire me today, from Chimamanda Ngozi Adiche to Uzodinma Iweala to Ada Udechukwu to Chris Abani.

This story is wholly fiction, yet rooted in historical events. A few sources in particular enhanced my understanding of time and place: *Fela From West Africa to West Broadway*, edited by Trevor Schoonmaker; James T. Campbell's *Middle Passages: African American Journeys to Africa, 1787-2005*; Chinua Achebe's *The Trouble with Nigeria* and *Anthills of the Savannah*; Eghosa E. Osaghae's *Crippled Giant: Nigeria Since Independence*; Marita Golden's *Migrations of the Heart*; George Packer's 2006 *New Yorker* essay "The Megacity," *Ebony* Magazine's May 1977 cover story on FESTAC, and Babawilly's Dictionary of Pidgin English. Special thanks to Knitting Factory Records for its CD *Fela: Live in Detroit 1986*, and to creators of the documentary *The Black Power Mixtape 1967–1975*.

Special thanks to my mother-in-law, Marguerite Fields, for all the times she bragged about me. And deep maternal gratitude goes to Tyler and Abebitu, who never once complained about the many hours Mom spent writing behind a closed door.

Most of all, I'm indebted to Rob, whose vigorous love and support still take my breath away. Thank you for the steady voice in my ear, reassuring me throughout the years that the work "takes the time it takes." That has meant everything to me. And so have you.